AGENT OF CHAOS: THE REGION TWO SERIES

BOOK THREE

JANET WALDEN-WEST

JANET WALDEN-WEST

This is a work of fiction. Names, characters, places, and incidents are either products of the author's imagination or used fictitiously, and any resemblance to actual persons, living or dead, business establishments, events, or locales, is entirely coincidental and not intended by the author.

Agent of Chaos: The Region Two Series Book Three

Copyright © 2022 by Janet Walden-West

Cover by Black Bird Book Covers

Editor: Jen Hinderliter—Alacrity Editing

Editor: Stella Wilkinson—Editing By Stella

ISBN 978-1-7372190-4-0 (ebook)

ISBN 978-1-7372190-5-7 (paperback)

Contact Information: janetwaldenwest@gmail.com

❊ Created with Vellum

To my sister Amy, for being the best real life sister anyone could be blessed with, and to our Dad, who taught us from the very beginning how to love and be loved.

CHAPTER 1

M arshall

MARSHALL SUCKED in and edged around the stacked boxes filling what should've been a wide-open OSHA-compliant kitchen hallway, but still banged a knee, causing a pallet of flour sacks to bump against the industrial pantry door.

"Watch what the hell you're doing." Jenkins glared at Marshall.

As far as Marshall could see, the guy didn't report to the head chef or the kitchen's boss-boss, but he was always around in the evenings.

"I could move this stuff in where it belongs," Marshall muttered. He was already working late, way after the kitchen closed, same as every night since he started here a couple of weeks earlier. Not that the extra hours were reflected in his check. But somebody—probably him—was gonna break their neck trying to squeeze through the cluttered passageway.

All the stacked supplies belonged in the pantry but nobody except this guy and the head chef had been allowed inside since Marshall started working here.

"Mind your damn business and do your job," Jenkins ordered, like he was management. Except management didn't wear jeans and long-sleeved shirts with weird bulges under both armpits. "Get done and get out, unless you want fired. Boss is checking in tonight."

Because he needed the cash, Marshall kept his mouth shut and didn't point out that unloading after-hours wasn't a line cook's job, and shouldered through the door for today's piled up deliveries. Except for cold stuff, none of the drop-offs were allowed in until after closing, either.

Even close to one a.m., the Mesa heat hadn't dissipated, trapped between the kitchen and hotel outbuilding's walls. The set-up created a wide, depressing alley.

At a sharp pop, followed by a click, Marshall hesitated. The layout left this area darker than the night was naturally, but it was more like a cave tonight. When the sound didn't repeat, he stepped into the lot.

Something other than pitted concrete crunched under his sneakers. Glass from the two weak security lights that illuminated the lot now littered the ground. Unease skittered up his spine. The bulbs had been fine when his took his break a couple of hours earlier.

Marshall stopped. Made himself hold his breath for a second, then let it out into the warm night air. No breathing too fast, no setting off the cycle that made his body think there was more to panic about than the low-level buzz of anxiety that was his day-to-day life.

Last thing he needed was losing another job so soon. The head chef here was okay enough. The kitchen manager though, Marshall's boss, was a jerk.

Like thinking it conjured the guy, Kincaid's sharp voice

2

barked from inside. "What is this shit? I had orders to make sure this place was empty by one, which means you damn well had orders to have it clear by one."

"Not my fault your employee is slow as hell," Jenkins answered, then his tone did a fast one-eighty. "Sorry, sir. I'll have this taken care of, and goods prepared for you in a moment."

Marshall grabbed the biggest box, his size coming in handy, balancing the weight on one arm and catching the door with his heel before it closed and locked him out, which would for sure get him canned, from the irritated sound of Kincaid's voice. As for Kincaid's boss—Marshall wasn't sure, but assumed he was one of the hotel owners. The one time he'd met the man, Marshall hadn't been able to get away fast enough from the frigid gaze, hairs rising on his neck at being the focus of the guy's attention.

Soft thumps sounded behind Marshall, almost lost under the argument indoors.

He twisted to look over his shoulder—and a force like one of the forklifts he'd used in a past job rammed him. A hand viced around his elbow, whirling him in a hard arc, creating a dizzy wall-people-wall-again kaleidoscope.

His back slammed against the wall, the box falling and containers of dry pasta clattering to the pavement.

Marshall blinked against a sudden glare—some kind of purple light, blazing in his face, blinding him. It swept from his face down his body, accompanied by a faint mechanical hum and then a beep.

"Human," a clipped male voice announced, and the light disappeared.

Marshall blinked against after-images, eyes watering. A sliver of light from the hallway, the door now held open by something other than Marshall's shoe, didn't much help. He tried straightening. He wasn't up for whatever crap Jenkins was pulling. Punching the guy would probably have the same result as actually punching his real boss, but whatever.

A heavy hand rammed him back against the wall. "Don't move."

Marshall's vision cleared enough to pick out a tall outline —and a gun barrel aimed at him.

"There's no cash here," he squeezed out, heart rate ramping up.

He'd never been in a restaurant robbery but everybody had stories about managers and owners being held up as they were leaving with the day's take. "I swear. We only cook," he added.

A soft curse met his announcement. Another voice, feminine, level, and in charge came from his right. "Stay here. Don't move, don't make any noise, and you'll be safe. Understand?"

"I—" He squinted. Other outlines joined them. The speaker, and a third, throwing a big shadow. Even bigger than Marshall.

All of them in gray and black camo, like some kind of urban soldiers in his favorite video game. All carrying very real guns.

"Understand?" That in-charge voice asked again.

"Yeah. Yes." He swallowed, throat trying to close around the words.

"Good. How many are inside?"

After a silent beat, Marshall realized she was asking him. Mouth dry, he got out, "Jenkins. My manager, Kincaid, and him. Mister Welch."

"Welch?"

"The—the hotel owner. I think." Marshall couldn't miss the shared looks, and his unease climbed higher.

She—the leader, had to be—asked, "Weapons?"

4

"What? We're just the kitchen. For room service and stuff. There's—we don't have weapons or cash."

His information earned another curse, but the leader's shadow motioned, and the grip holding Marshall in place vanished.

"Be still. Be quiet. You should be secure out here."

Nothing, not the guns, the movie-villain uniforms, the bruise probably already forming on his back, led Marshall to believe her.

The other two took opposite sides of the doorway. She held up fingers, folding them down one at a time. Three, two, one, and at zero, the three surged inside, her in the lead, the door crashing open in a *bong* of abused metal.

The quiet graveyard shift exploded in noise and lights. Flashes bright as daylight. A scream, like a wounded—or angry—animal rose.

Even he recognized the rapid bark of bullets. Concrete dust flew, peppering down on Marshall. Chips striking arms he'd throne up to shield his face. Bullets coming from inside, fired his way.

He pushed off the stupid wall, sprinting out of the way. And tripped over pasta boxes, his knees slamming against concrete and the shattered security lights. Sending him sprawling into the hallway. Into the middle of a nightmare come to life.

Jenkins, in front, between the kitchen and pantry, gun out —the bulge Marshall had seen under the guy's shirt. Shooting at the soldiers. And Marshall.

Then, so was Marshall's boss, a sleek gun in hand, acting like he knew how to use it.

Him, Mister Welch—materialized. Just there, where there had been empty space. He jerked on the heavy, reinforced metal pantry door. It groaned, metal tearing and hanging by one hinge.

Then the hall was empty again. Screams echoed from the opened storage room. Female. High-pitched.

Welch reappeared. Hauling two smaller figures, women, their hair wrapped in his fist.

And the hotel owner hissed, suddenly less...human. Face gaunt as a cadaver, skin almost translucent and showing the bones underneath. Too-pointed teeth shone from between blackened lips. Brown eyes blazing an impossible silver.

Jenkins stared. Then, mouth working, turned his gun on their boss.

In one swipe of his hand—now claws like something out of a really good special effects show—Jenkins' throat was gone.

Blood spraying, covering the pallets of flour. Spattering the two women, and the floor.

Kincaid darted behind Welch, into the pantry. Not freaking out, not scared of the man-demon-thing. A woman spilled out of the room a second later. Cowering from the gun Kincaid held.

As soon as the soldier leader saw, she held up a hand. Barked, "Hostages. We can't risk it."

The other two soldiers dropped their guns. The rifles on straps, slipping around and out of the way in a smooth motion.

Maybe it was over. Done.

Except they, the three in uniforms, hadn't been shooting to begin with. They seemed to be trying *not* to kill people. The overhead fluorescent lights bounced off the gleaming blades in their hands. After a life in kitchens, knives were one thing Marshall did know.

The huge guy's looked more like the knives kitchens used to butcher whole carcasses.

Bile and fear climbed up Marshall's throat, threatening to erupt.

After that, it was a chaotic, disjointed blur. Knives. Screams. People scrambling past the fighters, lost. One hesitated in front of Marshall. A woman. Dark hair, pale face, eyes enormous and full of tears. Terrified.

Marshall knew terror, almost as well as he did knives.

The woman turned to run. The wrong way, into the fight.

Marshall hustled, getting in front of her. "No, here, this way. Outside. Go outside." Somehow words made it out of his mouth, over numb lips and he held out a hand to her.

She shrank away, and spoke Spanish. But it was too fast for him and his limited kitchen Spanish.

"Sorry." He kept his hands to himself and pointed out, at the opening where the door had been. To the alley and freedom, and motioned again. Probably mangled it with his cruddy vocabulary, but added, "Safe. Outside is safe. Hurry."

The woman grabbed another woman, shoving her in the right direction. But she pulled back, speaking to her friend, tears leaving tracks down her cheeks, and both turned back for the room.

No,no,no,no. "Hey, no. Wrong direction—" Marshal caught a few words as the women spoke to each other.

Marshall did understand one word, and froze, cold sweat popping out. *Kid.* There was a kid still inside. And the mom or sisters weren't leaving. Were probably going back in. Right between a team of soldier-assassins, and his jerk manager's gun and…whatever the hotel owner was.

Purposely not thinking, shoving everything, including the rising panic away, trying to blank emotions and chaos out, Marshall whirled. Ran for the storage room that had at least one person, maybe more. All of them scared and probably with no idea of the layout, and if they went right, it'd be straight into the fight.

He grabbed the edge of the doorframe, stopping himself

as his shoes skidded. He hung his head inside, lights off in the room, turning it into some pitch-dark pit.

One filled with the scuff of people moving. Sobs. Wherever these people had come from, they needed help. The best help he could give was showing them a way out, and let them, and him, get away while the people with guns and giant knives were busy.

Marshall swung into the room, keeping to the crescent of light from the hallway lights that only penetrated a few feet in. He held his arms out, hopefully showing he wasn't armed, wasn't part of whatever was going on not even a whole room away. Then almost threw up for real, just enough light to show at least a half dozen frightened faces. And the kid. A boy, in a cartoon tee.

Marshall made himself into a crowd control barrier, using his body to help block the hall leading inside, and did his best with his broken Spanish, waving people out, trying to tell them which way was safe. Hoping he wasn't wrong.

Goosebumps crawling over his entire body, way too aware he had his back to ...criminals, at the very least. Whether it was because Marshall looked as freaked out and scared as they did, or only the lesser of the evils, an older lady turned to the group and as soon as she spoke, the entire bunch streamed for Marshall and the door. He covered as much space as possible, doing his best to keep anyone from going the wrong way, pointing to the outdoors. The older lady was last, pushing the boy along in front of her.

As they cleared the building, Marshall gathered himself, following. Getting out and watching their backs, in case. His heels cleared the exit threshold.

For the second time in one night, Marshall was flung out of the way, harder than with the giant soldier, his head rapping the outer concrete wall. Pain flared from the impact. Welch kept going, not even seeming to notice he'd elbowed

Marshall out of the way. The hotel owner was moving too fast. His passing creating a freaky breeze, tugging curls into Marshall's face.

Marshall jumped as another body flashed into the hall, one in a suit. The guy who always drove Welch, and held doors for him.

The man's attention whipped to Marshall. Those stomach-churning, unearthly silver eyes pinning Marshall in place. Teeth—that lengthened to fangs—slid from the not-guy's mouth. He—it—snarled. Not a human sound.

The blood pounding in Marshall's temples meshed with the growl.

Claws sprouted, as quickly as the fangs had. Visions of Jenkins, throat ripped out, filled Marshall.

A shout, a human one, rattled down the hallway. The thing whirled, bass growl filtering through the soles of Marshall's feet, right into his bones.

The monster, snarling at her, the leader. Marshall's pulse spiked and he pushed the start of a warning out, to tell her this wasn't a person. To run before it got her. He took a step in her direction. He could grab her, pull her this way. At least distract the creature and give her time.

The silver of her knife moved so fast, it left after-images. The thing shrieked and its head lolled to the side. Another swing, blade whistling, and the head separated. It rolled to drop by Marshall's feet, blood spraying across the toes of his Chucks.

Marshall raised his eyes from the impossible, gory scene, to hers. The soldier-assassin and her blood-coated knife.

Marshall backed, shoulder blades grinding into the wall. Fighting the blackness, iron band tightening around his chest, cutting off his air. Not able to remember breathing exercises, how to break the cycle. Not with a killer looming in front of him.

Panic crested.

Her lips moved, but sound didn't get past the panic. Then she was in front of him, knife gone. Brown eyes were the last thing he saw, before the dark closed over him, one he might not live to surface from this time, surrounded by murderers and monsters.

iv

"Crud." I pinched the bridge of my nose, although the blossoming headache was the least of my problems at the moment.

First, a civilian where, according to our intel, there shouldn't be one. Then a dead secondary human target. Plus a dead vampire, only a lowly worker, and the ranking vampire was in the wind. Clearly a Master, whose power had flickered around us like stinging sparks.

All on top of aiding and resettling the traumatized women and children, people the Master and his trash human accomplice had been trafficking. The people were the reason for our mission tonight. Today, now.

"It's not that bad, Liv." Jace, my lieutenant, cracked his neck, side to side, dispelling the last of the post-mission tension, same as after every fight.

That I finally knew one of my team's quirks and habits was a sliver of comfort.

A small comfort. *"Not that bad* wouldn't mean an escaped Master vampire with an in to organized crime, and his trafficking ring still viable. He'll move to another spot, another front or shell business, and keep moving human product."

Any Master that old and adept could've provided another piece of the puzzle to the inexplicable recklessness among vampires. Infecting people, then turning the new vampires loose to indiscriminately hunt, garner Company attention, and die.

Passing along the virus that mutated a human into a vampire required very specific conditions, primarily a Master vampire over a decade old, the point where the virus was fully matured. Even then, it was tricky, draining a human close to the point of death but not so far that organ failure occurred, before being infected. The majority of attempts still failed.

At least, it had until recently. Now we had a population boom. As well as starving, sick vampires, when neither condition should be possible. This Master might've been a key to the odd behavior ghouls were suddenly showing, and migration shifts occurring with windigo hordes. We now believed those anomalies were somehow also tied to the vampires.

Not bad also wouldn't mean an innocent civilian bystander being subjected to a violent altercation, and then discovering vampires existed.

We policed cryptids, natural animals who shared the biological ability, like a chameleon, to go unseen. Many also possessed attributes that could be weaponized, the whole reason for Company Alpha's existence. We prevented cryptids from coming to public notice, and protected civilians from any of the predatory cryptids sharing the humans' biome.

Technically, vampires weren't *vampires*, as our science crews pointed out every time an agent slipped up and used the slang. Nor were they cryptids. But, vicious, drank blood among other things, and healed quickly. So, vampires.

I frowned, but not at the human in front of us, probably a chef or kitchen worker, from the simple white jacket, now spotted with brown stains and grime. He still crouched in an unresponsive ball, where he'd basically dropped. On my watch, due in part to my actions.

He hadn't even twitched when I'd draped the reflective emergency blanket around him—two blankets, and even then, barely enough to cover his wide shoulders and chest— or when I checked his pulse and BP.

He had been like this for almost an hour. Long enough for us to check the victims for injuries, reassure them that we were the good guys, and help process them while Cleaners decontaminated the scene, disappearing evidence in their analytical, detailed fashion.

I edged back as another van pulled in, crew hopping out the instant it stopped. One agent opened the rear, revealing a pristine match to the destroyed metal pantry door inside, victim of an enraged vampire. The Intel arm at HQ would've had no problem pulling up building information—we'd already had the schematics, part of planning the mission.

Technically, our part was done. There were Company paramedics, and a counselor, on-scene to help the victims as Sera, the head of the closest Company safehouses, sorted them into units.

The healthcare workers were swamped though, dealing with the victims. Passing out water and food, answering questions, helping call any relatives or friends. At least none of the women had seen their human captors morph into monsters. As far as the women knew, this was an all-human crime. Which made it easier on them—they would be reunited with family and go home. Or we would help find them a new, safer one if they had fled their homes to avoid danger.

Guilt nibbled at me. I'd never done much of the dealing with civilians tasks. Partially, because Vee, my sister, was entranced by civi pop-culture and took any chance to interact with them. Partially because we had been that good, meaning few botched missions resulting in witnesses.

But that precision and those teammates were a thing of my past. I pushed aside the old flare of hurt and anger.

I had a new team, one I'd put together. Matteo, Jace, and I. The men sole survivors from two different teams, casualties of cryptids changing their behaviors, and the upsurge in vampires. I was a lieutenant turned C.O. who seemingly willingly left a team, the people I'd grown up with from nursery to Academy barracks. They were my family, and we'd been teammates from the time we were kids.

Now, we were leftovers.

Matteo joining us knocked me out of my poor-me loop. He sipped on a soda clearly liberated from the medic's stash, can looking more like a preschooler's toy in his big hand. Soda and snacks, part of the effort to prove we weren't another set of traffickers or out to exploit the victims.

Seeing me, another woman who looked like them, had also helped. Not so much with the kitchen worker, though.

Matteo's gaze followed mine, to the civi, worry scrunching his face "Oh, damn. He saw the vampire. Did we break him?"

I switched from what was going right, to what wasn't. Fingers tapping, putting facts together, I said what we were all thinking. "He had a full-blown panic attack. I didn't find any meds in his pockets, though. The only two cars here

14

belong to the manager, and the Master, this Welch. I did find a bus pass."

As we spoke, the man's hand twitched, then opened and closed like he was trying to get circulation back. The first movement or acknowledgment that there was an outside world, since his attack began.

We'd all had emergency medical training, but… my gaze swept the crowd off to one end of the hotel lot. Sera was deep in conversation with one of the victims, one whose face was still tear streaked.

"We're going to have to take point." I crooked my finger at Jace, who nodded.

Out of the three of us, he had the best rapport with civis. He stretched, long arms over his head, and put on his *'Hey, I'm a totally harmless, completely likeable guy'* face and headed for our civilian.

I didn't need to hear whatever Jace said as he squatted and touched the man's elbow. The results spoke for themselves. The man shoved heels into the cracked black top, trying to put distance between himself and Jace. Possibly still lost in what triggered his attack. Which, soldiers, monsters, vampires, take your pick.

"Aww, damn." Matteo started forward, then glanced at me. "If Jace freaks him out…"

Yeah. If pretty, genial Jace was frightening, a walking wall of muscle like Matteo was right out.

I dredged up everything I could remember from our crisis and EMT courses, while double-timing it to switch places with Jace. He moved before I asked, giving me an embarrassed shrug.

I kept my hands to myself as I knelt. The man's harsh, frantic breathing made *my* chest hurt.

"Sir, you are safe, I promise." I made my voice soothing and non-threatening.

I tried to see it from his perspective. Three black ops storming his kitchen. An aborted firefight. Plus, vampires—couldn't forget to add those.

And me, practically decapitating one in his lap, no disguising what it was or what I'd done. I winced at that misstep.

That hadn't been optimal, much like our performance, but it had been necessary. Jace had wounded the vampire, but it hadn't been a lethal shot since he'd been aiming for the Master. Who had tossed his underling in front of Jace as a living shield.

An injured vampire was vicious. One wounded by our weapons, all containing an alloy of the chem-compound toxic to cryptid and vampire physiology, was desperate and ready to feed on anything nearby in order to fuel its cellular regeneration.

In this case, the wrecked guy in front of me. The one I'd seen sending the victims to freedom amongst the chaos, using himself as a safety barrier between the women and a pitched battle. Hands down, it was ranked in the top two as the bravest thing I'd ever seen a civilian do, the other being my sister's then-civilian fiancé stand in an empty park in order to lure a sentient, apex cryptid out of hiding. Bruce had already discovered cryptids though, as opposed to having one pop up in his world and go for his jugular.

I dug in a thigh pocket and came out with the too-brave-for-his-own-good worker's wallet, taken while checking him out earlier. I needed to forge some kind of connection with him. I flipped the nylon square open and angled it to one of the halogen lights from the Cleaner's makeshift base of operations. Marshall Tate, six-two, Caucasian, blue, and red. License issued in Illinois.

"Mister Tate, I'm Agent Muñez." Maybe giving him a title could convince him I wasn't an armed criminal. "Mister Tate, is there anything I can do to help? Is there any medication you need? I can go inside for it if it's in a locker or the office. Our EMTs are here, but they're occupied at the moment."

He didn't answer, but he did stop attempting to merge with the wall behind him in order to get away.

I had a flash, one of my brother Josh. Us sitting up and talking about nonsense all night, a few nights in a row, after a power line fell during one of our early missions and he was trapped in a space barely large enough to stand in until HQ activated an Asset and had the power grid shut down.

If my talking eased some of Mister Tate's well-founded fear, I'd talk until I lost my voice. "Mister Tate, I apologize for our roughness earlier. We were led to believe the only persons present were traffickers, and their captives who were secured in a room alone. I made an assumption, and I was wrong. You aren't a hostile and I truly am sorry you were caught in our raid. We'll have our medic check you out soon, sir."

"Marshall."

I froze, processing his low, rough response. Marshall. His first name. Right. "Marshall..." What next? This so wasn't my sub-specialty. On impulse, I said, "I'm Olivia. Liv to my friends."

The thick tendons in his forearms relaxed a bit.

Okay. Progress. "Marshall, until our medic gets here, can you tell me where you're injured? Do you have meds inside?"

He tensed again. "M'fine."

I backtracked, looking for where I'd made the misstep. There was a chance it was some civilian guy thing. They didn't always react like Company men, instead like they weren't allowed to accept help, or ask for it, or something. "You were front row in a violent confrontation. If we—if I— hurt you, it's my fault." When I'd seen him in the entry, a wide-shouldered, imposing shadow, I had assumed he was part of the ring, probably their muscle. "Please let me help? Even if it is only to update a medic, since they are almost finished with the victims you helped save, and a real medical professional being freed up."

Silence washed over our corner of the scene.

Then that deep, quiet voice rumbled again. "They're okay? Those women? And—there was a kid." He uncurled enough to look at me, raising his head. "There was a kid, too."

His face was chalky-pale, with a scattering of freckles over his nose. Wary. But concerned.

He wasn't worried about himself, but mention of the women and boy overrode his aversion of me. That concern? I got it. We shared a responsibility fetish.

I hurried to reassure him. "They're going to be fine. Dehydrated, hungry, and frightened but aside from some bruises and scrapes, they're good."

No bite marks, either. It required a human near death, their immunity shot, and a mature vampire, over a decade old at least, to successfully infect a person. Even then, the outcome was iffy. These trafficking rings were about profit and food, not recruitment.

"Look. You can check for yourself." Slowly, I eased sideways, opening a space for him.

He watched my every twitch, every breath, tense as a cocked bowstring.

I tilted my head, toward the aid worker and crowd. "See?"

He chewed on his lip, obviously wary of taking his eyes off me, but finally darted a glance.

Then sat up straighter, watching the kid rip open another pack of convenience store doughnuts, and wipe a powdered sugar-coated hand down the front of his cartoon character shirt.

Strictly speaking, the doughnuts weren't any sort of official Company protocol. They were something my two sisters and I had discovered as teens though, and found nearly everyone enjoyed, and in a pinch acted as a bridge between us and victims in need of familiarity.

The kid tucked his prize close, holding his mom or sister's hand and joining the line to climb into one of the two passenger vans bound for the safehouse shelter. It was going to be a tight fit getting everyone in.

"Where are they going? Where're you taking them?" Belying his size, Marshall was on his feet, and several steps toward the vans, ready to intervene on the victims' behalf again.

I stood, and without thinking, caught his hand. Twice the size of mine, but not totally steady. Yet he was still more concerned with others.

"The lady up front, Sera? She is the director of a shelter. She's taking everyone in, where they can rest, shower, and meet their family. Most have already called friends or family. You can go ask them."

Marshall's gaze dropped. To my hand, holding his.

Crud. I let go fast. "I apologize."

"It's—you're okay." He chewed at his abused lip. "My Spanish isn't that good. They're safe? Nobody will—my boss. What was he doing with them?"

I tried skirting the question. "They'll be reunited with family, or we'll help find them a place and job if it's safer here."

"Safer from being kidnapped. They were kidnapped."

That definitely wasn't a question.

I nodded. "Basically."

"That's why we couldn't open the industrial pantry."

"I'm afraid larger restaurants make effective clearing houses for trafficking. People flow in, and it's easy to claim they are kitchen workers. A few came willingly, promised jobs, but their papers are held as blackmail. Others were sold into it. A few were flat out snatched of the street." My temper notched up at the ordeal they'd been through, and I tried sticking to facts. "Workers are faceless to most people looking in from the outside."

"Yeah. We're not important."

I didn't know what that meant. Marshall clearly wasn't an immigrant. His dull, flat remark sounded more like the people we usually helped, people who had been abused or taken advantage of.

I felt the moment when Marshall made the next, logical connection. "My boss—"

"He's in custody." I eyed the last SUV in the crowded alley. No need to add I'd knocked the guy out and zip tied him, and Matteo had not-so-gently dumped him in the cargo area. Humans who betrayed their own, sold them out to vampires —oh, then used them as a shield on top off the other atrocities—none of us had any kindness to spare.

We protected humans, but had little jurisdiction over them. After whatever Company members we had in the local LEO—law enforcement organization—deemed they'd gotten all the information on the vampires involved in the crimes, the civi criminal would be dealt with by human agencies.

I braced for what came next, as Marshall spoke. "The owner, my manager's boss. Mister Welch—" his throat worked.

Civilians always had trouble with this part, plus the man had already had a trying day. As matter of fact as possible, I said it. "Welch was a vampire, masquerading as a human. A very powerful vampire, and highly placed in associated human and vampire criminal circles, as well."

I stopped myself reaching out to him again. Civis weren't usually as physical as the average Company-raised person, a fact I had trouble remembering, or understanding. "He is gone, but you're with us and in no danger right now. We will apprehend him, no matter how long it takes, or the resources needed."

"It's...okay again, right? This is all done. For us, the regular people, and I can go."

Under those too kind, too hopeful eyes, I wanted to say yes and promise that his brush with what civis saw as monsters was over. But I couldn't.

Now came the crap part, the delicate task of informing a civilian, a normal person, that normal was off the table for a while. "Vampires are excellent trackers, both physically, and utilizing human methods such as surveillance, social media, contacts. We also have to assume this one had access to your employee files, including your address."

Marshall went an impossible shade paler. "I'm not important. Why bother with me?"

"Vampires are—" I stalled out on giving the official line, the innocuous reassurance we'd been taught to hand out to victims. Marshall had hero'ed up tonight, and he deserved honest. "Vampires are both vicious and petty. You've seen for yourself how they view us as objects, for sport or food. Welch is a Master, an older vampire where the virus mutations have fully integrated, who has produced multiple vampire followers. Vampire behavior is based on aggressive dominance ranking, so presumably Masters are routinely forced to prove they are too strong to have their territory or nest taken. That you—we—interfered with his domain, requires him to retaliate in some dramatically gory vampire way. More importantly, you worked here, you knew at least two of his human generals, and you are a witness to his part in an illegal trafficking operation. That operation is large, profitable, and international in scope. He will have a number of influential and angry vampire and human partners to answer to."

"I'm nobody. Why bother with me? I don't know anything about his business, except cooking in the restaurant part. I've only—I haven't been here long. That should count."

"There are tens of millions of dollars, and ties to weapons dealers, drug cartels, foreign groups, all at stake. You are a loose end."

He stared at me. When he spoke, his tone was hollow. "So I'm going to the shelter. My job—never mind. I don't have one now." Those big shoulders fell.

He should go to the shelter. Sera would evaluate him and decide if he could move to a different state and be secure, or if he needed a new identity, new career, and relocated, or possibly even to stay at an armed safehouse for protection until Welch was captured or eliminated.

Realistically, it would be the latter option.

Sera was close to capacity with the women alone, though.

And Marshall...he had been kicked in the teeth. For no reason. He'd lost his home, and his job. Whatever friends he had here as well. He also probably needed more oversight than Sera could provide while swamped.

The excuse sounded flimsy, even to me. I had screwed up, not doing further investigation once this mission was green-lighted. Letting a murderous vampire escape. Potentially putting Marshall squarely in the creature's sights. I kind of owed him.

At this point, what was one more mark against us?

I faced Marshall and took responsibility. "No to the shelter. You are coming with us."

CHAPTER 3

*M*arshall

MARSHALL ACCEPTED the soda from her. The assassin. Soldier assassin. Who beheaded vampires, which were a real thing, without even blinking. Who passed out cola and snacks.

He drained the soda, despite caffeine and sugar being a bad idea after a meltdown. His weird brain didn't need extra stimulation.

But right now, he couldn't think. Worse than usual after. Everything felt kinda outside him. The world fuzzy, a murky gray-green like spoiled food.

Except for her.

She was…bright. Soft gold-bright, a warm amber even in the night, in the shadows of the hotel alley.

Not the harsh, too strong glare of the spotlights the soldiers had set up, like the place was a natural disaster scene.

23

He should be grossed out. She had *stuff* on her. Blood, if what came out of vampires was real blood.

Instead, where she touched him, took his hand, it had been…easy. Easier, anyway. People were never easy-easy for him. The reason why being one more warm body in one more anonymous kitchen was his thing. Faceless, like she said. Most people would've already written him off after his meltdown. She had felt patient.

Marshall tipped the can to get the last drop, then crushed the aluminum, then again, folding it in half. Fidgeting, exhausted but twitchy, doing whatever he could as the conflicting ideas swirled and bounced, not processed and dropped into the correct slot, not fitting in his head.

He needed time to sort tonight out. Quiet would be good, too. Neither looked likely. He reached into his back pocket for his phone and earbuds. One of his apps, not the meditation one, maybe the ocean noise, and crank it up to drown out all this. Any timeout was better than nothing.

His pocket was empty. Marshall patted his other, because, yeah, sometimes if he was already thinking of one thing, he wasn't paying attention to what the rest of his body was doing.

Empty, too.

Last ditch hope, he dug in his front pocket then the one on his jacket. All empty.

He needed the phone. The simmering anxiety bubbled higher, threatening to take over. He scanned the area, and the last of the women boarding the vans.

The other two soldiers folded away the lights, while two women dressed in plain black slacks and jackets with the same bulge under their arms as Jenkins had, snapped metal cases closed, loading odd boxes and bags in a another black, windowless van.

He finally spotted her, his soldier. He pushed up from the

lone chair the kitchen staff used for breaks, remembered the can, and looked for a place to trash it.

One of the jacket and slacks women gave him a brief smile and took the can. For all he knew, they could read minds. She dropped the empty in a clear bag, sealed it, and added it to a box in the van.

Which wasn't any freakier than special agent soldiers, and kidnapped people, and vampires.

He tried fighting, keeping his breathing slow. His pulse still going too fast at not having the lifeline. Of having to explain. Marshall hurried over to the one in charge, pulling up her name—Agent Muñez. Olivia.

He stalled out when he got to her. Standing alone on the fringe, she was watching the scene. She gave a nod to the van people as they slammed the doors and climbed in, and to the shelter lady as the white vans pulled out behind the black one.

Lines bracketed her lips, a furrow between her brows. Hair in a tight bun, blood-stained uniform, guns and long knives, she should've looked dangerous, intimidating.

And she did, plus, completely in charge. But Marshall knew tired and sad, and she kinda looked both.

She turned, and those dark eyes locked on him.

He stumbled on what he'd meant to say. Instead, all that came out was, "My phone. I can't find it."

That patience he'd glimpsed earlier came out again. "I'm sorry. It's evidence now. As soon as we log you in, I can return this though." She pulled a beat-up canvas and Velcro square from a uniform pocket.

His wallet. He hadn't even noticed it wasn't on him. "My phone can't be evidence. I need it. Now."

She frowned, patience vanishing, and his gut pitched. He'd screwed this up. He took a breath, rearranging his facts into something she would understand. Psyching himself up to take another try at explaining *why* he needed the phone.

"We're set." A deep baritone Marshall recognized from earlier—the guy that had rammed Marshall into the wall, came from behind him.

Marshall stepped sideways, fast. That soldier and the third closed in. Making a pyramid, with Marshall in the middle.

Too close, taking up too much space and air despite being outdoors. The tallest looked more like a movie's version of a hero secret-soldier. Sleek as the leader, almost as pretty, same brown skin and dark hair, but in a fade.

The other guy, the battering ram—Marshall was big enough most people didn't bother trying to start anything with him, but this soldier was as big as Marshall, easy, plus the guns and arms that bulged against his uniform sleeves. No way were they gonna care about whether Marshall needed the apps.

He felt the weight of three sets of intense eyes, and sweat beaded along his lip. He wasn't sure how long he'd been—gone—or how much they'd seen. Still, they had to have witnessed part of his meltdown and checking out.

The biggest soldier frowned at him. Marshall's pulse took a queasy jump. It'd been a long damn time since anybody had started crap with Marshall. Not since he'd shot up six inches and sixty pounds in high school, and quit looking like an easy target, despite his weirdness and episodes.

These were killers though. He took another step back. The soldiers shared a look, and split up, flanking him. Blocking the alley exit and not even pretending otherwise.

Their commander walked past Marshall. "I am sorry, but the phone and contacting anyone is off limits until we all—" she hesitated like she was editing her thoughts "—until we debrief."

He didn't want to call anybody. Not that he had anyone who'd much care. The other though…"But—"

"I'll explain fully later. For now, we need to go. The first shift will be coming in to work soon." She opened the back door of the last vehicle, another black SUV, windows heavily tinted, and *looked* at him. Clearly expecting him to get inside.

The thing about him not going to the shelter rose up out of the chaos in his brain. "Where—where are we going?"

"To debrief at—" definitely editing her language "—our Region's central headquarters."

Marshall eyed the end of the alley, and his hands knotted into fists. Odds were that secret soldiers wouldn't come after him once he hit the sidewalk in front of the hotel.

Like they knew, the other two soldiers paced forward, even their walk holding a deadly vibe. Tightening the net around him.

Marshall ducked into the back of the truck as the door slammed closed on his life. However crappy it was, at least he'd known what to expect.

The SUV rocked as the soldiers climbed in. She looked over her shoulder. "We have a decent drive ahead of us. Do you need anything before we go? Aspirin? Water?"

He settled for shaking his head.

"Go ahead and get some rest. Tap if you change your mind." A tinted panel rose between Marshall and the others.

Leaving him alone, headed to some secret government site, with a trio of killers.

iv

"HQ, HUH?" Matteo didn't take his eyes off the busy highway, navigating the too familiar, too lengthy route to our Region's central command, instead of the shorter one to our main compound. His thumb tapped against the wheel to the beat of a favorite Daddy Yankee track.

I inched the volume up to cover this conversation, despite the privacy glass. "It is part of what HQ is for—anything beyond teams' and safe houses' capabilities." I tried to hide the resentment at admitting we couldn't handle this. But it still itched and annoyed me, like a shirt tag I couldn't reach to rip out.

I was having a hard time shaking the guilt that I hadn't vetted the intel thoroughly enough before green-lighting last night's mission. Plus, we had an eight-hour drive ahead of us instead of two.

Company didn't waste time and energy on what-ifs, so I

stuffed those worries away. "Besides, we might as well debrief in person. I can take a stab at spinning this a little more in our favor."

Leather creaked and Jace leaned up from the second row he had to himself, to join the conversation. "There's nothing to spin. We were tight. The place was closed, the lot empty except for the target's ride. I hacked that e-time card system myself, and it showed all the employees had clocked out and were long gone. We're good, but even we can't account for slime illegally keeping employees working without pay after-hours."

"Yeah, that Master vampire ghosted. But we didn't know he'd even show. We got the kidnap vics. All of them in one piece, and none saw anything cryptid or vampish. We got one of the human generals, the first tier planners we were after for interrogation. It was a clean op, Liv." Matteo finally glanced at me.

He was right. He and Jace both were. We'd hit our primary objective—freeing the people being trafficked. We'd also hit our secondary objective, procuring a high-ranking local member of the trafficking ring. No one would have seriously expected us to account for the Master, on the fly and without additional teams.

No one except me. Good wasn't enough, not for us. Exemplary was my goal. My team was top-notch. We'd worked together for nearly a year now, melding three different personalities from three different teams into a whole. Our trio did the work of a standard five-person team, and did it as easily as breathing.

And I was proud of the guys. I held my fist out, tapping knuckles with Matteo and Jace, getting grins in return.

They deserved my full support, not extra pressure. I was the one who had to make sure we were flawless, so that pressure all fell to me.

The guy in the back of our truck was also my responsibility. I flicked a flexible keypad down from the dash, typing, and the screen came to life. Showing the civi. He dwarfed the seat, but the choking grip on the seatbelt harness gave his real feelings away. His face was a pale, square-jawed oval in the low interior lighting.

He looked as wound-up, as freaked, as when the vampire had jumped him. No, more freaked. Probably because he wasn't busy saving vics and now had distraction-free time to think about what happened.

Still hanging over the back of my seat, Jace had no trouble guessing where my head was at. The cool, practical ability to read a situation was what made him my lieutenant and intel specialist. "That right there is a textbook flight risk."

"Back at the scene, I thought he was gonna make a try at me, and bolt," Matteo added.

"He saw too much." Even as I said it, I didn't have a clue why I felt the need to defend the stranger. "I doubt most civies would be thrilled or have their heads on straight after they'd been caught in a vampire raid."

I'd had the same emergency crowd control and mission-scene training as the guys, standard curriculum. However, my hands-on experience with civilians began and ended with one person. No one would call Bruce, soon to be my brother-in-law, a typical representative of civilians. Or even of agents.

He was a swearing, opinionated, one of a kind. The perfect match to my sister Vee. Part of the perfect team that had been mine, but wasn't any longer. I fished a bottle from the door and drank the lukewarm, slightly stale water left in the bottom. Not succeeding in washing the taste of abandonment away.

"HQ can do their thing, debrief our vic, do counseling

and whatever other aid, and resettle him." I closed out the subject.

"At least we'll get a couple of home cooked meals outta this detour," Jace said, and dropped back to sprawl in his seat.

The HQ cafeteria's menu was only home cooked if you'd grown up in the Company from birth. Which we all—every Company member—had.

Except I'd spent a few years learning what actual food, prepared by an actual person as concerned with giving us a real home to come back to as with providing proper nutrition, was like. I didn't miss the farm to table meals as much as I did what they had represented. Family. Someone who gave a damn that we came back, alive and functioning, and had made it a point to care.

I just grunted and let the guys take it as agreement, closing my eyes on their reminiscences about cafeteria tamales and what I now knew enough to identify as freeze-dried potatoes.

My time was better spent planning our defense for allowing a key player, and a Master vampire at that, to escape, instead bringing in a civilian in its place.

CHAPTER 5

$\mathcal{M}$arshall

BRIGHT LIGHTS FLARED and a high mechanical whine woke Marshall. He jerked, forgetting where he was for a minute, disoriented, heart pounding.

A purple light swept over him, lighting up his surroundings. Leather and durable fabric seats. Blacked-out glass.

The back of the soldiers' truck.

The light finally died—the one just like what they'd used on him at the hotel to decide if he was human. A claxon sounded, clear even inside the truck. The motor cut off, a fact he only realized when the door opened. Marshall blinked at the sudden brightness, rubbing burning eyes.

She—the head soldier—leaned in and motioned him out, against the blare of the alarm.

Marshall fumbled, seat belt finally clicking open. He scrambled out, muscles stiff from the long ride. He didn't know how long, but enough that the exhaustion that always came after a meltdown had won out over the anxiety, and he'd slept.

He stopped, taking in sterile white walls and steel. The soldier held her hand out, an eyebrow up. After a minute, Marshall interpreted it as her asking for his hand.

Wary, he held it out. She laid it palm down on a computer-tray device. A sharp prick bit the tip of his index finger, and he jerked. Her hand fit over his though, holding it down.

The alarm quit, silence backwashing.

She let go. "You can move around now. That won't happen again." She pointed to the finger-poking scanner thing, while he scrubbed his finger off against his already bloody kitchen jacket. "Blood test to confirm you're human and not infected. Your DNA is on file now."

Whatever that meant. Nothing good, every science fiction movie with evil governments and scientists he'd watched coming back to him. It seemed safest to go with, "Okay."

She stepped off what looked like a high-tech runway, motioning him to follow.

Merciless lights blazing down, they paced through the space-craft-ish building, and into another. A maze of glass and polished chrome and spotless light colored walls and white floors.

Marshall felt grungy in comparison. And, okay, he probably was. A ten-hour shift, then a couple more unloading and moving supplies. A—a murder scene, then the long drive.

"Lunch?"

He stumbled at the unexpected question. He'd forgotten he wasn't alone. "Uh…" Not sure what the proper answer was.

She held open a door. The clink of plates and silverware and wall of noise, too many people talking, hit Marshall. The huge cafeteria style space was full. Full of tables. Full of people.

Plenty of them turned, checking them—him—out.

"We managed to land here at lunch time. Welcome to the lunch rush." She walked in, not waiting for him.

He hurried after her straight-backed form. Skin prickling at being the focus of all the attention.

"Umm, the debriefing thing?" She'd said he had to do that, before he'd maybe get his phone back.

"I though food might be a good idea first. Give everyone a beat to get their land legs after our marathon trip in." Under the lights, her eyes were warm honey-brown. She stopped, right behind the other two soldiers.

Marshall edged further behind her, an extra step away.

Probably he should've been more intimidated by her. She was the one who had chopped a vampire's head off. But that patience he'd almost decided he'd imagined was back, turning her expression softer, more real.

She couldn't know he'd want the phone more than food. She was maybe trying to help. It wasn't her fault that what he needed and what normal people needed weren't the same.

He nodded and took a plastic tray she passed back to him, as she lifted another off the stack on the counter for herself.

"What do you prefer?"

He took a panicked look at the steaming holding pans. Tried to tell his body it wasn't a trick question. "Whatever. Whatever you're having."

He stuck behind her, head down as people called her name or just 'commander.' Her replies were quick, not stopping to chat, but nice. Totally at ease here.

She slowed and he jerked his tray higher to keep from ramming it into her back, his Chucks making too-loud squeaks. He hadn't been paying attention. Again. It felt like everyone in the room turned to watch Marshall nearly crush what was probably their favorite commander.

She didn't complain at the near miss collision. Just hooked a chair with her foot and pulled it out, then repeated the maneuver for herself and sat.

Gingerly, he eased into his chair, and registered that there were others at the table. The other two soldiers from the hotel. They were already digging into their food.

Which was a good excuse not to talk. He dropped his head and ate, not really tasting anything but the metallic edge of anxiety and leftover fear from earlier. When his plate was empty, he was at a loss. Small talk wasn't his thing. Small talk with hardened soldiers…

"Here." She took his tray, stacked it on top of hers, and scooted them across the table to the taller agent. "Your turn."

"Man, I did it last time we were here." Despite the complaint, the guy didn't look mad.

She didn't seem angry at the disobedience, either. "Yes, but we both know you're going to sweet talk extra dessert out of Prerna. Two birds, one stone."

She stood and stretched, her ease the opposite of Marshall's. "Ready or would you like something else?"

"No." He shoved up too fast, chair skidding, catching his heel and tangling him up. She reached to steady him, but hit the bruise on his back, above his kidney.

He must've flinched, because her expression went from relaxed to focused on him. Her lips pressed together, probably annoyed at him all over again. "You are hurt. Infirmary first."

Marshall didn't need nurses or whatever went with a visit, or annoying the commander more. Especially that last pitfall. "I'm good."

She eyed him, but didn't argue. "This way, then."

He followed her, paying attention this time. Now, he

couldn't miss seeing dozens and dozens of—them. Men and women like her, in black or gray tees and multi-pocket pants. Most of the soldiers at least exchanging nods with her.

Kids, too, in smaller versions of the uniform. Lots of older kids and teens, all shoving and goofing, briefly pretending to behave as the adults passed.

Except for the military thing, it was all echoes of his school years, a hell he didn't want to revisit, ever.

Other men and women in the same kind of suits or skirts as the team that had gathered all the evidence at the hotel strode past them, most to halls leading off to the right. All carrying tablets or files.

All, every person they met, was sleek. Graceful and dangerous, even in skirts. Polished, organized, and moving like they knew exactly what to do, where to go, and what to kill. And fully qualified for the job.

A woman in the soldier uniform led a pack of teenagers off to his right. Even the kids carried that dangerous vibe, in precise lines, faces intent

Basically, the opposite of Marshall.

Sweat trickled down his spine. The sooner he got debriefed, got sent to whatever shelter or new town without vampires, the better. He didn't have any of his clothes and stuff, but he'd figure it out. He'd done that part often enough. Move, take what little he had, drift to the next restaurant hiring.

Deep in the science-fiction maze, they finally halted in front of a simple black door, same as all that passed before. This one had a small plaque with *Public Comptroller* in neat letters.

She opened it, taking them through a waiting room area, with one of those standing desks in one corner, a guy younger than Marshall working at it. Sure and polished.

"Commander—" he started to leave his spot, standing even straighter. Maybe salute, if they did that here

She smiled and waved him off, but did halt at the door behind him. She knocked, then entered without waiting.

"Sir." She gave a shallow nod. Something in the way she stood now slightly more formal.

The man behind the desk, another suit person, not a soldier, motioned to a chair. The lights hit silver sprinkled in his short hair, the same style all the soldiers here had. "Mister Tate. I apologize for the inconvenience and complicating your evening. We'll keep this short and to the point so that you can relax a bit."

The guy had a laptop out, typing before he'd finished speaking. Too much like other teachers Marshall had once had. Like interviewers, people who wanted answers, but wanted them *now* and only in a certain way.

Neither of which Marshall could do. Not in a format most people had patience for.

"Commander Muñez, our thanks." The guy at least smiled, lines around his eyes crinkling, even if it sounded like he was kicking her out.

She turned to go.

Body and mouth not listening to his brain or common sense, Marshall lurched in front of her. "Don't—you're leaving?"

Instead of her, the office guy answered. "The Commander has other obligations, I'm sure. This will be quick, you have my promise."

She frowned, maybe at the guy or more likely, at Marshall. But she didn't glare or act like Marshall was being ridiculous. When she looked at him and spoke, her tone wasn't annoyed. "Would you prefer I stay for the debrief?"

He got out a nod, as the other guy interrupted, sounding

confused. Marshall had to effect on people. "Commander, you don't need—"

"There's no rule against the Agent-In-Charge sitting in, Sir, and I don't have any pressing plans." She took one of the solid looking chairs in front of the desk.

Marshall took the other, gripping the arms hard enough his knuckles popped. Knowing they heard it. That he was being weird again. Not able to help it though.

Then the questions began. Too many, too fast, all demanding times and details, in order. Without giving Marshall the space to line answers up his way. And he wasn't sure what the suit guy wanted to hear.

A soft touch fluttered over the back of his rigid hand, a there and gone wisp. The Commander, getting his attention. An eyebrow up, and kinda checking with him when he looked over. "Marshall?

He licked chapped lips. "Yeah? Yes?"

"Would you like me to rephrase the questions? These were created more for us than civilians, and we understand some of the terms used may require clarification."

Somehow, he didn't think that was true. Part of him was humiliated he couldn't even manage not flub an interview. The other part of him grabbed the lifeline she offered. "Yes, ma'am."

The skin beside her eyes tightened, but she repeated the other guy's question, at a normal pace instead of machine gun fast. Like there wasn't any hurry, one leg casually crossed over the other. Relaxed. In charge here just like with the attack and rescue. Even Suit Guy deferred to her, staying silent and typing in answers.

Marshall's body decided she was safer, angling toward her, and answered her questions.

When the snap of a laptop closing caused him to twitch,

he wasn't a hundred-percent sure what he'd been asked, or what he'd answered. It must've been good enough though.

"Thank you, Mister Tate. We truly appreciate your patience with us. We'll let you know if we need any additional insight or information. I assure you, we will resolve your situation as speedily as possible. The public's safety is our priority. In the meantime, my aide can show you to your quarters, so you can recuperate."

"No need. I still know the way." The Commander sorta morphed, turned more friendly than formal, and smiled at Office Guy.

She rose and Marshall leapt to follow, happy to shut the door on the office and the guy with his too smooth promises to what even Marshall knew was a not-smooth situation.

Whatever else she was—Commander and soldier—she was also more patient. Less blunt and hurried and impersonal. Maybe someone he could sort of trust. "Thanks. Thank you."

She gave him a smile, real and kind. But he couldn't miss the stress hiding underneath. Marshall was close friends with stress, in all its forms. "It's no problem. I'm heading that way myself, and can give you the mini-tour."

Whatever that meant. It couldn't be all bad, if a person obviously as important as her stayed there.

The office door popped open, and the standing desk kid hurried out. "Commander Muñez, ma'am."

She stopped and waited, while the kid handed her a piece of paper, dense with words.

Marshall's stomach pitched, threatening to lose the lunch he'd just eaten, now sitting like undigested bricks.

He took a breath when she read the paper and handed it back to the helper, not to Marshall. "Really?"

"We're at capacity, ma'am." The aid stayed put, doing that

formal thing, until she spoke. "I understand. You're dismissed, and thank you."

She turned, backtracking, going right instead of left this time, down yet another identical hall. "Looks as if the suites are maxed out. The barracks are this way. Group showers to the left."

Marshall slowed, trying to fix directions, what was where in this shiny maze, then hurried to catch up with her, before he for sure ended up lost.

She pulled open one side of a set of huge double doors, at the end of a wide hall. Showing off a giant room, with rows of bunk beds, and lockers at the foot of each. Filled with—okay, not kid-kids, but older teenagers. All staring at Marshall now.

Whatever she saw on his face, she let out a sigh. "Yeah, I know. Bunks, right? I swear they are immaculate though, and more comfortable than you'd think. I survived sixteen years on them, no joke. Oh!" She snapped her fingers, like she just remembered. "They aren't street fashion, but clean clothes plus toiletries for you are already on their way."

She moved to a bunk closest to one wall. "This is yours for the time being. That cool?"

He did the only thing he could. Lied, because he didn't have any other options and he couldn't piss this killer-soldier off, one that everybody else came to attention around. "Sure."

"Great." And she just...left. Walked out without another word. Left him there, not simply with a pack of merciless teenagers, but a pack of merciless teenage killers.

He'd have been better off with his criminal boss and vampires.

CHAPTER 6

iv

"HALT." My voice boomed over the outside course, sharp and harsh as a grenade.

The struggling cadets snapped to attention, one taking a step forward. She was the cadet who would one day lead this group. The one who was on her way to getting hamstrung by a ghoul—in this case, a junior Instructor playing the part—crouched behind a pile of junk metal and a water tank.

"Ma'am, yes ma'am," they chorused.

I channeled Instructor Annabeth, aka, the Instructor best known for busting our asses. I let my voice drop, cold and every word sharp as shattered glass. "Who is C.O. here, and on point?"

The rangy blond took another step out from her team, and closer to me, her smile disappearing. On a well-executed mission, no one needed to ask who was leading. "Cadet Graham, ma'am."

"Are you pleased with your team's performance today?"

"Yes, ma'am."

"With your performance?"

"Yes, ma'am." Braver now, sure of herself in the cocky way only teenagers managed, she added, "We are on-plan to clear the area—rooftops, buildings, and tunnels. Top to bottom, and ahead of schedule. The last hostile has been neutralized."

"You've completed your coursework on the wide-spread changes in cryptid behavioral patterns teams have reported?"

"Yes, ma'am."

"Then continue." As they reformed, and fell back into position, I held up a hand. "But you are on sweeps, Graham."

She started to ask why. Then got over that potential infraction in a millisecond, and swapped out places smartly.

I stepped back. "Proceed. Full force."

The team frowned and exchanged looks, since sweeps were usually tag-touch, not full contact.

She needed to learn though. Sometimes, learning hurt.

Despite what should've served as a warning, the team surged forward. Graham confidently charging past the tank.

The Instructor erupted, dirty water fountaining into the early Fall sky. His flat-armed blow hitting the Cadet square in the throat.

She crumpled to one knee, hands thrown out as braces, gagging, but the ghoul stand-in finished the required maneuver, a body blow that sent her skidding, flat on her back.

The Instructor removed the scuba mask, its top just above the waterline, allowing him to hide under the scummy surface. He nodded at me.

"Critical tactical hit. Team member dead," I barked out the penalty and paced to stand over the teen, now mostly curled on her side, spitting out bile.

"This is what you're pleased with? Losing a team member. On. Your. Watch." I squatted, eye to eye. "Then, when you fall, it creates a hole. One of those other ghouls—because I'm sure you did as rushed and sloppy a job verifying the areas behind you were cleared as you did here—will exploit that hole, that weakness and *eliminate your entire team.*"

Muted creaks announced sod-covered trapdoors opening behind the students, the two Junior Instructors serving as a ghoul pack popping from their dug -out pits and into view.

I rose, my shadow dropping over her. "Ghouls aren't windigos. Their metabolism is slow enough that they can hold their breath, and utilize almost any liquid above the freezing point. Your class also covered the switch to ghouls forming packs. Congratulations on killing your brothers and sisters, Commander. Because what is the C.O.?"

The Instructor nudged the cadet's ankle. Hard.

She got points for straightening and choking out, "The C.O. is responsible for her team at all times, under all circumstances, ma'am."

I turned my back on her, and her new bout of coughing from the acidic bile scouring her throat, with a lesson she'd never forget. One that hopefully meant she'd never lose anyone she loved to a monster's claws, and never have to watch a team member she'd known since birth bleed out or be torn apart in front of her. A lesson that might insure she'd never have to carry that unrelenting burden made of guilt and heartache.

The day's urban course class done, I stepped off the field and headed for the sparring mats, and someone on my combat level to work out my frustration. Everything in me hoped Graham would never be in a position to shoulder the disillusionment of a job well done not being enough, either.

From the patio linking the outdoors to the Cadet barrack's breezeway, Marshall stared at me. I didn't need to know much about civilians to read the horror clearly written on his face, or the censure in his eyes. Looking at me as if I was the monster. Without speaking, he whirled and vanished back inside.

I kinda wished someone had expended as much effort ensuring I understood how to deal with civilians, long-term and without disgusting them. Because Marshall had just proven to me as clearly as I had to the Cadet, that I'd failed that lesson.

* * *

SPARRING plus a long run had worn away most of my edginess and poor-me-mindset. Enough that when my phone blared out Queen B and *Formation,* my sister's ringtone and undoubtedly programmed in by my other sister, I settled on a bench outside the cafeteria. Legs crisscrossed under me, I answered and put Vee on speaker phone since the area was deserted. "Who did Bruce antagonize in spectacular fashion this time? Tell me Josh's favorite Harden jersey is still safe." Always a valid question, both when my future brother-in-law, and my brother Josh, Jace's twin, were potentially involved.

Vee's sigh came through clearly. "I swear, if demons really did exist? The producer on that episode B agreed to guest judge was definitely one. He introduced Bruce as the American version of you know who."

I whistled. Bruce didn't do comparisons. Or tact. Or modulating his volume. Worse, he and the British celeb chef best not named had a vicious, or at least vicious in Bruce's head, cross-Atlantic rivalry going. "Better you than me."

"Please. You know you miss this drama."

I clenched the phone and wished for a subject change because I did. I missed everything about my old life.

Oblivious, my sister continued. "Josh totally punked out, too. After our last mission, he took a side trip to HQ on—I don't even know what totally fake pretext, so B would be cooled off by the time Josh got back to the compound."

Crud. I braced for what was coming next.

"He brought back some gossip that you guys were coming in hot to HQ. With a civi. Kimi just checked—" i.e., hacked "—and it's true."

"Mhm."

My attempt at evasion tanked. Also no surprise.

"Deets, now, because not calling with details within an hour of hitting a compound or HQ completely violates the sister code. *You* brought in a civi. To HQ. You."

As much as I avoided civilians, Vee gravitated to them. She'd been fascinated with civilians, and their fashions, hobbies, and weird ideas like romance, and pop-culture stuff —which, okay, some of that part was cool—her entire life. She'd accidentally added one to our, to her, team, and was now engaged to him.

"Liv, talk. Where did you find this one? What were they doing that required HQ-level protection?"

I made a valiant last-ditch attempt at avoiding dissecting my failure. "It's not like I went out hoping to find one and bring them home. It wasn't a choice. He got caught in our sweep, and we were temporarily stuck with each other." Marshall had done his best to avoid all of us, making his feelings as to the situation and my failings clear, which was his right. "This wasn't my best mission, by far, okay?"

Silence stretched between us. I hadn't meant to say that much. Or show the bitterness I kept trying to excise from somewhere deep inside, and that I'd also failed at.

"Did you get any intel from him? The civilian?" Vee asked, trying to spin doctor this fiasco. Which was a very C.O. reaction, trying to make a bad decision less so for a teammate.

Except, I was the C.O. here. My mistake, my responsibility. I'd earned the position, and the weight that went with it.

"We didn't get anything from him that we didn't already suspect. This was a complete dumpster fire from start to finish."

The click of a door engaging filtered out over the terrace. I levered around and stretched, checking for bystanders who didn't need to hear a C.O. complaining, but no one was there.

Still, I lowered my voice and dialed back my attitude. "The poor guy was in the wrong place, at the wrong time. Literally. He played a big part in getting the other vics out safely, and he gave us everything he knew, but beyond picking out which of the three investors was the Master vampire, it was old intel. He didn't deserve this."

"Liv...none of that constitutes a failure. I checked your debrief report. You and the guys cleaned house."

Of course she'd checked.

I did the same with every one of her post-mission reports. Keeping tabs and assuaging the worry of my family out on missions and my not being there to have their backs.

I sighed and melted into the sun-warmed wood, getting comfortable. "Fine, it wasn't a failure. The guys are incredible. But it could have gone better. Much better."

"We both know perfect is a myth—like unicorns. It isn't attainable. You can't put that kind of pressure on yourself. No C.O. can. That kind of stress and intensity isn't sustainable."

Other C.O.'s didn't have to.

Other C.O.'s didn't have Oversight, the Company's ultimate ruling group, watching them, not because they were concerned for us but because they potentially doubted my loyalty, which could spill over onto the guys. Since part of the reason for the mistrust involved her team's newest member, Vee herself, and what she'd become, I didn't argue, not wanting to remind her, or hurt her.

Other C.O.'s also didn't have everyone in the Company,

from pre-teen cadets to emeritus agents watching. Conversations dying when Jace or Matteo or I walked in, then resuming as we left. They weren't taking bets on whether we'd fail, because that wasn't how anyone Company was—we supported and helped each other—but pitying us. The guys for the horrible loses of their siblings and teams, me for taking on what they all feared was going to end in the three of us dying.

We weren't supposed to exist. Yet we did, and I wasn't losing this, my team, my brothers, and my purpose. So, yes. I had to follow every rule. Miss no detail. Nail every mission flawlessly. Never give the guys cause to doubt their decision in joining or feel less than.

We had to be perfect just to be seen by our peers and extended family as good enough.

CHAPTER 7

ℳarshall

"WE GOT STUCK WITH EACH OTHER."

"A dumpster fire."

"Nothing useful."

Marshall had heard versions of that before. All his life.

He sank onto his bunk, the room mercifully empty for once. He'd been wrong, again, and not interpreted people and reactions right.

He'd thought—he didn't know what. That the Commander wasn't so bad. That in a complex full of killers, and future killers, and hard-edged office drones, that she was different. That for once, someone didn't think he was a problem to be avoided or solved.

The conversation outside that he hadn't meant to stumble over though, that was reality. She'd decided he was a screw up and she didn't have time for screw ups.

What he'd watched happen on the training course had been—bad. He wished he'd been smarter, faster, got between the kid and the violence.

Here was acres of perfect grass and buildings and fake cities and factories and tunnels, where other schools had football fields and tracks. Where she'd laid into the girl. She hadn't hit the kid, but no escaping she'd given the order for the other trainer guy to do it.

Instead of explaining to the girl, she'd barked. Punished. No patience or kindness anywhere on the field today.

His first instinct had been right after all. These were cold, hard people, comfortable with killing. He didn't belong here.

He still hadn't heard where he did belong. He was just— here. In the way. No job to do, no purpose. No clue about schedules, everyone moving fast, thinking even faster, aimed at important work. No word on when he could go.

He'd turned down talking to the doctors. Therapists or whatever they were called here. Bad as his situation was now, them finding out how messed up he was, it getting back to the Commander and the rest of this place, it'd be a new hell.

On time, a noisy crowd thundered into the cavernous rooms, seeming to make the space shrink around him. Older teenagers, including the girl the Commander had busted, swirled around. Talking. Shoving. Loud and busy and too much.

Marshall tensed when a quartet broke off and headed his way. The girl clearly the leader, same attitude as the Commander. The other girl and two guys followed her lead in everything.

The taunting had started small. Lights shone in his eyes at midnight, the culprit and their flashlight hanging over the edge of the top bunk. Marshall's bunk short-sheeted.

It'd escalated when he didn't respond. His stuff moved so

that he had to do a treasure hunt to find his shower caddy in the mornings. Dares to go on full backpack hikes to get his Company issued shirts back. Challenges to hit the climbing course to get blanket and pillow.

Shoving and arm-wrestling dares that he walked away from.

They were being brats. Picking up how to be aggressive, be heartless. Get ready to go out and kill.

They were still kids. He wasn't gonna lay a hand on them. After seeing how the teachers pushed and disciplined and yelled, he doubted he'd get busted for getting physical with them.

He still couldn't bring himself to hurt one of them. So he kept his head down and plowed through, the same plan he always relied on. Except before he'd always had a job to do. Plus, a place to escape to for privacy at least eight hours out of the day. Here, there wasn't even that time-out. All combining into a murky gray misery. With no end in sight.

As the group clustered in front of him, Marshall braced for another round. They'd been joined by four more kids.

His personal tormenter eyed him. "Are you a junior Instructor? When are you going to start classes?"

Marshall lifted one shoulder in a shrug. Never, but he wasn't saying that.

"Then what about PT training?"

He gave the same response.

The girl rolled her eyes. "Which Regional HQ did you come from? What are you here for. Like, your specialties?"

The guy from the other pack snorted. "Maybe he's here for you, Shell. You could use the help."

The girl—Shell or Graham or whatever shorthand they used here—who'd been on the receiving end of the Commander's temper, did some feint-and-sweep combo thing out of the blue, and the boy ended up on his butt. "I'm good enough to drop you."

Everyone laughed, not caring about rules and fighting. So used to being rough and kinda cruel that the guy took her hand when she offered and stood.

They all turned on Marshall again, eyes bright. Like a pack of hungry crows waiting at the dumpster for the night's food-trash.

The on-his-butt kid asked, "Are you going on Commander Muñez's team?"

That got him a shove from his tormentor. "Hello, Chip? Where are we standing? Oh, that's right, in cadet and junior trainers' barracks."

"So? I heard from Mikeal in Front Office that the suites are full. Muñez brought him in, so that's gotta mean something."

Yeah, that she'd gotten stuck with Marshall. Then ditched him as soon as possible.

"Ooh, that's why you don't do classes." Shell eyed him and ask-demanded, "Are you some kind of leftover, too? What was your other team and Region?"

"A team of leftovers?" Chip gave them a WTF-face. Like it was an impossibility.

Marshall got impossible. Like him working for these people, especially the hard, cold Commander.

The girl leaned in snake-fast and flicked the boy's ear. "Pay attention. That's already Muñez's team, and if anybody can make it happen? Definitely her."

Like talking about her conjured her, Marshall caught the flash of brown hair and confidence walking into the barracks.

"Keep it down," he muttered, getting all their attention again. "She's coming, and you don't want to make her mad again."

Now they were all staring at Marshall, then trading confused looks. Shell piped up. "Muñez? No way. She's freaking cool."

Only in this messed up alternate reality

At a throat clearing, the pack drew up a little straighter. Not looking as guilty or worried as they should be. "Ma'am."

She nodded to them, hair swinging with the motion, but spoke to Marshall. "Got a sec?"

The kids might not be smart enough to respect authority, but he was. Marshall shoved to his feet. "Yes, ma'am."

Her lips did that thing, pressing hard together. He'd screwed up again. "Olivia is fine, or Liv if you're comfortable with that."

Yeah, right.

"Could you give me your address?" She held out a piece of paper and a pen.

Marshall's mouth went desert-dry. If things had been bad before…he was about to really piss her off. If he refused, it would be bad. If he took the pen, it would be worse. He kept his hands to himself and blurted, "Why?"

She studied him for a minute before answering. "I need to do a clean-up sweep. The official Cleaners have been going non-stop on larger missions so I'm taking care of your residence. As I mentioned, our targets had access to your private information from your employment paperwork. Your license has an Illinois address, though."

He hadn't bothered updating it. He couldn't afford a car or maintenance. Plus, as often as he moved, there was a good chance he'd have already been fired and gone before he got the replacement.

She offered him the pen and paper again.

Anxiety chewed its way through Marshall's nerves. The room shrinking again, the kids circled around them. The

Commander in his face. The bed at his back, fencing him in, no place to escape.

She frowned and his stomach pitched. She looked to the kids, speaking to the girl, Shell. "Find some other place to be for an hour. This is ears only, and yours aren't those ears."

The cadets left, fast and collected as usual.

She faced Marshall again. "I respect that you don't feel comfortable broadcasting your address. I do need it though."

For the first time, it registered that she wasn't in soldier stuff. Instead of the plain tee and utility pants, she had on cargo pants, the kind that were made to look good, not hold weapons, and some kind of skinny white tank with lace along the top, instead of a gray soldier one. One of those short, short sleeved jackets over the shirt. Pale yellow, like spring and flowers, and somehow it suited her. Even her hair was different, in a ponytail but waves cascading down and the same streaky brown and amber as her eyes. She looked normal and not murderous and kinda approachable.

"I could go with you. Show you how to get there." Just them—and despite the knot of anxiety building between his shoulder blades at the idea of riding with her, better one soldier than three—and maybe convince her to leave him at his apartment. Or at least drop him someplace along the way.

"Marshall—"

He talked over her imminent no. "You said it—it's only cleaning out an apartment, checking things out."

She sighed and he flinched, because yeah, he'd screwed up again. She undid the button on her summery-pretty jacket and lifted one side—showing a holster and black gun under one arm. The hilt of a knife stuck up under the other. "Vampires won't be out, but that doesn't mean it's safe. It may not be for quite some time."

"Drop me off somewhere. Anywhere." He already knew her answer, even as she buttoned the jacket.

"We can't do that."

"I don't—" might as well be honest "—I don't belong here."

And he was speaking to her back, as she walked away.

"I know, and I am sorry."

iv

I DON'T BELONG HERE.

I slumped, head against the SUV's headrest, Marshall's flat statement still echoing even as I surveyed the block of cheap, rundown duplexes. It had only taken Front Office a few minutes to locate Marshall's last address in Mesa after his refusal.

According to the search, most of his time had been spent jumping from address to address, a dozen in the last couple of years. Like he didn't have a home, or didn't know where he belonged.

I understood where he was coming from.

Technically, I'd skirted the truth with Marshall. HQ's Cleaners were out on larger missions but I could have sent a local Cleaner team in to clear his place, box up, and deliver his personal effects.

Guilt over forcing him to stay in a situation he was clearly unhappy with, all because I hadn't been careful enough, ate at me. That he had also put himself in harm's way to aid other civilians and this was his treatment...

We were leaving for home, our primary compound, first thing in the morning. Basically, as soon as I rolled in from this side job.

Leaving Marshall stuck at HQ for the foreseeable future. Going by our last conversation, he hated the place even more than he disliked me.

I'd watched the cadets trying to feel him out, and get him to join in. Especially Graham. She would make a good C.O. one day, already looking out for others. Not ot in a way Marshall understood, though. In turn, they didn't understand civilians yet. He wore the BDU's of a Company agent, and they didn't realize that was simply because he hadn't come in with anything but the clothes he'd worn that day.

I'd watched him shy away from the rough and tumble overtures, and shut down. Although no matter what prank they committed, or roughhousing the teens engaged in, I'd also watched Marshall's patience and how he was careful to never use his size advantage to try to intimidate, or physically retaliate.

I wasn't any better than the cadets at offering him what he'd relate to.

Aside from this marathon delivery trip. When I'd left my original team, my civilian clothes, photos, favorite pillows, all the little things that accumulated over the years that eventually built to greater than the sum of their parts, was all I had. All the comfort available for a long time.

Hopefully, having his personal effects would offer Marshall a similar measure of familiarity and comfort. It wasn't much of a 'sorry we upended your life' apology, but it was all I had on hand for now.

Assuming no one had taken it upon themselves to liberate any of Marshall's property while he'd been away. This place was the epitome of anonymous, and committed to damn well staying that way. A strip of block buildings framed a stretch of dirt and sand. Each block apparently served as two apartments, a single door and window on each side.

The sagging sign I'd pulled in by advertised weekly or monthly rates. A hand-lettered piece of cardboard with a phone number was stuck underneath.

HQ might be full of rambunctious kids, but at least it was clean and there was no threat of someone busting out your car window in order to help themselves to anything saleable inside. Sliding out of the truck, I hit the lock.

Despite a real time SAT photo from the Intel branch, I eased down the pitted concrete walkway, skirting the pool, empty except for beer cans and debris. The possibility of the vampire Master or another backer having human eyes on this place was very real. I kept the gun down by my thigh, although no one here would blink at seeing it.

A curtain twitched in the first apartment then quickly dropped closed, inhabitant ignoring me. No one was sticking their neck out around here.

I double-checked the numbers spray painted on the side of each block. 2B was directly ahead, in a dead-end cul-de-sac of concrete and lost dreams—Marshall's apartment. My back pressed against the dusty concrete by his door, out of range of anything or anyone rushing or firing through the cheap wood, I stilled, listening. For the squeak of a shoe sole or familiar brush of claw against concrete.

Catching nothing but the shrill sales pitch from a car commercial playing on tv next door, I spun in front of the door and kicked. It crashed flat against the interior wall, proving nothing lurked behind it, but listing from one hinge, also proving I hadn't been the first person to abuse it recently.

I stepped in and swept the room, then repeated the action with the only other room, a tiny bath. Satisfied the place was vampire-minion and ghoul free, I backtracked and lifted the splintered door, smacking it more or less closed.

Even under the muted sunlight filtered through dingy plastic blinds, the place sucked. Block walls, with layers of patchy dirty-beige paint peeling off, framed a rickety metal bed. Now on its side, the torn linoleum flooring littered with mattress stuffing, where it had been slashed open. I toed the mattress over, double checking. The rips were ragged, from claws instead of a knife.

A table and chair that had started life as outdoor furniture were twisted into knots. Broken glass circled the heaps, what was left of a plate and maybe a few cups.

The laminate dresser that had probably stood between bed and kitchenette was splintered, its two drawers pulled out and clothes dumped. Colorful bits of paper were everywhere. I squatted and flipped over the one at the toe of my shoe. Part of a page, a comic. I tracked the confetti mess back to a larger pile of white that turned out to be the remnants of several cardboard boxes. Each must have been full of comic books.

I rolled the flimsy scrap around, half-formed ideas to realigning into new possibilities. A bit of wire and varnished wood peeked from under the box remnants. I let the paper flutter down, and shoved the mass of cardboard aside.

I winced, at what used to be a guitar, now smashed into kindling. A boot print was visible on a larger section of the body, proof it had been purposely stomped on.

I hated being right. Marshall's old boss' crew had paid a visit. Marshall still didn't understand how precarious his situation was. The trafficking lieutenants might even suspect

Marshall was a plant, a spy for us, and were after him for what they assumed he knew—shipment dates, locations, buyers' lists. Information he might've copied from the hotel manager's laptop or phone. They would logically also assume he knew where their cargo had disappeared to.

When they didn't find him, or a thumb drive and any clues, they'd trashed his belongings. What little there was of it.

I rose and scanned the two rooms again. If this was the sum total of Marshall's possessions... New agents were sent out with about ten times more, not even counting their cache of private objects, from personal hobbies and interests.

Angry for no reason I could pin down, I stomped out to the SUV, emptied one of our go-bags, and returned. Purposely not looking closely, the least I could do in preserving what was left of Marshall's privacy, I shoved clothes inside.

The bath hadn't fared any better than the main room, mirrored medicine cabinet smashed, toothbrush and supplies tossed out and shampoo dumped over the lot of it. Feeling guilty, I poked around, making sure I wasn't over-looking any medication.

As much salvaged as possible, I jerked the wobbly door closed on the remnants of Marshall's life, jammed sunglasses on against the late afternoon glare, and left, on my way to make Marshall's bad day a little worse.

* * *

SOMEONE BEAT me to ruining Marshall's day.

I crossed my arms, duffle bag banging against my hip, and cleared my throat. The noise was absorbed by the barrack's walls. "Cadets. Cadet Graham."

The future team froze. I gave Graham credit—she

stepped in front of the others, even as she tucked the can of whip cream, liberated from the cafeteria, behind her back in a sad attempt at concealing evidence.

The other cadets traded glances, and one flipped the blanket back in place on Marshall's bed. Not that it covered the pillowcase already filled with dairy product.

The prank was essentially harmless, and nothing Kimi and I hadn't done to Josh and Jace, and vice-versa. Except we'd grown up together, understood the joke would be reciprocated in kind, by someone we cared about, who'd have our backs the same as we had theirs.

Coming from strangers, in a setting he was new to, and unwillingly at that, and those strangers were armed? This would read as pure harassment from where Marshall was standing.

Which at the moment, was the outer barrack's breezeway. He rested against the wall, arms crossed but his posture screaming his weariness. Pretending his roommates weren't trashing his bed, because once again, he wouldn't risk confronting and accidentally hurting one of the kids.

"Ma'am." Graham spoke for the group, the rest now lined up at attention behind her.

"Should I give you a minute to work up a cover story?"

Her shoulders squared up. "No, ma'am."

"Report to the outdoor course. Three laps, in full gear." Three laps was cake, but the full gear took a lot of the fun out of it.

As the cadets aimed for the door, I held my arm out, blocking Graham. "As soon as your laps are completed, move your stuff to this bunk. Don't change the linens tonight."

She nodded, accepting it as fair punishment, and the four vanished.

"Marshall?"

After a beat, shoes squeaked on tile, and he came into view, dwarfing the doorway. "Yeah. Uh—yes, ma'am?"

"It's Liv," I repeated for the dozenth time. I unslung the duffle and held it out. "From your old apartment."

He flinched, either at referring to his place in the past tense, or my going at all and invading his personal life more deeply.

"Someone beat me there. They trashed the place pretty thoroughly. This was all I could salvage. I'm sorry."

He nodded, and gave me an emotionless, "Ok". Making sure not to touch my fingers, he took the load and backed a step away.

He was twice the cadets' size, but he took their pranks without a word or retribution. The same way he wouldn't ask me where the rest of his stuff was, and possibly rock the boat. Like he was the one imposing on us.

Turning to tuck the stupid duffle away, he hesitated, because, yeah, the bunk was no longer his. Gaze turned anywhere but at me, I still caught the way he tensed, shoulder's rising. "I don't—where should I go?"

Not here. I made a snap decision. "We're heading out. You're going with us." I'd find a way to explain our plus-one to Jace and Matteo. Perhaps I'd find a way to explain it to myself, as well. There was no rule forbidding me taking Marshall to our compound as opposed to him staying here until it was safe for him to leave and resume his life. His DNA was on file, and I was C.O. of the team that had conducted the raid he was involved in.

It wasn't the best idea when I was trying to show our professionalism, and our total loyalty, in the wake of my sister's decision that broke every Company rule. The guys and I were still perfecting our teamwork, which required all of my attention. Plus, Marshall didn't like me, and hadn't said one word to Jace or Matteo since he'd arrived here.

I couldn't bring myself to do the smart thing, not when it meant leaving Marshall here to be tormented.

He hefted his duffle and fell in behind me as I strode out. From his perspective, I guess it really was better the devil you know.

CHAPTER 9

*M*arshall

MARSHALL SQUASHED into the last row of the SUV's seats, wishing he could blend with the seat. It was probably weird —weirder—that he'd climbed in here, instead of taking the empty seat in the middle beside the tall soldier. Jace.

Sitting there meant they'd try to talk to him. Expect him to talk. Look at him, that freaky way they did, seeing everything.

Especially her. Liv, he reminded himself. She already looked at vampires, cadets, people, like she saw under their skin. Read the secrets hidden there. She would figure out he was a mess. Okay, a bigger mess than she already thought. That, that might paint a bigger target on his back.

His breathing sped up. Throat getting tight, his heart beating hard enough it echoed in his ears.

They hadn't done anything to him. It couldn't be far off though, something way worse than the kids had done, because these weren't kids. Easy to look at them and believe they'd *never* been kids.

They were the real thing. Real soldiers. Real guns. He'd already seen they knew how to use the weapons they carried. They *were* weapons. With no one to keep them in line, no one they had to fear, or who'd be watching them and sending them on punishment hikes.

They'd drop the polite front eventually. Or even if they meant it, he'd screw up bad enough or often enough to piss at least one of them off.

At least it was only three of them. Hopefully, he'd have room to avoid them, easier than with the kids.

The clang of a warning buzzer jolted him out of his bad headspace. Lights brighter than the noon sun blazed, sweeping over the vehicle, and he threw up his hand to shield his eyes.

"Sorry, man. Forgot to warn you. Those are UV, and vampire and ghoul repellent."

Marshall couldn't tell which man spoke, busy blinking teary eyes, his vision wavery. Whoever it was sounded contrite, but it had to be fake.

"Hang tight." That voice he already knew. Hers. She continued. "There'll be an alarm, but ignore it, in three, two, one—"

A shrill alarm pierced the truck. Under it, Marshall caught the rapid click of fingers on a keyboard, one that had folded out of the dash like something out of a superhero movie.

The noise died. Leaving his ears ringing.

"Right. The DNA scan is keyed to ours, so it goes off for unknown occupants. I've added your signature, so that won't happen again," she said into the quiet.

He caught the two men exchanging glances, then Jace

staring in her direction. Whatever it was about, her lips pressed together, hard.

Probably they wanted Marshall out of here fast, instead of putting his DNA in anything.

The truck turned off, and regular halogen lights illuminated a cross between a spacious garage, like for four cars, and another sci-fi set. Stark, clean white walls, though he couldn't miss dents and rusty-brown spots. He swallowed, throat tight again. Old bloodstains, because these people were killers. They might even have killed here.

Two doors slammed, the truck rocking. Which only left one other soldier. A seatbelt pinged. Live turned, facing him. "This is home sweet home for us. At least, it is seventy-five percent of the time."

"Not there? At HQ?" He blurted, needing something, anything to fill the silence that'd stretched too long.

"We're a deployed team, with our own Division in the Southwest Region. It shakes out to Arizona and a sliver of New Mexico. Normally we'd come straight here after a mission, but, extenuating circumstances." She shrugged, an elegant lift of her shoulder, same perfect, in charge way she talked, moved, did everything.

Extenuating circumstances. That was him, the opposite of perfect, the thing she'd gotten stuck with. Not knowing how to apologize for messing up their schedule, he went with, "Okay."

From her sigh—too like all the disappointed and disgusted ones he'd heard all his life—not the right answer.

At least she didn't yell. He'd make sure he didn't fuck up enough to get the treatment the cadet had, out on that training field. Except, fucking up was basically part of his DNA.

iv

MARSHALL FOLLOWED me out of the truck and through the entry chamber. Keeping as far from me as possible yet still escape being cut in half by the door. The same way he'd acted since we had jerked him out of his real life.

Despite his size, he seemed to take up half the space he should, hunched in on himself. His hand choked the duffle strap, tightening when the vacuum's puff of air lifted his curls. He didn't let go to brush them out of his eyes. I'd been right in assuming the bandanna he'd worn at our first meeting was more utilitarian than fashion statement.

His eyes widened again as the air swirled then died away.

I hurried to explain. "We're clear. That was a cleaner system. Part anti-bacterial, part other."

"Other. Not human," he said. Then twitched, like he was waiting for...I didn't know what.

"Exactly." I tried guessing. "It's calibrated and equipped to help eliminate cryptid, and to a lesser degree, vampire bio-agents. If it helps, you can ask me anything. I do understand how alien all of this is, and I'm happy to explain."

He nodded. I couldn't be sure if he was really agreeing, or if it was an automatic response, his default for every question.

As we stepped into the compound proper, I attempted to reassure him, based on how Bruce had reacted on first seeing our setup. "This doesn't look like most homes. Like I said, this is temporary, though. As soon as we track down the head of this trafficking ring, you'll be free to go."

His, "Sure" lacked conviction.

Trailing behind me, I couldn't see his expression, whether our home was too utilitarian and disgusted him, or was okay. There had been some renovations, but it still didn't look exactly like civilian living quarters. My team had been granted Region Two's Division Two, my original home and the compound, while Vee and the team had moved to Division Four in California.

I tried again. "It's plain, but you really aren't in any danger here, I swear. Aside from the armory and my office, you can go anywhere in the compound you like." I waved him forward.

When I didn't hear footsteps, I turned. Marshall stood in the junction that led out of the kitchen. Staring, like he was mesmerized. Reminding me that every military base didn't have a kitchen designed for a tyrannical, starred chef.

"I...wow." Marshall's attention jumped from appliance to appliance.

I snorted, and he jumped as if he'd forgotten I was there. "Um, you guys take food seriously."

"Let's just say one of my former teammates had exacting standards." I squashed the flicker of pain.

Still too easy to see the ghosts of hundreds of meals past,

Bruce slamming around the chef's range, barking at Josh to keep his paws out of the mise en place, Kimi laying out plates, all of us gathered around the scarred table enjoying the meal, joking, goofing. Being a family.

There was so much more to being a team than working well in the field. The guys and I were trying, but we weren't there yet. We might never be.

The giant table looked barren now, with only the three of us and our frozen pizzas.

I jerked myself out of my pity party. I had a new team and new obligations. The latest watched me, blue eyes wary, dark circles underneath.

After witnessing today's hazing, it didn't take deductive skills to know he hadn't slept well, keeping one eye open for the cadets' next prank. I'd failed to think through ramifications—I'd seen his reaction during our raid. I should have switched and given him the slightly more private bunk in the adult barracks, with the guys. Another blot on my iffy leadership record.

On impulse, I said, "Listen, whatever you think about our setup, this really is a safe place. No one here will mess with you, your room, or your belongings. You have my word. We can postpone the grand tour until later. Let's get you settled first."

He chewed at his lip, but gave me a nod, at least. It kind of killed me that he was still watching his back. I aimed for the rooms, then hesitated. The sleeping quarters made a weird y-shape off the kitchen, showers in the middle. To the left was the wing containing Jace and Matteo's rooms, plus multiple unused rooms. Marshall could have his choice.

To the right, the hall only held two rooms—my suite, the perk of being C.O., and one other room. All on its own, my mouth took over, and legs followed, going right. "Your room is down this hall, beside mine. It's quieter here, so you can get some sleep."

Which was so not true. The thick oak and adobe walls pretty much acted as soundproofing, and the guys weren't thoughtless teens. They got loud in the common areas, but respected private spaces.

Something in me couldn't stand Marshall's obvious anxiety. It would also be easier to check in with him if he was next door.

Marshall cut me a quick glance, not even a shred of trust in evidence.

I shoved open the first door and hit the lights. Trying to objectively see the room from his perspective. It was only one room, but it was easily four times the size of his old apartment and bath combined, the size a leftover from the days before technology evened the playing field between humans and cryptids, and large teams and two to a room were standard.

The furniture here was basic—queen size bed, nightstand, locker, dresser, and wingback chair. "The closet is over there." I indicated the far wall. "There are linens and extra blankets in the locker."

As I eased into the room to show him, Marshall moved right, probably attempting to avoid me, but only accomplished creating a bottleneck. The two of us crashed into each other. I caught myself, hand landing on his chest. Under the cotton of the Company tee, his heart raced. Showing his unease far better than his face or deceptively calm answers had.

He stared down where I touched him. Which, yeah. Violating his personal space in a major way.

I dropped my hand and stepped back, settling for tipping my chin at the metal locker at the foot of the bed. "I'll let you unpack. When you're ready, one of us will show you around."

I closed the door and retreated to the kitchen. And right into the mountain that was Mattao. He *oofed*, caught and turned me the same direction he was going. "Dang."

"Sorry." I cut around him, avoiding Jace's long legs stretched out from where he sprawled in a kitchen chair turned away from the table, and grabbed the first thing I came to from the fridge.

Taking a swallow, I regretted my choice, fake mango sports drink coating my tongue. "Gah."

"Never hate on the power juice." He rescued his and his brother's sugary addiction from my clutches, then got serious. "So. Marshall."

"Don't hold back." I dropped into a chair beside Jace.

They knew I meant it. I was leader, but we were a team, each member having a say. Plus, they were my friends, and had been since we were far younger than the cadets I'd busted earlier.

We hadn't had a chance to discuss anything, my and Marshall arriving as Matteo cranked the SUV motor. Putting up the privacy glass to talk about someone during the long drive seemed like a jerkish move, not a trust-building one.

"Man." Matteo rubbed his smooth chin. "A civi."

"A rule-bending civi," Jace added. "I didn't think we bent rules."

We didn't, not with so many strikes against us.

"He's a flight risk. Dude looks at us like we're the cryptids," Jace said.

"Can't blame him." Matteo grunted, a trace of guilt on his face. "I shove him into a wall, we blaze in, instigate a one-sided fire-fight, cut off heads, and hold him hostage. Ish."

Matteo had picked up the ish thing from my sisters. I didn't like *ish* tacked onto anything. Decisions, missions, choices should be clean, direct, with no room for maybes.

I slumped, until the chair back caught my ponytail and

stopped my downward progress. "I know. But the kids at the Academy are in that full of themselves phase, and don't understand how to interact with civilians, and I punted."

I rolled my head enough to check out their expressions. "Think it was the wrong move?"

Jace chugged half his drink before coming up for air and answering. "I feel kinda responsible, you know? The kids weren't being spiteful, but…"

"But the guy doesn't get that they expected him to join in," Munch finished. "Here's better, and it isn't like we have to worry about him coming into contact with Vee and the team and getting the Assessor's attention. We just didn't expect blatant rule flouting from you."

He tossed me a beer, took a seat, cracking his bottle open, and clinking it against mine. "'Bout time, Liv."

"Hell, yeah." Jace grinned and tapped his sports drink in, completing the unanimous vote.

I had to smile back. At least they believed I hadn't made a mistake, even if our newest resident didn't agree.

$\mathcal{M}$arshall

MARSHALL STARED AT THE ROOM. His room. The one the gun-carrying, scary as hell soldier-assassins gave him.

He touched the wall, double-checking that this was real, not a dream while he slept in the back of a SUV bound for a secret, high tech military compound located in who knew where. The textured finish glided under his fingertips, cool and solid. The room a soft ocher-yellow, like sunsets over the desert. Except quieter, a sleeping color.

With the new privacy, he took it all in, without worrying about being too slow and getting in anyone's way. The bed, heavy polished wood with a worn but shiny headboard. A similar dresser, wider than he was. Both antiques. A big chair in one corner, with heavy, ornate upholstery. As nice as anything his mother had bought, and warned him and his brother to stay off of or else.

He opened the locker, also reassuringly cold and metallic and real. Crisp blue and white sheets nestled in one half, thick matching blankets in the other, the scent of flowers escaping. The same fabric softener their maid from the cleaning service had used on her weekly visits.

This freaky reality, and pure exhaustion, swamped him. His butt hit the bed, and didn't even feel the impact through the cushy mattress. He checked under the spread, and yeah, it was one of those memory foam ones.

He didn't think of memory foam and military in the same sentence. He for sure didn't think they had this kind of stuff. Comfortable. Normal. *Nice.*

Except these weren't plain military, but black ops. Nobody had to spell it out. Even he knew that. Black ops anti-cryptid soldiers.

His gut did an *oh hell no* roll, images of severed heads too fresh. He rubbed at his stomach and tight chest. His hand lingered over his heart. Where she, the Commander—Liv— the scariest of all, had touched him. She'd seemed nice, too, the same as this room. And as out of place and unexpected. She didn't fit.

When he'd knocked into her, instead of worrying about him accidentally crushing her and barging into her personal space, she'd been trying to keep him upright. Worried about him, and that he had a place to sleep.

Soldiers, barracks, killer kids, kindness, and luxury beds. The clashing ideas hit and flew apart into a crazy mix in his head, refusing to line up in any kind of logical order, worse than when his dad had lost patience helping with homework and stood over Marshall, yelling about being lazy and needing to apply a better work ethic.

There was too much room for error here.

Maybe he could stay in here the whole time, and beat the

odds. One thing he did know was that lethal professional soldiers and smart, competent, and way too beautiful women only equaled one thing for him and his weird brain—hell.

iv

A DOOR CLICKED, the echo traveling up the hall.

Twenty-four hours, and his shadow slipping around a corner was as close as I had gotten to setting eyes on our new roommate.

I jerked the elastic holder out, letting my hair fall, then pulling it back into a tighter tail. The functionality of my ponytail one thing I could control.

"Dudes like a ghost," Jace said, entering the air-conditioned kitchen on my heels. He rooted in the fridge, coming out with another sports drink, and two or three-day-old Mongolian barbeque leftovers that had made the drive home with us. Escaping food poisoning really was his superpower.

I groaned, registering the dented take-out box. "Has anyone seen Marshall eating?"

Matteo trailed in and eyed the leftovers. When Jace

curved a protective arm around his bounty, Matteo settled for grabbing a box of cereal from the counter.

He dug in without benefit of milk. "Caught him in here around midnight, when we finished a CoW session." Matteo sprayed crumbs, using the shorthand for Cogs of Warfare, their favorite game. "I didn't mean to sneak up on him, but he bolted." He shook the cereal box, judging weight. "I think he had some."

"He's miserable." Jace pitched his voice low, like the subject of our discussion might overhear.

Both guys looked at me.

Right. This was a rule-bending C.O. issue. I strode down the hall, pulling up my Big Girl Commander Undies, and knocked on the door next to mine.

After an era, I got a, "Yeah?" the hesitant tone at odds with the deep voice.

I kept my tone light. "Could I speak to you for a moment?" As an afterthought, I added, "Please?"

Like something from one of our B-movie Night horror flicks, the door inched open in increments. Only enough that I got a glimpse of a slice of a blue eye and skin pale under a scattering of freckles.

"Hey. We never got a chance for that tour yesterday. If you aren't busy, now would be a good time for me." I tried out a smile.

"I—" The door edge creaked in his grip. I could almost see the panicked wheels turning while he searched for an excuse not to have to deal with us.

I relaxed against the far wall, arms folded.

Marshall caved, stepping out and closing the door behind him.

I peeled off the wall. "Grand tour. C'mon."

He stayed a full body length away, and slightly behind me down the hall.

The kitchen was empty, the guys either unwilling to get in the middle, or giving Marshall space.

"I'm guessing you already found the showers and kitchen."

Marshall hunched, shoving his hands in the pockets of a neon yellow hoodie, a survivor of the apartment devastation. "Sorry. I didn't mean to—"

I cut him off, irritated with myself and my lack of forethought. "I should have thought to show you where everything was in here, at least."

"It's okay." He hunched deeper. "Nice. It's a nice setup. I won't touch anything."

I gritted my teeth, then quit as a headache threatened. "Go for it. If the guys and I haven't managed to break it yet, you won't."

I tilted my head and he fell in behind me, again far enough away to convey how very much he didn't care to be near me. I pointed left at the junction of the shorter hallway leading out to the kitchen. "My office. If you need anything and I'm not out on a course, that's where you'll find me. Feel free to knock, although it's off limits when I'm not in there."

Getting zero feedback, I kept going. "Game room and den common area. It's where you'll find us the rest of the time."

Sure enough, Matteo and Jace were on either end of the pool table, racking balls for a game. "Yo, man." Jace saluted with a pool cue.

Marshall's eyes widened, scanning the double room, taking in the wall-sized screen, and the mass of boxes and cables attached. Basically, every system known to gamerkind. Disc boxes piled in one corner. Throw pillows—which probably had recently served as missiles—in a pile near the oversized, ugly-ish couch, loveseat, and pair of legitimately ugly barrel chairs drawn up in front of the screen at the perfect gaming angle.

Crumbs from the previous night's battle covered everything. "I was so not kidding about chupacabra's discovering this place is a vermin drive-through, and invading while we sleep." I toed an empty sports bottle.

Marshall tensed, although Matteo didn't even bother shifting his attention my way, committed to lining up his shot. "We'll get it cleaned." The crack of balls signaled him breaking, and Jace turned back to the action.

Marshall shot me a furtive glance.

I sighed and continued our tour. "They will clean up. It really isn't slob-central here, I promise."

"S'okay," Marshall said, his tone verging on confused.

I popped the door and stepped onto the narrow pipe-rail balcony that ran the length of the backside of the house.

Marshall blinked at the change to bright sunlight, while I jogged down, the metal steps echoing. He followed more slowly, his attention going all over the yard. Probably scouting out potential escape routes. Still distracted, his sneaker toe stubbed on the last step, one taller than the rest, and he stumbled.

I grabbed, bracing his shoulders, before he pitched face first into the sandy dirt.

His face went from paper-white to blazing, clashing with his hair. "Sorry, I'm—I wasn't paying attention. I didn't mean to try to squash you."

"It's cool. All of us have misjudged there, even knowing it's higher than it should be. I've always suspected a vampire designed it, as a joke on humans."

He blinked at me, lines creasing his forehead, recognizably confused now.

Or uncomfortable because I still had hands on him even though I'd had to reach up. My palms flat on his upper chest, since I'd have had to reach even higher to touch his shoulders, their span rivaling Matteo's. The way Marshall had

78

reared back from Jace's simple touch at the hotel raid flashed through my head.

I backed off, into the yard, sand crunching. And kept my hands to myself, sticking with pointing out features. "Outdoor course, track, though most running is cross-country if you wanted to join us, gym with weights and space for—" I hesitated at mentioning hand-to-hand sparring, and went with "—workouts. There are showers and medical grade whirlpool in back."

He turned as I did, while I gestured at the last building and field. "Armory and shooting range. They are off limits. Company policy, not that I don't trust you."

Marshall's face faded back to pale, and he swallowed, loud enough that I heard. Because, again, a civilian, and I'd forgotten their general response to violence and blood, and his even more so.

"I won't go out there." He closed down again, eyes on the ground.

"Marshall." I stepped in close so he couldn't not see me. "I understand this is sudden and very much a stranger in a strange land situation. But you aren't a prisoner. Aside from armory and office, you can go anywhere in the compound you like. Sit out here." I flicked a finger at the bench, covered in turquoise and gold outdoor cushions, situated to watch the bird bath and artistically arranged succulents my sister Kimi had set up. The plants were looking a little brittle without her here to care for them.

Anyway. "If you get bored, pull up our streaming services, or hit the library. It's in the rear of the game room."

My attempt at reassurance went flat, Marshall taking a step back.

Enough terrorizing the guy for one day. I gave up and climbed the stairs, Marshall a silent shadow trailing me. We passed through the house in silence, until we got to the kitchen.

I couldn't miss him sneaking glances at the double fridge, or Bruce's leftover second-tier pots and pans hanging over the prep island he'd installed.

Sometimes I was so slow. We'd stormed in on Marshall in the hotel kitchen. Presumably his thing. His 'wow' when he'd first seen ours came back to me. If he was anything like Bruce, with his rabid love of all things culinary, maybe this could be his safe place, and give him some sense of normalcy and control.

I made another snap decision and touched his elbow, getting his attention. "You should make yourself at home in here. We're all cruddy cooks but you know your way around. I was serious when I said root through the fridge and pantry and see what you can throw together."

Apparently, snap decisions weren't my wheelhouse. Marshall flinched away, nodding, and left for his room without a word.

I slumped against the fridge, metal cold against my back. The empty kitchen absorbed my sigh.

CHAPTER 13

M arshall

MARSHALL HOVERED, one hand on his door to shut it fast if he was wrong.

But it sounded like they all went outside, feet pounding on the metal ladder-step thing leading from the deck to the ground. The one he'd tripped on, nearly crushing her—Liv. Heat rode his face at the reminder of falling all over himself, and in front of one of them, soldiers who moved like they were part non-human, unnervingly fast and smooth and sure of themselves.

Especially her. He cringed at the lingering ghost of her disappointed sigh earlier. She'd pretty much ordered him to cook, even though she'd already made up her mind that he'd suck. He'd seen how high her standards were and how she acted with people who didn't meet them.

The silence heavy, he peered into the kitchen, then went the rest of the way. The chrome and copper dazzled him.

Okay, he probably would suck compared to whoever used all of this before him. This was the kind of range and equipment he'd only seen a couple of times, one in a Gold Coast hotel where he'd only been a busboy, the other a four-star place in Tucson where he'd only lasted the night.

He left the kitchen long enough to stick his head in the tricked-out game room, something he hadn't imagined assassins had. It was empty and the band circling his lungs loosened.

He hurried back, throwing the fridge open. Spotless but empty shelves gleamed back. Half of a jug of milk, one egg, cartons of yogurt, a few beers, and lots of electrolyte drinks.

Marshall dropped to one knee, pulling open crisper compartments. Just as bare. Some wilted lettuce, already turning slimy, was the only thing in the front drawer. Way in the back, he spied an onion. Shriveled but usable. Near it, a plastic packet. Processed cheese, most of the yellow squares still inside.

He swallowed and braced, opening the freezer section, taking stock. A couple of frozen burritos, the cheap kind from convenience stores, a single-serving pizza, all meat, and a depleted carton of chocolate chunk ice cream.

He closed the door on the blast of cold. Heart sinking lower with every cabinet he opened, finding only cereal and more cereal. The pantry off the kitchen was his last hope. Flipping the light on, his heart quit trying to bottom out. Boxes and containers of grains lined the shelves—barley, oats, quinoa. One lone box of pasta, shoved to a far corner like it had offended someone. The next, nearly bare shelf held a couple cans of tomatoes, and a row of spices. He checked a folded over bag of flour, and sneezed at the musty-stale smell.

Still, compared to the rest of the kitchen, this was the mother load. He grabbed the flour to pitch in the trash, then pushed it back in place. He hadn't been given leeway to toss stuff. Instead, he scooped up dried spices and cans. He'd fix —something.

He set a pot on, turning salted water up to boil, and adjusted the oven temperature. Praying this would be enough to buy him some space, and lessen the harassment that had to be waiting when their patience ran out.

His fingers stilled, midway to dropping the pasta in the water.

Nobody had yelled or snapped. The Commander had been kinda nice earlier, between his nearly crushing her and bolting like he was giving her the cold shoulder. But the irritation and complaints had to be coming. No way were they happy to have him here. His stomach clenched hard enough to hit his backbone at the conversation he'd overheard where she had complained about getting stuck with him, and the look she given Marshall when he'd frozen in front of the barracks full of cadets.

Then she'd been—okay. Patient. Hadn't barked or thrown stuff when things weren't going her way. Other than the cadet on the field, she hadn't gotten rough or petty. Hadn't even yelled at the other two soldiers over the crumbs and disorganized mess, even when they blew her off. And no way was she *disorganized.* Everything about her was sharp and clear. That direct gaze, those hard, ninety-percent cocoa eyes that caught every move.

The way she stood, pulling every eye her way. Not needing to get loud to get a room's attention. Her voice was always level and real—like somebody you could think of trusting, no overreacting like Marshall. No lying like his old boss. Easy. If he ignored how pretty she was, she felt easy to be around.

Hot bubbles popped against his hand, the water boiling

over, knocking him back to reality. He shook the sting off and turned the temperature down, dropping the pasta in.

Whatever. The yelling would come. It always did. Like when she finally really realized who she'd gotten stuck with, and he didn't work fast enough, fucked up simple directions, got lost in his head, his body telling him something basic was life threatening and shutting down. When she expected him to do something everyone else could—everyone but him.

* * *

HE WATCHED the clock beside his temporary bed, waiting until the numbers flashed past midnight. He'd learned his lesson last night, thinking they'd all be in bed, all military lights out like in movies. Instead, he almost ran into the biggest soldier, foraging for food. Soldiers weren't *supposed* to keep restaurant hours.

At one, he slipped out into the dark hall. He'd clean up from dinner, and load the dishwasher. See if they'd left any lasagna.

It wasn't much, but most people who liked pizza also liked lasagna, and it wouldn't taste terrible if it sat for a while after cooking, since he wasn't sure when they'd be ready for dinner. This version was only noodles, cheese, and sauce made with the tomatoes and onion he'd salvaged. There hadn't been any meat, or any real vegetables.

His empty stomach twisted, nothing to do with hunger. He didn't know what he'd make for lunch. He could cobble together real oatmeal with cinnamon for breakfast, but the lasagna had cleaned out the other useable staples.

He blamed getting lost in worry and what-ifs for not noticing danger until he ran into it.

"Marshall?"

He froze, pulse rate ramping up, caught. She stood at the

sink, frowning at him, soap bubbles popping as she pre-washed the empty lasagna pan. So much for dinner.

"Hey, don't—" he swallowed, shoving words together while he had the chance. "I'll clean. I was only waiting until you were gon—until everyone was finished."

She slotted the pan in the dishwasher and closed the door, switching to run the damp cloth she'd washed with across the counter, her lips moving.

He had to concentrate over the blood pounding in his ears, to hear her, and still missed too much before he separated her voice and his pulse.

"—clean up."

"I will. I should've already, I know," he promised.

She gave him a weird look, and frowned. "Seriously though. You cooked, we'll clean up. Jace and Matteo are capable." She flipped the cloth over a rod to dry. "That lasagna—"

"I'll do better," he swore, on a wave of failure and shame. "There wasn't—" It didn't matter. She wouldn't care about his excuses. "I will."

He retreated and slammed his door on whatever she said. He didn't need to hear that she was disappointed. His head was already clear enough in telling him how screwed he was.

CHAPTER 14

Liv

THIS WAS GETTING to be a thing.

Marshall went scary still, cereal box in hand, as we all spilled into the kitchen.

I caught Jace's whispered, "Craaap." He and Matteo both halted, leaving me taking point.

I had fought for the position. Time to own it. Pulling on crisis training, I smiled and walked past Marshall. Grabbing water bottles, I pitched them to the guys.

Marshall watched me, only his eyes moving. "I thought— it's early. For lunch."

"Mid-morning break, man." Munch kept it chill, plucking his sweaty tee, arms torn off as usual, away from his chest.

"We'll be outta your hair soon." Jace didn't have one bit of trouble seeing Marshall had assumed we'd be outdoors, that he could safely stage a grab-and-go, and really wished he'd been correct.

"That oatmeal stuck to our ribs. Surprised you needed a snack break." Matteo used his water bottle, pointing at the cereal box.

Marshall dropped it like he'd been accused of shoplifting. "Sorry."

The oatmeal had been good, as well as filling. A suspicion formed, knocking and demanding my attention. I drained my bottle and tossed the empty into the recycling box, trying to be as casual as Matteo. "You're welcome to the cereal, if you didn't get enough earlier."

Marshall mumbled, "I'm fine." Retreating befor his soft lie died out.

"Ooo-kay." Jace exhaled and sprawled in the first chair. "So much for not spooking him. At least we got breakfast out of it."

"Dinner, too," Munch said. "Didn't know anybody had gone shopping, but hey, Marshall put it to good use."

"Neither of us have been out." We never did until the sports drinks and burritos ran out. And we'd been borderline when we left for the hotel mission.

I hit the fridge, jerking one of the two doors open. The expansive shelf space always dwarfed our few items, but now they were barer than usual. Even the milk was gone, undoubtedly into the morning's oatmeal.

I abandoned the fridge, slamming cabinet doors open, one after the other, as if they'd magically been stocked by a delivery service. "Crud."

"Liv?" Matteo paused mid-glug.

Jace put it together first. "He didn't. Did he?"

"I don't know how Marshall managed to pull together a dinner and breakfast from nothing, but I do know he didn't have any of either for himself. Nothing had been scooped from that lasagna pan when we found it."

"The other night—he wasn't shopping for a snack." The

water bottle died in a crackle of plastic, crushed in Matteo's big fist.

"Nor was he just now." How had I missed it?

"He fed us, but he didn't eat first." Jace scrubbed a hand over his fade. "That's messed up."

"When I suggested cooking, I thought I was giving him a way to relax. He took it as an order to feed us."

"Or else." Disgust tightened Matteo's face, at himself and us. "If he's this literal, we gotta be more careful."

"I'm about to rectify that. Okay, right after a shower," I said, as Jace eyed my soaked shorts and tee. "Make yourselves scarce."

CHAPTER 15

M arshall

MARSHALL WASN'T surprised when the knock sounded. He breathed, held it, breathed again, slowing his heart rate as much as he possible. As sure as he could be that he wouldn't melt down, he unclenched bloodless fingers from around his knees, and stood.

Facing the music, ready for a chewing out, or worse. No one here would blink at punches being throne. The two guys —he wouldn't start anything, but he'd fight if he needed to.

Then there was the Commander. She was a leader, and a killer. Size disadvantage or not, she was a real fighter. Those were facts.

He still knew he'd never put a hand on her, no matter what she did to him.

Instead of drawn up, ready to get in his face, when he opened the door she was slouched against the far wall with her ankles crossed. "Hey. Got a minute?"

"Yeah. Yes." Suspicion made it come out sharper than he'd intended.

"If I ask you a question, will you be honest with me?"

"Yes." Although he couldn't puzzle the trap out, his thoughts veering to whether he'd end up back at HQ or that shelter.

"You didn't have dinner last night, or breakfast this morning, did you?"

"No."

"Right." She tipped her head back, like there was something fascinating on the ceiling. Some undiscovered Sistine Chapel painting, except this one with monsters and Arizona sky. "I'm assuming that was due to there being little here to work with."

That didn't sound like a question and he stayed quiet. Safer that way.

"Let's go." She straightened and flashed a keyfob at him.

Okay. Getting kicked out, then. He didn't know if he was relieved or fucked, brain splitting off on multiple tangents—where he could find a place to stay in whatever town this was, where the cheap motels might be located. "I'll get my stuff. I just need a minute." He hadn't unpacked, not that there was much let *to* unpack.

A low curse came from behind him, and he tensed.

"Marshall, no. Look at me?"

He turned back to her, not like he had any other option.

She'd crossed the hall, hand out like she meant to touch him. Following his gaze, she dropped her hand, and backed closer to where she'd started from. "I only meant let's go shopping. If you're cooking, you need supplies. Even if you aren't, we're one yogurt away from starvation here. We need to restock groceries."

He twisted and turned her speech, trying to figure it out. Because she didn't sound angry or even irritated. For the first time, he really looked at her. Instead of the basic BDU's they trained in, or even the gray-scale camos from the night of the attack, she had on real clothes. No jacket and gun, but a pink and green shirt in that floaty stuff that looked like summer, glowing brown skin visible, and those light jeans. The skinny kind that followed the line of her body and legs.

"A quick, painless shopping trip—milk, pizza, chocolate, possibly veggies?" She said, her cheek dented in, like maybe she was biting the inside of it.

Like she was worried instead of mad. Which he couldn't process. She had no reason to worry, but—she was.

"Okay." He gave the only answer he could, and joined her.

* * *

IN THE REAL OUTDOOR LIGHT, her eyes were less bitter chocolate and more spun-sugar brown. Like boiled sugar, almost caramelized, the kind they stretched to decorate fancy desserts. He concentrated on them, and the play of light across them as they drove, helping occupy his brain so it didn't latch onto problems instead.

She'd tried to talk to him at first, all the way from the compound to here—a city. Scottsdale. The one they'd passed through on the way from HQ probably, but it hadn't stuck in his head, too much else that day crowding out things like where he was. Missing important information, like always.

"Marshall?"

He started at the soft question The truck was parked in a lot. Still running, 'cause it was always too hot to sit in a closed car in Arizona, even one with tinted windows.

He darted a furtive glance at her. She'd already unbuckled and was swiveled in her seat, facing him. Staring. Panic fluttered at being under that direct look.

Whatever she saw, she slumped in her seat and rubbed

between her eyebrows, like she had a headache, or was getting one. Likely because of him. "Sorry," he blurted.

"For what?"

Her question didn't hold the usual edge most people put in, when dealing with him. It, she, sounded real. And confused, again.

He understood confused. "You know. For messing up your routine. Pretty much everything."

"Marshall, seriously." He tensed but the way said it, as soft as when she'd had to knock him back into the real world, didn't change. She wiggled and leaned toward him, like his attention mattered. "Listen to me, please?"

Nobody had asked-asked him anything, not in that way in —long enough he couldn't remember. He nodded.

"You have nothing to apologize for. You haven't done one thing wrong. Your immoral, greedy boss, and his greedy, vicious, human trafficking vampire Master did. They brutalized innocent women. They put you in danger. Then we, who are supposed to be mitigating some of that stress, are instead causing you to feel even more in danger. I am so, so sorry I haven't handled this better."

Shock jerked his head up, locking eyes on purpose. He didn't read anything but truth there. She was blaming herself. And that wasn't right. "You didn't. Mess up, I mean."

"Neither have you."

"I'm not explaining this right. I do that all the time."

"Yeah, me to. My ideas don't always translate to real life the way I intend."

Shocked again at the sadness dragging her voice down, he hunted for a way to reassure her. Instead, he got lost in the gentle wisp of her fingers on his arm. Almost light enough to be his imagination, except for elegant fingers right there, warm and real, then gone. He nearly missed it when she started talking again.

"For instance, I didn't think about asking you to perform one of those bread and fish feeding the masses miracles, like our adopted father talks about. I never meant that suggestion as an executive order for you to feed *us*."

He digested that, making sure he'd really heard her. "It wasn't? I mean, you really didn't?"

"Not at all. My thought process went something along the lines of 'Hey, Marshall's a chef. We have a chef's kitchen. He'll like that.' Epic fail, huh?" She gave a grimace-smile.

"Oh."

She stayed turned to him, quietly watching him. Not hurrying him or glaring like she begrudged the time it took him to process and put his thoughts into a format other people understood. Which was different. Nice different. "S'okay. Sometimes…I miss things or don't interpret right."

"Thank you for being gracious." She gave him a tiny, real smile.

He got braver. "This is?" He checked out their destination. Not a store. A farmer's market, one of the permanent ones with, with shops and stalls.

"We do need supplies but you don't have to cook with them, or cook at all. Just help me choose, and pick up whatever you want. Although, let me say, dinner was great, and thank you for that."

The hot rush that meant he was blushing, bright red like a clown, climbed his neck. That and surprise. "You—you guys —liked it? The cheese wasn't good." And now he was insulting them. They'd picked the boring sliced kind in the first place, which meant that they liked it. "I mean, not good for cooking, not the disgusting kind of not-good."

"I'm well aware that processed cheese is only a couple of steps above petroleum by-product with yellow dye added." She laughed and ducked her head

Like she meant it. Like—he double-checked. Yeah, she wasn't laughing at him, but at herself.

"The lasagna really was great. It's been a while since any of us had a home cooked meal." Some kind of sadness flowed through her open expression.

Whatever caused it, he had the swift, strange urge to fix it. As usual, his mouth worked without clearing it with his brain first. "I can cook. I mean, I can do meals."

She did that dented in cheek thing again. "Tell me you're listening?"

"Yeah."

"You are basically our guest. It's our mission to keep you safe until you can go back to your real life. No one in our compound, not me, not Jace, not Matteo, would ever do anything to harm you or make you uncomfortable. If we do, it's out of our ignorance of civilian preferences and customs, and please let me know, so we can correct the issue. You don't owe us anything."

Since she seemed to expect an answer, he went with, "Okay."

"I mean it, Marshall. We'll do everything we can to make this transition as easy for you as possible. Though—maybe meet us half-way? Not look at us like that?"

"Like what?"

"Like we're serial killers."

His mouth worked on its own again. "You killed people."

"Cryptids. We eliminate predatory cryptids, and for our purposes, vampires are included in that group. Essentially, we eliminate monsters. You are definitely not a monster, and are under our protection." Steel laced her voice, chasing some of that softness away.

Her eyes stayed kind, though. She'd said he wasn't a monster, meaning she wasn't angry at him. At least, not yet.

"Do they make you?" Because he was pretty sure

murderers didn't spend time ensuring sheets and comforters matched, or keep chocolate chip ice cream on hand, or shop organic to help the environment. Meaning there was a chance none of this, the weapons, the violence, was really her. He understood being forced to do things, and desperation.

"Does who—what are we talking about here?" Her eyebrows crinkled and she tilted her head, like she really was trying to understand him.

And cold, soulless murderers didn't bother with the patience to untangle his logic.

They'd never come out and said what she and her team were, what HQ was, but come on. "The government. Do they make you and the—" he caught himself in time to change from *big-assed soldiers* "—your friends kill people? Make all those kids learn to?"

He wouldn't blame her if others were forcing her against her will, or if they'd threatened her friends, people she cared about. Some real reason.

She pinched at the bridge of her nose, frown altering, and his gut reclenched.

"For brevity's sake, let's call us a branch of the government, similar to Homeland Security, and leave it at that. I was raised to protect humanity, trained and fought hard for my position. I love who we are and what we do. However, I have had a recent crash course as to how most civilians view us, or at least our work. You seem like a good person, so I'd prefer not to have this disagreement. Can we table it?"

He nodded, too fast and jerky, but he didn't want to argue with her either, and not because he was afraid she'd behead him, or ship him to some secret government prison.

Like she read his mind, and for all he knew, that was possible and her group learned to do that as well, she said,

JANET WALDEN-WEST

"Can we agree that HQ and my team aren't the bad guys? At least, as far as keeping you safe?"

"Yes. Yeah, okay."

"And you aren't afraid we'll harm you?"

"I'm not afraid of you." His stupid mouth felt compelled to add, "Much. But you don't have good taste in cheese."

She blinked at him, long lashes dropping down over what he'd decided were spun-sugar eyes. Then, like the sun rising by degrees, until, *wham*, it was full-on morning, her smile grew and turned into a laugh. The sound filled the SUV, free and joyous.

Which lit her up like she was under a spotlight. One of those glowing gold ones that made people look...perfect.

And she kept laughing 'til it turned into a snort.

Then it was true. He wasn't afraid of her. Nobody could be afraid of someone so alive and full of light. Someone who didn't care that she snort-laughed like a goofy kid in public.

She wiped her eyes, laugh tapering off. Even though her lips weren't curved, unless you looked hard enough to catch the faint tilt, yeah, she was smiling. "Fair enough. You are not the first chef to call me out on my cheese choices."

"I'm not a chef. I'm only a line cook."

"You make lasagna magically appear, and somehow make oatmeal palatable. That is mad chef skills."

Embarrassment burned through him. Under was something else though. A new sensation, bright blue, like pride, if he'd ever done anything to be proud of.

No more oatmeal. "What do you like?" He needed to know. Only because cooking with your diners in mind was important. Not because he wanted Liv to smile like that, at him, again.

iv

AT LEAST OUR new guest had a sense of humor. And I'd finally gotten closer to understanding the keys to unlock him.

I wasn't taking back the chef compliment, although he didn't have a typical chef temperament. I'd yet to meet one so self-effacing. One compliment, which he had more than earned, and Marshall was willing to tag along with me to poke at produce, although he still maintained the body-length no-fly zone between us.

For the first time, I didn't worry he'd bolt if the opportunity presented itself. All I needed to do was keep conversation off cryptids and our mission, and on food. Which, juggling act, since my long-term association with any civilians who knew about cryptids was based on two people, not a statistically viable sample group.

They both handled the reveal well, but McKenna was a

human federal agent, accustomed to violence as part of her undercover work. Plus, she had a thing going with Ridge, the Instructor who had accidentally teamed up with her. The other was Bruce, and the loud, pushy, fanatically loyal social media star wasn't exactly representative of humanity in general.

I tried looking at Marshall's situation, or at least how he might perceive it, from his perspective. Bruce and McKenna's introduction to cryptids had been with anangoa and ghouls, respectively. Both species looked like exactly what they were—predatory animals. What the average person would call monsters.

On the other hand, Marshall had only seen us sweep in, starting a fight. Until Welch, the Master, and his vampire driver had gone into full hunting mode, they'd appeared human. Marshall hadn't truly been up close and personal with a vampire's powers, enough to understand that the virus mutated and warped the victim until only a human-seeming shell remained.

Mostly. Guilt crept in, forcing me to remain factual. Because my sister and adopted father *had* fought the virus, and kept their humanity, despite the mutations that changed them into vampires. They wouldn't admit it, possibly even to themselves, but the battle between human and virus was ongoing, every moment they were conscious. A constant fight, so they could remain with the people they loved. What they did was heroic and horrible at the same time.

It was also a one-off, and nothing Marshall would ever learn of.

Whether it was thinking of them or the location, the ghost of lives past dropped over me. I'd rambled through enough markets with my sister and Bruce, then only with Bruce when she disappeared. If I squinted, this could be one of those trips.

Bruce complaining about the selection, and arguing with vendors over whether eggs really were free range and antibiotic free, while Vee and Kimi hit a favorite stall, loading up on ice cream, and Josh flirted with the abuelitas at the food truck court.

I blinked, and the illusion shattered. Instead of family, and a mouthy, tattooed chef, it was simply me. And the big ginger refugee who hadn't completely taken me out of the government serial killer category.

Marshall had stopped, casting sideways glances at a table, then at me.

I made myself smile, and raised onto my tiptoes to look over his shoulder at whatever had caught his eye. "See something you like?"

Red engulfed his neck and face at the innocent question.

The guy was going to stroke out on me at this rate, well before I pinpointed how to talk to him. I wished for Vee and her civilian fascination again. She always knew how to talk to people, as natural as breathing for her. Yet another hole in my new life.

"I don't know what you guys like. Where to start." Marshall looked from me to the tables.

I eyed the one he faced—red, white, and purple potatoes, multi-colored carrots, weird tiny cabbages, and a rainbow of tomatoes. All items that had been on our menu before. "This looks like a good possibility to me. Consider this free rein. You pick, I pay. You create *if* you feel like it, and we'll enjoy whatever you prepare. Go wild."

He studied me. Possibly seeing me in a new light for the first time, too. Slowly, like he was waiting for me to attack and smack it out of his hand, he chose potatoes.

After a few stops, he found his groove, checking items, muttering to himself. I caught him reaching for his hip pocket again and again. Precisely where guys kept their phones. Bruce didn't write out ingredient and shopping lists, but I'd noticed most chefs did.

Marshall's phone had been confiscated immediately by the Cleaners, and turned in with the other evidence of the cryptid confrontation. Marshall had been insistent that night about needing it, when most people would have asked for other necessities. Especially since his had been a basic, bare bones model and nothing new or fancy.

I'd completely forgotten about it, and by this point, there was little chance he'd get it back from the forensic lab at HQ. Which was the sort of thing scary black ops assassins would do. I began to see that Marshall kind of had a point about us.

I must have sighed, because Marshall twitched and shot me a wary glance.

"You don't like apples?" He jerked his hand off the bushel he'd been examining.

"I do. We all do. Apples, mangoes, those sweet lemons." Fruit required minimal to no prep, so was always on our menu.

"Meyer."

At my blank stare, Marshall said, "Meyer lemons. The sweet ones." He ducked his face away, like he'd been out of line even speaking.

"Which is a one-hundred-percent chef thing to recognize," I said, trying a smile out on him. I pointed at him with the pan of sweet rolls I'd chosen. "Own it."

He blinked at me, like he was analyzing and processing. Then the faintest smile crept out, answering mine.

That one expression completely changed him. He actually full-on met my eyes. His weren't generic blue like I'd thought, but the color of the sea glass I'd collected from Galveston on my first trip to a beach. That determination and intelligence I'd seen in the hotel kitchen surfaced, chasing away the...hollowness.

Before, Marshall seemed hollow. Eerily similar to vampires. Look underneath their blood sports and parties, and there was this void. Like the possibility of living untold centuries came at the cost of losing their purpose, leaving them with an emptiness that turned to heartlessness.

With Marshall, that gap had felt bleaker. More hopeless than heartless. But when that one smile escaped, he shone. Now he was someone I could understand wearing the superhero shirt he'd donned this morning, and not ironically.

As quickly as the smile appeared, it vanished. He did that lip thing, which I suspected was part of his decision process. Giving Marshall space and time, I paid for the pastry and moved to check out the next table's bread options, remembering the vendor from days past, and hoping they had a French loaf.

He caught up with me. "I can do that." He tipped his chin at the loaf. "Make bread for you, so you'll have fresh every day."

"Baking. You bake?" Suddenly, my day looked not exactly perfect, but better.

"Yeah."

"To be clear, we're talking about actual gluten-containing baked goods?"

"I can do gluten-free, but I'm better at traditional."

"Muffins?"

His brow furrowed. "Cornmeal or sweet?"

"Yes."

"Sure."

"You do understand that Matteo alone can go through a loaf a day? Then add Jace and I, *and* you."

"That's cool. I'm more used to making big batches for restaurants." His shoulders squared up, and a measure of that wariness he'd carried since meeting me dropped away.

I'd been right about giving him something concrete to

accomplish. The familiarity and sense of regaining some control visibly relieved and steadied him, a piece of the ground that had been jerked from under him returned.

I abandoned the table in a hot minute. "Prepare to be the most popular person in the compound. The guys may oust me and name you new our C.O., and I'd go along with their decision."

His face went neon, but the micro-smile reappeared.

After my breakthrough, Marshall remained less skittish and more communicative. He went so far as to suggest stalls as we wandered through displays. He also shyly took the heavier bags without asking, only the tops of his ears pinkening as his fingers tangled in mine, sorting the load.

"Thanks." I didn't argue, stopping at the exit and scanning the open space between the crowded market proper and the relatively empty parking area. Double-checking for anything out of place.

"Ma'am?"

"Liv," I corrected automatically, and continued from dirt to gravel.

When I checked, Marshall hadn't moved, frown lines cutting across his forehead and attention going from the lot to me, and back. "You think there could be any of them? Welch?"

I had to remember to filter my usual actions through how a civi might interpret them. "Surveillance, and checking possible ambush points, is all habit for us. We're well out of the area where the ring can easily track you. I'd never have suggested an outing otherwise."

Marshall cut across the parking and stowed supplies in the back of the SUV. A knot of tension between my shoulders eased a degree at the evidence he trusted me enough to take my word for my ability and his security.

His trust demanded equal respect. Once he settled in his seat, I tapped the console between us. When the compartment opened, I slid back the tray with its backup knives, and pulled out one of the half-dozen phones inside. I held it up. "Untraceable burner. We carry them as standard procedure, in the event of damage to ours, which happens fairly frequently. If your absence from social media would raise suspicions, you can post, but please keep interactions to the absolute minimum. No location or event pins, mentions of us, or shots with us, the compound, or anything associated in the background. I'll have to enter any numbers you want to call, and your activity will be pinged back to my Company account. If you can live with those stipulations, it's yours. Again, the restrictions are standard safety protocols, not anything personal."

"You can do that?"

Apparently, yes. It wasn't as if my sister hadn't allowed Bruce the same leeway when he'd first sheltered with us. "I trust you not to put us or yourself in danger."

Marshall's fingers twitched toward me, but then he curled them under, into his palm. "I don't want to mess up and accidentally do that. Get you hurt or in trouble."

"Untraceable," I reminded him. "That you're concerned tells me I'm right and you'll be careful. I'll pull up the cover story HQ created for you, clear the numbers with me, and then you can contact whoever you need to. Be vague. I'm sure your story is basically following the script of you taking a private catering gig, and being required to sign a non-disclosure agreement with the employer."

"There's nobody I need to call."

Perhaps I hadn't done such a great job reassuring Marshall that I was on top of security. "The phones are safe. I can put you through to one of the HQ tech agents since they'll do a far better job explaining the security measures.

You won't be putting family and friends in jeopardy. My word on that."

Marshall spoke fast, almost before I finished. "No, ma'—Liv. I believe you. There's just nobody who'll notice me not calling or whatever."

I tried wrapping my head around the idea of no one noticing his absence, while he eyed the phone.

He had to be exaggerating. I waggled the case. "It's yours if you want it. Unlimited data, streaming, sports, whatever your interests are."

Marshall gave in to his obvious desire, taking the phone and cradling it reverently.

CHAPTER 17

*M*arshall

"WHERE DO THESE GO?" Marshall held up the bags of produce and supplies. Lots of supplies. She—Liv—hadn't acted like waiting on him to decide was too much trouble or questioned any of his suggestions. Had even sidetracked a bunch of times, asking what he liked, tossing it on the growing tab.

She took the biggest canvas bag, one of the fancy reusable hemp ones she'd found stuffed in the back of the SUV, easing the strap off his shoulders. Her warm fingers sent chills down his arm, and a weird curl in his chest. "We don't exactly have a system. It's been a while since there was anything edible here that wasn't pre-packaged or frozen. Where do you suggest?"

He'd lost count of the times Liv had asked his opinion, and assumed he knew what he was doing, instead of assuming he was incompetent. She also assumed that he had anything useful *to* say.

Her, her actions today, those were another thing that didn't fit. He tucked the thought away to examine later, in private.

He put his load on the generous kitchen island, and took the heavy bag back. "I can put things away. I'll show you after and you can tell me what needs changed." He wasn't over-stepping boundaries or pushing Liv's goodwill.

"You have a better idea than I do of where all things kitchen should go." A chime sounded from deeper in the house, and Liv turned toward the shorter hall. Then checked herself and faced him again. "I hate to dump all this on you but I need to take that conference call. You can leave anything non-refrigerated for later or—"

He jumped at the chance to be useful. "I can do it. I don't mind."

Her quick salute and, "Thank you," stayed with him as he inspected storage options. The privacy let him turn over and over the facts, examining them from different angles—shop-ping with a soldier, one who patiently waited as he debated carrots versus cauliflower, and who asked his opinion, then listened.

The same soldier who chopped heads off but who also touched his arm like she worried he'd object, and who smelled like coconut lotion and summer days. A soldier who he really wanted to make the best whole-wheat loaf ever created for, and not because he feared she'd complain if he didn't.

The ghost sensation of her hand on his, and her playful salute lingered all the way through prep.

* * *

MARSHALL RELAXED on the bed while he messed with the phone, learning its settings. He'd felt naked without the lifeline

it represented. Liv had been true to her word, the phone activated by the time he finished cleaning up the kitchen. He'd
found all his favorite video channels for music and cooking.
He didn't care about making calls and didn't have any social
media accounts. The other stuff though, the channels and apps,
those were sorta priceless. The ones to re-center, that sometimes worked to keep the panic at bay. Even nature sounds to
block out conversations when all the input turned overwhelm-
ing, or when his brain needed something easy to focus on at
night, instead of getting stuck obsessing over some random
non-event that had happened weeks or months before.

He breathed in the pure, green-gold of relief. He had
supplies. He had a phone and a way to double check recipes,
make the kinds of lists he needed.

A light knock, already familiar, sounded. Liv's equally
soft, "Marshall?" proved him right.

He pushed down on the ugly black swirl of worry and
panic. If Liv didn't like the food, she'd tell him. He didn't
think she'd be angry if it wasn't what she'd expected, or yell
about wasting food and money.

His mouth was still cotton-dry as he opened the door.

Once again, Liv was propped on the opposite wall, as far
away as the hall allowed. Lik she understood not crowding
people.

"Am I interrupting?" Her hair was down, and she tucked
it behind her ear.

"No, I was—" He held the phone up, and crap, she might
not have meant to surf and download without clearing it all
with her first, and he'd probably downloaded some vampire
hacker virus, and given up the compound's location, if
vampires had hackers.

Her smile cut through his runaway train of thought.
"Glad you figured our WiFi out. The Regional call totally
sidetracked me."

"Was dinner bad?" The question popped out, instead of answering her or making actual conversation like any normal person. But he couldn't come up with any other reason she'd seek him out.

"Are you kidding me?"

She looked at him like—he wasn't sure, aside from not any expression he'd ever had directed his way before.

"I can do better. Change whatever you didn't like," he promised.

"Let's stop right there." She held up her hand in the universal time-out sign. "Dinner was *amazing.*"

Oh. "You liked it?" He poked, second-guessing. Checking to see if she was only being polite, because he *could* do better once he knew what things she liked, what she didn't. Sort of refine the recipes he used.

"Very much. You didn't?"

He shrugged. It didn't matter if he did. "Yeah, sure."

"Because you tasted as you went." Her tone was as weird as her earlier expression had been.

"Yeah, you gotta. You can't cook without checking, seeing what needs balanced out."

Liv sighed and his chest constricted. Already he got that the sigh meant something was wrong. Him. He was wrong.

Liv pushed off the wall, and he braced himself.

She thrust out her hand. "Here."

He stared down at—at a plate. The one he hadn't noticed in her left hand, down by her side as they talked. The plate full of carne asada and avocado burrito he'd made, none of the frozen cheap ones like they'd had in the freezer, the unmistakable red of the sauce he'd prepared, grated cotija on top. "I—"

"Don't even try lying. You didn't eat. That? That is *not* going to happen again. I respect that you can't stomach eating at the same table with us, but you will not be going without meals while you're here." She thrust the plate at him again, dusky color blooming along her cheekbones.

Emotional. Liv was *mad*. But not at him-at him. For him.

Her voice flowed over him as he got lost in the wonder of her reaction. "I know dang well you didn't eat last night or this morning."

"There wasn't enough for four."

"That isn't how it works here. No one gets left out. We share. You don't have to like us but you do need to understand that in no way is it acceptable for anyone under this roof to go without basic life necessities, especially for any one of us to take at another's expense. None of us are more important than the other." Liv's voice climbed, plateauing at the end of her speech. Not yelling but passionate.

For some reason, this was important to her.

Suddenly, it was important to him she understand. "Eating with you isn't disgusting."

She frowned but didn't interrupt.

"That's—it's your team dinner time and all."

"Like that restaurant thing where staff eats before service, all together? Family meal?" Her cheek dented in, then some of the furrows smoothed out of her forehead. "Huh. Okay."

Not exactly but it didn't feel right anymore admitting he hadn't wanted to eat with them. Not if it hurt Liv's feelings, and now he suspected it would.

"All right. I get habit. As long as I've made my no-starving point." Liv's eyebrow arched. "I have made my no-starving point, correct?"

Unfamiliar emotion clogged his throat. He cleared it before he could answer. "Yeah. Got it."

"Prove it." She waggled the plate.

He took the silverware she'd also brought and took the warm plate. She'd reheated the food. The first time anybody had cared if he had a meal in...years.

"Thanks." Because he couldn't leave well enough alone, he kept talking. "You—all of you—liked it? The meal?"

"You are a popular guy around these parts." Liv stretched, exposing a hint of smooth skin as her shirt hem rose. "If you get bored, you can come hang with your adoring public. The guys are gaming in the den." She narrowed those spun-sugar eyes. "*After* you eat."

"I'm eating," he promised.

It was getting easier and easier to promise Liv anything she wanted, when she looked at him like that. Like she saw him, and was still okay with him after.

CHAPTER 18

iv

I FLIPPED the fuzzy *book dragon not book worm* emblazoned couch throw over my folded legs, half listening to Jace and Matteo trash talk over the sounds of virtual AR fire, the other half straining to hear a repeat of the creak-groan that signaled someone stepping on the weathered middle plank in the hallway, right where it joined the kitchen.

"Got a live one?" Jace muttered, just for our ears.

Matteo cocked his head, as the creak repeated. "Incoming."

They pretended deep concentration, bent over their controllers, commandeering the best chairs, always arranged in front of the giant screen.

Project Draw Marshall Out had turned into a team effort. Walking in after PT and being greeted by the welcoming aromas of grilled steak and homey vanilla from fresh-baked muffins did that.

When Marshall hadn't joined us for dinner, the guys started brainstorming. They'd noticed his wardrobe—he hadn't worn the Company tees since I'd salvage his personal belongings—all pop culture and superheroes, and I mentioned his trashed comics. According to my team, all those details added up to a ninety-percent likelihood that our guest was also into gaming.

And gamers couldn't overlook the newest CoW release. By *release*, I meant Kimi had hands on it at least a week before it officially dropped. According to my calculations, it was sixty-forty as to whether she had connections inside the company who provided her perks, or whether she'd liberated it herself.

Between the market outing and a new, highly covetable game played at mega-decibels, hopefully Marshall would at least check in. Opening the door to proving that despite upending his life, we weren't awful, and he could relax here.

Reading me like a good lieutenant should, Jace took part of his attention off the battle between our team and Kimi's and murmured, "If he doesn't hate our guts, this will be too much for him to pass up. Ask Kimi."

As leader of the entire Company gaming fanatics crew, she'd know. But this was about my team and cementing our bond. Trusting each other at every level. "I believe you. Keep in mind, no work talk."

"Keeping it chill," Matteo promised.

The biggest reason Marshall might not bother with us was all on me. I hadn't exactly been chill when I all but shoved leftovers down his throat earlier. As the guys set the table for dinner, I'd checked the dishwasher, finding no plates or cups inside, only prep utensils. The idea of Marshall having spent all that time and effort shopping and preparing a meal, then sitting alone in his room, hungry and listening to *us* put away *his* food...

In hindsight, I hadn't handled the situation well. Hopefully, I hadn't tanked Jace and Matteo's plan.

My self-flagellation stopped as I caught a sliver of auburn hair and black shirt in the arched entry. Marshall, hovering and clearly not committed yet.

"Easy." Matteo's steadying caution could pass as talking to the game, but it was the same support as when we waited for the green light on a mission sweep.

I played the ace up my sleeve. Nudging the crumb covered plate on Jace's chair arm, I asked, "Are there any muffins left? I only got one."

"Dunno," he said. "Probably not."

Rubber soles squeaked on the antique kitchen flooring. A minute later, Marshall returned, but still hovered outside the arch, not committing.

I upped my game, licking my finger and rolling it over the plate, picking up the last of the crumbs. "Dang. These were better than the ones from the patisserie downtown."

The squeak repeated, Marshall's beat up Chucks and our polished floor combining to betray him. Moving like he was threading his way through a field of sleeping ghouls, Marshall edged into the room. "There's one more muffin. If you wanted it."

Score. I'd yet to meet a chef who could ignore a hungry fan. "It's been kind of a long day. Do you mind?" I snuggled deeper into the couch.

Marshall retreated. After a minute of no reappearance, I uncurled, sure I'd pushed too hard and debating whether to knock on Marshall's door again and apologize, or give him space.

As my toes touched wood, Marshall moved into the doorway, plate in hand. I jerked my toes back. When he hesitated, I smiled, and he came the rest of the way in. He kept his head down but a wary eye on the guys, and made a wide arc around them. He stopped an arm's length from me, and held the plate out.

Grabbing a muffin hadn't been enough for Marshall. He'd split it, added a pat of the real butter—from the market stall owned by the dairy Vee swore had happy cows—the butter now melting where he'd warmed the bread.

It kind of felt like Marshall was offering me more than a simple plate. "Thank you. I was full on burrito earlier, but these are terrific. Plus, snacks are a thing here."

"For real," Matteo rumbled.

Marshall twitched at Matteo's deep bass, but didn't retreat. "I can make extra tomorrow."

"You are the man," Jace said. "*Some* people here got no respect for leftovers." He looked away from the screen to cast a not entirely fake covetous glance at the muffin.

"Seriously? You're calling people out when you're the one who always end up with the last piece of pizza?" I accepted the plate with an appreciative smile. "You'd think there would be a little respect for the C.O, but not so much."

"But you still love us," Jace said.

"Clearly. If I'm going to sacrifice pizza for anyone, it would be you two." I bit into the muffin, sweat bread, tart raspberries, and creamy butter mixing, and groaned. Marshall really was that good.

His face went as pink as the berries in the snack.

With perfect timing, the guys hooted. "Upgrade."

Marshall paused and cast a furtive glance at the screen. Then proved my lieutenant worth all the pizza leftovers he wanted. "That's—I didn't think CoW went live 'til next week," Marshall said. Then tensed like he'd been out of line even speaking.

"Perks of having a tech-forward sister," Matteo said, as Jace snorted. "Hey, you hear about the hidden skins add-on? It wasn't a rumor. Look."

Marshall hesitated, then leaned in enough for a clear view. "That's for real?"

"True story." Jace stuck out a long leg and hooked the stool usually by the pool table. "You gotta see this, man. This mod? Unlocks in level five."

Suspicious as a goat wandering into a chupacabra den, Marshall took the seat. I could read how hair-trigger his tolerance was, shoulders tight, and muscles bunched. He was prepared to either fight, or flee. It hurt to watch his mistrust, and I had to wonder what awful circumstance had instilled that reaction. It went way past discovering cryptids existed, and putting his life on hold in unfamiliar territory.

The guys tag-teamed, talking at Marshall and each other. He only spoke in short syllables, but he did answer. He stayed until Matteo's avatar bit the dust, courtesy of my sister's.

Matteo swore, and Marshall tensed, shoulders rising.

Jace only grinned. "Pay up, bro."

"Yeah, yeah." Matteo stood, collecting bottles, cups, and popcorn bowl as he went.

"Loser cleans up," I said to Marshall."

"Don't ever play against Liv. She cheats," Matteo said, sailing one of the small pillows my way.

I caught the missile and tucked it behind my back, giving Matteo a Cheshire cat grin.

"At CoW?" Marshall's attention ping-ponged between us.

"At everything." Matteo laughed and grabbed my plate. "Except basketball but that's only because she could have a career in women's NBA if cryptids ever went extinct."

Marshall's gaze settled on me as Matteo left.

"No proof, no crime." I winked.

"That's Liv-speak for 'I cheat'." Jace stretched and stood, starting on the other side of the room, gathering recycling. "I'm out."

Marshall jumped up, the stool rattling. He caught it before it crashed to the floor, then eased out of the room.

"Night, Marshall," I called after him. "Thanks for dinner."

After a beat, "Okay," floated back from the hallway. "Night, Liv."

I called our mission a success.

CHAPTER 19

M arshall

WITH THE CREAK of the outer door opening, the heavy clomp of boots carried to Marshall, along with a momentary breeze scented with baked sand.

The air cut off as the door closed, and the pack of soldiers rounded the corner. There was a muffled *oof*, like maybe one of them ran into something, and then all noise ceased.

Marshall pushed down on the wild flutter in his chest, the one threatening to let black creep in the edges of his vision until everything not in his head disappeared.

Instead, he pulled up on the creamy blues and golds, the warmth of the reheated plate Liv had brought him, the way she'd thanked him, twice, for a meal. And the way the other two soldiers had acted. Not like assholes. Not even when one last big at CoW. To date, there hadn't been any barked orders and threats.

He forced his tight throat to form words. "Hey."

The silence held for a heartbeat. Then Liv's coffee and cream voice filled the room. "Good morning. Are we in your way?"

He blinked hard, focusing on what was in front of him. He hadn't thought Liv and the others would resent him still in their space.

But he'd been wrong before.

He shoved more words out. "No, this is good. Breakfast is almost ready." He kinda hated the stupid question under the statement. Right. Think of them as diners. Customers waiting on an order they'd placed. "It'll be a minute. Okay, two minutes."

"You're cooking for us again?" The biggest soldier, Matteo, his voice hopped higher on the last note, sounding more like a kid's whose voice cracked in excitement.

"Yeah."

"Cool. That oatmeal stuck with us until lunch, last time."

That was the other one. Jace. The one who stole Liv's muffins.

The dangerous flutter amped up a notch, but Liv wasn't an oatmeal fan. She did like French bread, and muffins. "It's toast. French toast casserole. With bacon." He dared a look over his shoulder as he stirred the caramel sauce.

Liv was in front, like always, the big guys behind her. He couldn't read her expression, and his mouth took off on its own. "You guys aren't vegetarian, so bacon. And probably you need the protein for the—" he stumbled "—the workouts and stuff."

The beep of the timer he'd set saved him. He pulled out the casserole, cutting it in squares, and drizzling sauce over each, then adding the bacon.

He tensed at the presence suddenly at his side.

"Here." Liv took two of the plates and carried them to the table. Passing them to the men, who sat backs straight, eyes

118

wide and hands folded in their laps, like they were in church.

When Liv returned, he handed her the third plate. The one he'd just added extra sauce to.

Her elegant fingers, extra warm from being outdoors, brushed over the top of his hand. She paused, something that looked a lot like a mix of confusion and loneliness peering out from its hiding place.

He recognized loneliness and it punched him in the gut that Liv, smart, capable, in-charge Liv, had that shadow in her eyes. Another of those alien urges to make it better for her hit. "Since you like muffins, I though French toast." Which had to be the suckiest reassurance ever uttered.

Except Liv's expression altered, softer and open.

"Oh, hell yeah," Jace boomed. "This is amazeballs."

He and Liv both jumped at the enthusiastic response, Liv taking her plate and breaking contact. When Marshall checked, Jace was half-way through his breakfast. Matteo wasn't talking, probably because he was too busy demolishing his food, the bacon already gone. He did toss Marshall a thumbs-up.

"Bacon, sugar, and caffeine. I.E., the key to our hearts. We really are that easy," Liv said and rolled her eyes.

Marshall got that she was playing, not mocking.

Then she did that narrow-eyed thing. "Why are there only three plates, Marshall?"

He flushed but nodded at the two-seater bar at the other side of the kitchen, and his plate and mug. "I made two batches. Maybe there'll be leftovers this time."

Her expression cleared and she stopped at the coffee maker for a cup before joining the others.

He ran the towel he used as a potholder through his hands, thinking. They hadn't minded him last night. He took one of the stools at the bar and finished his breakfast and coffee to the background track of three covert super-soldiers enjoying his bacon, and discussing their day.

* * *

Lunch followed the same easy pattern, except this time Matteo was first through the door, poking his head in, hopeful as a kid. The guy drew in a deep breath, and a grin wreathed his face.

"Grilled chicken and greens," Marshall said, because that look, he knew—hungry people hoping for food.

As early as they'd gotten up that morning, and as sweaty as they'd been at breakfast, they'd headed back outside after. Marshall had worked in a baseball team clubhouse briefly, and players' menus were always lighter at lunch, lots of protein and fresh carbs. Soldiers were sorta like players, both athletes, if he ignored the weapons.

"Showers first," Liv said as she paced in, hair up in a knot-twist thing and face gleaming.

"Since when?" Jace ducked around her, rooting in the fridge, coming out with drinks. He tossed her and Matteo water, and then opened and drained half a bottle of electrolyte drink in one go.

Liv's smooth throat worked as she drank. After, she rolled the cold bottle down the side of her neck, and chest. Right over the tank plastered to her, and Marshall had no business noticing anything about her chest. He jerked his gaze away from glowing brown skin with a lighter pink ridge peeking out, a healing cut.

She used her bottle to point at each soldier. "We shower since we have a guest and reason not to live like feral dogs. Marshall, do you really want three sweaty people at your table?"

Heat climbed his neck. But she seemed serious, caring

what he thought. Still. "You guys worked hard, and it's your house."

Liv snorted. "Which is a polite way of saying we stink, but you're too kind to say so. Showers. Hit 'em." She made a swooshy circle in the air with her free hand, and the other two swept down the hall to the showers.

Marshall had the table set when they all piled back in, chicken arranged over greens. Now with a boiled egg and cheese added for even more protein.

The guys fell on their plates, while Liv made a pass and poured another cup of coffee. Making Marshall glad he'd made an extra pot and left it on.

Liv took a seat, same as that morning. Now, she pulled the chair to her right out. She gave his plate, still on the counter, a look, gave him a longer one, then the empty seat.

Heart triple-beating hard enough it felt like it was tap-tapping his ribs, Marshall lifted his plate and slid into the offered chair. He ate, easier to do than he'd imagined with the soldiers he'd once seen storm in with guns drawn, eating right across from him.

Maybe because they had names now—Jace and Matteo. And Liv was beside him, brow lifted in that cool thing she did, making sure he joined in and ate his share.

iv

I DROPPED the laptop on the bar counter and went to start coffee, only to find fresh brewed and waiting.

Marshall came out of the pantry, a room I'd almost forgotten existed, arms laden. A dusting of something white and powdery decorated his dark auburn curls.

"Uh…" He halted. Then sneezed, more powder lifting. Flour, from a bag split along the top. "Sorry. I was gonna throw this out." His eyes widened, and a bit of that wariness he'd lost lunch returned. "Not wasting your stuff but this is old, and stale since it was opened."

Ah. Because Bruce would have been the last person to use flour here, and that was a good nine months ago, when the compound officially become mine.

"I can put it back," Marshall said. "It's just—it might make you sick if anybody cooked with it."

It wasn't as if he was tossing anything important.

Although I hadn't touched the pantry. Or Kimi, Josh, and Stavros' old rooms, those standing empty. Jace and Matteo had taken the two at the very end of that hallway. Possibly reading the keep-out message I'd been unconsciously sending. I'd even put Marshall in the room on my hall instead of one of my siblings.

This was my base now. Mine and my team's—laidback, funny Jace, and kind, ferociously loyal Matteo—my brothers and my teammates. Who deserved better, to know that this was unequivocally their home too, and how much I valued them outside of missions, every single day. It was past time to make the place all ours. Time to embrace the new instead of acting like it was some sort of cruddy consolation prize.

"Go for it. I have no idea what most of this is, or where it should go, so use your best judgment," I said. For the time being, Marshall was part of the new and deserved to have a comfortable space as well.

"I won't make a mess," Marshall said, for at least the third or fourth time since he'd arrived.

I played with the comment as he disposed of useless, stale foodstuff we should have tossed long ago. I matched up today's downplaying of his knowledge with his earlier assumption he was getting booted out when I only wanted to talk, his hesitation at the market despite him being the expert, his horrific, heartbreaking assumption we got fed before he did.

And the combination started a fire burning somewhere deep in my soul.

Assuming you had nothing worth contributing, and that everyone looked at you and expected failure—that was too much like HQ's view of us. That our rag-tag team wouldn't coalesce. That we'd never perform at the level required to be an effective barrier between cryptids and humanity. That we were all broken, no longer useful.

HQ never said as much. Neither did its agents, or other teams. They wanted us to succeed. They were on our side. But that we hadn't had a cadet team sent here as part of their externship after graduation, that was truth. Deep down, our superiors and our peers didn't believe in us.

"Marshall?"

He paused on his way to trash and recycling, eyes wary. "Did you change your mind?"

"Just the opposite. Ready?"

"Is this one of those 'are you listening?' things?"

"Yep." I had to smile. "Here goes. This is your kitchen for the duration. Do whatever feels right to you. Got me?"

"But that's…" He watched me, as if waiting for a trap to close.

"There are no buts, no strings attached, no qualifiers. You know what you're doing and you aren't going to accidentally burn the compound down with a soufflé gone wrong."

"You don't know that."

"I do." Rules, probability, hard-earned experience gained through missions and time disagreed. Rules, data, risk versus benefit, and strategy were the bedrock of everything. Anything else, emotional reactions, experimenting, innovating, all posed unnecessary risks. Spur of the moment decisions based on feelings was Vee's thing, and it had gotten her ripped from her family, infected with the vampire virus, kill chips inserted in her and our brother, and losing Oversight's trust.

It had also saved Bruce's life, given us a father, and created an even more effective means of performing our core mandate, to protect humans at all costs.

I looked Marshall square in the eye, not allowing him to evade, or to ignore my meaning. "I have had years of training, and the benefits of centuries of others' experiences. Once in the field though, instinct also comes into play. Mine says that you are solid. Besides, if you intended to poison us and steal the truck keys, you would have done it yesterday."

"I wouldn't," Marshall said, indignation clear, along with a scowl way too much like Bruce's, at implying Marshall would ruin food for something as paltry as revenge. Then his expression changed, voice deepening into that bass I felt vibrate in my bones. "I wouldn't hurt you. Or the guys, Jace or Matteo. I wouldn't ever."

The part of me entirely too fond of the romantic movies clogging my streaming queue went all warm and fuzzy. The same part that had melted at walking in and having someone waiting for us, meal ready. Concerned that we had protein instead of cereal. The part of me I'd forced to go dormant, in order for me to survive. "We're not so bad for government-issue killers, huh?"

"You're—good. You're a good person."

I drummed my fingers against the laptop, watching Marshall. He blushed, which I expected. He met my eyes and held them, determination plain, which I didn't.

"Would it bother you if I hung around your kitchen? I usually do the boring daily reports in here," I said. "However, I can go to my office."

His answer was swift. And sort of surprised us both. "Stay." He grabbed a dishtowel and scrubbed at a non-existent stain on the island. "You should stay. This is closer to the coffee pot."

I snorted and settled into my usual spot. "You're a secret smart ass. You'll fit in here perfectly."

CHAPTER 21

*M*arshall

YOU'LL FIT IN PERFECTLY.

Marshall rolled that comment around and around, laying on the bed and staring up at the ceiling as old school metal power chords resonated from the phone on the nightstand.

Probably Liv hadn't seriously meant it. No one—*no one*—had ever said it to him though, even joking. He either got dismissed as a fuck-up, or overlooked, too boring to notice unless he got in the way.

Today though, he'd gotten a 'freakin' awesome dinner' and backslap from Matteo, which, okay, despite Marshall's size, had almost put him through a wall. Then Jace had kept Marshall upright and grumbled at the other soldier. Who'd hung his head and *apologized* to Marshall with an 'Aw, crap. Forgot you weren't used to barrack's high-fives'. Which was also cool.

Same as Liv sitting in his temporary kitchen, working on

secret government business. Her quiet presence was weird, that weird but nice kind.

When he'd gotten brave enough to switch out her empty cup for fresh, she'd blinked at him like he'd dazed her. And when she recovered, she gave him that smile. The one that meant 'thank you,' and 'you did it right' and felt like pure sunshine after a freezing winter.

Liv was soothing enough that he'd forgotten she was there a couple of times, and talked to himself and his phone. All the supplies they'd picked up were rapidly dwindling. This time, he'd decide what he wanted to make, get the ideas and what he needed, then double the amount, all lined up ahead of time. Less stressful that way. Plus, he wouldn't waste Liv's time, trying to fit together pieces of ideas flying around in his head while she stood and waited.

So far, they'd seemed happy with everything he made. He grabbed his phone and flipped it around and around, helping him think. There was still part of a loaf of bread left from dinner. But he wasn't feeling it. He rolled off the bed and headed for the kitchen.

When he checked, there were plenty of eggs to bake with. He set the oven temperature and pulled out bowls and baking sheet.

"*Uncle Tom's Cabin?*"

At Liv's question, Marshall twitched, metal mixing spoon ringing against the side of the mixing bowl. He'd forgotten he'd put music back on. He reached for the phone, realized he had brown sugar all over his hand, and switched to wiping it off with a towel.

"I didn't mean to startle you." Liv halted in the space between house and kitchen, like she was afraid to move again.

"I'll turn it off," he said.

"It's great. Retro as heck, but great."

He double-checked that Liv meant it, because he already got that she did things to make other people comfortable.

She must've learned how to interpret him too since she shrugged. "We had an instructor who saw them all live— GNR, Poison, Skid Row. If they had big hair and electric guitar, she was all over it. We ran a heck of a lot of courses, and did a staggering amount of homework to metal tracks. Hearing it feels like home, I suppose."

He wondered what home meant to soldiers.

Once he didn't act like spook on her, Liv came in. Instead of the stool, she wiggled onto the bar, legs swinging. "What's your story? Who hooked you on power ballads?"

He jerked his way inappropriate attention off her legs. She wasn't wearing training gear. A skirt. Liv had on a skirt and it was kinda perfect and his tongue stuck to the roof of his mouth. She looked like the Liv who cared about what he thought, not like a cold soldier.

And he quit that train of thought, the one imagining what it would feel like to have those long legs wrapped around him.

Liv's cheek dented in. "That was invasive, and I had no right to pry." The soft click of her heels hitting the floor as she hopped off the counter brought him back to reality.

"My music teacher." He reached for any topic, anything to keep her from leaving. Because she'd gone from intimidating to the kind of good he wanted to be around, even if he didn't always understand her.

He tossed more words out there. "My music teacher liked hair metal, and nineties grunge. Nirvana. Alice in Chains."

"Ah." Liv said it like he'd answered more than one question. "High school?"

"Middle. We, uh, I went to a good school district." His parents had enough money and they lived in a nice neighborhood, not that it had changed anything for him.

"I'm not really up on civilian school structure. I mean, I know enough to talk about homework assignments with my sort of nieces, but that's pretty much the entirety of my experience," Liv said, apology written all over her face.

Like she'd done something wrong, or offended him, and Marshall had no clue what to do with that twist. He did have a growing desire, like bread dough rising and doubling its size after every proofing, to make Liv smile again. To keep all the worry or hurt or whatever away. To be the person she turned to in order to feel better.

She sighed and bent her head, the most perfect waves in the history of hair falling forward to hide her face for a second, before she flipped them over her shoulder. Which was bare, thanks to a sleeveless shirt, which meant she wasn't dressed for hanging out at the compound. Jace and Matteo bounced in, filling the huge kitchen with their energy. Both of them in real clothes, too. Matteo's shirt even had sleeves, although they fit snug around his biceps.

The three matched, in that way friends did, all on the same page. So, soldiers went out. Of course.

Marshall turned back to the bowl. He told himself it was good that he'd have the compound to himself. Tried to convince himself it was even better that they trusted him enough to leave him on his own.

"Yo, man. Is this like an obsession for you?" Jace peered over Marshall's shoulder.

"They're cookies. Snacks are a thing." Which sounded stupid, coming from Marshall.

"I'm all over me some cookies but can't you do that when we get back?"

"They'll still be fresh when you get back tonight, or in the morning."

Jace grunted and staggered a half-step. "Dude. What was that for?"

As Marshall mechanically dropped even-sized balls of dough onto the sheet, he glanced back. Matteo and Liv bracketed Jace, arms crossed, Matteo fresh from shoving Jace. Both soldiers glaring at Jace.

"Marshall, you do know we're going out?" Liv asked.

"Sure." He put the filled cookie pan into the oven and set the timer.

"Because Jace told you about our plans two hours ago, and invited you?" Matteo more growled than asked.

"Uh—"

The object of their irritation swore. "Aww, damn. Josh called, and I totally forgot." Jace turned to Marshall, contrition written all over him, expression like a puppy getting yelled at for chewing up shoes. "We gotta take our fun when we can. Friday night out is a standing tradition when we don't have a mission. I honestly forgot I hadn't mentioned it." He peered at the timer. "Seven minutes. Beers will wait that long while you get ready, and these finish cooking."

"You don't have to say that. Friday is your thing, for you guys."

A muscle worked in Matteo's jaw. "Man, we're serious. Pretty boy got busy with his two-hour beauty routine and forgot to tell you is all. C'mon. We'll wait."

And, okay, Jace did have great skin. Not as great as Liv's, but still.

She cut in. "Jace was supposed to ask if you wanted to join us. This isn't an order." She held a finger up, the keyfob dangling. "Buuut, Friday night out. A few beers. Karaoke if it's more than a few. Fun."

He studied her face and body language, and found no evidence she was only being polite, embarrassed at being caught ditching him and thinking he expected to be included.

"We don't get too crazy, since there's always the possibility of a call-out mission," Matteo added. "Beer and pizza, no drama."

"We just—how can you be hungry?" Popped out. "For real?"

"I warned you," Liv said.

"Dinner was hours ago," the other two chorused, like they'd answered the same question often enough their response was choreographed.

"Get ready. We'll wait," Jace said.

The oven beeped and Marshall bent to retrieve cookies, in a cloud of chocolate-scented heat. He blamed the bloom in his cheeks on the oven. If he changed, it would only be into more of the same.

"Tee shirts are perfectly acceptable," Liv said, like she'd read his mind. Again. And maybe that was her superpower. "Maybe one without sauce on it though?" She fingered the edge of his sleeve, and yeah, he'd splashed soy on it earlier during prep.

She held on a second longer. Eyes asking him if he was okay. If he was okay going out with them. With her.

"Don't eat those while I'm changing," Marshall said to Matteo, who snatched a guilty hand back from the tray, trying for an innocent *'I would never'* vibe, and that—that was pretty damn awesome, too.

iv

I CLOSED my eyes for a few seconds, then opened them, read-justing to the close-to-midnight darkness as the club door *shushed* closed behind us. Taking a deep inhale of air only slightly tainted by exhausted and the mixed smells of beer and fried food, I stretched, enjoying the cooler air on damp skin.

From between Jace and Matteo, Marshall tracked my movement.

He'd been quiet on the drive in, and he hadn't joined me and Matteo on the dance floor. The stiffness in his wide shoulders had disappeared after the first communal pitcher of beer, and he'd been comfortable enough to laugh at Jace's over the top Imagine Dragons karaoke performance, and Matteo's shameless flirting with the bartender.

"What's next?" Marshall asked, taking a prudent step back to avoid the guys roughhousing.

At least now he took the antics as they were meant, all in fun, instead of bailing at the first hint of anything physical.

"Food," Jace said, answer muffled thanks to his head-locked position under Matteo's armpit. He popped an elbow into Matteo's kidney and twisted free.

"After all that dancing, I'm in need of topping off," Matteo agreed, same as every post-club outing.

Marshall looked to me.

"Totally agree. The usual fill-er-up?"

The guys took a left turn at the end of the block, their version of yes.

"You're good at that." Marshall stayed the few steps behind, with me. He shoved his hands in his pockets and matched his pace to mine. "Dancing, I mean. Did you take lessons?"

"It's for fun, which contrary to some opinions, I do believe in." I fanned my face, debating knotting my hair out of the way. "I'm only self-taught. It's something my sisters and I started." Primarily indulging Vee's fascination with all things civilian. Dancing had been one of her more awesome obsessions.

We ambled down the street, light on human traffic at this hour, families already home, partiers still in clubs.

On impulse, I said, "I can teach you?" His attention had been on me every time I glanced at our table, even when he was talking to Jace. I'd also noticed how his fingers moved with the music, like he was playing an instrument.

Marshall's head whipped my way. "I'm no good at stuff like that. Way too clumsy."

"Is it okay to tell civilian guys they're graceful? Those rules are really confusing."

At Marshall's nod, I kept going. "You're pretty together and graceful in the kitchen." During prep and cooking, he moved like he forgot to worry about who was there,

133

comfortable in his skin and fully immersed. I'd had ample time to notice as I worked, and he hummed and did his thing today.

It had been familiar, but his tall, wide frame and lowkey silence were different enough from Bruce's fast paced, take no prisoners style to be soothing instead of rousing the ache of loss.

Even in the dark, this section where the streetlights became less decorative and further apart, I couldn't miss Marshall's head shake. "It's only cooking."

"But you enjoy it and your good at it." It annoyed me that he downplayed his skill. "Own it. Seriously."

"What I do isn't important, not like what you and the team do." Stubbornness laced his voice.

An interesting change, although he could've chosen another topic to dig his heels in on. "Matteo, Jace, and my stomachs' disagree."

He huffed but moved closer. Enough that my skirt brushed against his jeans as we walked. He'd changed into yet another black tee, this one with a stylized bat on the front. Which I really wanted to steal as a gift for Stavros. Picturing Marshall without a shirt on...

We didn't equate sex and relationships the way civilians did. Our emotional needs were met by our team members. Sex was for fun, and there were plenty of willing partners at HQ, or on neighboring teams. Basically, anyone not from our year-group. Between putting a team together, and keeping Oversight appeased, my sex drive had been MIA. At the idea of a shirtless Marshall, it finally woke.

A stray breeze flitted around us, tickling my bare arms. It was easy to imagine Marshall's hands taking the breeze's place, running over my skin. My nipples pebbled, and I shivered.

In the artificial twilight, backlit only by the occasional

streetlamp and neon from signs, Marshall cut an intimidating figure, stark black and white, hair the deep color of spilled blood. The openness in his eyes turned him from potential villain to potential hero.

He slowed, busting me staring at him, some question forming on his lips. Jace's short whistle, letting me know he and Matteo were already cutting left again into a side-street, stopped whatever Marshall wanted to say.

The two halted at our destination. Marshall checked out the neon glowing over the narrow door, the only sign of what the business inside was. He looked from the sign to me. "I can make you pizza."

"Enjoy not cooking, for once."

"You said you liked it when I do. Cook for you." He'd stopped, his back to the twenty-four-hour pizzeria, face in the shadows, but voice husky.

Another shiver went through me. "I do."

"I'll make you pizza next." He dipped his head, enough for me to see his eyes. They were as intense now as when he watched me on the dance floor. At odds with our mundane topic.

"Thank you." My voice had lowered, to match his. "But tonight, have something you didn't have to work on. You deserve—"

Marshall came that hair closer, more the way he leaned into me than actually moving. His washed-soft shirt brushed my bare arm, warmth from his body seeping into mine.

In the intimacy of our little pocket of darkness, I lost what I'd intended to say. Instead, I took the half-step that erased the slice of empty space between us. My body language mirroring his, leaning into him and my body seeking more. His heat, his kindness, the heady novelty of being the first and sole focus of anyone's attention.

My sandal caught in a sidewalk seam, barely a blip and

not enough to threaten my balance. As fast as a thought, Marshall had me. His hand cupped around my elbow, rough calluses and smoother burn marks against mine, his kitchen scars over my fighting scars.

"I've got you. It's okay." His deep, low reassurance wrapped around me.

I believed him. Those patient blue eyes promised me that he was there. It was impossible not to believe Marshall and the new glow, a spark of hope, under his reassurance.

"Yo, the usual? Or sushi pizza?" Jace called out from where he hung half in, half out of the restaurant's door.

Marshall dropped my arm and put a length between us. The wariness dropped back in place like a mask.

I flipped my head upside down and shook my hair out, pretending I had something in it. Shaking off whatever had happened, or almost happened.

Marshall was our guest. Our charge to protect until we made the outside world safe enough for him to go back to the life we'd interrupted. He didn't choose us—he was stuck with us and making the best of it. If he paid extra attention to me, it was simply him attempting to figure out the rules of the world he'd been unwillingly thrust into.

CHAPTER 23

*M*arshall

MARSHALL STARED after Liv's retreating back, restaurant door opening and closing on her, and Jace and Matteo's loud argument over toppings.

The hit of sweet basil and sharp pepperoni only made Marshall's stomach roil. He'd screwed up. If superheroes were real, that'd be his superpower.

Liv was being Liv—kind and watching out for everyone around her—and he'd pushed it to places she'd never meant to go. She'd jumped on the chance to get away from him and his weirdness. Hell, his weirdness had doubled down, and was full-on creepiness at this point.

The voices he couldn't ever one-hundred-percent tune out picked up energy and volume.

Liv was professional, and smart, and in control. Made for being the center of people's world and in the sun, even if she worked in darkness. That was her thing, bringing some of that light in and banishing shadows.

He couldn't hold a job for more than six months. Couldn't keep himself together, much less a team.

He was the opposite of her and Jace and Matteo, and they had to see that by now. Tonight had been a pity thing for them.

The neon flashing in his eyes sent spikes through his brain. Marshall lurched around the edge of the building, into the murky black relief of the alley. Back here with the dumpster, and out of sight, where he belonged.

He pressed into the restaurant wall, eyes closed. Rough brick finish biting into his back. Hoping the here-and-now pain would keep him centered. Get it together before Liv and the rest of the team came out and caught him mid-meltdown. The only thing that would make this situation worse was seeing the hint of respect for him in their eyes die out.

A metallic *bong* reverberated up the alley. For a second, Marshall tensed, turning away from Liv or whoever was coming out of the pizza place. Then the thump repeated, coming from the dumpster. The opposite direction of where Liv would be.

Marshall concentrated on the ugly realness, the stink of cooking oil gone rancid in the heat, and the ammonia of animals marking their turf.

A shadow flowed from around the rear of the dumpster. Probably raccoon or a coyote. He'd already learned how bold they were here, and the thump had sounded too heavy for a cat.

A shrill *skree* split the air, setting Marshall's teeth on edge, like accidentally biting into aluminum foil.

Coyotes didn't make that sound. Or plaintive sobs. These coming from this end of the dumpster. Marshall squinted and made out a huddled form at the base of the giant container.

The kind of sniffles that meant they were trying to cry quietly, not be seen or heard, came again. Like…a kid. There was a kid out here. And somebody else, who the kid was afraid of.

Marshall took a step toward the dumpster, and pitched his voice softer, trying to sound reassuring and safe. Safer than whoever the kid was hiding from, at least.

"Hey." He held his hands out, showing he didn't have a weapon and wasn't grabbing or trying to start anything. "You okay?"

There was a hitched snuffle, like the kid was snot-crying and trying to hide it. Marshall tried again. "It's okay, for real. You can come out." He squatted on his heels, anything to look less scary.

He'd seen enough hungry street kids hanging around the backs of restaurants. Hoping for something they could scavenge, or because the place handed out the day's extras at closing. It didn't take much for Marshall to put himself in those kids' place. "C'mon. Really. My friends are getting pizza. If you're hungry, I'll share."

Whether it was the promise of food or the coaxing, the kid inched into the light.

Small, maybe pre-teen, maybe a badly nourished teen. His —Marshall was pretty sure it was a boy—face streaked with tears and shirt torn. A bruise covered half of his face.

The eerie *skree* came again, and the kid darted a panicked look between the figure slinking around the end of the dumpster, and Marshall.

No way was whoever it was, another kid or a crappy adult, whaling on the terrified boy again. Slow fire kindled in him. He rose and held his hand out. "Hurry. I'm not gonna hurt you, and I'll make sure nobody else does either. Just —come on."

He'd get the kid away, get them some food. Call someone. Not the police, since they never bothered with this stuff, street kids and bullies. Liv might have an idea, someplace like their safehouses.

The kid bolted and flung himself in Marshall's shadow. The dumpster skidded a foot, like a giant shoved it. A guttural snarl ricocheted off the metal, echoing up and down the alley. The taller figure prowled forward, predatory and sure.

Marshall's heartbeat ramped up. Keeping his eyes on whoever—or whatever, because if vampires were real, other things might be too—was stalking them, he reached back and felt for the kid. A sweaty hand grabbed his. "Slow," he whispered, backing a step. The kid clung to him, a slight, dead weight pulling on Marshall's arm.

The thing—definitely a thing—dropped to all fours, mouth open and inhaling, like it was smell-tasting them. Then it rocked back on two legs, eyes locked on them, and lunged. Charging. At Marshall and the kid, and the creature hit the weak light from the street, and holy crap, a Great White shark with legs was trying to kill them. Something like a human shark anyway, double rows of serrated teeth gleaming like a death sentence.

Marshall flung the kid behind him, at the street and the only chance of escape. *"Run."* The not-human shark close enough its scent, rotting meat and decay, hit Marshall.

"Marshall?" Liv's voice preceded her. Liv, in her flippy skirt and pretty shirt, and unarmed. Who wouldn't be in this filthy alley and in danger if it wasn't for him.

"Drop. Get clear!" Her voice snapped like a whip, but it didn't matter. He couldn't, too big, too clumsy. Not fast enough. But he could slow the monster. Give the kid time to get away. Give Liv time to get backup, the guys, weapons that had to be somewhere in the SUV.

The creature gathered itself and launched. A foot slipped, causing it to bobble. Changing its angle, hopefully enough for what Marshall intended.

Marshall ducked, the thing sailing past him, close enough the stink choked his sinuses, rubbery weird skin brushing his. Claws digging into the concrete and throwing up sparks, the monster checked its momentum, ready to turn back. Make another try at Marshall.

Instead, Marshall shoved upright behind it. Grabbed, getting an armful of monster, locking his arms around it, underneath its. Pinning its back against his chest, its thick neck not able to turn enough for a bite. It thrashed, nearly lifting him off his feet. One of its arms came free. Claws grazed the side of Marshall's jeans, a tip getting caught in denim and scratching in a bright flare of pain along Marshall's thigh.

The thing fought harder, and Marshall's grip slipped an inch. Then another.

"Turn. This way, now." Liv's voice came again.

He more tripped than turned. Liv was there, small gun in one hand. With the other, she drove a too-silvery blade into the creature's eye, red-green goo splashing.

The thing yowled, and whipped its head forward, right at Liv. And she jammed a gun against the side of its head. The blasts blew weird blood and pinkish stuff meant to be inside a body, not on the outside, everywhere. Over the dumpster and restaurant back wall. Over Marshall's arms and side.

Ears ringing, edges of his vision turning dark, adrenaline threatened to drown him. Nothing feeling real, nothing to hold on to and ground himself in the now.

A touch on his face stopped him. He jerked, and slipped on blood and worse, nearly going down.

"Marshall. Marshall. Let go." Liv's voice registered. Quiet. Compelling. Offering him a landmark into reality, a line to hang on to.

She had a hand on his chin, the touch that had brought him back. Her other hand cupped around the side of his face, trying to keep him from seeing. "Marshall, you can let go. Please."

It registered that he was holding what was left of a body. He dropped it, fast. Blood splattered on his jeans.

"Don't look." Liv got between him and the body.

Not before he saw, though. Slick gray skin. Claws on its hands and feet. Those teeth, white and lethal in the light, in the remains of a bullet-shaped skull. All alien.

But it was wearing ragged sweat pants and a hoodie. He'd helped kill someone who looked like a monster but wore hoodies. He'd had a part in ending a life.

"I can't—what did we just *do*? That is a—"

Two shapes hit the mouth of the alley, joining Liv. Marshall jerked and his shoulder blades slammed into the wall behind him.

"Find the child," Liv said. The shadows turned into Jace and Matteo. They split up, going in opposite directions as they hit the street.

"Don't. He's a kid. Don't hurt him." Marshall stared at her.

Liv closed her eyes for a second. "I know, and we won't harm him. We need to see if he's injured, and get him either medical care or to a secure HQ safehouse." She pulled up her shirt and holstered the gun, the one he hadn't known she was carrying, in a band that hugged her middle like a second skin.

Catching the direction of his gaze, she dropped the fabric. "Are you injured? Did it hit you? Talk to me, okay?"

"I'm—" His skin was still pebbled, but with cold this time, and his jaw hurt, like he was standing outside during a

Chicago winter, and his teeth were chattering. He tried again. "Fine. I'm fine."

Liar. The voice in his brain were yelling because, no, he wasn't okay. He'd help murder someone.

"Ghoul."

He jumped, staring at Liv, realizing he'd said at least the last bit out loud.

"It was a ghoul, not a person, and it's over. Damn, Marshall. You scared the hell out of me, interfering with a highly territorial cryptid's hunt and tackling it." She held out her hand, the way he had to the kid.

He reached to take her hand, and saw the blood on his. After, he barely registered moving, reality jumping in and out of focus. The darkness of the SUV. Clammy-wet denim sticking to his legs. Staring at his hands, blood dried into the lines of his palms, flaking in spots, from where he'd killed a sentient being.

iv

As we passed through the main gate and its infrared scanned us, I typed madly, keying in the codes for ghoul DNA and organic samples, no live specimens. The last thing Marshall needed was the alarm screaming because it detected an unregistered cryptid presence entering the compound.

He had gone a shade of white I didn't know breathing humans could achieve, even his lips pale, far worse than the night we'd met him.

He'd also compulsively scrubbed his hands on his pants the entire time—while the guys disappeared the ghoul carcass after failing to locate the kid, while I called in the Cleaners for a more thorough sweep of the alley, and the drive back to base.

As the alarms accepted us, the garage door opened, then closed behind the truck. UVs flaring to life, Matteo cut the engine. He and Jace stayed still, watching us via the rearview mirror, waiting on my cue.

From my middle seat right beside Marshall, I touched his elbow. "Hey." I kind of hated myself as he jerked away, opposite elbow banging into the doorframe.

"We're home," I said softly, projecting *it's all good, totally safe here* vibes. "You can hit the—"

My vibe attempt crashed and burned, Marshall bolting from the SUV before I finished. The breezeway's door whooshed opened, the interior door between it and the kitchen slamming seconds later.

I dropped my skull back against the headrest at the same time Jace said, "Fuck."

"About sums this night up." Matteo's big hands flexed around the steering wheel. "Got a kid in the wind who may be hurt, and saw too much. Got Marshall, who sure as hell saw too much. What was he doing in that alley?"

Trying to get killed.

I shivered, the scene I walked in on still fresh. An unarmed Marshall facing down a hungry ghoul, one desperate enough to stalk live prey, putting himself between it and a street kid, latching on to the powerful cryptid. Claws and teeth within inches of Marshall's throat. For whatever reason, this one's behavior had become the norm in the last year, and I'd looked over far too many crime scenes photos where the human victim hadn't survived.

Pressing my thumbs against my lids, I eliminated the horrific vision in a burst of colorful floating spots. I had screwed up, again, and Marshall had nearly paid the price. It didn't matter that the ghoul was a half-grown juvenile, or starving. They were still lethal.

Jace hung over the seat, frowning at the blood and bits of ghoul flesh on the seat Marshall had occupied. He echoed my thoughts. "You sure he's not hurt?"

"Not sure enough." I climbed out and went after Marshall. The guys would detail the truck, and put out feelers with our street contacts to watch for the boy and alert us, while I took care of our guest and reports. That's what teams did, covering each other. This one time though, reports could wait.

I scanned the kitchen. Then took a right and nearly ran Marshall over. He stood in front of his door, hands out and staring at them.

"Hey." I slowed, inhaled calm, and hoped Marshall bought into it.

"If I touch the knob, I'll get—this on it." Marshall didn't look at me, eyes glassy and almost like he wasn't here-here.

"Stay right here, okay?" I darted for my room and grabbed a packet of makeup wipes. Marshall hadn't moved when I came back.

I motioned at his hands. "May I? Please?"

He blinked, pupils too large, but offered me his hands.

I cradled them, wiping blood off scrapped-up knuckles. "You're home. It's over, hear me?"

"We killed someone."

I kept my touch gentle, cleaning away every trace of blood from big, capable hands, calluses telling a story of his life. Hands that had saved a child tonight. "You didn't harm anyone. I did." I probably should've left it at that, but Marshall wasn't the only one rattled by the evening's events, even if for very different reasons. "What were you even doing?"

"It wanted to hurt that kid. Then it would've kept going and got you. I couldn't let it."

I wanted to swear, and never stop. Marshall had protected me, when it was my job to protect him.

"You had a gun." Those not-quite-focusing eyes shifted to

mine for the first time. "And that weird knife. Why did you have one when we were out for beer and bad karaoke?"

"I'm always armed, and with chem-treated weapons. Always. We're never truly off the clock, unlike police or standard special units."

Marshall jerked his door open, bolting inside, and slammed it in my face.

I scooped up the used wipes and went to file my report. If Marshall had begun to see me as anything good and trustworthy, I'd killed that connection as surely as I had the ghoul.

CHAPTER 25

*M*arshall

THE BLACK PIT, the one that stole in and swallowed him whole, spit Marshall out a degree at a time.

First, the recognition that the iron band that'd clamped around his chest, getting tighter and tighter ever since the alley, was gone. Then, that his lungs still worked, and he had control over his breathing.

Next came the chill, artificially cooled air hitting his skin and turning the fear sweat to a clammy film.

Finally, his vision cleared.

He was on the floor, in the corner of a room. He blinked and breathed, staring at the striped comforter and the bedside table. His room in the compound.

He let his head thump back against the wall. His room, where he'd made it barely in time to keep Liv from witnessing a full-blown panic attack. The worst he'd had in years. Way worse than after the raid on the hotel.

There had been blood then, too. None of it had been on his hands. An ugly, harsh laugh ripped out of his throat. Now he got where that expression came from. He bit his lip, choking off the laugh before Liv or the team heard.

Matteo, who really couldn't stand crumbs and compulsively cleaned up his teammates' spills, and who had a tendency to stick his tongue out like some kid when he concentrated. Jace, who goofed, and forgot song lyrics, and stole muffins and cold pizza from Liv.

Liv, with her butterfly-light touches. Trying to shield Marshall from unpleasant sights, and who wiped his hands, careful and precise. Hand's that had been coated in a dead sort-of person's blood, because Liv had killed the person. Coldly, efficiently. Matteo and Jace would've done the same if they'd gotten to the alley first. They'd had done exactly that to the crew working for his ex-boss.

Marshall hauled himself off the floor, pins and needles running through his legs and feet. He paced until the sensation quit, moving the quickest way to stop the discomfort.

He didn't have a clue how to get that to work on the rest of his life.

When he checked his phone, it showed it was already morning. He'd been lost in his own head that long. He trudged to the showers, stuffing his dirty clothes in the trash. He didn't have many to spare but he couldn't look at those again.

Bone-deep freezing, he grabbed his hoodie. The image of another hoodie and an alley stinking of fear and death superimposed over it.

He destroyed half a carton of eggs, accidentally crushing shell into yolk or yolk falling down the drain, his hands shaking. But he had breakfast done by the time the team came in. Instead of their usual casual energy, they were even quieter and more subdued than when he'd first come to the compound.

Marshall kept his head down, and kept busy. He might've made it to privacy before he completely melted down, but no way had he been normal. He couldn't remember most of what happened after. After the alley.

Which was a bad sign. Probably, he'd acted weird, freaked them out, the way he did other people.

Instead of conversation and jokes, today was only chair legs scraping across the tile flooring and the creak of wood, a chair protesting Matteo's size, and the swish of fabric mixing with the gurgle of the coffee maker.

The clearing of a throat, obviously meant for him, forced him to look up. Okay, more look sideways. Liv waited by his elbow, nowhere near as close and casual as the day before. Silently, he scooted plates down the counter for her to pass out.

He poured himself coffee and stayed standing. Using the excuse of washing pans, while everyone else ate. Breakfast was only bread, eggs, and avocado, plain toad in the hole. His stomach had rebelled, hot saliva filling his mouth when he'd tried touching the bacon. The slick meat had stayed in the refrigerator.

When chairs scraped again, he braced for complaints over the basic, meatless breakfast. Instead, Liv brought him the empty plates, and silverware. A bigger shaped hovered behind her. Matteo clasped Marshall's shoulder, a brief, firm grip. "You did good out there last night."

Marshall scrubbed dishes, and tried to fit Matteo and his kindness into the same picture as knives and blood-spray. Into a world that required skirts that camouflaged guns, the world he was in now.

iv

JACE SIDE-EYED MARSHALL, THEN MOUTHED, "MOVIE?" at me.

I nodded and stuck the last pan in the dishwasher.

Marshall didn't check my work or remind me to pre-rinse. Instead, he closed the loaf of bread away, then sort of stood there, staring at a spot on the wall.

"Do we have popcorn?" I asked the back of his head.

He twitched, but turned and more or less looked at me. The yellow hoodie clashed with his hair and paper-white face. "Yeah. You didn't get enough at dinner? I'll double the recipe next time." His tone was still too flat.

"We are well fed, trust me. Matteo will complain through the entire movie if he doesn't get popcorn, though."

Marshall frowned, completely lost.

"Tradition, man. Nothing beats the ritual post-mission B-movie marathon." Matteo stretched, hands linked behind his back, and ambled toward the den's common room at half-speed, giving me time to do my part.

"I'm thinking of turning in early." Marshall ducked his head, which only highlighted the purple shadows under his eyes.

If I thought there was even a miniscule chance of him sleeping, I would have kept quiet. "No can do. Tradition is everything. Go on, and I'll toss some popcorn in the microwave."

He hunched deeper in his hoodie but followed Matteo, all the social progress gone, him back to not willing to argue with us. Probably doubly hesitant now.

'I killed someone,' kept looping through my head, and I didn't know how to explain or make it okay.

With the guys out of sight, I massaged the spot over both eyebrows, then hit the cupboard. I'd erred once. Twice wasn't an option. I gave Marshall points for pretending he was fine all day. If *fine* meant not meeting our eyes or saying more than three words at a time. The barely noticeable tremor in his hands when he'd dished out the salad tonight said otherwise.

Corn popped, I balanced the oversized orange bowl festooned with tiny bats, Jace's idea of funny, and entered the den. Marshall hunched on the loveseat, sunk into the hoodie and hands shoved in its pockets like he was freezing.

"The team leader should rate first choice of the good chairs." I grumbled at the guys, who played along and grabbed the twin recliners.

"Calling shotgun beats titles," Matteo said and appropriated the bowl. "The couch is just as good. Mostly."

The couch was awesome, but didn't work for the plan we'd thrown together on the fly, relying on discreet sign language during dinner. "Mind sharing?" I asked Marshall.

"I can move," he said to the floor.

"There's no other spot that provides acceptable movie viewing." I grabbed my book dragon throw from the couch arm, and climbed over Jace's outstretched legs.

Marshall twitched, like he meant to get up. Perhaps I should have respected his choice but the trust he'd shown in letting me hold his hands and clean away blood grated against the hint of terror I'd glimpsed when he bolted for his room and his obvious sleeplessness now. He'd allowed me to help once. I hoped he'd allow it again.

I plopped beside him on the loveseat and whipped the afghan over us both. "I don't understand how the rest of the place can be normal yet it's always freezing in here."

Marshall swallowed hard but stayed. Under the throw, he abandoned hoodie pockets, and his hand wove a repetitive path, picking at a frayed spot on his jeans, then scrubbing against his thigh the way he had on the drive home, in an endless loop. My chest ached the same as when I didn't block fast enough during sparring and Vee got in a lucky punch to my chest, except this pain was from Marshall's obvious distress and my failure in preventing it.

Slowly, I reached across, intercepting his loop. His hand was chilly when I touched the back of it. He blinked and focused on me, and didn't jerk away. I curled my hand around his, letting him know he wasn't alone, the same way I did with my brothers.

I bit the inside of my cheek, and tilted my head, silently asking Marshall if this was okay. If I was crossing a line, or if the physical contact with another person helped.

He propped our joined hands on his knee. I wiggled deeper into the cushions, as the opening soundtrack played. A few minutes in, the tendons that'd stood out in his neck relaxed. By the movie's midpoint, he'd slouched lower, matching me.

As the guys yelled at the screen and the actor took the

wrong train, headed away from where he'd promised to meet the rest of the heist crew, Marshall let out a deep breath. His shoulder and thigh touched mine, hesitant. When I didn't protest, he left them there.

The movie ended and Jace cracked his neck back and forth, as Matteo stood and set the popcorn bowl and remote by us. "I'm out."

"Me, too. Gotta return a call from Josh."

Marshall tensed, poised to move if I did.

I reached over him for the bowl and remote, and wiggled back into my nest. "I had too much coffee earlier, so I'm still wired. Want to keep me company?" I tipped the bowl his way.

When Marshall took a handful, I asked, "Buddy cops or kissing booths?"

"Say kissing booths. She loves that stuff. Best way ever to butter her up and get out of a morning run." Matteo grinned.

I threw popcorn at him and his grin grew.

"Plus, rom-coms are *awesome*," Jace yelled from the hall. "Don't hate."

I checked with Marshall. Pink tinted his face, which was an improvement over the previous chalky look. "Yeah. Kis— uh, booths. Booths are good."

Marshall didn't seem to share Matteo's bias, getting into it and a laugh slipping out over the characters' awkward meet-cute. Still, there was only so long you could fight exhaustion.

The second time his head dipped, and he jerked upright, he said, "I'm sorry."

I dusted salt off my hands and turned the movie volume down, twisting enough to see Marshall. "For what?"

"Ruining your movie. Dinner. Everything."

Since he'd been fine with it earlier, I laid my hand over

his. "You have nothing to apologize for. I know you didn't get any sleep."

He angled his face away, leaving me with his profile and the muscle clenched in his jaw. "I'll do better. At least not keep you up, too."

"Stop beating yourself up. Of course you can't sleep. My sister couldn't sleep unless the lights were on for a month after her—" I switched, fast "—after a tough cadet exercise."

Silence filled the room, the murmur of a fake date gone wrong the only noise.

"You were going to say a kill of some kind. Your sister's tough mission and killing something." He faced me, pupils way too big. "Except this time, I killed a—a being. I helped kill it. Him. I think it was a him."

"It may have been a male of the species, but it wasn't a *him*. It was a thing." I had to at least try to make him understand the facts, ugly as they were.

"Specifically, a ghoul. Ghouls are vicious. So nasty that until recently, they didn't even have packs, like windigos do. They barely tolerate each other during breeding season." I took his hand again. "They are cowards and opportunists, and when you are talking opportunistic ghoul prey? That means children. The elderly. The mentally ill. Many homeless fit at least one of those categories. Who knows how many children living on the streets *didn't* have a Marshall to save them."

"Does it get easier? Murdering, I mean?"

I let go, frustration swamping me. We didn't speak the same language, and I wasn't succeeding in translating.

"I'm sorry, Liv, but that's what we did. Murder." He at least angled to me again. "How did you deal with—with the first time?"

His plea for direction hurt a part of me I hadn't known existed. My answer wasn't going to help him. "We gradually build up. We're twelve when the field specialist Instructor lines up staged hunts at a dedicated training site, and releases a small pack of windigos. By thirteen, we move up to a ghoul and other Level Three cryptids."

Horror etched Marshall's face.

My first up-close civilian experience was with Bruce. He hated our lives, loathed the Company, and hadn't been shy in sharing his opinion when he first arrived in our world. Marshall though—he looked at me not as if I was dangerous, but as if I was a criminal.

I sighed. "It's who we are."

He swung all the way around, hand on my shoulder. Passionate and forgetting about rank or rules. "It's not. You didn't drop me off on a corner after your mission, and you could have."

"Our first mandate is protecting humans. Any vampire, or even human partner, would've tracked you down in a hot minute."

His expression turned stubborn, calling me out, and he shook his head. "You didn't leave me at your HQ, and Jace said that's protocol and what almost always happens."

My turn to look away. I also didn't have the vocabulary to truly explain my decision to myself.

Marshall didn't take then hint. Or he didn't care. "You haven't yelled at me for throwing your schedule off, for messing up in general, for all the extra work I caused you. That I'm still causing you. You made sure I had my—you made sure I had food. That's not part of a black ops' job description."

"You didn't ask to be caught in our raid, nor did you intend to be caught up in our war against cryptids. I'm not about to blame you for acts outside your control. Aside from that, you work hard to fit in, which we all very much appreciate. You are an easy person to like, and even easier to get along with."

His face went as red as the bouquet of apology balloons the heroine was offering the hero, across from us on the flat screen. "You are way too nice to me, all of you, with meals and a room and the night out. You're *nice*, period. But you murder people, or things, or whatever you have to call them to make what you do seem not so bad. Then go get a beer like…"

I stared at him and he swallowed and finally stopped. I counted heartbeats, pushing through the resentment. An exercise I'd perfected in the last year. "Until you've seen a cryptid crime scene, and the remains of innocent people strewn across a backyard, you don't get to judge my or my team's actions. The larger predatory cryptids have no concept of compassion or kindness."

I pushed back the part of me pointing out that my sister and adopted father were technically cryptids. "So yes, I will eliminate them, using whatever means are at my disposal. If that makes me a monster of some sort in your eyes, so be it. I will never apologize for my career or allow anyone to judge my team."

I drew in a much-needed breath, stopping myself. I'd lost my composure and professionalism, something I kept doing with Marshall.

Who hadn't moved, the loveseat too small to put any real distance between its occupants. Yet he gave the impression he had. He scrubbed both palms against his jeans. "I didn't mean to insult you."

"Yet you still believe you were complicit in a murder."

He stuck with nodding, undoubtedly leery of another rant.

"Think about this—what were your other options, in the moment, with the ghoul charging you? Over short distances, ghouls can move faster than cheetahs. So your other option was to stand there and die?"

"I pushed the kid out of the alley. I could've blocked the opening 'til the kid got away, and you or the guys had time to —I don't know. Stop it and take it in to HQ, like you were gonna do with my old boss."

"Marshall, damn." I grabbed both his big hands, pressing like I could press truth through skin and bone. "You are worth more than losing your life serving as momentary bait. I won't ever change my opinion on that, any more than I would as to the importance of the Company's existence."

We both figured out at the same time that I was practically in his lap. His gaze went to our hands and where we were joined. I couldn't interpret his expression, but it couldn't be positive, and I let go. All I'd accomplished in the last twenty-four-hours was making error after error.

My face felt as hot as Marshall's had looked earlier, especially when he stood and added, "It's late. I should—" He didn't finish the thought, in too much of a rush, wide back already disappearing out the door.

I wrapped up in the afghan, and trailed past his closed door to my room.

* * *

THE NEXT DAY'S menu consisted of more vegetarian meals, not even a red sauce in sight, and Marshall kept a mug of coffee in reach at all times. He'd gone through enough coffee already to put Colombia's economy in the black for the year.

I locked my heels over the bar stool rungs and twisted side to side, loosening tight muscles, while Marshall dumped beans in the grinder without measuring, then immediately transferred the powder to the coffee maker and held a cup under the drip. At least he was speaking to us again. I had no illusions though. The whole The Team Are Murderers issue wasn't solved, merely back-burnered for later.

Hitting send, I closed the laptop and pushed it to the corner of the bar, still no word on the boy Marshall had saved. "Do you have a stomach lining left?"

Marshall jumped, splashing hot coffee on his wrist. He swiped it on a towel and shoved the cup back under. "I guess."

"It took you five minutes to remember which was the bread knife this morning. You look like a zombie."

He whipped around, scalding liquid arcing across the counter. "Are zombies real?"

"No, of course not. That legend seems based on this Bolivian parasite which—" at his horrified expression, I switched gears. "Right. Let's just go with no. Of course there's no such thing as zombies."

He shuffled to the glass canisters and spooned a mountain of sugar into the pitch-colored liquid in his mug. Particles of sugar pattered on the counter, lost in his twitchy movements.

I leaned over the counter, and steadied the mug with one hand, and caught his wrist with the other. "Marshall, stop. You have to sleep."

"I can't. I'm fine."

I put the cup out of reach and kept possession of his arm, which violated personal space, but he needed an intervention. "Nightmares are awful, true. However, lack of sleep eventually pushes you into this state of psychosis. Please believe me when I say that is far worse."

He sagged against the counter and defeat deadened his voice. "I can't."

"Have you ever had an addiction—alcohol, drugs, anything?"

He blinked at me, processing, then shook his head.

JANET WALDEN-WEST

"Seizures? Allergies?"

Another negative shake.

From sweeping his apartment, I already knew he didn't take any regular prescriptions. "We have a couple of decent sedatives on hand in the infirmary. One will buy you a few hours of sleep."

He chewed at his lip. "Will it stop the nightmares?"

"I can't guarantee that, no."

"Can I wake up fast if it doesn't?"

I hated saying it. "No. You cannot go on like this, though."

He glanced down the hall, toward his room. Then away fast enough to give himself whiplash.

And wow, had I not been thinking. Nightmares. A dark, narrow, ghoul-filled alley. Very similar to the dark hall and windowless bedrooms. The perfect storm as far as nightmares. This though, this I might have a solution for.

"Given our divergent views, and recent events, this is probably a ridiculous question. Could you trust me enough to try something that might help?"

Either he took pity on me, or he was that desperate. "Yeah. Sure."

"Back in one second, I swear." I strode down the hall, rummaged through my stash, and met Marshall, still standing exactly where I'd left him.

I clamped my elbow tighter on the pillow threatening to escape, and hitched the light throw higher. "Ready."

I climbed the massive beams inset in the wall at the junction of the hallways, serving as ladder, and flipped the trapdoor open. Late autumn air greeted us on the flat roof, my favorite outdoor space.

Marshall climbed the last step, and peered around me as I tossed several real pillows onto the violet and gold indoor-outdoor cushions already on the platform swing. "Liv—"

"Hear me out. Sometimes a radical change works to short

160

circuit a behavioral association. In this case, the association between sleep and nightmares. Also in this case, an open space with great natural light instead of a dark, closed off area." I was also betting on his almost pathological aversion to saying no. I'd add that infraction to my tab, to feel guilty over later.

"Are you—I don't know if that'll hold me."

I climbed on, bounced on my knees to demonstrate, then pointed at the crazy-heavy beams that created the frame. "This was a beast to assemble, but it has held an entire team at the same time."

"You and Jace and Matteo?"

I'd meant me, Kimi, Vee, Josh, and Bruce, but I nodded. It had also held the three of us.

Probably going on the assumption that if it held Matteo, it would hold him, Marshall edged onto the platform. Out here, the sun mercilessly highlighted the dark circles under his eyes, and he kept the hoodie, even as my skin warmed under the cloudless sky.

I arranged the pillows, and tugged on Marshall's cuff, since he was still on the edge, almost hanging over.

He joined me. I debated whether to go, which was the common-sense, polite thing to do, versus staying, which might push his boundaries. Even after years with Bruce and visits with his family, it was still difficult to gauge civilian reactions. That, and remember they had weird rules about being physically supportive or casually affectionate. Still, leaving felt like I was abandoning Marshall.

"Up front, you can be honest and say no to what I'm about to ask. Would you mind if I stayed out here?" I asked.

"With me?"

"I can use the floor." The colorful beanbag type chairs arranged around the low, wide table in the center of the roof were comfortable, and well used.

"What about work and boring daily reports?"

Which was a very polite way of telling me to leave. "I'll give you some privacy."

Marshall surprised me, reaching and snagging my BDU pocket. "I didn't mean—it's your roof." He frowned. "Like, it looks like you. Nice. Easy-comfortable. I just don't want to waste more of your time if you've got stuff to do."

I wasn't sure what easy-comfortable translated to, or why is gave me a weird little pop of happiness. "Training is done. My reports are filed. Matteo did an early sweep, nothing is stirring, and no chatter from our street or Asset contacts. This is downtime until another sweep, a mission plan is issued, or an emergency call-out."

He didn't let go of my pocket, heat from his hand joining the heat from the sun. "Why do you want to stay?"

Since it sounded like a judgment-free question instead of a challenge, I answered. "Sometimes having someone with you short circuits nightmares."

"Yeah?"

"Sometimes. If not, having someone to wake up to helps," I added softly, the patient blue eyes fixed on me making the honesty feel natural. Jace, Matteo, and I had more than our share of bad dreams, though time was finally wearing down the sharp edges of traumatic memories.

"Yeah, I can get how not being alone would be better."

He let go of me, and I curled up, back against one of the posts, arms wrapped around my knees. Just because he'd agreed to my staying didn't mean he wanted me close.

"You're too far away. For the blanket." He shook out the light, open weave throw that barely counted as a blanket. It caught the breeze, and puffed.

I scooted in, and it settled over us in slow motion. Neither of us seemed to know what to do next, Marshall tensed up again, and I didn't understand why. To have something to do, I used a toe against the corner support to push us into motion.

The balm of sun and the hypnotic slide of the swing worked on me. I dug my spine into the padded mattress, and a yawn snuck up on me. I covered my mouth, but was too late.

"Yeah, it's pretty cool out here," Marshall said, instead of getting offended. "I mean cool-great, not cold-cool." His head moved as he took in the wrought iron railing circling the roof, the table and bean bags, the stack of empty pots in the far corner, the shadiest spot and where Kimi once had a bougainvillea and Bruce had kept his mini-garden of herbs.

I rolled my face enough to watch Marshall, and when he turned back more quickly than I'd anticipated, it left us staring at each other. Marshall examining me the way he had the roof. Whatever he saw, a little more of the tension drained away.

When a tiny shadow passed over us, one of the yellow and black birds that enjoyed Kimi's plantings, he jerked his attention away.

The bird was joined by its flock, and they settled into their chirping conversation. Clouds scudded overhead, not enough to block the sun, melting into a display of ever-changing designs as the breeze played. Marshall made the perfect windbreak, and my muscles went limp under the warmth and the sway of the platform.

"You should sleep. Even if I don't," Marshall said, tone apologetic.

"M'kay." I half-closed my eyes.

When I checked again, Marshall's eyes were closed, the roof having worked its magic. In his sleep, he shifted, and his shoulder butted against mine and stayed. Close enough that messy curls scented with our supposedly unscented sham-poo, and ginger from lunch, tickled my forehead and nose.

I brushed the wayward curl flat. Flat wasn't its natural state, and it popped up as soon as I moved my hand. On the same principle as a curling iron, I carefully wrapped the curl around my finger, then slid my finger free. Which worked much better. Marshall sighed in his sleep and nudged closer, bringing curls with him. To keep from sneezing and waking him, I spent the next few minutes taming those closest, twisting them into real curls that sort of behaved. They weren't anything like the different fades that were standard for male agents, instead soft and fluffy and kind of fun.

Which was not the line of thought any C.O. needed to entertain towards a civilian, most especially a sleeping one, and one who considered me little better than a ghoul. I abandoned the last curl, and tucked my arms close.

A choked off yell shook Marshall, and he rolled, muscled arm falling over me.

I touched his shoulder, hoping the additional contact helped. "Hey, we're okay. You with me?" I rambled, since tone was a heck of a lot more important than the words.

Marshall rolled further onto his hip, homing in on my voice. Lashes as long and fluffy-looking as his hair swept open at half speed. "Yeah," he said, words hoarse. He cleared his throat. "Yeah. You aren't a monster, Liv."

The change in topic took me a second to translate. When it did, that alien spot of warmth hit again, and my tone held the same hoarseness. "Thank you."

He blinked again, some of the sleepiness retreating. "You've gotta have better things to do." Despite the statement, he didn't lift his arm or shift away.

"I might've mentioned how committed we are to our downtime. Right now, I'm basking in the sun on a fabulous Fall afternoon with a new potential friend. Because honestly, I take caramel French toast and non-monster labels as friend-ish stepping stones?" I hoped.

"That's—being a sorta human dream-catcher is friend-ish, too." He glanced at where his arm was, and color ran up his neck.

"Keeping me company and acting as my windbreak as I bask also seems like a friend thing." I nestled into the pillows as an invitation to stay, if he wanted.

He hitched closer, studying me. Tense again, as if he was waiting for something to be taken away. Another yawn snuck up on me, and he relaxed again, a yawn answering mine. "If I'm not up in an hour, wake me. You guys haven't had enough protein the last few days, and there's some organic chicken in the fridge."

Protein was good. Him drifting off before I answered was better. I snuck my phone out and texted Matteo to order and pick up a couple of all meat pizzas. And if he had to kill anything on the way, not to share that fact with Marshall.

* * *

"MAN, YOU'RE HARDCORE." Jace folded the last slice of pizza in half and finished it in two bites.

"I was gonna fix dinner, too." Marshall slid the baking dish out of the oven and hot cocoa scented the kitchen. Despite the pizzas, he's insisted on doing dessert.

"I fell asleep and the missed the alarm." I put on what I hoped was an innocent expression.

Marshall frowned and gave me the hairy eyeball. "You aren't very good at lying."

Matteo clapped Marshall on the shoulder. "Nobody begrudges having pizza. It covers four of the five food groups. Brownies cover the fifth."

Our guest chef brought out plates and a serving knife. "That's not the food pyramid."

"Government revamped it. Probably you just didn't hear. Like demoting Pluto as a planet."

I snorted and bubbles popped in my milk, the only proper accompaniment to brownies.

"I'm backing Matteo on this one. Besides, taking a freaking day off. You sure as hell earned a couple," Jace said. Then winced at bringing up ghouls, or at least a ghoul-adjacent topic.

Marshall ducked his head, suddenly intrigued by cooling baked goods. "I won't miss breakfast." He handed out plates and brownie squares. At least he didn't sound guilty like he thought we'd judge him for slacking, or seem afraid of us. More as if he was fired up to get back to something he enjoyed.

"Can you make more of that bread thing with the avocado?" Matteo asked, spraying brownie crumbs.

"Uh, sure. There's an avocado left."

The guys high-fived as I snorted another laugh, but it was nice to see them so excited, and happy. "CoW in ten," Jace added.

Marshall didn't beg off. Either Jace and Matteo were back on his good side, or the lure of gaming won out over caution.

Once the kitchen emptied, I pinched off a bite of dessert. "They mean it, you know."

"That they like Toad in the Hole?"

"Well, yes. Though I'm referring to the part about your strength and resilience and deserving time off. That was admiration." I licked my finger clean and hopped off the barstool. I felt a night cross-country run coming on.

CHAPTER 27

$\mathcal{M}$arshall

MARSHALL DUCKED the slap from the ghoul with a human face and his father's heavy eyebrows. For nothing, since he turned and was surrounded by jeering humans, old teachers and ex-bosses and vampires. Dozens of voices echoing their disappointment in him. All while the ghoul and zombies covered in bugs circled, looking for a chance to attack.

When something non-dreamish touched his arm, he jumped, heart slamming, sick fear leaving a metallic taste in his mouth. He jerked, and light, clear and bright as opposed to the murky dream-fog, penetrated. Real world light meant the bedside lamp he'd purposely left on.

Which now throwing a long, menacing shadow, something towering over him. He shoved, attempting to get away, not getting purchase on slick sheets, only tangling and trapping himself.

"Marshall, it's Liv. Easy, it's okay. It's just me." Liv's hypnotic voice cut through the last of the fugue.

He stopped, fighting now to slow down. Breathe. Hold it. Exhale. Too fast set off an attack. He couldn't do another so soon. Didn't want Liv to see one, either.

Her hand rubbed up and down his arm. "I am so, so sorry. I heard you but you didn't answer my knock, and I wasn't thinking when I rushed in."

He swiped at his face, fresh shame swamping him as his palm came away damp, fear-sweat or tears or both. Right in front her. He wiped his hand along the sheet, on the chance Liv hadn't noticed. "I'm fine."

She made a *hm* sound, although she kept up the steady sweep, her hand real and grounding. "Nightmare?"

He avoided her eyes and shoved the rest of the way up into a sit, and blinked hard, eyes gritty and burning. The sleep today helped, but he was still tapped out. "Yeah, I guess." He kept it as vague as he could.

Liv's sigh jerked his head up.

She rubbed her face like she was as exhausted as he felt. "I suppose it was too much to ask that one nap break the cycle."

"It's okay. For real."

She frowned. Which didn't trigger the usual need to apologize and bail. Liv didn't yell much. When she did, she did it trying to make people feel better or help them, which was weird. But also kinda great.

"This is my fault and I'm sorry. You never should have been in a position to have to make the choice you were forced to. For what little it's worth, I apologize for not protecting you the way I should." Her hand rested on his knee, a tentative brush, and then gone. "You're doing a far better job of handling the shock and being uprooted from your life than we are of holding up our end of the deal."

He didn't think, grabbing her hand, and words spilling

out. "You saved my life. You did it twice, and saved all those women and that little kid, and probably more people than I can keep straight. You're like some superhero agent. Don't be upset. Please."

"Marshall. Damn." She lifted her other hand and touched his cheek, brow crinkled and her head tilted.

Confused. He knew confusion in all its shapes and Liv was confused. Could be it was exhaustion making him stupid but all he wanted was to press into the caress like some giant cat. Get closer to her and her kindness and her—her Liv-ness.

She kept going. "You have slept six hours total in the last three days. Going on four. Which is largely my fault, yet you're concerned about my ego."

"I don't want you to ever feel bad because of me. You didn't mess up. You haven't this whole time I've known you. Today was your idea and it worked. I slept." He hadn't though he'd be able to. With Liv's even breaths beside him though, somehow he had. Hadn't thought of monsters, or worried about slipping up and being weird in front of her.

"And now?" Her cheek dented in. Which meant worried-Liv.

"That was—it wasn't all ghoul stuff. More the mess always in my head." That last slipped out but felt right as it did. Something told him he could be real with her, the way she was with him.

He'd caught her hand, and now his thumb was sweeping over the back of it, and Liv didn't frown or try to shake him off, nodding instead. "Trauma can stir up all kinds of old baggage and swirl it together into a nightmare stew."

"One that isn't your fault," he countered.

She gave a half smile and bubbles of happiness popped in his bloodstream in response.

"Would my staying in here tonight help again? The way it

might have this afternoon?" She held her free hand up, since he hadn't let go of the other. "No qualifiers needed, a plain yes or no, and it's perfectly fine to say no if you prefer to be alone."

He swallowed, throat hurting from the mix of dry air and worry and whatever this was, lighting the moment up in warm pink-golds. Hoped Liv didn't hear, in case she'd take it wrong. Liv here, curled up next to him again? Like she cared? Her breath on the side of his neck as she slept, her heart beating against his arm?

The pulse of excitement was stupid. This was probably part of her job, because all the other inexplicable weirdness was, so why not this too.

It felt real though. He already knew she cared about people. This though, it felt like she cared about him. Not like with the trafficking victims she didn't know at all. Although not like she did Matteo and Jace, who were her brothers. Somewhere between those two extremes. His hair was still in the neat curls she played with and twisted earlier. He'd finally drifted off to that light touch.

He gave the only possible answer. "Do you want a pillow?"

"Yes, please." Her smile was all Liv, too, and he couldn't remember one damn reason he'd ever been afraid of her.

He pushed the bigger pillow to the opposite side of the bed. Instead of walking, Liv climbed over his calves and took her spot. She smushed the pillow flat and laid on her side, facing him, then flipped damp hair out of the way.

Because Liv had showered before bed and wasn't wearing BDUs or even jeans. Suddenly it was hard to concentrate on anything but the snug tank and shorts that left long legs bare. Her skin was extra glow-y, and he caught hints of coconut from whatever lotion stuff she'd used after showering.

Those patient spun-sugar eyes stayed fixed on him, like he was actually interesting.

Except he wasn't interesting, or as put together, in a ratty tee leftover from some job last year. Not that anything would help his looks much but the electric orange couldn't be doing him any favors. He tucked one foot behind the other, hopefully hiding the hole in the sock, the one right over the caped crusader's mask. At least these sweatpants didn't have holes in embarrassing places, and the frayed strings at the cuffs weren't noticeable. Much.

Liv tucked one arm under her pillow and yawned.

He rolled to turn off the stupid lamp.

Liv latched onto his sleeve. "Leave it on? There's no shame in avoiding dark places for a while. I was serious about Kimi sleeping with every light on for a month." She tugged lightly until he hitched back around.

"Thanks." He eased lower and grabbed the blanket, awkwardly flipping it over her since he'd also seen Liv didn't like cold. Then he rolled on his left side, mirroring Liv. Unlike him, she was interesting, and he could stare at her all night. Anytime.

She squished the edge of her pillow flatter, making it easier to talk. "Thanks for taking me out of the government serial killer category."

"You guys aren't serial killers and I was a jerk saying so. You're all good. Like, the kindest, most decent people I've met in a long time. I don't know how your job makes you that way, but it does."

Her smile was different this time. Smaller but more personal. Almost shy, she lifted the blanket up over his chest, sharing, her cheeks dusky pink. "You bring out the nice in people."

He had to look away for a minute. He'd heard *doormat* plenty. And *hopeless*. Nice though, that was different. He needed to tuck that safely away until he had privacy to pull it out and examine it. "I guess Matteo likes my breakfast ideas. What about you? I can make anything." He grimaced. "That didn't come out right—not that I'm some great chef, I mean I can learn."

"I told you, you get five stars from all of us." She raised on an elbow and peered at him. "You seriously take meal requests?"

"Uh, sure."

"Whoa." She flopped down. "You just became Matteo's best friend. He's easy. He'd eat a chupacabra if you put bacon and jalapeño on it. Jace is a sucker for our version of home-made, the stuff they served in the cafeteria growing up."

Marshall made a *go-on* noise. This was more than Liv had ever said about her past. He wanted to hear all of it.

"Carne asada, meatloaf, chimichangas, posole, flan, roast stuff. All the usual suspects. Oh, potatoes, although they can't tell real mashed potatoes from two-minute instant ones."

"You really know all about each other, huh?"

"We're a team."

She said it the way some people said 'we're a couple' or 'we're a family'. They were more like the idealized ones on TV than any he'd seen in real life.

"What do you like?" Whatever it was, it went straight to the top of this week's menu.

"I'm on board with all above. Hey, do you make pasta?" She inched higher again, something akin to excitement peeking out, more interest than she'd ever really shown for food before.

"What kind?"

"A friend makes this ricotta and corn agnolotti with a pork belly ragu. It's probably been two years since I've had any."

Agnolotti. As in hand made, high-end stuff, not noodles

from a box. "Most people don't mention instant potatoes and pork belly ragu in the same breath." Or ever.

She nestled back in the pillow, her enthusiasm dimmed, and he wished he could erase the last thirty-seconds, get a do-over. He'd find out what went into agnolotti, and braise the hell out of some pork belly.

"I have a friend who used to utilize us as his test eaters."

"Oh."

"We were on the same team until I—" the hesitation was barely noticeable, but it was there "—until I gained clearance to put my own together. My friend is an autocratic snob. He made what he felt like, and we ate it, end of story. He's brilliant enough that no one argues, aside from an unfortunate beef tartar incident."

"You miss him." Which wasn't Marshall's business. Of course Liv had friends, and friend-friends.

Liv played with the tag on the pillow. "Not only him. You have to understand. We grew up together and trained together and knew by the time we were ten that Vee, Kimi, Josh, and I would be a team. Then have our own Division after graduation. But there's only one team commander. Vee was it, all the way. After—after a set of events occurred, I took the chance to leave and create a new team." A shadow passed over her face. Some kind of deep sadness. Loss, too.

Every cell in his body wanted to erase some of Liv's sadness. "You're the best Commander."

She only gave a half-hearted laugh.

"For real. You have all this patience. You don't lose your temper, you don't yell and browbeat. You know people's favorite food, and pretend not to notice when Matteo cheats at board games. Then there's that saving line cooks thing, I vouch for that one."

Liv rolled closer, their pillows overlapping. "Tell me about line cooks."

Suddenly, it was easy to. More Liv magic. "It's a job. I can always get work, pretty much anywhere." Then when he screwed up, he could find another line. One commercial kitchen was the same as another. Generic bodies, where he could blend in.

"Do you like traveling?"

Did he? He'd never looked at it that way. The places he'd been blurred together, nothing standing out about any of them. "I guess I haven't found where I belong." If there even was some mythical Narnia for underachieving weirdoes whose brains melted down on the regular and took their bodies along for the freak out.

"Where did you start from?"

"Chicago."

Liv made a face.

"Too cold." He said it before she did, getting a laugh, because again, cold and Liv didn't go together.

She tucked her hand under her cheek and shivered. "How does the Southwest rate on the traveling line cook sliding scale?"

"No snow and ice and no losing days of work is nice. No tornadoes in the Spring for sure is."

"The heat?"

He shrugged. "Kitchens are always hot, and we spend twelve or sixteen hours there anyway. Sometimes, I wake up and have to check what city I'm in, because we don't get much downtime most places. Sorta like you guys, I guess."

Tiny scowl lines appeared. "Your schedule is more brutal than ours."

"I get paid." Except he hadn't lately. What little he'd had after the last move had been stuck in an envelope in his apartment, and the envelope hadn't been in the box Liv brought.

He huddled under the blanket. He could sleep at a YMCA

for a couple of weeks, until he had enough for a by the week place. It wasn't like he hadn't survived that way before. He'd learned long ago to sneak leftovers so he'd get two meals a day in whatever kitchen he landed at.

"Hey."

He snapped out of the haze to Liv frowning. "Whatever you're thinking about? Maybe don't."

"I wasn't."

"You were. Whatever it was clearly sucked, because you lost your shine."

"I shine?"

"In a very lowkey Marshall way, yes."

"Is lowkey another word for boring?" It had to be. Although Liv didn't sound like that was a bad thing.

"Definitely not. It's unique to you. Our kitchen is much more interesting with you ruling it."

A frisson of pleasure curled in his chest, wisps of pink and orange.

"Much better. Now, sleep while you're still thinking about whatever made you smile. That's my best advice for good dreams."

"If you have better things to do, I'll for real understand. You don't have to stay." He *wanted* her to, but that was on him.

She just rolled her eyes, but her wry half-smile took any sting out of the action. "If this weirds you out, I get it, and you can say so. Growing up, living, and working the way we do is obviously different than the way you, or most people I suppose, live. We're more casual about personal space, and affectionate than civilians, and sometimes I forget that."

She looked relaxed. Like she really wanted to be here, as much as he wanted her here. "I know I say it a lot, but this is nice. Really nice."

"Yeah, it is." Liv reached over and stroked her thumb over his eyelids. "Close your eyes. You're exhausted."

"This is also why you are hands-down the best Commander. You don't lose your temper, you know when people are tired. You *care* that they're beat, and do something to help."

"Some people might call that controlling," she whispered. Like someone had accused her of that.

Someone needed punched. Marshall only just kept from saying it aloud.

With his eyes closed, Liv switched to running her finger over his eyebrows, inner corner to his temple, a light, hypnotic pressure. "You protect people, you don't control them."

"Even if I tell you to hush and rest?"

Liv touching him was on his Top Ten list, somewhere above music, hell, above gaming. She'd basically announced touch was an agent thing, so he went for it. "Maybe you should get closer. In case I try to hog the blanket. Don't want you to risk freezing. You're way too delicate," he teased, heart beating fast.

Her laugh, and her rolling over and inching close, then letting him fit them together, his knees bent behind hers, was his reward.

He drifted, feeling safe. Glad Liv was safe. Playing with compliments, with her view of him being strong and interesting. Where to check to learn to make agnolotti and a ragu that'd replace some ex-partner's as Liv's new favorite, one small way to pay her back for caring.

CHAPTER 28

iv

I CALLED TIME, stepping out of my crouch and Jace straightened, dropping his fists. I shucked the sparring pads, and rubbed my face on my sleeve. When I looked up, Marshall was still leaning on the upper walkway's pipe-metal rail, arms braced and content watching our session.

Somewhere between the rooftop intervention and our overnight sleep experiment, Marshall's insomnia seemed to have broken. I hadn't heard any nightmare-related noises from his room the last two nights, despite my staying up late in case. I really was relieved for Marshall's sake even if it meant no more sleepovers. Sleeping with Marshall wasn't at all like curling up with the guys.

Marshall really had removed us from the Bad Guys list, as well. I doubted that he saw cryptids as the danger they truly were, which would have been a problem if he wasn't a short-term guest.

Pulling off his hand wraps, Jace faced away from the walkway so Marshall didn't hear. "He won't watch us do knife drills, but he's chill about sparring. He and Matteo spent an hour last night going over a nine mil when Marshall asked if gaming weapons were accurate."

I grunted. A basic nine mil would also be something Marshall could learn and maintain. Arming civilians wasn't an action I usually supported. However, sending Marshall back out in the world didn't sit well with me. From the sound of it, Matteo shared my opinion.

"I wondered there for a minute when Marshall practically lived in the kitchen twenty-four hours straight," Jace continued.

So had I. Whatever Marshall was now experimenting with seemed to balance and relax him, grooves absent from around his sea-glass eyes. "Maybe he needed to deep-dive into one area he can control."

"Do you hear me complaining? That breakfast pizza thing was hella better than even cold pizza."

"You never leave any pizza to get cold," I said.

He pointed at me, a victorious smile flashing. "Word."

Marshall wasn't the only relaxed person around here these days. I tossed the pads to Jace and headed for the house and my reports.

The scent of coffee and roasting meat made my choice of office easy.

I laid the laptop on the bar, pulled up the armory list, and unfolded the paper list I'd used to hand check, row by row, weapon by weapon. We needed more chem-loaded rounds, my second time requisitioning more in the last two months. That had become our new normal, the swell in cryptid sightings and attacks still increasing.

Vee had been correct when she'd theorized several years earlier that there was something changing in the cryptid biome. We had all initially ignored her. I'd carry that guilt forever, from the attack that left her infected with the vampire virus, took her from us for over a year, and now had her, Stavros, and our all-human Josh implanted with lethal chips. I had ignored her and now we all lived under Oversight's scrutiny, their finger hovering over the chips' detonator. Vee and Stavros were also tasked with supplying Oversight's Lab division with research specimens, among other demands. And my team secretly reporting to Oversight on Vee and her team.

I forced myself to stop dwelling and act like a C.O..

Marshall's presence helped, him humming under his breath and hitching up ragged pants as he dumped a handful of something in a deep pot.

I worked on requisitions as he moved from cutting board to prep to the oven. Hitching his pants every other step. I glared at his jean's frayed edges, belt loops hanging by threads. The rags we used in the garage were less threadbare than Marshall's wardrobe. What there was of it.

"Okay, I'm calling it," I said as he repeated the tug and hitch for the hundredth time.

He peered in the pot, lowering the heat, before turning to me, far less wary and more comfortable now. "What are you calling?"

I waved at him. "This. The burgeoning burlesque show. You're one missed meal or stretch from those jeans either falling off or disintegrating. Which will lead to a chain reaction." I tapped my finger on the counter as I presented the coming catastrophe. "First, Jace will get in on the mooning action. Then Matteo. It will only escalate from there, as they try to outdo each other, unless I act on it now. Let's go."

"But—"

"I've logged enough kitchen hours to recognize that you are at the point where that pot simmers for hours—the guys can be trusted not to let it burn—and you mentioned our supplies getting low again. We'll hit the market, then find you clothes that stay put, and in one piece." I was so not recalling how solid Marshall felt when he'd tucked me against him that night, or suddenly wondering what was under his jeans. I stood fast enough the bar stool skidded.

"I won't wear these again." His gaze shifted away.

"It's every pair you own. This has been going on since you arrived." He also deserved far better than trashed remnants.

Marshall's shoulders tightened, visible across the length of the spacious kitchen. "I'll find a belt. These will last. A while."

"Or, we go shopping." I closed my laptop, stacked the lists neatly, and headed for the den. "I'll let Jace know where we're going, and to watch our dinner. Meet you at the truck in a couple of minutes."

"I can't afford anything." Marshall's voice was barely audible over the bubble of the pot's contents, and whirr as the A/C kicked on.

What he said registered, and I spun back to the kitchen. "I'm not sure I understand?"

He stared at the floor, hands shoved in his pockets, leaving me a view of chestnut curls and wide shoulders. "I hadn't been in town long. I paid the deposit, and first and last on the rent. Then I kinda didn't get my first paycheck."

It was probably rude by civilian standards, but I needed to understand if what he was saying, and how I interpreted it were the same. "How much do you have, or is in your account? The Office division can get you access without leaving a cyber trail here if that's your concern."

Marshall refused to meet my eyes. "I have a couple bucks. I'd stashed the rest in the apartment because I hadn't been off to open a bank account, but—" he lifted one shoulder.

In the destroyed apartment that I hadn't searched thoroughly enough, because paychecks and subsistence living weren't the sort of thing Company people ever thought about. "Damn it."

"Sorry." It felt like Marshall withdrew, though he hadn't moved.

"No, I am. I never thought to ask." I reeled in the cold fury —at exploitive vampires, horrible humans, myself—for failing to think about the basics of civilian life.

This I could fix. I strode back, flipped the laptop open and tapped away as I talked. "You're working here and have been for nearly a month. I'm pushing through a financial notice. If you're working, you are dang well getting paid."

I hit send and straightened. If he had remained at HQ, he'd already have been provisioned with whatever he asked for. "In the meantime, each team gets a quarterly stipend since we burn through a lot of street clothes, between sharp objects, claws or fangs, and blood stains."

"I'm only paying my way, and the rest of that, your money, it's not meant for me."

Not only had I missed important issues, I'd been completely oblivious. "You have to hear me. You are not working to pay for your keep, or room, or whatever civilian equivalent. I'm sorry that I wasn't clearer. You are a guest here. We all love that you are kind enough to take over meals. Don't think I haven't noticed all the clean and hung up clothes and gear in the laundry room, and that trash is sorted for the recycle bins, instead of decorating the den and game room. But until you lose a bet, you don't owe anyone here anything."

I switched tabs on the laptop, typing again. "As a matter of fact, the financial notice I sent also means you have short-term Asset status. Meaning the stipend does also cover your needs." If anyone complained, which wasn't likely, I'd cover it out of my account. We all had trouble processing and remembering civis didn't have what we took for granted—whatever we needed, whenever we needed it.

"I'm not kidding Marshall. Consider this me flexing my C.O. muscle. I'll meet you in five minutes."

* * *

MARSHALL HADN'T SAID a single word to me in the SUV, looking out his side window for the entire drive in.

He softened unconsciously at the market, falling into his normal habit, muttering about menus and asking if I liked things. After he tapped his phone for the list he'd recorded on one of the apps or checked photos of dishes before buying ingredients, my role was reduced to carrying bags.

After my obliviousness about financial issues, I was paying more attention now. I was also considering other areas I might need to reexamine. Things like Marshall never employing written lists. I'd caught him watching cooking videos, but he never glanced at the printed lists on the screen, or took notes. I played with that loose collection of observations, and added Marshall's relief at getting a phone, despite him making no calls or sending any texts.

"That's all I need."

His statement pulled me away from my mental puzzle. I handed cash to a vendor and in return got a cheery, "I'll have squash blossoms next time." Another ghost of the past when Bruce made weekly trips, spread between different markets and different days.

Marshall grabbed the bags, like the thinking part was done and he'd finally realized where we were and that I'd been the bag girl this time.

I cranked the SUV, turning the A/C on full blast. The truck dipped as Marshall climbed in. His seatbelt clicked and

I backed out. He didn't argue when I pointed the truck deeper into town.

At least, not until I pulled into a slot in a busy shopping center, one with a couple of major chain stores that I used. There was plenty of selection here.

"I could go in and get a belt and be out fast," Marshall said to his reflection in the side window, since he wouldn't face me. The ease from the farmer's market was long gone.

"Alternately, we go in and buy clothes." I let my belt retract with a *thunk*. "Your unlamented former boss was a literal monster, who trashed your belongings out of spite. I know what I salvaged and brought you, and it wasn't much. You deserve better. Now, you're a Company Asset and no one in the Company goes without." I didn't know if this was one of those bizarre civi male things about gifts or charity.

Marshall shifted and his fingers picked at a stray thread, completely miserable for a reason I didn't understand. "They probably won't have anything. My size."

I started to speak, then stopped to think instead of blindly reacting. He was as tall as Jace, shoulders even wider, although not quite as big as Matteo. There was more of Marshall—he wasn't as bulked up as Matteo, but built solid, even with the weight he'd obviously dropped from stress. Our conversation from the night out dancing came back to me, when I'd offered to teach him, and Marshall's comment about being to big and clumsy.

This was another miss on my part. Either Marshall didn't like how he looked or...I didn't have a clue. I needed more information. "If this store doesn't have what you need, then we'll go someplace else, or order from your usual spots. We have a drop locker and a postal box. Can we check first though? I need a couple of things." A ghoul had recently icked on my favorite skirt, but no way was I bringing that detail up.

Marshall trailed me through the store. He was a far better shopping companion than the guys. Jace took forever, checking out the entire health and beauty section and sight-seeing, while Matteo amused himself by sneaking the weirdest items possible into our purchases.

I worked through the women's section—and stealthily toward the men's. Marshall only sighed when we turned a corner and racks of guy clothing met us.

I shoved through to the middle, to the shelves of tees. Vee and I had found a birthday gift here for Stavros once, in the form of a cartoon minion creature wearing a Dracula cape. It was reasonable to assume there were also pop culture and superhero characters, which accounted for ninety-percent of Marshall's wardrobe.

He stayed by the cart but I dove into the shelves. Total jackpot. "Holy crap." I held up a purple shirt with a raccoon holding a gun. "Going by your shirt examples, I though these things only came in black and gray, and I was fifty-fifty on the gray being faded out black ones."

I thrust my find at him. "How do you feel about well-armed rodents?" Because I kind of loved the tiny trash panda.

Marshall's face pinked up. "Raccoons aren't rodents, but that's the wrong color and too small."

I folded it and stuck it back on the shelf and continued snooping. Sizes went through multiple X's. I grabbed one I recognized. "Here. You like spider guys."

He shook his head. "It won't fit."

"C'mere." I tugged on his sleeve. "Maybe ditch the hood-ie?" It wasn't cool during the day yet. The oversized shirt seemed more a comfort thing—or a means to hide.

Marshall tensed when I circled behind, trying to pivot and follow me. I laid my hand between his shoulder blades. "Quit. I have flawless shopping instincts."

"Liv, it won't work." He didn't break contact though.

I did, to hold the shirt against his back with one hand. Then bunch the excess fabric at his sides with the other. "Flawless, see?"

Marshall did an awkward twist and grab, and held the shirt in front of him, double and triple checking.

While he measured, I chewed on the inside of my cheek. Playing with bits of information, creating an outline to organize and slot them in. Once I had enough of the right facts, they would eventually form a coherent picture. Like the possibility Marshall didn't see himself the way I—we all—did. He couldn't gauge sizes versus his true size.

"Huh." He held the shirt out, still not satisfied.

I plucked the shirt away, and dropped it on top of mine.

Marshall grabbed and stuffed it, and the raccoon I'd found in a different size, back on the shelf.

When I reached around him, he blocked the shelf with his elbow. "It's red. Redheads can't wear red. It's a rule."

I glanced at the electric yellow hoodie he was wearing, then at his hair. "Seriously?"

"It was on clearance."

I ducked around him in the opposite direction, and snatched a green tee before he could body-block. "Redheads wear green. It's a rule."

More gently this time, he took it away, and held up a black one with a caped guy.

"Acceptable." I pointed at the buggy. "Keep going."

He sorted through stacks, not even looking at anything not black or gray. Which only left a few options.

"Two shirts do not a shopping trip make."

"Bright stuff isn't my thing."

He tried blocking me again as I aimed for the shirts. An epic fail on his part since he wouldn't even jostle me, like he was afraid he'd knock me over, much less put hands on me. A fact I added to my facts-about-Marshall outline, for now, took full advantage of. "This one?"

"It's too loud. It'll draw attention."

What it was, was dark navy. "It's *blue*. Blue is almost black. They're right beside each other on the color wheel. Blue and black get invited to all the same family reunions. Plus, it works with your coloring."

Marshall moved a step closer, our sides brushing, and took another look at the shirt. "If you like it, okay."

I tossed it in before he changed his mind, and picked another, a lighter blue. "This blue matches your eyes. It's perfect." Which was true. Totally a thing a friend would point out.

He let me add to the pile and only vetoed one, something about a Marvel and DC grudge. He also stayed closer, right at my side.

Tee's exhausted, I scanned for more blue on the other side of the department—lightweight jeans, my original target. I wasn't brave enough to push for cargo pants and shorts. I'd work up to that later.

Two steps later, I realized Marshall wasn't with me. He cleared his throat, hands shoved in his pockets again, the same embarrassed-apologetic expression as when he'd said none of the shirts would fit.

I made a show of propping against one of the support columns that also served as a mirror for shoppers. "Pants aren't as interesting as shirts with armed wildlife. You're on your own."

Relief lightened Marshall's face, erasing the pinched expression. "It'll only take me a few minutes."

"We're in no hurry." I narrowed my eyes, and intoned in my best movie announcer voice, "Keep my no-mooning rule in mind and choose carefully."

He actually laughed, a deep, rich chuckle. The sound as

open and easy as he was when he relaxed, and charmed a smile out of me. It suited him, the real him underneath the wariness.

Still, I wasn't naive, so kept an eye on my—on Marshall, while I amused myself exploring the men's sleep section.

Marshall eased by and tucked the rolled-up jeans in the cart, like they were contraband.

More likely, an attempt to disguise that he'd only picked a couple of pairs. So, I didn't exactly feel bad in holding up the sleep pants with a colorful innuendo on the fly.

Marshall smacked my hand and the hanger down and out of sight. "No."

This was turning out to be fun. "Let's be real. I've seen your so-called pajamas, which aren't even real pj's, and they are the stuff Matteo relegates to grease rags for the garage. If you thought I'd lose it over accidental mooning, imagine my mental and emotional state at you instigating some mass sleeping naked rebellion, because half our emergency call-outs are at night, and it's instinct to bolt out of bed and check with other teammates."

"Nobody would do that," he protested, hanging the pants back.

"Two words. Matteo. Dare."

Marshall frowned then tacitly acknowledged the risk, selecting a gray tee and pants.

"Same rules apply when it comes to going commando." I pointed at the underwear display to our right.

"Liv!"

"It's clothing. Are you briefs or boxers?" Suddenly, I very much wanted to know.

Every ounce of blood in Marshall's body had to be in his face and neck. "I can't buy underwear with you watching. That's—no."

The guys wouldn't have cared. Bruce though—he had.

Civis and their baffling, random rules. "I think that might skirt a discriminatory line."

"Liv," he moaned like one of those zombies that did sort of exist.

"I'm not looking." I covered my eyes with one hand.

I gave it a minute. "I don't hear the sounds of picking."

"I'm still looking, okay? Don't rush me."

I grinned at the grumble, which suited him the same way the laugh did. Bossy Marshall was...unexpectedly fascinating.

"Get the super-guy boxers. You know you want to."

"You *said* you wouldn't look. Looking isn't very Commander-like."

"I saw those earlier, thank you very much."

"Oh."

I widened my fingers, watching him. He limited himself to a cheap pack of generic boxers, and flung them in like they were covered in scorpion venom.

He looked up and scowled. "You are too looking. I didn't believe Matteo before, about the cheating thing. Now, I think I do."

"Guess you were right to be suspicious. Besides, it's not like shopping is inherently embarrassing."

Sea-glass eyes narrowed. "Then you pick sleep things and underwear. Fair's fair."

"Me?"

He folded his arms, that intriguingly stubborn streak reemerging. "You said it's not embarrassing and that you needed clothes. Let's go get some for you."

The urge to play...I wanted more playful Marshall. Only because playful meant he trusted me again.

I wheeled left. Women's lingerie butted up against men's, separated by a row of columns, creating the illusion of a barrier. I glanced around the displays and pointed. "Get to it then. Pick me something."

Marshall got out, "That's personal."

"Agents have a very underdeveloped sense of personal space and boundaries, according to a friend. Go ahead." I lifted a brow, daring him. Plus, my wardrobe had once been three times larger. I might as well update it, the same way I'd decided to make the compound ours.

His stubborn streak showed again, accepting my dare. But Marshall was still Marshall. He skirted the lacier lingerie, apparently on the theory that a ghoul or equally lethal creature might be hiding among the underwire and satin. He aimed for the tamer sleep shorts and pants and cotton shirts. After a second, he flicked through hangers in earnest, scowling, then muttering "Yeah," in triumph as he pulled a set out.

He held the shorts and shirt out—black with some auburn haired chick in leather and knives on the front, and a red spider outline underneath. "They don't have any tank tops like you usually wear," he said, suddenly apologetic.

I had no business noticing that *he'd* noticed my usual wardrobe choices. "No problem. I'm a killer spider?" So much for him taking me off the bad guy list.

Like he heard, he stepped closer, putting us in touching distance. "Not like that, not in a bad way. At first, the other team members think she's this amoral, ruthlessly practical assassin, but she's really got this big heart and keeps the team together."

"Thank you." I reached for the hanger and clasped Marshall's fingers, and he didn't hesitate to squeeze back.

He didn't blow off my thanks or blush, either. Only nodded, as intense as when he'd been sending victims to safety.

I refused to tear-up in a chain store. "You find us a checkout and I'll meet you in a couple of minutes."

"Why?" Suspicion replaced the softer expression, and he gave me a stern look.

"I need feminine items." None of the guys I knew cared about walking through the feminine care isles, and Bruce routinely picked up tampons for Vee. Kenny, our future brother-in-law, not so much. Like, *severely* embarrassed-weird the one time we'd had a group shopping trip, when his family had visited. I bet on Marshall sharing the same inexplicable civi phobia. "You can tag along while I pick my brand of—"

He held up a hand and retreated in a squeal of hastily moving buggy wheels.

As soon as he was out of sight, I swept back through the men's section.

Marshall made it a point not to look when I scanned and bagged our haul, and I got away with my subterfuge.

$\mathcal{M}$arshall

THIS ONCE, Marshall let Liv arrange bags in the cargo area, and climbed in the big truck and—breathed.

A shopping trip shouldn't leave him edgy and unbalanced worse than a surprise sixteen-hour shift.

But he couldn't keep up with Liv. Bouncing from potential embarrassment to potential embarrassment, even if she didn't laugh at him. Then processing the way she bullied him. Except bullying never meant picking stuff to help him out before. And the teasing. A new kind, and new from her. Like she wanted—no, needed—like she needed him to laugh, *and* to argue with her.

He closed his eyes, arranging the moments by flashes of color attached to the feelings, for later. He'd sort them tonight, in the dark of his room where he could concentrate.

The driver's door slammed, but the motor didn't turn over.

"Are you in there?" Fingers skimmed his arm, the touch already familiar. He'd pick Liv's touch out, no matter if he had a bag over his head, no vision, no hearing.

"Sure." His stomach gurgled, nearly drowning his reply out.

"What are you in the mood for?" Liv didn't hesitate, wheeling the truck into traffic.

"I'll make something when we get back."

"I'm starving now, and I need a break from the boys. Any restaurant suggestions?

"I've never been here before. Whatever you want is good."

At a light, she peered over her sunglasses. "There's nothing you don't care for?"

He shook his head. "I'm not picky."

Liv took him at his word. The sushi place was a small, eight-table place well off the main drag. Those were usually the best kind, the ones locals kept in business.

Liv picked a table at the rear, by the exit door, and took the seat that put her back to the wall. She nudged the other chair from its spot in front, and moved it to her left. "Don't sit in front of windows," she said quietly as a waitress brought sheets and pencils.

That little bit of concern, even if it was her job, hit him and he inhaled around a ball of thanks. The card was the same as in every sushi place, in the same order. He penciled in tuna rolls instead of embarrassing them both.

"While we're out, what else do you need?"

"Nothing."

"We can afford to restock your favorite bathroom supplies without going broke," she said, flipping paper off the end of her straw and sucking up water.

He grabbed his instead of staring at her lips. "There's plenty of supplies already there."

Her toe banged against his ankle. "Come on. What's your

shampoo or hair product preference? Shower and shaving stuff? Moisturizer? Matteo swears he doesn't, but he totally steals my hydrating masks. Jace's routine on the other hand is like an art form."

"Whatever's on sale."

"Cologne? Aftershave?"

"I don't use any."

Liv rubbed her forehead. "You're killing me. Gaming controller favs and headphones? Tablet for music and streaming?"

"There's plenty of gear already in the den. I use my phone, when I can afford a service, but mostly I work hours where it's not worth bothering."

"Work, home and crash, and work again." Liv held out her fist. "Solidarity."

He bumped knuckles.

Liv gave up long enough to situate wasabi and sauce, and inhale a couple of mango and chili rolls. But quitting wasn't her way. "What about bookstores? Ebooks are fine, but sometimes you want paper and a bookmark in your hands. There's a chain and a great indie on the way home."

He rolled up sticky rice and shook his head. Shoved the food in to buy time. "I'm not a reader."

Her chopsticks tap-tapped against her plate, thinking, and he braced. Liv was smart and read people like she saw inside their heads. He'd known she would figure this out— just not so soon.

Her chopsticks stilled. "Comic books or graphic novels don't count? It looked like you had a major collection, before the break in."

"That's different." His stomached clenched and he pushed the plate away. Liv didn't give up, ever. *Get it over with.*

Aloud, he said, "Go ahead. Ask."

Her voice was pitched for only the two of them. "I noticed

you don't use the library or make written notes, ever, not even shopping lists, and that you prefer podcasts and videos to articles. You use the voice app on the phone instead of the keyboard function."

"I can read."

"I know. But? With our job and cryptids, we have to factor in things most never even think about, and this might be something I need to know. I'm not nosing in out of curiosity."

He got the answer out in one long breath. "I'm dyslexic, severely dyslexic is what the tests said with—with some other stuff because being stupid and half-illiterate isn't enough by itself."

Fingers worked around his. Then worked his clenched fist loose and curled around his hand. "I kind of though maybe. A friend in our year-group is dyslexic, but hers is primarily flipping letters or similar numbers."

"Mine isn't—that."

Her thumb swept over the back of his hand, an endless loop. "I'm listening if you're cool with explaining. If not, if it's too much, that's also cool. Either way, thank you for being honest with me."

He risked checking, finally taking his eyes off the laminate tabletop. She didn't look disgusted or patronizing, the top two responses.

She'd caught the edge of her lip between her teeth and was leaned over the plate, all her attention on him. "This is the part where you tell me if I'm crossing a line."

The restaurant was empty except for the two of them, thanks to that weird lull between lunch and dinner. Behind the cash register, the waitress-cashier hunched over her phone.

Liv's strong fingers kept up the soothing half-circles. He'd already opened his mouth, no going back now. She probably deserved to know, before she expected something from him, like reading the note the office guy at HQ had handed them, or writing out his stupid address when she'd asked for directions to his apartment, and he screwed it up. "I can read, but it takes a while. The letters, it's like they're moving all over the page. Sometimes it's easier than others."

"Like when a debriefing agent doesn't bark at you to read over a report form and supply answers in the next breath."

"That's what normal people do."

Her chair squeaked, then his shook, as she butted their sides together. She shoulder-checked him, gentle enough it barely registered. "According to one of my few civilian friends, we're outrageously well-funded black ops who train in a faux city-within-a-city, pretty much from birth, to police creatures that don't really exist, and we don't understand finance, free will, or interpersonal limits, and wouldn't know normal if it was in ten-foot letters with neon arrows pointing the way."

"You don't have to say that. Reality is reality."

Liv didn't scoot away and her shoulder stayed against his. "Look, Matteo's sense of up and down can't translate when he is under water. I hate fire and have issues dealing, especially on the fly."

He took his hand back and shifted so they weren't touching. "It's not the same. At all."

"Agreed. Definitely. However, reading and writing are like breathing in your world. It's a necessity, one taken for granted, and apparently, you're seen as having something wrong if you can't." Her eyes were—not hard. More flat. Serious and hiding something, some pain. "The ability to jump in and eliminate cryptids whether it's at the bottom of a pitch-dark well or muscling through a fire-producing cryptid's defenses *is* breathing for us. We are supposed to do it, not think, and it is taken for granted that any agent will deliver."

Silence settled in, only a Spanish language station and the clink of dishes filtering in from the kitchen.

Liv maybe-wasn't saying it was all the same, so much as giving him something important and equally serious, because he'd been open with her. An exchange of trust.

Because he was a jerk and didn't know how to apologize for thinking he knew it all, the same way other people reacted with him, he tried out, "But you and Matteo are agents?" He made it a question. Hoping Liv translated this in her uncanny way, too.

"We are supposed to handle all the situations I mentioned. However, there's no one definition of how to get to that point. That's what a team means—we don't expect every agent to be or work the same. A team fills in each other's weaker spots and further strengthens strong ones. Southwestern, Central, and South America have more of a cross-section of both fire-based and water-dwelling creatures than nearly any other country. Which is a long and horribly clumsy way of saying fuck narrow definitions of what is or isn't normal, fuck aquaphobia, and fuck dyslexia as some sort of measure of worth, and fuck other people's judgments."

She sipped her water, giving him space, while he rolled around her speech, the glimpse of passion, and decided it translated as Liv didn't think he was useless. That she wasn't spouting some bullshit about knowing how he felt and how his life was, but sharing that they had a connection.

"Hey." She nudged him. "Comics?"

That shorthand made sense, too. "This one teacher gave me a bunch in fourth grade. Seeing the pictures first made it easier to figure out what the letters made and what the words were supposed to say. I didn't get as frustrated and quit, probably."

"A workaround. Perfect," Liv said, voice mellow with approval.

And that was that, Liv satisfied.

* * *

MARSHALL NEEDED to rethink what satisfied Liv.

Especially as she drove the wrong way after leaving the restaurant, west instead of toward the compound.

He shot furtive glances at signs and surroundings. He didn't get it until she pulled into a strip mall and parked in front of a store, its windows covered in twenty-by-forty movie posters. A vintage, life-size science fiction movie hero cutout guarded the glass door.

Liv swiveled in her seat and pointed a finger at his chest before he could speak. "Don't say one word. Life is not limited to sheer survival and need. We may be brainwashed soldiers who love what they do, but we believe in balance and enjoying life, too. Fun makes the rest easier, and keeps us fresher and not burnt out. Pick out comics, or I swear I'll switch out every knife in the kitchen for plastic picnic ones, because I am familiar with chefs and the sanctity of their bond with their knives. *And* I will assign Matteo co-kitchen duty. For a solid week. He will be with you every minute you're in the kitchen. Every. Minute. Good luck keeping him out of your mise en place ingredients, or from constantly opening the oven door to see if dessert is ready."

"That's harsh." It wasn't much of a complaint, not with the goofy smile he couldn't hold in, following her out of the truck and to the store.

Pegging him as a fellow geek, Marshall got the familiar

nod and, "Hey man," from the guy behind the store's long glass counter-display unit, busy sorting cards.

Marshall also caught the squinty, borderline judgmental look and double-take when Liv walked in, a beat behind Marshall because she scanned the lot, the other cars, and the building roof lines before entering. Like a B-movie bodyguard.

Her outfit kinda added to the impression. Liv hadn't taken much time before they left the compound, like she thought he'd change his mind if she took five minutes to match up clothes, so she had on the plain gray tee from after her morning workout and shower, under another of those light jackets, also gray, that he now knew were to conceal a gun and whatever other weapons she carried. Same for the jeans and the blade tucked somewhere between the ankle and her boot.

She hung her sunglasses from the vee of her shirt, and did that one eyebrow thing. Asking him if this place worked for him.

He hesitated between hitting the wire racks along the wall with the new releases, and the tables in the middle of the store, holding the hand-labeled cardboard boxes full of back issues. It depressed him to think about replacing fifteen years' worth of books. Starting over from nothing was the theme now.

Marshall caught movement in the big circle security mirror in the corner. Liv drifted from section to section, not touching but examining every item like this was an exotic museum. The clerk watched her the same way.

The guy finally left the counter and worked around to Marshall. "Help you find anything in particular?"

"I'm good."

"Your friend looking for anything specific? Like glittery-vampire fanfic adjacent?"

"She'll tell you if she is." There were plenty of women involved in gaming and comics, but some people were still jerks about it. If the guy started some crap with Liv, trying to prove she wasn't a real fan, Marshall wasn't here for that, even if Liv wouldn't notice or know to be offended.

The guy struggled with Marshall's answer. Then spotted the issue in Marshall's hand, heroine crouched in the center of the cover.

Marshall felt the mental puzzle pieces click together as the guy nodded. "Yeah, man. What's her cosplay?" Still not talking to Liv like she was a real person, but to Marshall.

The jerk deserved to be messed with. "She's not cosplaying. She's naturally borderline disturbing, and has this fetish for kicking guys' asses. You wouldn't believe the bail money I've shelled out, or the restraining orders against her."

A puff of amusement sounded from behind Marshall, and Liv materialized at his side in one of those freaky-stealthy moves, linking her elbow around his.

The clerk sputtered, "Sure," and retreated.

Marshall picked a final comic. He limited his addiction to two series so he could afford to keep up every month. He spared a glance at the boxes, but turned for the checkout.

Liv didn't budge, which brought him to a halt, since they were still linked. She peered past him. "What's in the boxes?"

"Back issues."

Liv used their elbow lock to haul him around. "Rebuild your collection."

Instead of the excuse he meant to use, "I don't know where to start," came out.

Liv shook her head and her hair whispered over his shoulder. "Pick one thing, and go from there. That's how to rebuild," she said, like it was advice she'd learned first-hand, the hard way.

His hand went to the pre-reboot, the Natasha-heavy

years. Because his subconscious registered that Liv smelled nicer than aged paper, and that where her sleeve had pulled up, warm skin slid along his, and her hair still feathered along his shoulder, giving him a hit of coconut and the coffee he'd made her that morning. The sensory feast brought back the night she'd curled in his bed. Trusting him at the same time she shared comfort with him.

Liv remained beside him while he sorted and chose the six oldest issues available. She sighed, the gust breezing across his cheek. Weird how, and how fast, that sound had moved from meaning he'd screwed up, to meaning somebody cared.

"Getting through these will take a while. I'm seriously set," he promised.

She shoulder bumped him again, and didn't argue. The shorthand and the matter of fact acceptance felt strange. Good-strange, the kind he'd have to be careful not to get used to.

WHEN HE LOOKED up from sorting his new purchases, they still weren't home.

This shopping center was more upscale. A neon guitar hung over the shop Liv parked by.

"I saw your guitar," was all she said. "I couldn't salvage it."

It hurt to do, but he shook his head. "The books are awesome. This is too much, though. Guitars are crazy expensive."

She swiveled to face him, one knee drawn up in the seat. "I've seen you with the instructional videos, your fingers twitching along like you're playing. They also do that sometimes when you're stressed out. I'm not prying, simply stating a fact."

"However my brain is wired, music is easy. I can't read the music tabs, but once I watch a guitarist play, I remember the chords." He inhaled and went for it. "Playing helps me relax, re-channel energy or self-sooth. Like, not freak out 'til the panic backs off, when things get rough."

If she'd noticed the dyslexia clues, she'd noticed the other problem, too. The first time could've passed for a one-off. Not the ghoul one though. Admitting it to her didn't bring on the usual shame and crushing press of hopelessness.

"Marshall, you already know what I'm going to say, so let's skip it and go pick a guitar."

"You didn't trash mine. You're not responsible for replacing it." He folded his arms and met her stare for stare. It wasn't like she could physically *make* him leave the truck and go in the store.

Okay, she could. But she wouldn't.

She didn't level threats about kitchen purgatory this time. "I'm not offering out of a sense of responsibility. This is about your life getting blown up, and one shopping trip making it a little less awful. I know nothing about guitars and whatever goes with guitars though, so please come pick yours." Sincerity flavored her rich voice. That, and true concern, because Liv cared.

"This—" His voice failed, and his eyes stung. He ground the heels of his hands against them, rough and fast.

"I didn't mean to—"

"Don't. You don't get to laugh at me or feel sorry for me because I'm not like you." It came out harsh, but that's all he had in him right now.

The center console complained, and then Liv was suddenly on the edge of his seat. She grabbed his fist and when he didn't bark at her again or jerk away, scooted in enough to wrap her arms around him. Or, at least as far around as she could reach. "There's no way I would laugh.

Why would any of us? You're strong, even when it hurts you. You don't believe in violence, but you don't judge us for what we do. Change is—when life pulls the rug out from under you and you lose the life you thought you'd have, it can be devastating, or result in basically shutting emotions off. Yet you've taken every twist thrown at you, put your head down, and kept going. Do you have any idea how admirable that is?"

When gravity won and Liv started to slip off the narrow bit of seat she'd perched on, he caught and lifted her into his lap. "You guys, you're the best people I've ever met," he got out, around the bands crushing his chest, and his breathing turning too fast, not able to tell terrified-dangerous adrenaline from heartbreaking-relief adrenaline.

Liv wiggled enough to free one hand, and ran it up and down his back. "There's no agent, anywhere, who hasn't needed to let go, get all the awful out, and reboot. Do what you need to. We can sit here. No one can easily see through the windows or bother us. Or I can get us home."

Her lullaby-soft whispers did the opposite. He fixed on the soothing roll of her voice. One solid thing, Liv and her certainty. It anchored him. Too different, a new thing, something curious to concentrate on and push the panic back before it took over.

He got in a deep breath, then another. His heat went back to a normal pattern.

Liv's breath warmed a spot on his temple. Her arm curved around him, and she rested against his shoulder. Half his size, but she grounded him.

"I'm sorry," he whispered.

"Why? I'm serious. We have all had these moments where we had to close a door and just let go. I mean, I theoretically understand that what I'm talking about and what you live with aren't the same, not even a little. No judgment is what I'm trying to say, and wow, am I bad at this."

"You're great at it." They sat, Liv relaxed against him now, him memorizing the way she fit, the way she felt in his arms, because yeah, at some point he'd brought her in closer.

"Your legs have to be going to sleep," she said against his cheek.

He kept the shiver contained, the one that her lips brushing against his face created. His lap wasn't the best place for her at the moment, and it had nothing to do with lack of circulation. Pretty much the opposite.

Carefully, he lifted her off him before he offended her, and sat her gently into her seat.

She dug in the console, came out with a bottle of water, and handed it to him. Matter of fact, no weirdness.

As he drained it, she asked, "Are we going in? And if so, can I be your groupie person?" She flicked her visor down and checked the mirror critically. "I don't *technically* have on enough eye liner, but I can probably sell it."

He snorted, and choked on lukewarm water. His cough turned into a real laugh. "Yeah, go for it. I have an opening for a good groupie."

* * *

MARSHALL SHOVED the dishwasher closed on licked clean plates. He flicked the machine on and trailed down the hall. The hall that was always well lit now, day or night. He didn't know who was responsible for the lighting. This once, it didn't matter. No one here minded around the clock lights, or cared about wasting electricity, and phobias.

Liv came from her room at the end of the hall, a pack of cards in her hand. "If I haven't mentioned it, dinner rocked."

She kissed her fingertips and planted them on his forehead as she walked past.

The giddy-braveness that only Liv brought out rose up. "I think it was implied when you stabbed Jace with your fork."

"He shouldn't have swiped the last piece right from under said fork. He knows the rules."

Which was pretty damn cool. It wasn't handmade pasta and ragu but it was the first step in mastering the process. When he and Liv had arrived home, the pork he'd left braising had filled the house with the smoky scent of perfectly cooked roast and garlic. And had Jace and Matteo circling the kitchen like starving wolves. Which led to Liv offering to unload and stash their stuff while he defended dinner.

As Liv left to get some payback on Jace, Marshall opened the door to his room. He'd dump out the new clothes to wash, then join the team. Okay, dump clothes and stare at the gleaming Gibson guitar. Liv had zoned in on the higher end instruments as soon as they'd walked into the store. When she said Company people didn't really understand civilian salaries and costs, she hadn't been lying. He'd barely got her turned and herded out of the store before she blew the whole team's allowance or stipend on one trip.

She also hadn't raised a brow at him cradling the case the whole ride home.

Now, he flipped the double latches and opened the case, on the stand that she'd added after seeing other guitars on them, and touched the inlays along the neck. He closed his baby up. He'd put new strings on and tune it after everybody went to bed. Breaking it in was a private, personal thing.

Raised voices carried from the den, the cheating versus not cheating argument he'd expected already underway. Jace's righteous yell carried over the other two voices. "Marshall! You gotta referee man. You're the only other person who doesn't cheat."

"How can the cards be marked? The seal on the box wasn't broken," Liv countered. "Matteo saw."

"He's as bad as you are."

Marshall tuned out the squabble as he turned to the bed. He counted bags, then recounted, slower, in case his math had been off. There were still too many bags, though. Liv must've mixed hers in with his. He used one finger to lift plastic corners up, Liv's *girl things* statement still fresh.

His jeans. His tees. The sleep stuff and boxers Liv had enjoyed teasing about. He half-closed his eyes, horror movie-viewing style, and eased the fourth bag open.

Instead of Liv's purchases, the bag held a couple more sets of the pj's, all way too big for Liv. He swallowed and opened another bag, finding more neatly folded jeans, same size and style as those he'd grabbed, plus a sky-blue fleece zip hoodie. The last bag was smaller—the super guy boxers Liv had dared him over, plus maybe a dozen pairs of socks, every color, like his thoughts, each with some kind of superhero on them, no two pairs alike.

He sat hard on the bed, its lux mattress creaking at his weight. Socks, because Liv paid attention to details like holey socks. The blue hoodie because she said the color suited him and because she believed in beauty and fun, not just survival.

His chest ached. This wasn't anxiety or the prelude to an attack though. He poked at the soft, heady thought. It felt pink and orange and red, a mishmash of sunrise colors.

So, this was what happiness looked like.

He touched the socks. Rubbed a red and black pair between his fingers, thick cotton springy and new.

A compound full of assault weapons and single-minded soldiers trained to kill. Who respected him. Who liked him even after seeing him at his worst. Video gaming worlds, and fighting over food he cooked, and thanking him for it, and being part of Jace's in-jokes and the staggering shoulder slaps Matteo handed out to friends, and lights left on with no commentary about acting like a man.

And Liv. Who stuck knives in stomachs with emotionless precision. Liv, who made up reasons to sit through bad movies all night, and hauled blankets onto rooftops, and snuck in supplies and hoodies, because she didn't like him going without.

Liv, who smelled like plain soap and something coconut, and fit against him like they were part of a puzzle, and who didn't care that he didn't think like, or act like, most other people. She was bright. A new wood-fire, the first fireflies of the summer, the burst of hundreds of brilliant fireworks.

He tilted his head back and stared at the ceiling that'd probably seen hundreds of people come and go. He'd never bothered thinking about the future. What was there to plan? He'd work lines, go where the jobs were, spend a couple of bucks when he had it. It wasn't good or bad, just life.

Now though, he'd glimpsed a different kind of life.

Everything would be so much grayer after Liv. His future stretched out, starker and uglier now. The team would find Welch, and his other trafficker vampires and human accomplices, then eliminate them all. He didn't really belong here, in the chaos and friendship. He'd have no reason to stay in the only place that'd ever felt like a home.

He'd be out on the street, with decent clothes, a new guitar, and some cash. But no friends. No Liv.

It took him a few minutes to answer Jace's repeated calls for a referee.

CHAPTER 30

$\mathcal{L}$iv

I TOSSED MY CARDS IN, and left Jace and Matteo to duel the game out, without any queens, since all four were tucked face down in my discarded hand.

"Do you want dessert?" Marshall asked. The tap of cards being reorganized nearly drowned him out, despite sitting right beside me at the table in order to police us.

The shine I'd glimpsed on the drive in from the music store had gone dim. He hadn't said a dozen words and he moved slow, not with his usual methodical, focused efficiency. For now, I'd put his mood down to exhaustion, my fault for pushing too hard today when I should have given Marshall space. While he'd finished dinner, I'd done a quick and dirty dive into panic disorder resources so the guys and I would have a better idea what to do or not do, when to maybe offer a shoulder and when to back off. Tomorrow, I'd start making up for my error, and do a deeper dive.

"We have dessert?" Matteo did a double take, his cards dropping far enough for Jace to steal a look.

"Yeah. It should be done chilling."

"Point me that way." I rose, stretched, and nudged my chair under the felted table.

Marshall was already through the archway, before the echo of my offer died out.

I plopped onto the loveseat. Time to see how Marshall felt about rom-coms. Hanging out with him and a movie wasn't a bad way to end the night. He didn't hog all the leg room like Jace or talk back to the screen like Matteo.

He also gave incredible hugs. He committed, none of that loose arms and minimal contact thing civilians seemed stuck on. When he'd picked me up like it was nothing, and wrapped around me in the SUV, it had felt like nothing outside of his goal mattered. And I'd been that goal.

Marshall slipped back in, drawing on some server skills he'd picked up in restaurants, juggling multiple plates, and left two on the card table. He didn't say anything, but at least sat beside me and handed me my plate.

"Where's yours?" I cut a chunk of what looked like cheesecake with mango arranged around the edges, and more of the fruit turned to a custardy filling on top.

"I'm good." He sat on the edge of the couch, elbows on his knees. More slumped and mindlessly studying aged wood under his feet than watching the game.

Since I was ninety-nine-percent positive I'd hammered home the no starving rule, that wasn't it. I poked my knee against his hip, and tried feeling him out. "Want to see if there's anything more scintillating on than watching Jace clean Matteo out? Say, romance with a side of comedy?"

"Sure." He fished around between the cushions for the remote.

I waited until Jace dealt and both guys were engrossed in

arranging cards to say, "You don't have to put up with us if you're beat, or bored."

His answer was to settle back into the loveseat's squishy depths, sliding against my knee as he went, and settling so that my knee was pressed against his thigh. "I like hanging out in here with you. With everyone," he tacked on, finding my queue and flipping through the options.

"Oh, there." I pointed my fork at the screen and Marshall clicked on the media's version of a chef's kitchen, and people in white jackets scrambling to meet a timer. Bruce had guest judged on this one once, while my and Vee's teams had tagged in with that Division's team to track a steep vampire population explosion in L.A.

That was right before the guys and I took over this Division and compound, and Vee's took over their new home.

Like kids and cats, the noise and flashes of movement caught the guys' attention.

That, or Matteo was hoping his competition would lose interest, and Matteo would get out of a losing hand. "You ever thought of doing that TV thing, or the ritzy stuff?" He traded cards for food and inhaled a quarter of the slice in one bite.

"Bruce, a friend of ours, has hit a couple of shows, and a lot of the charity events," I translated. Bruce had a competitive streak at least as wide as the Grand Canyon, but mostly he seemed dedicated to helping fund every cancer research group in the Western United States.

He'd beaten—so far—a Stage Four diagnosis, but not solely through medical means, something the Company didn't and couldn't know, since it involved DNA from the vampire virus. Another secret Vee's team, and now mine, kept. No agreement with Oversight would save the eight of us if they discovered what my sister had done in order help Bruce.

The same knowledge was churning in my Lieutenant's brain, as Jace glanced at me, and away.

Safely oblivious to the shadow we all lived under, Marshall played with the remote, spinning it in circles on the overstuffed couch arm, finally answering Matteo. "I can't do any of that stuff. I never went to culinary school or worked in any of the important kitchens. I only do basics that chefs and their sous don't bother with, where there's not much to screw up."

He said it with the same matter of fact delivery as I'd say windigos smelled like rotting garbage. The bite of tart cheesecake might as well have turned to ashes, dry and choking. I forced myself to swallow before I accidentally insulted Marshall.

"Nah, man, this is fucking awesome." Matteo held up his empty plate as evidence. "Everything you make rocks."

"True, that." Jace tossed his cards in the pile, and caught my eye again, frowning either at Marshall's lack of confidence, or at whatever my face showed.

Pink climbed Marshall's neck but he only said, "Chefs like that have to be interesting. The only interesting thing I've ever done was get in your way while you shut my old boss down."

"We are the shit. And you helped with that raid and rescue." Matteo poked out a giant fist for Marshall to pound. "You oughta hang with us on the regular."

Marshall shoved to his feet fast enough both soldiers jerked. "I need to check the kitchen."

"Hey, he only meant—" I leaned to snag Marshall's pocket, and reassure him that Matteo wasn't suggesting cryptid hunting.

The main alarm, disguised as a landline, went off. So did each of our cells, with the universal team call-out tone, mine and Jace's from our pockets, Matteo's jittering across the card table where he'd set it, knocking piles of chips over in a clatter of plastic.

"Weapon up." I waved at them and they sprinted for the armory.

"Liv?" Marshall reached to grab me, a mirror of what I'd done with him seconds earlier, but then let his hand drop.

"HQ has information on a cryptid event either about to blow up, or already in progress. We have a call-out mission."

All the embarrassed blush drained from Marshall's face, freckles standing out.

"It's business as usual, no biggie." I squeezed Marshall's hand, hating the way it clenched and that I was cruddy at reassurances. "Watch a movie or tag in with Kimi's CoW crew—she's always online this time of night. Or hit the sack, and we'll see you sometime after dawn, probably."

I left him standing in the den, while I confirmed with HQ and reviewed the mission information. Then reminded them that there was a civilian in residence.

If none of us checked back in within forty-eight hours, a crew would collect Marshall and get him back to HQ, and finish our job, taking out whatever killed us.

iv

I CUT the motor as the reinforced garage door lowered, cutting off the mid-morning sun. Painfully bright UV interior lights blasted to life.

Jace groaned and jerked the bill of his cap lower. "I'm dismantling that thing one day."

"Can't without the alarm alerting HQ," Matteo mumbled from the middle row.

"Kimi did."

I got out, slamming the door on the old litany, repeated every time we dragged in from a long mission.

"Think Marshall's up?" Jace fell in beside me, as I moved through the connector between garage and house, Matteo behind us, decontamination scans sweeping over us.

"Keep it down just in case. We'll survive one morning of cereal and frozen breakfast burritos."

He stretched, long fingers nearly tickling the light

fixtures. "Sure, but you gotta admit it's hella nicer not to have to."

As if Jace spoke and it was made so, we cleared the scans and the house door opened, sweet vanilla and cinnamon trickling out with the A/C. Someone's stomach growled in response.

I stumbled and Jace hesitated, Matteo banging into us from the rear, a hazard of the stupidly narrow hall. Matteo threw giant arms out, catching me and Jace. "Damn.

Which…yeah.

We all stared at the muffins. Lots and lots of muffins. Multiple cooling racks took up the counters, all holding baking tins. The breadbasket thingie sitting on the eat-in bar overflowed with more muffins.

Marshall sat a last pan down in a rattle of metal on tile, then faced us, working the kitchen towel he employed as a mitt through his hands. "Uh—in case you guys came in hungry."

Anxiety and concern pinched the corners of his eyes. Eyes that raked over us, lingering at the stains covering my shirt.

"How long you been at it?" Jace asked. Matteo went straight for the tin Marshall abandoned, scooping up a muffin full of chocolate chips, and smelling of cinnamon. He juggled the hot pastry from hand to hand.

Marshall squinted at the wall clock. "Since you left."

He dropped the towel over the last pan, like he could hide the evidence. "I can freeze all the extras for later."

He skirted around Matteo. Putting himself a step closer to me. "Are you okay? Hungry?"

"Yes, and starving." More so than the hints of vanilla and kitchen air warm from all the baking, his stark concern welcomed me home. It had been a very long time since anyone had been here to greet me.

The worry eased, smoothing out some of the creases in Marshall's forehead. He darted covert glances at the stains covering all three of us.

I took a step back. "Showers first. That not living like feral dogs rule is still in effect."

Jace caught on and ducked out of sight and down the hall, since the gunk smeared on his boots couldn't be mistaken for anything other than brain matter. Matteo thanked Marshall around a mouthful of pastry, before also bolting for their rooms.

I shoved my hands in my pockets to kill the instinctive urge to hug Marshall, and settled for, "Thank you," as I retreated for my shower.

TEN MINUTES LATER, I walked back into the welcoming warmth of the kitchen, the guys trailing behind me again. They were either being polite, or more realistically, leaving it to me as to how much to share with Marshall if he asked.

The bulk of the muffins were out of sight, only the full basket remaining. Mugs and plates covered the counter in place of baked goods.

I sniffed at the steam coming off the closest cup, greeted by the fresh green of chamomile. Instead of coffee, real cocoa, plus vanilla, sat out.

I propped by Marshall while he folded eggs over easy for me. Bacon and ham was already divided out on each plate. "Wow."

He double-checked that I meant it in a good way. "Chamomile in case you needed sleep."

"The chocolate?"

"It goes better with muffins." Then he muttered, "I'll put on coffee."

"I prefer hot chocolate," I voted, preempting creating more work for Marshall, tipping my head at the guys. "They prefer to humor me, and expand their horizons."

Jace and Matteo gave *what the hell* shrugs and rolled with it.

Marshall slid eggs from pan to plate, then attacked the mugs.

"Is hot chocolate a religion with you?" I watched as he frothed vanilla, raw sugar, and the chocolate together.

"Pour." He nodded to the carafe to my left.

I did as instructed, feeding a slow stream of heated milk into the mix.

The guys eyed Marshall's final touch, whipped cream crowns dusted in cinnamon, but took an experimental sip. A gulp in Matteo's case, leaving him with a dairy mustache.

I slipped into my seat, shoving the other out for Marshall as Jace moaned. "Oh, dang. This is going down with B-movie Night as an official tradition. Man, you are frigging brilliant."

Tuning out their chatter, I sipped chocolate and picked over bacon and warm, buttered muffin. Relishing the mix of voices, the laughter and one-liners, and the press of familiar bodies squashed around the table. With my gaze unfocused, it was home, the way it had once been with Vee, Kimi, Bruce, and Josh.

An empty well in my soul filled, the way real wells did with the first nourishing rains after a hot, barren drought.

A knee bumped mine and I blinked, detail coming back. Marshall rolled his leftover muffin crumb around his plate. "Is this all right?"

Underneath the table, I hooked my ankle around his, the new socks cottony puffs against my bare ankle. I got that he meant more than the menu choices. "Perfect. It is perfect." I raised my voice and motioned at the table. "Jace wasn't joking. All of this is amazing. That you stayed up all night and came up with this welcome home is wonderful."

Marshall's eyes widened at my taking our conversation so public.

Then widened again when Matteo held his mug out, toast style. "Yeah, brother. You got our backs. That ain't no small thing."

My throat ached, for Matteo, and for Jace, their loss so much worse than mine. One they'd never completely get over. What Matteo really meant was a *thank you* for caring. For treating him, all of us, like we mattered, in a way that only family usually managed.

Jace and I clanked depleted mugs against Matteo's in agreement, although Marshall didn't lift his. He didn't seem able to. He didn't duck away, blow off Matteo's gratitude, or belittle his contribution to us though. "Okay."

Totally relaxed now, Matteo stretched, biceps bunching, the whole reason his tees and sweatshirts were usually sleeveless. He stood and started gathering our empty plates.

"What's next?" Marshall watched me.

"Lazy day, ideally. Major relaxation, complete with napping," Matteo answered.

"Then a run to work out the kinks," I said. "A short one."

That got rolled eyes, but no disagreement.

Marshall rose and blocked Matteo's path. "Go on then. Clean up and dishes are on me today."

The bigger man cocked his head, something I couldn't quite translate spooling through his brain. He finally nodded, respecting the conviction in Marshall's voice.

The guys headed toward that napping Matteo also hadn't been kidding about, since we'd been up twenty-four-hours plus, and another call-out could hit at any time. Still, I sat in the easy silence, finishing the last drops of my chocolate. Marshall flipped over to the playlist I'd put together and sent him a couple of days earlier, and set the kitchen to rights in his methodical way. He bent, sorting contents in the bottom pull out section of the fridge.

On my way past, I dropped a light kiss on his soft curls. It wasn't enough of a repayment or thanks for what he'd given us. It would have to do until I figured out something more concrete.

CHAPTER 32

 iv

THE HOUSE WHISPER-CREAKED AROUND ME, pretty much the only sounds. Matteo and Jace took their sleeping time seriously.

My muscles were that heavy laxness that came from hard work and a hot bath. My head refused to shut up and get on board, though. Despite my command, I wasn't virtuous enough to hit the track or cross-country. Even the new season of my favorite telenovela didn't hold any interest today. The library was a lost cause. I'd long ago read and re-read everything on the shelves.

I aimed down the hall for my e-reader and an online book-buying binge.

Warm amber light cut an illuminated swatch across the hall floor, splashing up onto the wall at an angle, Marshall's door three-quarters open. He'd looked done in the evening before, even without adding in the all-nighter.

Checking isn't violating privacy. I'd peek in fast, then close his door so he could sleep with no risk of my prowling, or one of the guys getting up to forage, accidentally disturbing him.

I peered past the edge of his door. Marshall sat on the bed, back propped against his headboard, a comic from our shopping spree open. He was also wearing the new sleep pants and tee, web-hero themed socks poking out from the cuffs. One of the pairs I'd picked out.

I leaned around the doorjamb. "How are you not asleep?"

"You aren't." He laid the book on his lap, gaze sweeping over me. Double-checking, the way he had when I first arrived home from the call-out.

"Let's say I'm looking into the possibility. Eventually."

"What happens before eventually?"

I slumped against the frame, admitting defeat. "I got nothing."

A complex emotional cocktail passed over Marshall's face quicker than I could process. Whatever they were, he cleared his throat and said, "This is what I always try. Could be it'll work for you." He looked at me, at the other side of the bed, then back at me. Totally stealing my go-to move *and* using it against me.

I had to ask anyway, in case he was merely being polite. "Are you up for company?"

He answered by scooting closer to the edge, leaving half the bed for me.

I claimed my spot and folded my legs, lifting his comic with one finger to check out the cover. Which told me nothing, other than artists didn't adhere to the laws of physics or nature when it came to female anatomy.

Catching my expression, Marshall said, "You can't judge, because you bought these."

"Not true. Your money, and your purchasing decision. Although, I was a willing participant. Crud. I'm an enabler."

Marshall huffed one of those rumbly laughs, as I rolled to my stomach and stretched out, examining the neat stack of titles on the locker at the foot of the bed.

The books were all in clear bags, with a piece of cardboard in the back to prevent squashing and a piece of tape keeping the bag closed. "What are these about?"

"Superheroes."

"Yes, but what else?" I twisted enough to prop on one elbow. "There has to be more to them than some person gets splashed by an off-book lab experiment or meets an alien, and then solves every world problem, ever."

"You really want to know?"

Some of the reserve that had vanished over the last week returned, Marshall's gaze flat and a little challenging. I got the feeling that what I thought was an innocent question either might not be in the civilian world, or there was subtext I was missing.

I tried again. "Yes, I really want to hear the attraction for you, and no, I'm not being a jerk. I hope?" I rolled further on my side to face him. "Confession?"

He nodded, fixed on me.

"I never considered anything civilian especially fascinating, or understood my sister. Vee has this borderline obsession with it. I mean, a civi job or life compared to being Company? Even after Bruce joining us, I didn't get it."

"Right. Dull and pointless," Marshall muttered, shoulders tightening.

"That's not what I'm saying. I think I do get it now because of you. I wouldn't want to be anyone else or have any other life, but I enjoy talking with you about yours and hearing your take on work or food or these." I gestured at his book. "It is different and interesting. So yes, I would love to hear why this is your hobby."

He studied me for a long minute, then relaxed. "The stories aren't about crazy powers. They're about people who have to get through the day, and yeah, there are always new problems because of what they are now. Plus, the same old problems everybody else has, the things nobody gets a pass on."

The bed creaked and Marshal moved so that he was beside me. He lifted a book that matched his socks. "Like, this guy can climb buildings, but his boss hates him, and he never has enough money to take his girlfriend on a real date, because he's always missing work to go stop some neighborhood robber, or twisted scientist spewing out biological weapons."

I rolled back, using Marshall's bent knew as a brace, propping my chin on my hand. "Superhero-ing should come with major government or private backing, full medical, and all the newest tactical gear."

"It never does though, not for regular people." He turned another book my way. "Like here. He saved people, but he also tore up the city, and a bunch of private businesses that people depended. Now, he's being sued, looking at new laws being passed, and maybe jail time."

"That is definitely where Legal comes in."

He ignored me, flipping a third book. "See this one? She doesn't have powers. No flying, or invisibility, or super healing. Only training and working hard and being smart. The villains trained her, so now that she's switched sides, she doesn't even have that. Her old family hates her. She has to prove herself all the time in order to stay with the heroes, and some of them still don't believe or trust her at their backs."

"I can sympathize with her." I wiggled higher, more of me

draped over Marshall's powerful thigh. He was warm and the pants carried the hint of our ocean fresh scented detergent, that in no way resembled a Galveston beach, but was familiar and comforting in its own way. The book he held up had the same heroine as the sleep set he'd picked for me, too generous chest and weirdly miniscule waist, but in real street clothing I could see being serviceable in a fight.

"Do you—you can read them, if you want. If you don't have anything else."

And then I did want to, to get another look into Marshall's world and all the things he enjoyed. "They're sealed up, and you aren't supposed to touch them much, right? I don't want to ruin yours. I'll buy my own next week."

"Some people do the collector thing, but I read mine all the time. They're—you know." He shrugged, and found a seemingly fascinating spot on the opposite wall to stare at.

Companionship. Comfort. All he had of either, reading between the lines. "Which one should I start with?"

Marshall gathered the whole stack and sorted.

I stayed half in his lap. Telling myself this wasn't any different than the way I acted with Jace or Matteo. Hanging out with a good friend. Even though we were more hands-on than civis, Marshall never seemed offended when I forgot he wasn't Company. This though? This wasn't accidental. A civilian in a cartoon-themed ensemble shouldn't cause my heart rate to speed up, or cause me to invent reasons to stay. Yet here I was.

He chose, and offered me a book. "This isn't the first issue. Some people get confused if they don't start at the beginning, but you won't."

"I have an in-house expert if I do." I settled on my stomach, working the bit of tape free so that it didn't flip and stick to the cover.

Marshall returned to the head of the bed. For some

reason, my spot suddenly seemed less inviting. A chill pebbled along my bare arms and legs.

"I'll get a blanket." Marshall's voice came right on the heels of my shiver, as if he'd still been paying more attention to me than to his story.

"Mind acting as my blanket?"

He hitched over so that brushed cotton touched my side and legs. I stretched, toes digging into the blanket and snuggled in, flannel just the right degree of toasty from his body heat pressed firmly against me. Giving me what I needed, like with muffins and coco and staying up to make sure I came home.

By a couple of pages into the story, I'd deciphered Russian saboteurs and the basis for my heroine. The writing made up for the unrealistic anatomy.

"Liv?"

"Hm?"

"I'm glad you came back." His deep bass vibrated through me where we pressed together, bringing on a different kind of shiver. "I'm glad the whole team came back." Blunt, scuffed fingers circled my ankle for a moment.

I traced around a panel of the heroine sitting at some enormous central command table, under the judgmental stares of the other heroes. "Do you want to hear another confession?"

"Yeah." He didn't attempt to hide his eagerness.

"What I said earlier? I'm not sure I can express how amazing it was to have you here waiting for me. Not the part where you lost more sleep, but the part involving coming home to someone. It seems like a lifetime since that happened."

"Was it somebody special?" His voice was still that reassuring rumble, but there was some sort of strain underneath. "I shouldn't have asked that. Ignore me."

"One of my best friends used to wait up every time we went out, playing solitaire in the kitchen until we rolled back in, if he wasn't on a job, or calling if he was. As far as someone special, I've never had one of those. Most of us don't. To be precise, I didn't think any of that was real—the romance aspect, the soul-mate thing."

The weight of his fingers rested on my ankle again. "Me either. Somehow, I didn't get the notification that cruddy restaurant hours and the line cook lifestyle weren't huge dating draws."

I snort-laughed, and reached back to pat his shin. Theoretically, I now believed romance existed. All I had to do was look at my sister and Bruce. That everyone needed that kind of partnership, I wasn't sold on. The Company and the team structure had worked for hundreds of years, without agents requiring romantic love.

We also had brutal hours and a secretive career. If I ever decided to try out romance, I had built-in choices, with any agents not part of our year-group, or even official Assets. Marshall, far less so, though.

Which brought up a new topic. "Speaking of jobs, what are your plans once you're free again? Are you going back to Mesa?" Mesa was part of our Division, and we patrolled through regularly.

Visiting with Marshall wasn't against Company rules, as long as I was scrupulous about insuring I never drew cryptid attention his way. In the past, when I'd bothered to think about that rule, it hadn't seemed difficult. We kept the Company off of cryptid radar by eliminating any we interacted with. Basically, we found predatory cryptids as they migrated in, and eliminated them before they could migrate out.

Things had gotten more complicated, though. Vee had been collecting data on aberrant cryptid behavior, for several years before she was infected. We'd humored her, but hadn't believed it was anything significant, simply another of her temporary obsessions.

My disbelief had resulted in my sister becoming a vampire. Somehow, at least one Master had discovered what we did, who we were. The Master had a pack of vampires, possibly somehow with windigos as pets or shock troops, waiting to ambush Vee.

Stavros, our adopted father, had also known of the Company, though. Whether others might—that was another reason he and Vee had been allowed to live. Who better to discover what other vampires knew, than a vampire who had lived as a solitary ghost, dedicating his existence to eliminating other vampires?

The air compressor clicking on shook me out of the ugly track my head had gotten stuck in. The silence also registered. I rolled to my back so I could see Marshall.

His head was bowed, but not like he was reading. He finally answered my question. "One kitchen line's the same as another. I'll find one wherever you drop me off."

"We aren't shoving you out on the first empty corner we find." I switched positions, hand on Marshall's shin. "We'll go wherever you prefer, okay? Sedona, Taos, here. That isn't limited to our territory, either. My sister's team has Southern California, and will help. Aside from Southwest HQ's private force, Texas has its own team, too, but their C.O., Terrance, won't mind us crossing over. El Paso, Houston, Galveston, they have great options." All were relatively close to our patrol routes.

"Doesn't matter." Marshall said it with emotionless finality.

A chill snaked through, having nothing to do with the A/C.

CHAPTER 33

Marshall

MARSHALL STARED AT THE PAGE. The words squirmed, moving in and out of impossible shapes. He clenched his teeth until his jaw ached. Start with one letter. Add another. Slow, and it would make sense.

Easier than thinking about sitting and piecing together this book in some dingy room, killing the few hours off from some anonymous grill.

Liv's soft voice rose and blew the partially constructed word apart. "Can I ask another intrusive question? Always keeping in mind that if it falls into the overly personal spectrum, and you tell me it's none of my business, I'll never be offended?"

When he glanced, she was not-watching him, eyes on her page but attention on him, in that way she had.

Reflexively, acid scalded his throat. He grabbed the mug off his nightstand and washed acid and shame away. Reflexes were wrong this time. Liv wouldn't laugh over how long it took him to finish a page, or snark about how he'd be better off redoing some basic task he'd flubbed today.

He believed in Liv more than reflexes, as her hip pressed the side of his knee and she sprawled beside him.

"You can ask me anything." Even if the question embarrassed him, he'd answer. Liv got to ask because she bothered to care.

She closed the comic, using her finger as a bookmark instead of carelessly tossing it face down. "You haven't made any calls to friends or family." She left the unspoken question for him to tackle, or ignore.

"There's not much to tell. I move a lot." There was never anybody to keep in touch with.

She rubbed his knee, an innocent gesture, but the ghost weight of her fingers lingered after she lifted them away. "No family? I am so sorry."

"My parents are fine, and my brother is still in Chicago, as far as I know."

"You're estranged." From the sadness and deepening frown, that wasn't the response she'd hoped for.

He didn't know where she was going with this, but he'd answer anyway. Maybe figure out a way to get rid of the sadness. Liv didn't deserve anything but happiness. "We talk and all."

"When was the last time? I mean, I realize it won't be every day, like my sisters and brother and I do. Even Bruce's family is only every few days. Except for texts."

Marshall did the math—after the casino kitchen, but before either of the Mesa jobs. "Late January, February, somewhere in there."

Liv sat up fast enough her book spread open, the paper fluttering like a startled bird. Her expression had gone from sad to kinda horrified. She folded her legs up and faced him, fingers tapping a rhythm against her thigh. "I'm not sure, but this is probably way, way over the line except—" She paused, like she was searching for words and lining them up. The way he did sometimes. "Intellectually, I understand Bruce's family is considered quite close, but even so—a family you only hear from once a year. No desire to contact them in the middle of a seriously traumatic life-altering event."

She inched her fingers until they touched the tips of his. "You don't care for volatile situations and aggressive people. Taken together, those facts paint a certain picture. Would my picture be accurate?"

He parsed through the thoughts, while Liv sat quietly, patient enough to let him work the ideas out. When he lined them up so they fit, he grabbed Liv's hand, folding her fingers in his. Needing to reassure her, take the worry off her, any way he could. "Hey, no. Sure, we got smacked now and then, but it was only for the usual kid stuff, when we didn't listen or kept on and got on their last nerve. They didn't abuse us."

Her fingers flexed, then twisted and closed around his, her eyes shiny for some reason, and oh, hell, he couldn't make Liv crying-sad. Not because of him.

He hurried, getting the words out to reassure her. "We were never close, and now we do our own thing. That's all."

"Because?"

Whatever power Liv had, he laid his book on the night-stand, and faced her. Trusted she wouldn't use him, his moments of weakness, the ugly parts of him, as leverage later. "I don't think they wanted to be parents. Not like those people who will go through all those procedures, or waiting and costs to adopt, because they want kids. I overheard my mom talking once. You had to have the right job, the right house, the right kids." He hadn't been the right kid.

"They mostly ignored us. They worked a lot, and there

was lots of after-work networking over drinks, and weekends boating or whatever with clients. All kinds of different summer camps for us. Yeah, they probably drank too much, but that only meant we sorta raised ourselves. Lots of people we knew did the same thing." He shrugged, trying to show Liv there was nothing for her to be upset about. "It was a nice neighborhood, so nobody worried about any of us coming home from school and doing whatever until bedtime. Once we got tired of pizza and microwave junk, I messed around in the kitchen until I figured out how to cook easy dishes. One of our neighbor's grandmother liked us and taught me her recipes."

That was all he knew to tell Liv, more than he'd ever said at one time, and probably more than she wanted to hear. He used taking another drink of cold tea as an excuse to pause a minute and check Liv's reaction, watching from the corner of his eye as he swallowed.

At some point, he'd twisted so he was cupping her fingers again. She'd curled her legs around so that she leaned more toward him. And was really listening to him, making it the most natural thing in the world to keep talking.

"Cash, my brother, he had it harder than me. He was the oldest, and smart. He was into grades and soccer and stuff, so our parents rode him harder." Cash was the kid they usually brought out at client's family events, where they needed to look good.

Whereas, his parents didn't know what to do with him. The too quiet, too big and clumsy kid with no motivation. They'd dumped their expectations and demands on Cash. Marshall, they mostly gave tight smiles and moved on to another topic.

"They didn't understand your dyslexia?"

"It was embarrassing." He set the empty mug away. It wasn't something they'd ever said, but they hadn't needed to.

He was an embarrassment. "It wouldn't have looked good. Once they found out I wasn't being lazy."

Liv's hand knotted into a fist, and her lips thinned out, pressed together hard enough they lost color. He switched to rubbing his thumb over the back of her hand, enjoying the glide of skin on skin, as much as being able to soothe Liv.

She pulled in a breath and held it for a second. "They didn't put you in the classes or programs you qualified for? Our year-mate did a couple every day, then came back into the other classes with us."

At a loss again, he shrugged. "They left me alone, so it was all good. They didn't like me going into restaurant work, but I was already used to kitchens, and it was one area I did okay in. It wasn't like they expected me to go to college. There didn't seem any point in culinary school, even if I could've got in one."

"That is—" Her lips did that thing again, pressed together, then going back to bright rose-pink as blood returned.

And he wasn't thinking about those lips pressed to his. Turning them that blush color, swollen from his kiss. At all. He sure as hell wasn't thinking about her passion turned to another use, them naked and tangled together on this bed, him watching Liv come, again and again. The *last* thing he was thinking of, for sure, was being the center of anything Liv related, having someone who cared that much, all the time.

He emptied the mug even though it was down to bitter dregs that'd escaped the infuser. After he had his brain back on track, one that wouldn't offend Liv and end with her bailing and not talking to him again—probably after she punched him—he changed to a safer topic. "Anyway, I don't have to worry about my parents or brother wondering why I went dark. They won't notice 'til closer to Christmas, maybe later, if they go skiing for the holidays."

Liv flexed her jaw like she was working out tension, then drilled him with one of those *'are you paying attention?'* looks. "Marshall, with all due respect to your parents, which is somewhere in the negative numbers, your family is composed of idiots. Idiots and oblivious jerks."

He finally got *his* jaw, sagging from Liv's furious defense, closed. "I wasn't the ideal son. I could've tried harder and I didn't. We just don't have anything to talk about now, nobody's fault."

"You are their *child*. That's all the incentive they should need. Plus, there is no way they will find anyone as patient and generous and complex and as—as Marshall-esque as you. They are fatally stupid for not recognizing how unique and wonderful their kid is."

His face had to be flaring brighter than his hair. "Liv, come on. I don't know what to do when you say stuff like that."

He changed focus before *he* said anything fatally stupid. He needed to bubble away all the things she'd said and her conviction, and have them for later. "What about your parents?"

"We're Company. Orphans, unwanted babies, especially girls in some cultures, that sort of thing. We don't have parents. We do have instructors, members, and agents who care and nurture us thought." She waved her hand, like none of that was weird. "However, civilians, normal people, shouldn't treat their children so callously. You deserve better."

She kept saying that about him, that he deserved good things. He cleared his throat again, way too many emotions and not-thought-out words trying to escape and maybe ruin Liv's opinion, fumbling for—anything. Like the barren foot of the bed he was currently staring at. "All the pillows are up here. Do you want one?"

Liv crawled the rest of the way up, punched an unsuspecting pillow, pretty much doing the opposite of fluffing, and tossed it beside his. The sturdy headboard *whumped* the wall as she flopped back.

Liv sat beside him, hip nudged against his. She unstuck her hair from where it had caught between her and the mauled pillow, flipping waves out of the way.

They waterfalled over his neck and shoulder, glossy brown strands clinging to his shirt. The ghosts of plain soap and coconut floated up, and he wished he could catch and save the scents the way he did feelings.

She snatched her comic and found the spot she'd stopped, and went back to reading. More or less.

"It is a crime how they don't appreciate you." She flipped a page in a rattle of paper.

"It's no big deal." He'd made his peace. He didn't fit into his parents' and brother's world. Trying only made them and him uncomfortable.

Liv leaned forward enough to reach behind and fluff the pillow. When she sat back, her shoulder wedged against his. "For whatever it's worth, Jace, Matteo, and I appreciate you."

The colors on the page wavered into abstract watercolors. He blinked hard until figures came back into focus. "That's— thank you."

* * *

ONCE HE PUT them in order for her, Liv read through all the issues, with occasional questions that showed she really was invested. The A/C kicked on, and off again, and the world shrank to their breathing and the warmth from where she returned to sit, arm against arm, after switching a completed book for a new one.

She didn't offer to leave after she finished the stack, and he was only on the second new issue.

"Want a muffin or hot cocoa?" He asked.

"There's no danger of even Matteo demanding lunch or dinner today. You are officially off the clock." She yawned and stretched, looked at the door, then yawned again. Not actually making any real move to go.

He wasn't ready to lose Liv's company. All of his desperate gambles had paid off so far, and he went for it again. Because he wouldn't have any of this for long, and he didn't have anything to lose by hoarding as much Liv-time as she'd allow. "You should lay down. In here. You already have a pillow beat up the way you must like."

"Hm?" She turned her head in a soft rustle of hair against the pillowcase.

"Sometimes getting up and moving is enough to wake your body up. Like nearly falling asleep on a couch, then you get up to go to bed, and end up laying there wide awake forever instead."

"Valid point."

Victory sang through him, skin tingling. "I'll turn off the light."

"Don't bother." Liv snagged the quilt folded at the foot of the bed and drew up over her as she returned. Like she was made of quicksilver, she oozed down under the blanket until she was laying flat, then flipped the edge over her shoulders. "You need more pillows. The regulation allotment is seriously lacking."

He snapped out of his victory daze. "For what? We have two."

"Two are the absolute minimum, *minimum*, for head to neck comfort, plus the added third huggie pillow, also a bare minimum sleeping requirement."

"What's a hugging pillow?"

She propped on an elbow, the blanket sliding off, and shook her head. "The gaps in your sleeping education sadden me. *Huggie* pillow," she enunciated. "The pillow or other object one hugs around for optimal sleep performance."

Toss up if he was adrenaline-drunk or just stupid, but no way was he leaving this revelation alone. "What kind of other objects count if you're low on pillows?"

"Huggie pillow status is highly coveted and difficult to come by." Holding up fingers, she ticked off possibilities. "A stuffed object that meets the necessary size parameters and doesn't have weird fuzz, bows, or scratchy synthetic hair. Then there are dogs, which I only discovered recently. Dogs are excellent, as long as they're large enough not to risk squashing if you roll in your sleep. For instance, our friend's niece has a retriever that is perfect." She flicked up a third finger. "Accommodating friends who don't hog blankets, snore, or get up to pee every hour."

His heartbeat ramped up to what had to be stroke level. "You've had a rooftop opportunity to observe how I sleep. Do I snore?"

"You made adorable squeaky-snuffley noises, and maybe a little drool. No snoring though."

"Seriously, Liv?" His face burned hot enough it felt like he was on fire. It matched the fire inside him for once. He mock elbowed, making sure he didn't budge her.

"I *said* they were adorable." She dropped back flat in a puff of blanket resettling, and grinned up at him.

Her teasing was so different than anything he'd ever experienced. Gentle, inviting him in on the joke, not one at his expense. "I'm not squashable, and as long as you behave, I won't roll and squash *you*. I do have weird hair, but it's all-natural, and no excessive bathroom breaks. Plus, I'm an okay blanket in a pinch. Those last two balance out the hair thing."

He watched for any sign of disgust or annoyance, signals that he hadn't interpreted her right.

Liv only crooked an arm behind her head, raising it a bit closer to his. "Confession three? I might have played with your hair while you drooled. Seemed like a fair trade."

He nudge-elbowed her again, testing out this new playful thing, and got another grin. "Yeah, well, I might've liked it." More like loved it, pretending to sleep so she wouldn't stop, processing her touch. The easy kind he hadn't had in forever.

He lifted his left arm enough to offer her a spot, yet not so much it'd be noticeable if she pretended not to see.

"I won't disturb your reading?"

He shook his head. "You don't bother me." At least, not in a bad way.

Liv simply rolled onto her side and traded her pillow for his chest. She tucked her arms in close, between their bodies like she was cold. The position flashed the purpling bruise that ran from her upper back and disappeared under her tank top, and who knew how much further.

He rested his arm around her shoulders, all the protection he could offer her. "If—I might be useful in case you have a nightmare, too."

No idea how much later, he finished the book. Having Liv here hadn't distracted him, which he had anticipated and lied to her about. He couldn't miss her head resting so close, or her weight propped on him. Instead of self-conscious and nervous, it focused and soothed him. Lucky for him, she hadn't mentioned a rule about huggie pillows and hard-ons, because his brain might find Liv soothing, but his body had the opposite reaction.

Which was his problem, not Liv's. He inched to drop the book on the bedside table, and kill the lamp. Liv sleep-grumbled—her eyes had closed before he'd finished his first page —and she slung her leg over his, locking them together.

She'd already cuddled closer, pages earlier, her arm now over his chest instead of between them, a kind of boneless relaxed he'd never imagined possible, especially from her. She was always alert, always poised to move, to go, to lead. When she said hugging pillow though—not an exaggeration.

He worked the blanket around and covered her, hiding the ugly bruise on her back. Life was precarious, and more bad than good. For now though, he was here and Liv was snuggled close, at ease and trusting him.

He rested his cheek on top of her hair and gave himself over to memorizing every touch, every breath, so he'd have this perfect memory, one pure moment with Liv, after she and the team went on with their lives and he was alone again.

iv

I HIT the ten-mile mark and slowed, jogging the quarter mile to cool down. The guys had waved me off five miles ago, already moaning about allegedly short runs.

I thought better when I was in motion—running, hitting the obstacle course, even driving. Today was running. The guys' slacker attitude might have come from lack of sleep. I'd slept fine. Better than in ages.

Except for the part where I woke up before Marshall, warm and safe, his arms secure around me and his even breathing lifting the new hairs along my temple to tickle me. He'd rolled enough in his sleep that we'd nested with our legs interlocked, like we'd done this before.

I could have wiggled free and slipped out. Instead, I'd stayed and enjoyed myself. Marshall was wide and solid, a perfect replacement pillow. All of his usual tension was absent, and he curled around me like a living shield, utterly relaxed for the first time.

The dark and the quiet gave my brain leeway to do things like picture Marshall's horrible apartment, his illegally skimming manager, and Marshall's resignation about finding another version of that life, not even caring where. My stomach had turned at the image, worse than at the stink of a freshly killed windigo.

Which then led me to his lack of a support net. At that point, the wash of cold anger at his careless excuse for parents woke me up more thoroughly than an icy shower.

As I'd mentioned when Marshall asked, Company members were basically orphans, babies whose parents couldn't care for them, those separated from families due to war or uprisings, or flat out unwanted. The Company structured it so that the children in each year-group were raised as siblings, our closest ties forming with the other future agents who would be our team. That self-contained bond, unmarred by distracting outside ties, was what allowed us to perform like one mind with multiple parts. That level of understanding was the key to giving humans as much advantage as possible so we could confront predatory creatures with dangerous powers and traits, with the highest probable chance of success in saving civilians, and our surviving each encounter.

So no, we hadn't had parents in the civilian sense. However, I had learned from Bruce's big, devoted family how parents loved and protected their children, even after they were adults, and how siblings had each other's backs, almost like us.

Fine, perhaps life didn't owe anyone anything—wonderful family and friends, health, great career, whatever. By that reasoning, it shouldn't get to pick and choose who it drop-kicked in the teeth, either.

Marshall was a capable adult. Presumably, he lived his life fine by his standards. Which didn't leave me any less furious about hole in the wall apartments, and only a guitar and a few books as company. Worse, I hated the thought of him turning back to the wary, closed-off person we'd first met.

The Marshall of the last few weeks was the real one— generous, full of life, funny, and protective of street kids, us, anyone he saw as needing help.

I fished my phone out, tapped the first icon, and laid the case on the bench by the birdbath and plantings, while I stretched tight hamstrings.

One ring before voice mail kicked in, Vee answered. "What's up?"

"Loosening bruises after another ghoul infestation."

"A proto-pack?"

"Four adult males, all acting as freaky as that first anomaly Ridge and the cadets encountered, what, two years ago?"

Her voice sharpened. "HQ?"

"Cleaners. The report should be up by dinner," I answered in our shorthand. The cryptids had been unusual enough for me to tag them to go to the Lab division. It was too little, too late as far as believing and protecting my sister. Now, I went into every mission or call-out on high alert, not automatically assuming any cryptid would behave the way it was biologically programed to.

"I'll check once we get in. Do you—" She cut out for a second. A snarl and thud reverberated. "Okay, back now."

I switched, bringing my heel back and up to loosen the other hamstring. Although I was sure she *was*, I said, "Tell me you aren't."

Another thud sounded, loud enough it felt like it should've rattled my speaker. Followed by an exasperated string of mixed archaic Spanish and Nahuatl from Stavros.

JANET WALDEN-WEST

Officially, he was Huisy 'Stavros' Villca, a Bolivian Special Forces soldier, taken by vampires for their version of gladiatorial games, and rescued from the pits when we rescued Vee.

In reality, he was the grandson of a conquistador, conquered Aztecas, and those conquered by the Aztecs. He'd been infected by the vampires who raided his hacienda over four-hundred-years ago. In taking revenge on his attackers, he'd also accidentally discovered that if a freshly infected person's first meal was another vampire, the double dose of virus DNA mutated in a manner that allowed the new vampire to tolerate sunlight, to a degree. He'd made sure Vee had the same advantage when he infected her.

Another thump and exasperated reprimanded sounded from Vee's end.

"Stavros says hello."

"That so wasn't what he said. More 'You answered that device? Do not answer phones during a fight, Victoria. No matter we only battle vermin, such arrogance is a sin.'," I mimicked in a decent reproduction of his lilt. Perfectly aware he could hear both sides of our conversation, I added the melodramatic sigh he swore he never gave, but did, usually because of one of us. And that we usually pointed out, just to watch him throw his hands up. He really did the dramatic hands thing, too.

"Close enough." Vee's end of the conversation cleared up.

"Windigos eliminated?" I took an educated guess. She had always been impetuous, and as a baby vampire still learning to control her heightened emotions, that impulsiveness was magnified. Even as a vampire, though, with a powerful old Master at her back, she'd never fight distracted against ghouls or other vampires. Thus, process of elimination equaled windigos.

"Completely."

No wonder Stavros was extra exasperated. He hadn't stooped to hunting lower cryptids until he joined us, and he remained sure that were beneath him and his whole Scourge of the Lord, demon killing holy mission. Plus, the vaguely canine windigos were *rank*. "Ooh, did they ook on Josh? Worse, did he hurl after?"

"This is a hurl-free zone. B sends grouchy-love."

"Back at you guys. He's along?" For a year after Vee disappeared, presumed dead, Bruce had joined us on missions. Doing his best to kill every vampire, a futile effort to even the score for them taking Vee from us. A far less futile path to suicide via hunting as well, one I'd been slowly losing ground on preventing until Vee returned.

"Nah, but it's implied. Josh and Kimi were packing the base up, and B's off terrorizing sous and line cooks."

Meaning the team was done in that area of their assigned Division, and either moving to another on their patrol route, or back to their main compound after a circuit. Her statement pulled together the threads of the solution I'd subconsciously been working.

"Ask him about lobbing a job recommendation." I released my heel and rose onto my toes, then down, finishing the stretches. Bruce knew everyone in the culinary world, or near enough. Even people who hated his abrasive, in-your-face guts respected him.

This was perfect. He'd help find Marshall a decent position at a real restaurant, one where the owner wasn't in collusion with a vicious, vampire-led crime syndicate. One where Marshall might stay, and work up the ladder.

"Come again?" Vee said, knocking me out of my rosy planning-Marshall's-career moment.

"It's for a civi who will need a job soon-ish." The soon-ish part basically sucked. Marshall had become such a positive, key part of my day. Of all our daily lives.

"Dang, hermana. Another civi? I thought Kimi was gaming trash-talking and teasing the guys when she mentioned having one playing on your team."

I banged my heel against the heavy iron bench leg. If I'd called five minutes earlier, Vee might have been too distracted to make the connection. "No, this is the one we picked up on the Mesa mission."

"The one from over a month ago? No, wait, *two* months ago? That you dropped at HQ?"

"The barracks' atmosphere wasn't working, so I brought him with us since we'd finished our yearly Division sweep, and won't be heading away from the compound to check secondary bases for months."

"Holy fr—"

"¡Niña¡ How many times must I remind you not to blaspheme." Stavros' most common reprimand came through clearly.

I snickered as my sister muttered, "That wasn't even blasphemous-blasphemous. *Holy* is used in non-church connotations." Which was her most common complaint.

"Anyway," I attempted to get ahead of any more questioning, "He is a truly good person, and he can't go back to Mesa, so butter Bruce up, please and thank you. Oh, and make sure to add we want some place really respectable, and safe. Like, no food trucks in the Valley. A position that will really pay the bills so Marshall has options." Bruce understood finances and would know what was or wasn't a livable wage.

Silence ticked by as sweat finished soaking my sports bra, and I considered hitting the gym shower, where we could still talk privately while cooling off.

Vee finally broke her uncharacteristic silence. "A stable position in a fine dining restaurant, and an apartment similar to the condo."

"Yes, exactly." Vee and I were still able to lob ideas off

each other, getting what the other meant. The condo was what the Company had set up here once Bruce joined, since he was a very public figure, and required a place other than a secret compound to bring visiting family and friends. "I assume a kitchen job wouldn't pay well enough for a condo, so let's say the moderately priced version."

"I'm going to repeat, what the heck, Liv?"

"Marshall didn't deserve to have his life upended, and become collateral damage in our war. That's all."

"Oh, that is *so* not all. Add the rest of your list—you'd prefer this new job and apartment be in your usual patrol loop, the closer the better. Where you can see this guy on a regular basis."

"Monitoring ex-targets is well within the rules."

"True. Except civis hold no interest for you. If I wasn't around to do it, you literally drew straws with Kimi and Jace to see who got stuck with the making-nice to civis part of a call-out. Okay, B's parents and brother and sister and the girls, sure, but only because they are family now."

Her voice lowered with a muffled *shooing* sound that meant her lips were brushing the phone. "Stavros is burning carcasses and can't hear us over the fire. What is going on? Do you need—I don't know. Anything?"

"I'm not sure?" After double-checking I was alone except for the crows and a lizard sunning itself on the stair handrails, I pitched my voice to match hers. I spilled everything, to the person who'd had a crib beside mine, then a bunk bed over me, who'd shared a first mission, and compared notes on first kisses, first sexual experiences, first time grieving the fallen. Maybe she could help me understand this, the way we had every other milestone.

"Marshall is—he isn't like us or Stavros or even Bruce's family. He hates what we do, not the way Bruce does because of his whole Company using us paranoia, but because violence toward even cryptids feels wrong to Marshall. Yet he stayed up all night when we were gone on the ghoul call-out. He was waiting for us with chamomile tea and cocoa. *Jace* drank hot cocoa with whipped cream."

Not able to stand still, the injustice prickling under my skin, I paced from the bench to the gym and back, as I talked. "Marshall does things like that *all* the time, despite him basically living through this horribly neglectful childhood, and the apartment I cleared of his belongings wasn't fit for even a ghoul to nest in, and he acts as if he doesn't deserve anything good, for some reason, or as if he doesn't matter. And it is *killing* me that he'll go back to that life. We see ugly things almost weekly, but this is absolutely soul-killing depressing."

I finally ran out of incoherent facts, and dropped to the bench, impact jarring from my butt bone up to my skull. "Commander to Commander, what do I do in this situation?" I knew the rulebook answer, though.

My sister voiced the official stance. "Let HQ do their job. Aiding civi vics is their domain, and they would help Marshall relocate."

I ground the heel of my hand between my eyes, trying to squash the awful feeling, building up behind them. "I know."

"But, forget that. Sister to sister, here. It will take most of the morning to clear out the stragglers from this stupid horde, and clean up, but then I'll pin B down and go over every four-star place that owes him a favor, or that's totally scared of him and will agree just to keep him away. You and I can put together a—hm, a care package? Ooh, yes, a care package on top of whatever B magics up."

According to Bruce, we weren't paid what we were worth. I was fifty-fifty on believing him, versus it being pure grudge on his part. I did know that we didn't have normal people bills, or much free time. Which left plenty of funds for whatever hobbies we had. Vee had just offered hers to go with mine, and us cobble together some legitimate-seeming story about Company relocation benefits for Marshall.

"You work on details, and I'll work on B," she finished.

"Love you. Pass it on."

"Love you. I'll call later."

I tucked away my phone and aimed for the obstacle course, this time as a way not to think about unsettling things like my sister's opinion on why keeping in contact with Marshall was so important to me. Or face that no matter what I'd said, any place but here didn't feel close enough.

Before I overthought it, I pulled my phone back out and texted Vee. *See if B has a line on any legit job options in Phoenix, first, before expanding out to other areas.*

CHAPTER 35

iv

As I WALKED into the kitchen, Marshall stopped mid-whatever it was chef's did with spatulas, nd checked me out, frowning. "Cherry pie?"

I quit humming to answer him. "For dessert? Yes, please."

He pointed the spatula at me and my opened laptop, then shoved his free hand underneath the utensil as sauce splatted down, catching the blob in time.

I made a *no clue* face.

Neatly, like he did everything, Marshall laid the implement in the sink and wiped his hands. Clean enough, he reached over the laptop screen and tapped the volume. Hair metal blasted out, and he turned it back down. "You were humming that."

"Don't judge my musical tastes, because they're also your musical tastes." I abandoned the laptop on the bar and dug a water out of the fridge. "So does that mean we don't get pie?"

He turned his attention to the range. His back and shoulders held some sort of tension. Not fear, but a new, different kind. Conversely, the tension had always been there, and I only noticed now after having seen him the day before, relaxed and with all his defenses down.

One big shoulder lifted and dropped. "I could. I wasn't sure how much to make." He grabbed a bowl of something diced and glanced at me before turning away. "You didn't have breakfast or lunch."

"I wasn't hungry at breakfast. Who could have been?"

I caught myself, and rolled my eyes. "Matteo." We said it at the same time.

"Fair point. On my way out this morning before the guys joined me, I might have stolen the last chocolate chip muffin from the basket, and stashed it for lunch, since I had a noonish call scheduled." One with most of the Region Two Division Commanders, discussing the latest freaky Lab findings from the ghouls I'd tagged. More half-starved specimens, when normally a ghoul hungry enough would willingly eat anything around it, including other ghouls. Plus, these also had the inexplicable mutated brain morphology we'd first encountered with a pair of imported anangoa, the mission where Vee met Bruce.

So far, the working theory was a virus only communicable to cryptid physiology, similar to how all cryptid physiology respond to chem weapons.

"Okay." Marshall's odd tension vanished like I'd imagined it.

I wandered up and raised on my toes enough to peer over his shoulder. "What is for dinner?"

"Porchetta. It's sort of an experiment I started yesterday."

"You have an exemplary track record with experiments. Hey, you look nice." I dropped flat-footed, and leaned far enough out to take in the whole effect. He had on the light blue shirt I'd talked him into at the store. I put my flare of odd possessiveness down to satisfaction over being right, nothing else. "Told you that's your color."

Blue suited him, alive and hopeful in a way black wasn't. I admired the whole package, reminded again of how broad his chest was. I gave into temptation and ran my hand from his shoulder down his back, downy-soft fabric and solid muscles sliding under my fingertips.

They hit his waistband, fabric bunching. "These jeans are borderline too large."

His face was bright when he turned his head to me, though the effect might have been from the oven. The look he gave—it reminded me of my possessiveness moments earlier.

My fingers forgot what to do, brain also threatening to fritz. I blurted out the first thing that came to mind. "Can we go shopping again? It'll be winter and there will be all these new superhero shirts, and I feel I'm far more qualified now to make thoughtful choices. Pleeease?" I held my eyes wide, like a cartoon character, hoping it diverted attention from my reaction.

"Could I stop you?" A tiny grin grew into a real smile, one that traveled and settled in his eyes.

"Nope, but it is more fun when you're along."

His smile dropped. "I probably won't be here by then."

If I had my way, if I hadn't misjudged, he'd at least be close by.

I tested out the waters, evaluating whether Marshall was only humoring us until he could get away to a non-cryptid life, or whether there was a true bond with us. Okay, between the two of us. "I really hate to bring it up, but HQ hasn't hit any new leads. If Welch and his connections are still actively trafficking, they are part of a larger, more sophisticated operation capable of hiding their actions.

Homeland, FBI, Coast Guard, and the private sector anti-trafficking coalitions are all coming up empty."

Marshall stilled, but the muscles under my hand stayed loose as he nodded and spoke. "We—you guys—aren't close to finding the people? Monster cryptids and criminals," he corrected without my prompting. "The head vampire."

"I'm sorry, but no. If they are hiding and taking a break, our only option is waiting them out. If they are as widespread as we're beginning to believe, they're buried under layers of shell companies, legitimate business, and offshore accounts, which makes tracking them more complicated."

"And finding them will take time."

"I'm afraid so." Which was one of the reasons I hated botching our shot at apprehending Welch. "Even with Company resources, it all means gathering and sorting huge amounts of research from multiple groups and areas of expertise, then turning all that data into anything useable. Spring and Summer are typically the busy time to move human cargo. It's already late Fall. If we don't get any hits in the next month, maybe less—"

"I'll be here for months."

"Right." I couldn't decipher Marshall's tone, beyond him not being overtly upset. Not upset was promising.

He reached for another ramekin of spices, but I was in the way. Instead of nudging me aside, he said, "Hand me the thyme?"

The row of ingredients was closer to the back of the counter. I could've stepped out and around to reach them. I wouldn't have bothered with that formality with the guys though. After sharing a pillow, surely Marshall and I were on the same informal comfort level.

I draped over him, a hand on his shoulder for balance, and reached for the herb.

"The other green one." He absorbed my weight without a

twitch, and turned his head to track my progress, amusement obvious.

I changed ramekins. "This?" When I checked with him, it put us face to face, only a breath between us.

He nodded and a curl escaped his bandana, brushing my forehead.

I looped the stray around my finger and tucked it back in, then offered him the herbs.

He accepted the bowl and sprinkled it over a rolled loin, moving slower, in smaller increments than usual. Like he was trying not jostle me off. My chest pressed against his back, keeping us connected.

He hadn't minded before, so I dropped my now-empty hand back down to his waist, right at his waistband. Playing with belt loop and the edge of the tee.

"Do you like turkey or ham for Thanksgiving?" He asked, a husky buzz to the question.

"Pizza?"

"Why?"

"It's what's usually open."

He sighed. "Which for Christmas? Or Hanukah? I forgot to ask what you celebrate."

"Both. Um, frozen pizza because nothing is open."

"Not this year. You deserve better, too. I'll take care of yu —of dinner." He shifted enough that I caught his expression, a mixture of determination and something new. Something that resembled contentment. He didn't hate being stuck here, with us, for the next few months.

"Yes, sir." The same thrill as when I won a sparring match buzzed through me. "This is your kitchen, and what you say goes. Let me also say how awesome that is."

Marshall shifted even closer, and like he thought I might fall off, reached back, pressing me tighter against him. His shirt bunched, and my fingers slipped onto hot, bare skin.

He inhaled, more growl than breathing. When I hesitated, he said, "You're okay. Good—you're good where you are."

I took the chance and rubbed a slow circuit up his spine, then back down. "This?"

The growl deepened. "Yeah. That's—"

The gate security system came on with a snap and flash of information scrolling across the screen by the bar, and we both jumped, me for the screen, him to put distance between us.

"Matteo and Jace didn't go anywhere today," Marshall said. "All of you are in the compound."

We were here, and HQ or the C.O. would have alerted us if any of our neighboring teams needed our help, or emergency access to our infirmary or armory. I'd also already spoken to most of them earlier during our video conference.

We'd had one cryptid ambush here, vampires burrowed under the sandy dirt yards from the fence, rushing the compound as gates opened. I tapped my code in without looking and the counter's strip of decorative tin retracted, the hidden shelf sliding out, revealing two Glocks, and chem-treated blades and extra ammo.

The cheerful *tink-tink* pattern of a gate code typed in from a Company vehicle, and accepted, sounded. A beat later the DNA scan of whatever was inside the SUV with its extra dark windows completed, and automatically collated against our internal database. *Approved Occupants* flashed in the corner of the screen.

I smacked the keypad and the weapon's shelf closed, my heart nearly stopping, then racing. Almost loud enough in my ears that I didn't hear myself speak as I read the names listed. "You have got to be kidding me."

"Those aren't traffickers? Cryptids?" Marshall said, all ease vanished, undoubtedly picking up on my stress.

"No." A total lie, since we lumped vampires in with true

cryptids. I made my shoulders drop, faking relaxed. "It's my sister and our adopted dad."

Unless it was a world-ending, all agents on deck crisis, her arriving when there was anyone other than her and my teams in residence was potential grounds for Oversight to activate the poppers, the tiny bombs planted at the base of her and Stavros' brains, and over Josh's heart. With her arriving when there was a *civilian* here? Oversight's warning kept time with my pulse—that should anyone outside the eight of us ever discover what Vee and Stavros were, if any of us give Oversight reason to think Vee was infecting a human in order to create a team of Company trained vampires, there wouldn't be anything left of the compound and any living thing within a mile's radius.

There was a chance she and Stavros had a second call-out mission after I spoke with her, something tougher to kill than windigos, and they'd burned through their supply of harvested blood from the vampires they hunted, the diet that allowed Vee and Stavros to tolerate daylight. They'd need a secure indoor spot to hide until dark, or they'd face the same fiery end as any other vampire.

I hated the idea of her hurt, images of a trashed SUV and desert soaked in her blood too easy to access, the way images of team members falling had to be for Jace and Matteo. But if they weren't here because someone was horribly injured, human or vampire, and this was the closest safe place...

I had to consider whether she'd had the same thought I did, except in reverse. That *my* having Marshall here was putting her and her team in danger. That she didn't have Kimi or Josh in the SUV with her meant something, but I didn't know what.

I loved my sister, but she was master of spur of the moment, out of the box thinking. Sometimes her impulsive decisions worked beautifully.

Sometimes, they crashed and burned, with devastating results.

Whatever this unscheduled visit was about, it held the potential for me to lose family, lose what I'd built for the guys, for myself—and lose Marshall.

I tried a smile for Marshall's benefit as I continued piling up lies. "Hang out in here until I see what's up, okay? It might just be a quick in and out to replace some gear, as they head to a call-out. Sometimes cryptids cross Division territorial lines, and the team that initiated the mission usually sticks with it."

The fact that I bolted for the garage didn't help my believ-ability, but I needed between Marshall and the SUV containing Stavros and Vee.

The guys must've shared my concern. The small outer side door to the garage, the quickest way inside since garages didn't have bio scanners, slammed open, Mattaoe's shadow oversized and menacing as he came from the armory and inventorying. Jace raced in from my office, where he'd been finishing a report, nearly running over me.

"You get a call? Who's hurt?" He demanded.

"No, and it's only Vee and Stavros. They were out on a mission while Josh and Kimi packed."

A sliver of the harsh terror that hid under both his and Matteo's professionalism left. That trauma from watching their siblings die wouldn't ever totally go away, but Jace put on the brakes, and Matteo looked down and scowled at the tablet he'd forgotten he held. The screen was now spider-webbed with cracks and he tossed it onto the metal tool cabinet in the corner as the garage doors rose.

"Think they're beat up?" Matteo asked.

"No clue."

Although we all had mandatory EMT training, one agent on each team was also a medic, taking additional classes.

Matteo was ours. Even knowing if Vee and Stavros were injured, all they would need was a quiet spot and a run to the butcher shop for beef or pork blood, until they could go after the next vampires they found, he still got that expression, where he was mentally preparing for triage.

"Stavros has got to quit being such a big vampire baby and embrace texting," Jace grumbled, going on the logic if Stavros was the worst injured, Vee would've already messaged us, whereas if Vee was injured, our tech-resistant father couldn't inform us.

Although I agreed, sister loyalty ran deep. "Kimi is trying to teach him, I promise."

The SUV glided in, and Matteo was by the passenger door as quickly as I took the driver's.

Mine opened to the view of close-cropped black hair, familiar dark eyes in a square-jawed face, skin copperier than mine or my sisters "Hola, hija. All is well," Stavros said.

Had that been the truth, he wouldn't have greeted me as *daughter*, but as Olivia, always honoring my position as team leader, the same as he did with Vee, while he acted in my old role as her lieutenant. *Hija,* though, that slipup meant he was emotional, for a vampire reason or a father one.

I bent into the truck, looking past him to Vee. If you didn't know her well, she seemed equally calm. Except, we'd literally been together from infancy. Plus, she was a crap liar. Everything from the slant of her shoulders to how her hands rested in her lap, as close to her thigh rigs and knives as possible without touching them, told me she was in danger mode.

The fact that she and Stavros had the rigs on, blades that were really machetes, too large to comfortably sit in for any length of time, told me that I'd been right to worry. So did the way the hairs on my arms rose. Vampirism was a virus, not anything mystical or otherworldly, but a predator was a predator. My body recognized the primal danger, picking up on whatever aggressive pheromones the two were shedding all over my garage,

"How did we go from a completely reasonable conversation this morning regarding Bruce and job hunting favors, to Defcon One?" I spoke over Stavros' head, because this decision was all Vee. "Why didn't you call?"

"Hello? My sister is in crisis. And we were already close. The team will join us as soon as B finishes out that fusion pop-up tomorrow evening. This is technically on the way back to our compound."

"Oh, sure. If 'on the way' means a couple hundred-mile detour. Your mental mathematics evade me. Conversation plus job ideas does not equal crisis."

"There is a human here. One who is not of our Company."

Jace twitched, either at Stavros answering or at the unsettling coldness under his usually level, collected voice. Stavros didn't rush and didn't do anything without thinking through all ramifications. He was deliberation personified. This was as good as walking in, guns drawn, for Stavros.

"Yes, and he has been fully debriefed by HQ, and it is also fully within HQ rules and my role as Commander to decide where he stays, until it's safe for him to reintegrate into civilian life. All paperwork is in order, signed off on by HQ. We all know HQ's name is on the approved form, but that it's Oversight saying yes or no. You know this."

"He's down as a temporary Asset," Vee said. "You didn't say anything about *that*."

And Vee hadn't said anything about not trusting *me*. The pop of hurt caught me off guard. We had separate teams and separate Commands, but we were still family.

"Sure. Marshall lost most of his belongings plus his job thanks to our raid, and without us even asking he has been working since he got here. Him working as hard as we do and not getting paid wasn't cool," Matteo said, feeling the situation out. "He legit earns his pay, no lie."

Stavros twitched, like he'd been stung. Since he never showed pain even with another vampire's claws embedded in his chest, his problem wasn't physical. The way he tilted his head a fraction in Vee's direction, like he was listening, was as good as a neon arrow pointing to the culprit. Vampires weren't psychic and couldn't speak mind to mind, but thanks to the virus, they could feel human's emotions to a degree, and even more clearly, those of other vampires they shared a biological bond with. When Stavros first arrived, he'd had to spend hours in the desert, our everyday emotions swamping him after centuries alone.

I switched attention to my sister and caught the challenge and protectiveness she'd just drowned Stavros in. I glanced at Jace, right by my shoulder and tensed about this discussion in our shorthand, unsure if this was a sister sort of problem or a Commander sort of problem. Then I stared—hard—at her, brow inching up. Color flooded her cheeks and guilt replaced the alien territoriality and suspicion. She dang well knew she was being over the top, and that this was extra stress for Jace, already worried about his twin and the tiny bomb inside Josh.

Guilt hit me, too. Vee hadn't even been a vampire for two years yet. That she'd overcome the virus' changes was amazing, that she'd accomplished that feat so quickly, even more so. That we got our sister back was one of those miracles Bruce and Stavros believed in. She was accustomed to leading, which in our world meant hard decisions and doing what was best for her team. Mix that with what had to be the low-level worry and grief about what she saw as putting Stavros' and Josh's lives in danger because of her getting infected and coming back...

"Major drama llama. Just saying." I sighed and motioned for them to get out of the truck already. As Stavros complied, I stepped in and hugged him, waiting out his hesitation. I'd figured out that the reaction when any of us were affectionate wasn't offense, but his continuing shock and happiness at being loved, and having family to love again. He processed his wonder, and returned my embrace.

"Bet Marshall will make us hot cocoa again," Jace said from behind us. "You gotta give it a try."

Vee worked her way around, hugging the guys in turn. She finished with me, a semi-apology hug on both our parts because I'd missed her the same as I knew she missed me.

"I'll never say it to Bruce's face, but Marshall makes the best hot cocoa. Real whipped cream and cinnamon and everything." I headed for the breezeway, still making sure I stayed between Vee and Stavros and the civilian inside, because I was also responsible for the lives of my team, and Marshall fell under that heading. At least for now.

Part of me that wasn't a C.O, or even agent, also really wanted my sister to like Marshall, and that thought was almost as unsettling as interpreting Oversight's leniency, biological kill switches, overly emotional new vampires, and suddenly testy ancient ones.

arshall

THIS VISIT WASN'T that drop-off and leave thing Liv mentioned.

As a whole herd stampeded through the decontamination breezeway from the garage, Marshall gripped the range handle until knuckles popped. Telling himself these were like diners. Generic diners. People he cooked for and that moved on. No big deal.

Except these weren't people he'd never have to see again. These were Liv's people. People important to her.

As soon as she'd read who they were on the video screen, she'd looked at him, her face paling, and everything about her changed. All the playfulness, the way they'd fit together, gone. She'd asked him to stay inside, away from her family, because she was worried he'd fuck this up.

His chest tightened, because Liv was right.

These agents would take one look at him, and figure out

fast he was a bigger freak than anything they hunted. Then they'd point out all his flaws to Liv, how useless he really was, that he wasn't good enough for her or Jace and Matteo. She'd see and be disgusted over her mistake. He'd be an embarrassment again.

Forget there being any more rambling, easy conversations or shared couches, or watching her try his food, and nights together. Definitely no more of that weird admiration from her that he didn't understand, and didn't want to lose. These people signaled the end of Liv's friendship.

Liv was Liv and wouldn't be rude, and neither would Jace and Matteo, but Marshall would be back to a stranger they couldn't wait to see leave.

You knew it wouldn't last. For a few minutes though, he'd hoped it would. No end in sight with the trafficker hunt. Liv here in the thyme and rosemary scented kitchen, watching him do the one thing he usually got right. Her pressed against him, that connection that grew every time she touched him, every time he held her.

A burst of laughter from one of them echoed into the kitchen and Marshall flinched. Oil from the pan he was tending popped at his jerk, spattering range top and him. He swiped the droplets off on a towel, not bothering with cold water, not with the sink all the way on the other end of the kitchen, right by the entry and *them*. People Liv had a real history with, who didn't melt down in public, forcing her to always make allowances and take extra time.

"So we've got what, a whole thirty-six Bruce-free hours? Sweet decision, carnala," Matteo said.

Jace got in on the joking, like Marshall had any doubt how welcome the others were. "Oh, dang. We have time to swear Terrence desperately needed backup in Texas, and hit Galveston. Bonfire and cervezas on the beach."

"Okay, that is always a legit idea. But, not quite enough to justify listening to B's tantrum once we get back. Maaaaybe if it was forty-eight hours."

Marshall's body turned before his brain had any say in the matter, pure instinct, that voice so eerily familiar, almost Liv's. Liv had said *her sister*, earlier. Whatever that meant to them, she looked enough like Liv to be a birth sibling, same golden-brown skin, same intelligence shining from dark eyes.

Except this version was too much, even though she was kind of tiny. Small, at least compared to Liv. Instead of spun-caramel, her eyes were espresso-dark and fierce, like the hawks and eagles Marshall had seen at zoos as a kid, where Liv's were more watchful, like she was watching over a flock or family. Her sister's hair wasn't thick waves, or even the neat bun Liv used on missions, but pulled high in a severe ponytail and then folded over, leaving her face bare and angular. Instead of street clothes or BDUs, hers was more of a uniform, tight black jacket that had to be crazy-hot even indoors, over some kind of equally tight turtle-neck and solid black pants tucked into high boots, Liv's kind of thigh harness but giant knife hilts sticking out of both.

The man stalking in behind her, if Liv hadn't said he was adopted, Marshall would've assumed he was their father. His skin was cooler, more copper, and his hair was true black. He wasn't much taller than Liv, not reaching Matteo or Jace's height, but he controlled the room. Maybe the air too, from the way Marshall's lungs seized up, a brief, panicked hitch. He wore the same dangerous all black uniform, with matching blades, and no way was he gonna approve of Marshall.

Marshall hadn't moved but those predatory gazes swung and fixed on him at the same instant, their eyes seeming almost glowing under the lights. The force pinned him like a giant hand was holding him down. He fought the pressure on his lungs, slowly suffocating, true panic cresting.

"Guys." Liv didn't seem to be aiming it at Jace and Matteo, especially since the word was followed by a soft thump, like someone elbowed another person. Liv's sister, from the way the woman huffed.

The spell snapped. Marshall sucked in oxygen and spun to the stove. He curled his hand into a fist, driving the edge of the metal spoon he'd been holding into his palm, concentrating on that pain to push the pit opening around him back. Losing it here, in front of Liv and her family, wasn't an option, no matter what his head was screaming at him about danger and hiding.

"Yeah, there ain't much worth getting Bruce extra fired up. Normal fired up's bad enough." Matteo abandoned the group to amble over and lift lids on the other pots on the range. "Whatever this is, two thumbs up, man. Smells good enough to make up for missing a beach party."

Marshall braced in time to catch Matteo's good-natured slap. The friendly assault pushed more of the panic aside. Not gone, but back to lurking. "It's—it'll be ready soon." Soon, and then Marshall could go.

Like there was some current traveling between him and Liv, he felt her approach. "Guys, meet Marshall. He has been kind enough to not only hang out with us, but feed us, too."

"And round out our gaming crew. He's our secret weapon," Josh added.

"Kimi did say your performance had improved," the not-Liv said.

Marshall forced muscles that still though this was a bad idea to unlock and meet the others. His neck and face burned, no way to hide the reaction. He hoped they'd put it down to the range's heat.

Liv lifted a brow, checking with him. Even if she did stay

mid-way between him and the other too sleek people instead of coming back to stand with him. *Like that'll ever happen again.* He did his best to ignore the voice always quick to remind him of his shortcomings.

Her voice gentle, the way she acted when they first met, when Marshall acted like a worse basket case than usual, Liv said, "Marshall, meet my sister Victoria—Vee for short, because we all get tired of signing full names to daily reports."

Liv's almost-twin cocked her head and smiled. Her smile was all white teeth, the kind his ex-boss had on the rare occasions the guy—the vampire—smiled.

"This is Stavros, our papá," Liv continued. "Basically, adopted into the family whether he wanted to be or not."

The man Liv had just so casually called her papa, tipped his head barely enough to notice, the aloof move a match to his voice, formal and unforgiving, accent not like any Marshall had heard before. "It is good to make your acquaintance."

The guy didn't sound like there was anything good about the meeting or Marshall.

Marshall settled for a stiff nod that probably made him look like a jerk, and twisted back to the pan he'd been tending. "Dinner will be ready in a few minutes if anybody's hungry."

"What is this?" Matteo was back to poking at pots, like a kid who couldn't wait.

"Porchetta."

"No way! You said cook but you totally kidnapped your own chef," the not-Liv burst out, sounding more real for the first time.

From the corner of his eye, he caught Liv tensing.

"I'm not a chef," Marshall said, before they all expected

more than he was capable of and he humiliated Liv when he didn't come through.

Nobody argued, and Jace order-offered "Where's your gear? Get it in here so we can eat." Boots thumped against tile, followed by the whoosh of the connector door opening.

Marshall wasn't alone though, the muscles knotting between his shoulder blades warning him. Metal scrapped on the old tile, the bar stools being slid out.

"Believe it or not, I didn't plan to roll in at mealtime," Victoria—Vee said.

When Liv cleared her throat, he realized too late that the statement had been aimed at him. "Sure you didn't," she answered for him.

"Stavros and I can grab something out of the freezer, or cereal," Liv's sister said, of course familiar with the compound and what was usually in it.

"There's enough. Plenty," he stumbled, because, hey, not stringing a sentence together wouldn't convince them even faster that Liv made a mistake bringing him here.

"Marshall is more generous with portions than Bruce. Love the guy, but he refuses to believe tasting menus aren't the way to go when people spend the day—" Liv hesitated, editing her answer "—working out and patrolling."

The tops of Marshall's ears burned. Liv had switched out *fighting* and *concealing bodies*, already having to put in extra effort because of him.

He tuned out any more conversation. Concentrated on the food, on getting it done and plated, then he could get out before he embarrassed Liv further.

iv

TYPICAL VEE, she was on her best behavior at dinner, both as apology and because we were all pretty dang happy to be together. She'd also subtly altered her attitude toward Marshall, the ridiculous borderline predatory thing gone.

When she tried to draw Marshall into the group's chatter, out of his sight I discreetly signed a warning and she shifted gears. In turn, one glare from her and Stavros abandoned what we'd all concluded had been typical, painfully polite seventeenth-century dinner manners that included conversing with seat mates.

Marshall served, and once he had nothing else left to do, kept his face down during the meal. I wasn't even sure he'd touched his food. I couldn't ask, and risk bringing him more attention that he obviously wasn't comfortable with.

Once Jace gathered everyone's plates and utensils, Marshall left the table like he was bolting from a starting line. Without a word, he finished cleaning in record time. He closed the dishwasher with a muted click, as if he was afraid even that might bring attention his way.

Jace checked in with me and at my nod, asked the room, "Yo, who's up for poker? Better yet, pool? Maybe you can redeem your last stunningly sad loss. You'd expect better reflexes from a—" he caught himself, muscle clenching in his jaw even as Vee and I both whipped to face him "—from agents."

Vee kicked Stavros' ankle, and earned a put-upon look down his aristocratic nose, but also knocking him out of that hair-trigger reaction place he'd gone at Jace nearly saying *vampire* and outing them in front of Marshall. "Very well. I'll not bet more than the tiny candies if your sisters are included though," he said as Matteo hopped up to grab the bag of chocolate kisses from their hiding spot, the subterfuge a habit even with Bruce and his draconian snack rules long gone.

I smiled at Stavros. BV—before Vee—he had been a ghost, alone, no living creature knowing his name, no one having spoken it in hundreds of years. His whole identity from the time he was infected was as a vampire, what he considered a demon, a damned creature. As penance, he was meant to carry out God's will by killing other vampires until he died in battle.

He'd considered candles and sleeping bags an unnecessary luxury, his only gear a crucifix that had to have come from some long-ago Spanish mission, Christian bible, and fighting gear. There most *definitely* hadn't been gambling allowed. He was coming along nicely now as far as actually living, at first because he loved Vee and wanted her happy after ignoring her Company oath and turning her before she died, then because he loved us too.

"Are you implying we cheat?" I asked, hiding my grin and giving him innocent eyes.

"I am well aware your sister sometimes attempts to, just as I suspect you do, but far more deftly."

"Oh, she cheats," Jace answered.

"I think we're offended." I checked with Vee. "Are you offended?"

"Uh, yeah. Enough that I think shunning is in order." She turned her back on the guys.

Before Jace could ask, Marshall ducked around the bar and was halfway down the hall to his room.

"That did not go the way I planned." Jace stared down the hall. "Should we?"

"Give him some space for now. There's a whole lot of poorly thought out ideas going on here." I looked from Vee to Stavros.

Stavros transferred his gaze to the ceiling, examining the heavy timber beams possibly almost as old as he was. His go-to when embarrassed. "Perdóname, Victoria. My apologies for—"

"My decision, my place to apologize, if apologies are in order." Vee took the responsibility, the same way she took charge, born for the role of leader.

However, so was I. Trying to keep in mind the emotional turmoil we all had waded through in the last two years, I met her head-on. "Stop. Think for a minute. Then talk to me. Why are you both overreacting? Because objectively, you are."

Vee went from comfortably slouched to on her feet, facing me.

She ignored Stavros' soft, "Victoria" the same as I ignored Matteo's, "Maybe both of you take a beat?"

"You allowed a civilian, an unknown quantity, into our home and lives. This risks *everything*." Her hands were curled into fists. "At first, I thought it was a joke, because Liv and a civi? Never gonna happen. But, wow, has it. You didn't want *a* good job for him, you wanted a good job *here*. So you can keep associating with him, and what happens when some vampire or new sentient cryptid comes through, and uses him to get to us, or gives up our secrets?"

I kept the 'this is *my* home now, not *our* home' comment buried, because it was petty, it would hurt her, and the choice to leave had been mine. "Yes, deciding he would be better suited to life here than at HQ was impulse. However, I cleared it with Oversight five minutes later, and was fully prepared to take him to Sera's half-way house, which has armed protection, if Oversight refused. Marshall being here wasn't a risk, until *you* came here, and without talking to me beforehand. You see that, right?"

Vee hesitated, then looked to Jace, honestly asking for his input. "You're seriously okay with this stranger? Answering me, as Josh's brother?"

"I'm fine with it, as Josh and your brother, and as team Lieutenant." He scrubbed a hand over his fade, which was in need of a touch up. "Marshall isn't a security threat. At least, not any more than me and my big mouth slipping up."

Matteo gripped his teammate's shoulder. "You've never once come close to slipping in front of other people. Difference with Marshall is that it feels like he's always been around, like he's part of the group, you know?"

I froze, Matteo's statement hitting me like an arrow burying itself precisely in the center of a bullseye, more so than Vee's barb about my wanting Marshall living nearby. The idea should've been ridiculous. Yet—

"Oh." Vee's soft, surprised exclamation pulled me back to reality. She stared at me, lips parted.

She'd been quiet enough the guys didn't notice, still talking. Jace nodded his thanks at Matteo. "Hadn't thought of it that way, but truth. Fact is, even if I had, I don't think I'd have freaked the fuck out the way I would with anyone else, civi or Company. Marshall is solid."

"Man, we're walking a tightrope and common sense and training say we shouldn't trust a civi, but hell, I do. Marshalls like that." Matteo switched spots, arm around Vee's shoulders, dwarfing her. "I'd hack out my own liver before risking you guys. Flat out, I can't survive losing any more family."

Stavros' sigh held way more subtext than should've been possible. "I am well aware there was little to no risk of exposure, until Victoria and I rushed here, creating the exact scenario we feared. I can't but honor your truthfulness."

Vee and I both looked like we were watching a sparring match, attention jumping back and forth from each of the men.

Stavros gestured at Matteo. "Though Victoria has exceptional control over the changes we are cursed with, today's reaction wasn't the fear of a Commander, but the fear of a sister, a far, far more potent emotional trigger. That I did not do my duty and offer her my calm until she achieved it on her own—though old, I have never had anything that I feared losing. Until Victoria found me, and you all opened your hearts to me. The terror of having but losing my family again overrode all else, and instead of supporting Victoria, my emotions fed hers."

"Flashbacks," Jace said, lines he should be too young for, carved by grief, showing. "If you aren't prepared, they will lay you flat on your ass."

I abandoned my spot, wrapping my arms around Jace. He lifted his arm, tucking me under. Matteo caught and pulled both of us in, the three of us sharing grief and comfort, his other arm still around Vee.

"All of this is to say that I do owe an apology." Stavros touched my head, a gentle hand smoothing hair down. "I have complete trust in your abilities and discretion as a soldier, and even more so as a sister and daughter."

* * *

THE GUYS FINALLY LEFT, the crack of balls signaling the start of a game of pool. Vee and I had stayed though. I went by feel, pulling the tequila from the top cupboard while she snagged glasses.

"Margaritas?" She paused by the blender.

"Today calls for no frills."

We ended up on the stools, side by side at the bar. I poured shots and passed her one.

"Thank you for not going all righteous Commander and tossing me out," she said.

"I do still love your favorite-skirt-stealing butt." I held my glass out and we tapped, then emptied the distinctly low shelf tequila. "Besides, I just bought a new skirt."

"Lots of new going on, huh?"

I refilled our glasses, but didn't pass hers back, staring at the tile, image distorted through the clear liquid. "New isn't always bad. Pretty sure I learned that from you. Do you really think I'm being careless or that I'd do anything to hurt you? You came without Kimi, Josh, and Bruce, and if it were me, I'd leave them out of it if I thought I might be walking into an ambush or fight."

"Not even a little, and I was so out of line and totally awful today, and I'm sorry. Really, really sorry." She started for a cuticle to shred.

I stuck the glass back in her hand instead. "Send me the limited edition set of *The Kissing Booth* books—the signed set —and I'll call it even."

"I'm not that sorry."

I'd known she wouldn't turn loose of the contested books.

Which I was reasonably sure Kimi had smuggled to her room on the down low.

"So, Marshall." She played with her tequila instead of drinking. "I should have asked a few more questions. He's…"

When she didn't finish, a foreign surge of protectiveness washed through me. "Don't start on him, because he's done nothing to deserve it. You came here prepared to hate him."

"No, that wasn't what I meant. If I didn't know better—which I do, and super sorry, again—I would have though you'd told him what Stavros and I were from his reaction when we walked in."

"He's reserved until you get to know him. He's had cause to be, from what he's shared with me."

Her not even slightly buzzed gaze fixed on me, way more sister than C.O. or vampire. "Either you're lying to yourself, or you've somehow lost all ability to read body language. He was dumping adrenaline and fear like a breached oil tanker. His heart rate doubled, and for a minute he was breathing short and shallow. I think he was borderline panic attack."

I sipped my cruddy tequila as she continued.

"Any perceived conflict seems to be a trigger. I can't imagine what actual violence does to him."

Vee didn't need me to confirm her evaluation. She'd aced the same psych courses I had, then added acute vampire senses on top of that. I squashed a thread of disloyalty when I said, "I know. He manages."

"He may cover well, but the anxiety is very much there. Like—" she sorted, or translated from vampire senses to real words, "—like there's this path inside, worn in the way a real one would be if it was used constantly, except his feels deep. Plunging into a ravine deep, so much so that you can't really climb out, and are forced to follow the same road, again and again."

"He didn't freeze when we blew into his kitchen with

weapons, and flushed out enraged vampires, not until after he'd put himself between the vampires and the hostages. He saved a street kid a week ago, which, yes, it was my fault he was ever in a position to feel tackling a ghoul was the only option. Both of those hurt him emotionally, but he's made huge strides adjusting."

"Liv—"

"Don't throw shade simply because you don't like him. You weren't there, and didn't see how amazing he was."

Vee looked at my hands.

I exhaled and pried my fingers out of the fist. It was ridiculous to get angry at her for stating facts.

"I never said I didn't like him. I'd like to get to know him —you never get all up in your emotions over anything. Or anyone. Although let me point out, if I were petty, I'd casually mention how often you've rolled your eyes and accused me of that exact same thing."

"Good thing you aren't at all petty," I muttered.

"You really do like him."

"I do. The guys do. He's our friend."

"I noticed Jace and Matteo big-brothering him." She did that thing, carefully choosing her words again. "I think maybe you don't want him close by because he's a friend. You feel more than that. Kind of like I did with Bruce?"

I opened my mouth to correct her, and tell her she was seeing relationships lurking in every shadow because of her engagement, and that she was in the minority as far as agents actually wanting or needing romantic attachments. As in, one of only two agents, out of thousands around the world. What came out wasn't even close. "I think we've gone over all the reasons that can't and won't happen, beginning with the fact I'm not sure Marshall is interested in me romantically, followed by the fact that I'm not sure if civilian romance is something I'm really interested in, touching on his deep aversion to violence and harming cryptids, and that he had a life he had to hit pause on, no matter how unappealing we find it, and ending with how we are all on probation and how I cannot imagine any scenario in which Oversight would bend their rules."

"Your reports on Stavros and I are thorough and really great, and the one Assessor of the pair tasked with overseeing our experiment is super impressed with you guys. Oversight basically trusts you now. Mostly. Plus, your team has an outstanding record."

"My team is on probation, whether you want to admit it or not. We are neck deep in some sort of cryptid reorganization, and almost a year later still have no clue what it means or the end game, if there is one. Emphasize to Kimi that Oversight has a zero tolerance policy when it comes to agents without the appropriate clearance level accessing records. Emphasize the no tolerance part *heavily.* I'm going to check on Stavros and the game." I shoved the tequila bottle away, because the entire bottle wouldn't erase this conversation and the ball of confusion lodged in my chest.

CHAPTER 38

Marshall

MARSHALL PLAYED the first few chords again. The weird half note whine was gone. He'd finally gotten strings on and tuned.

He sighed and flexed his fingers. The first attempts were strings popping every which way, because his fingers wouldn't stop shaking. He checked the bedside table and his phone. It had taken him hours, screen showing it was close to midnight.

Voices had carried, moving back and forth across the house, mostly between the den and kitchen. None down this hall. Not that he'd expected anyone to stop here. He repeated that lie, not doing squat to convince his brain it was true.

At a knock on the door, he started, his phone clattering to land face down on the nightstand. This for sure had to be his imagination, or next door. The rap sounded again, kinda hesitant. The strings gave a metallic whine as his fingers slipped.

Hope flared to life. "Liv?"

The door cracked open a hand's width. "Sort of-not-really? It's Vee."

"Oh." Which sounded like he didn't want her here. He didn't, but—"Did you need something? I can warm leftovers."

A slim, bare foot nudged the door wider. If she'd looked like she and Liv could be sisters before, now she was undeniably related. She'd traded the intimidating leather for the same shorts Liv preferred, and a generic Company tank top. Her hair even seemed more real and approachable, down from the fierce tail, waves flowing down her back. "Am I disturbing you?"

"No."

Almost shy, she held out a fork and plate, one with a slice of the pie he'd put together after Liv's earlier joke. "You didn't seem hungry at dinner."

His face burned. He'd already been weird enough that they'd noticed.

She kept talking. "I have the same problem—distracted at mealtime, then I'm starving by this time at night."

"Ah."

"This is a terrific pie. I never thought strawberry and rhubarb sounded edible. What the heck is rhubarb, anyway? Like, its leaves are toxic but you're supposed to eat the other parts? Then I had some of yours. I mean, Matteo isn't a good metric to judge by. The guy will eat anything. Honestly, Stavros isn't much more discerning despite that whole displaced royalty front. But I trust Liv's judgment."

Good that Vee liked it. He didn't have any reason for the stab of disappointment, that she hadn't asked him to join them for dessert. That she hadn't stopped by at all. "I'm glad. That everybody liked the pie."

"Liv hasn't had hers. First HQ called about a project Liv and I are collaborating on, then our—Liv's—neighboring C.O. called to compare some migration notes."

He was pretty sure Vee wasn't telling the whole truth. She had to have the same rules and all as Liv, about who and what she told, but it was kinda cool she bothered to tell him anything.

He tuned back in as she continued. "I hid her a piece for when she is free, and I thought you might like the last one. So." She held the plate out. "If not, I'll put it—okay, honestly? High odds I'll get tackled for it before I ever get to the fridge."

He fiddled with the guitar, fingers briefly touching strings, not to play but just to think. This wouldn't be the first time, not even the hundredth, that he'd misread people. Ice-cold killers didn't ramble about vegetables, or bother with unimportant strangers. This was such an echo of what Liv had done, making sure he got his share, too. Vee wasn't Liv, but she wasn't the person he'd assumed, either. He owed her an apology even if she didn't know. "Thanks. Thank you."

She tilted her head, a version of Liv's eyebrow-question and glanced at the food.

"Yeah, snacks are a tradition here." Which she of course knew more about than he did, and he shut his mouth.

"Seriously. Hand delivering desserts is also a thing." She walked in, a little hesitant still, and set the plate on the farthest edge of the nightstand, then retreated to her spot in the doorway. Like she understood bigger than normal personal space and made sure not to crowd him.

When she didn't leave, he pressed firmly on the flutter of nerves. He hung the guitar on the stand, glad he hadn't changed to sleep stuff. He took the plate. "What do you like for breakfast? Or not eat?"

"You take requests?" Her eyes widened, and if supersoldiers could look like excited kids, she did. "Dang. That's a change."

"Liv said that the first time I asked her." Because he'd missed his share of common sense when it was being passed out, he said, "Do you have the same friend?" He shoved a chunk of pie in before he asked more. Did Liv date their probably-mutual friend, and no matter what Liv had mentioned, were they more than friends, and was that who Liv was thinking of and missing those times she'd seemed so sad?

Vee's expression sharpened, and she tilted her head, like she was seeing something odd or discreetly sniffing his room, which had to be his imagination. Then she morphed right in front of his eyes, the last of the fierceness gone, replaced with a softness he wouldn't have guessed at. "Heard about our dictator chef, huh? That's B, Bruce, my—fiancé."

She smiled, a tiny one, no teeth, the way she ducked her face almost like she was shy or embarrassed. "I'm still not accustomed to saying fiancé." She pulled a thin chain he hadn't noticed, from where it disappeared under her tank, a ring strung on it.

All of a sudden, the pie tasted better. Possibly this was the best pie he'd ever made. He blamed the sugar rush for further loosening his tongue. "You can do that?"

Vee's smile turned wicked. "Basically, B does whatever he wants, and expects anyone in a position of authority to fall in line. Dating and getting married have never come up in Company history so there's no rule forbidding it." She crossed her arms, propping against the door frame, not seeming self-conscious about old marks around her biceps and forearms, and way serious scars along her throat and chest.

"True story—I meet B more or less the same way you ended up here. I saved his indignant, hallucinating butt from a bad life decision involving back alleys and a female cryptid."

"Heroes run in your and Liv's family." He shoved another gooey bite of fruit and crust in, hoping to God it would keep it from saying anything else weird.

"You pick up the best people hero-ing," Vee said. "According to the guys, you're practically Company. Your first run-in with cryptids, and reaction, was far more flattering than B's."

"That's—they're only joking around."

"Liv told me the same version of events."

He bent his face over the nearly empty plate, so Vee didn't see how much that meant to him. That Liv and the guys might really see him that way, that he might've helped them in some fashion.

Vee kept talking, satisfaction now clear in her tone. "Also, I hear you're the only honest person in this compound, so you are obvs needed tomorrow evening. Jace might not have been wrong in accusing us of taking liberties with the rules. Turns out that Liv and I have that in common. Night, Marshall."

He looked up and she was already a foot down the hall, only her voice floating back. He scrubbed at his eyes, more tired than he'd thought if he'd zoned long enough for Vee to walk out and him not notice.

"Good night," he said to the empty room.

CHAPTER 39

ℳarshall

Since he was alone in the kitchen, Marshall nudged the tablet's volume control with his elbow, turning GNR up. Hands busy, he settled for humming along, another of those instinctive workarounds, that keep the sliver of his brain not focused on the task his hands were doing busy enough that it didn't drop into what-if anxiety mode.

He kept the whisk moving, not giving the sauce the opportunity to burn. They'd gotten distracted the evening before and Vee hadn't mentioned her food preferences. Liv liked the French toast, so it was a good bet her sister might as well. Everyone also seemed cool with pork. Or fanatical. It was kind of a fine line.

"Let me get Legal on the phone. Liv can't force you to listen to this. I mean, we wouldn't force cryptids to listen to this." Vee's tone and delivery were enough like Liv's gentle teasing that he only darted a quick glance to double check his interpretation, lifting the pan from the heat and pouring its contents over the toast.

Vee grabbed a handful of sliced mango. "Hey, nice shirt." She motioned with fruit when he turned, then sucked bits of pulp off her fingers. "I got B the boxers when the movie came out, after he took his nieces to see it."

The tips of Marshall's ears warmed, his thoughts automatically jumping to shopping with Liv, and boxers, and choosing for each other. "That's an awesome gift."

"Not really." Liv strolled in and re-stole a chunk of mango from her sister. "She didn't tell him they were glow in the dark, plus we'd been celebrating that night, i.e. there was a quantity of alcohol consumed. Bruce's reaction was impressive. And loud."

This was the first Marshall had seen of Liv since she got stuck in meetings. He nudged his jumbo coffee mug behind the pan, because he might've stayed up way late, in case she stopped by his room, the way she had the night before. Before the semi-disastrous way he'd acted around her family, like she'd brought killer cryptids in, not real people.

She hadn't showed up, giving him a chance to apologize. This morning's breakfast was his Plan B apology. A wisp of satisfaction wove through him, light green and happy. This was also evidence for Vee that he wasn't a weirdo, plus another apology to her, and thanks for the night before. She lived with a cook. She'd understand food shorthand.

"I maintain that it's the thought that counts." Vee elbowed her sister, defending the remaining piece of fruit.

"I feel your thought process requires deeper consideration." Stavros was as unsettlingly quiet as when he had first arrived, and in the kitchen between blinks.

"B liked them." Vee defended her actions.

"The volume and length of his blasphemous swearing brings your interpretation of events into question. He is already overly proficient." The guy's scowl alone would've intimidated a ghoul or vampire but Vee and Liv only rolled their eyes, like the guy's opinion was a joke between them.

He'd changed from his supervillain uniform into the team's everyday tee and BDUs and somehow, he was even more disturbing.

Whatever. Even if he hated pastry and ham and turned out to be the world's biggest douche, the kind who demanded gluten-free vegan meals and a million picky substitutions, Marshall would deal. Vee was cool enough to make up for their father.

Vee said, "Marshall, as a neutral third party, how do you rule on glow in the dark underwear as a gift?"

His pulse inched up, in anticipation, not fear. This wasn't a test. "I think anybody who knows you guys should be prepared for bizarre underwear gifts."

Vee laughed, and Stavros snorted agreement.

He waited for Liv to agree or shoot him one of her secret, wicked grins. She didn't look at him, turning her back to them, and pouring coffee.

He reminded himself that in the last forty-eight hours, she'd been out on an extended cryptid mission where she'd gotten banged up, had surprise visitors, and been involved in one marathon meeting after another, meaning cryptids were up to something extra bad. She had to be tired.

Plating the pastry, he took time to wipe edges and arrange the fruit, since nobody pounced like starved street cats today. He pushed down the tension at confronting the semi-circle of faces seated at the table, all trained on him, and passed out plates.

"It's frou-frou." Matteo eyed the edible display, then popped a bite of pork belly in his mouth. "Huh. I forgot frou-frou tastes *good.*"

"I don't usually have time to fix presentation." He eyed

Matteo the way Matteo had the plate, and got a conspiratorial laugh. Marshall grabbed his plate and took the last seat on the occupied end of the table, one by Jace, Liv not having saved him his usual spot to her right.

"Ask B for dining-manners training tips," Vee offered.

Matteo groaned. "He's a hardass. Sit, shut up, don't eat until he explains the food's dang life history."

"He understands the value in holding onto civilized actions." Despite the gravelly voice, Stavros bowed his head, surprising Marshall with a quick blessing, although Marshall missed some of it, the wording not familiar.

More surprising, the rest of the team quieted and honored the formal moment, not moving until after Stavros crossed himself, and cut a bite of food into a neat square.

"Whoa. You and B agreeing? Worse, you approving of anything B-sanctioned? We aren't provisioned for the apocalypse," Liv said, her gentle humor getting an almost-smile from the severe soldier.

That set off a back and forth among the crew. Marshall ate, content watching them enjoy each other, the air of friendship and good humor almost enough for him to get a contact high. Especially when they took time to compliment him or the food between teasing and conversations.

All of them except Liv. He felt the weight of her gaze on him, although every time he checked, she was turned in another direction, or picking apart the remains of her toast. She didn't ask him anything, or ask him for anything, jumping up to refill her mug instead of passing it to him to froth, the way she preferred now.

She didn't hang out by the dishwasher, passing him the empties, while going over the day's plans, either. Instead, she physically aimed Matteo at the pile of dishes with a curt, "Your turn."

"Grump much?" The soldier said as he hauled wobbly stacks of stoneware to teeter beside the sink.

Marshall leaned back, checking that the rest were gone. "Did Liv get bad news in that meeting from the Texas person?" Texas was where Liv said the smugglers made port.

"Nothing past a whole lotta unanswered questions, which is the new normal. Cryptids are freaky scum and you never know why they do anything, other than kill. The level of *what the actual fuck* has hit new highs lately. Especially when Vee and Liv did their private meeting after."

At Marshall's go-on grunt, Matteo paused in stacking, frowning at the innocent tilework over the counter. "Their dynamic is brainstorming and bouncing what-ifs around. The shit they hatch that way is brilliant. They hadn't seen each other in person in months, Vee's team hitting a series of hot spots in the north of their Division, us after the traffickers. Here's hoping they do their magic and get a handle on what's behind the recent shakeup."

"Right." Marshall hadn't missed how tight Vee and Liv were, the strong bond between them even when they disagreed.

Matteo righted a leaning cup, and misread Marshall's expression. "There's nothing coming down the pipeline that we're aware of. We wouldn't keep that from you." He clasped Marshall's shoulder and squeezed, forehead crinkled. "No bull, no joke, man."

"I believe you. Go on. I've got the rest of this."

Matteo saluted him and left for the morning training.

Liv joked about them, but anybody could see how happy she was that her family was here. They weren't a problem. Meaning if it wasn't bad news about work or family, that only left him.

He'd screwed up last night. He took responsibility for that. Squaring his shoulders, he speed-loaded the dishwasher. Breakfast had been a start, but he needed to prove he'd pulled his head together, and wouldn't throw off the teams' routines or embarrass Liv, calling her judgment in letting him stay into question. He could do that for her.

* * *

LUNCH HAD BEEN a repeat of breakfast, although this time Stavros had also thanked Marshall, and seemed serious about it. Liv only turned and propelled Jace to act as Marshall's cleanup crew.

The rest of the kitchen done, Marshall made sure the counter was spotless and dry, and put on fresh coffee. He dusted off the stool on his side that Liv preferred, then pulled out and did the same for the other, since logic said Vee would have the same daily responsibilities as Liv.

"You would for real make Martha Stewart and all those social media show-offs lay down their crowns and weep in defeat." Vee surveyed his work.

"Liv does the afternoon reports in here." Then he added, "Not the confidential stuff, only—"

"The eyeball numbing everyday junk," Vee finished for him, then sniffed. "Ahh, coffee."

Marshall grabbed a mug from the cabinet. "Cream, sugar, or black? I can froth milk, too."

Vee joined him on his side of the bar, keeping a body length between them. "You do not have to cater to me or Stavros."

"I don't mind. I'd rather help." He touched the sugar, and she nodded. Same for the cream. "Not that I'm helping with anything important, but I can take the kitchen and meals off their shoulders so the guys and Liv don't have to waste time on basic work."

"Don't discount your contribution. I mean, making day to

day life run smoother and give us one less item to think about is great. That's part of what B does for us but it isn't the most valuable contribution though." She took a sip and made an approving noise. "Even more importantly, he makes sure we have someone to come home to. To come home for, really."

She took the extra stool and rested her elbows on the counter, cup cradled between both hands. The steam cast a mysterious, transparent veil over her face. "We didn't know how valuable that type of support was until B came along. Honestly, I'm not sure any of us could function without him anymore, at least, not at one-hundred-percent effectiveness. That extra one or two-percent can be the difference between coming out of a fight to the good, or missing a step and ending up in a rough spot." Vee's tone was respectful. Reverent.

He swiped at a section of old tile and new chrome. He'd do—he'd do anything to hear somebody talk about him that way. No, to hear Liv and the guys talk about him. To find some real means of making their lives easier. He ground his fingers into the chilly chrome, keeping his head in the reality of the here and now, not in impossible wishes.

Nothing like that was in his future but he'd do everything he knew how to now, while they were stuck with him.

When he twisted to ask Vee if she liked chicken or fish, her head was tilted, eyes narrowed on him. The steam gave the illusion of tinting her brown eyes silver. Hair on his arms stood up in a wave of goosebumps.

"You need to see the charts Terrence emailed." Liv walked in, searching for her sister.

And it was simply normal Vee sitting at his counter when she said, "No kidding. Gimme a second. Don't even with the coffee thievery," she warned, scooting her mug away as Liv reached.

"Name me one time when I thought, 'Wow, I have been wrong in my enjoyment of a pure cup of coffee, unblemished by obscene amounts of cream and sugar. I must steal Vee's,'" Liv said. "Being a thoughtful sister, I'm carrying it to the office for you."

Marshall stilled, the mug he'd already had out for her in hand as soon as she appeared, coffee pot in the other.

"Marshall busted you. I'd rather work in here, too."

"My office is called *office*, a room dedicated to all things written, typed, or generally admin related, for a reason. I'll even trade you your old half of the desk for today."

"You forgot the addendum about it reeking of cigar smoke, even fifty years after that guy retired to HQ. Pass."

Marshall filled the cup and heated milk. Stay or go, Liv would still need it.

In a neutral voice he hadn't heard since they'd first met, she asked, "Will we disturb you? Vee talks as she types. Spoiler alert, she is the worst typist in the history of ever."

"As if," came from down the longer hall of suites, followed by Vee returning, and the thump of a laptop onto the counter. "Besides, Marsh and I have bonded." She made a back and forth motion between them. "We totally get each other."

He set the frothed coffee to the right of Liv's seat, in case.

Her lips did that thing, smushed together, as she tapped the rolled-up reports against her thigh. "Marshall. Not Marsh."

Liv wasn't playing.

Vee plopped onto her seat, flipped her laptop open, and without taking her attention off Liv, said, "Marshall, your opinion on nicknames? They're something I only do with my favorite people."

The dry air crackled between the two women, like water on a heated griddle.

His options were piss off Liv or piss off her sister. Unless this was a sort of unconscious test, Liv expecting him to melt down because Vee treated him like a normal person. He swallowed, pulse quickening, as he weighed options.

Vee spun around on the stool, attention on him, and her tone gentled. "It's fine if nicknames aren't your thing. Stavros flat out refuses, and, obvs, I still love him."

He and his mouth needed to have a discussion about consensus, because it opened before he'd decided which decision was riskier. "I've never had a nickname." Shots about his hair and IQ didn't count. Not in the way Vee meant.

She locked her heels on a stool rung and leaned over the bar, fist out. "Welcome to the fam, Marsh."

He tapped knuckles with her, sucked in by the warmth and welcome radiating from her eyes, and the smile that really seemed to welcome him. Like this was way more, and way more important, than joking around about nicknames.

Probably only Vee being polite, another skill the Company taught Commanders, the tools they needed to keep civilians calm in a crisis.

Still, her reaction made it easy to go back to flipping through photos on the tablet Jace had dug out for him, double checking ingredients he needed and in what order.

The one time he felt the weight of eyes on his back, during a lull in their on-again-off-again conversation and typing, he checked and found Liv watching him, expression unguarded. Like she'd seen something she wanted but was afraid to ask, or that it wasn't right to ask. Catching him, her face went back to that neutral thing, that wasn't really neutral if you knew her.

He'd work harder, until he proved he'd gotten over himself, and gotten things right. Out of their way, helping where he could, not throwing off the team's daily rhythm. He offered Liv a quick smile and got back to work.

* * *

LIV CLOSED her laptop and stood, stretching arms up and behind her head just as Marshall rose from sliding the roast in the oven. He blanked, whatever he'd intended to do next obliterated by her shirt rising enough to catch a glimpse of lean muscles and brown skin. Its silky feel, the way it glided under his fingertips, slammed into him. The sensation was burned into his memory.

So was the heat of her body, draped over his, trusting him to hold her. A whisper of coconut wrapped around him, replacing the here-and-now bite of fresh ground pepper and sharpness of rosemary, even though he was too far away to catch her scent.

He couldn't have made himself move even if a pack of vampires had rampaged through the place. Liv finished by rolling her head, loosening neck muscles. She straightened, and caught Marshall staring-staring, which was probably over the line and creepy. Instead of acting like she didn't notice him, the way most people would've avoided him, she stared back.

What felt like pure electricity arced between them. Her lips parted like she wanted to ask him something. Whatever it was, the answer was yes, because anything Liv wanted, he'd find some way to make it happen. He tried to put that in a look, that all she ever had to do was ask.

Whatever she saw, it finally freaked her out and she spun to her sister. "Let's hit the obstacle course."

Vee did that head cocked thing, something triumphant and—challenging—definitely a challenge, in the look she and

Liv shared. Then Vee smiled. "Later. I'm still working on the extra report I owe HQ." She settled behind her screen.

Back to not seeing him, Liv glared at her sister, pivoted, and left.

He exhaled, and wished for a do-over. To at least erase the last sixty seconds. He hoped a perfect meal and him reining in any further weirdness would be enough for Liv to forget whatever line he'd just crossed.

"Ignore Liv," Vee said, because, of course she read minds like Liv did. He kept the groan in.

"Seriously," she continued, and at least she was still speaking to him. "Liv gets touchy whenever things go off book—missions, interactions, cryptids—and don't follow the rules. I swear, she takes it as a personal failure," Vee said, fingers attacking the keyboard as she spoke. "Sure, rules are good and useful, but so is the ability to roll with change. She just needs permission, I think, to go with her instincts when they don't fit inside the framework of our rules."

"It's cool how you guys know each other that way." He laid out yeast and supplies. Bread prep required energy and concentration, and seemed like the option least likely to blow up in his face.

"We grow up together, take all the same courses, live and work together. The definition of intrusive and suffocating, according to B," she muttered, banging the delete key hard for some infraction, then resuming typing.

"Belonging isn't suffocating."

She paused, fingers hovering over the keyboard, then seemed to remember what word she'd wanted.

The click of key strokes and whump of him kneading dough settled over them. Vee was as soothing to have around as Liv.

"Can I be intrusive?"

He smiled, since Vee couldn't see thanks to her screen.

"When Liv says that, she asks anyway, whether you say yes or no."

"Not swearing or immediately leaving the area when asked is a yes in our world. Liv mentioned Mesa was off the table as far as you returning. Where are you hoping to relocate to?"

He punched the dough harder than necessary. "Wherever I find a job."

"No preferences?"

"Kitchens a kitchen."

"B's pretty connected. I can ask him to hook you up. What's your thing—regional food, fusion, molecular gastronomy?"

"Whatever's hiring." He stopped himself, because he sounded like an asshole. "I mean, I don't have any specialties. I'm only a basic line cook. Don't bother your fiancé. I'll find a job."

"It's no bother. We take care of our own."

He wrapped the dough and set it aside to rise. "I've never seen people have each other's backs the way you all do. It's— nice. A lot of people probably wish for that bond." *Belonging.* Which was way too much to dump on Vee. Anyone who made it to Commander was smart. All he needed was for Vee to read between the lines and share his impossible daydreams with Liv, and her be weirded out and awkward for the rest of the time she was stuck with him.

He muttered an excuse and ducked out of the kitchen.

iv

"HOW MUCH LONGER ARE YOU going to keep this up?" Vee met me as I walked off the obstacle course.

Flyaways tickled along my face, the breeze kicking up a brief dust devil that swirled madly, then faded out of existence. The same couldn't be said for my sister. When something caught her attention, she latched on, relentless. An admirable trait, unless you happened to be the object of all that sheer determination.

I jerked the ponytail holder off, bent forward and finger combed my hair. Totally not because I didn't want to face her. "I'm finished on the course. Thinking about hitting the gym and bag next."

"You know dang well that's not what I'm talking about."

The tips of her scuffed boots appeared, basically under my nose. I wrapped the band as tight as possible around my hair and flipped upright, the tail falling perfectly down my back, loose hairs back where they belonged.

"Then nope, I don't know." I gave her our universal *I can't even with you right now* glare.

"Let's recap, then. You were *happy*. Happy-ish anyway, with a daily side of fresh-baked muffins. I know you were. I heard it in your voice on that call, which was one of the reason I overreacted. Then I felt the—" she made extravagant loopy gestures with both hands "—all those seriously content vibes that still lingered when I walked into the house, even under the agro and worried pheromones we were both kind of shedding."

"Of course the guys and I are content." I ignored the voice pointing out that wasn't even a little true, all my fear about not measuring up in HQ's eyes, the fear of not giving my team what they needed to be effective and safe and none of us ever have to go through the nightmare of losing people we loved. Of not giving them *enough* for them to move from the quietly grieving stage on to truly living again. Of the worry for Vee and Josh and Stavros and Kimi that had been my companion most nights, and that my reports would fail in keeping Oversight from Vee's doorstep. And mine. That Jace and Matteo would be the ones paying for my failings as a leader.

I'd been the one to go to them, to promise we could make it work, the three of us form a new team and family.

"We both know that's not true, either." A bit of guilt leaked in around her edges. "You were happier, and clearly spending time with Marshall, aside from living in the same house sort of time together. Then I pointed out that you were more than fond of him, and now you're ignoring him, he's wracking his brain trying to understand what he did wrong and how to fix his mistake, and you are miserable.

You're both miserable. At least tell me you'll go back to friends once I leave."

I hadn't missed the way Marshall had kept glancing at me over breakfast and lunch. How he'd had my usual spot prepared for our afternoon of my doing reports and research while he did his thing and worked on dinner. Or the unasked questions when I'd broken my end of our agreement.

I'd missed his solid presence right beside me at both meals. The other side of the table where he'd ended up between the guys felt like miles away.

After I won the disputed drawing of straws and got to choose the movie the evening before, I'd missed hanging out with him and sharing half of the loveseat. Instead, I'd taken the usually comfy beanbag between the chairs and screen. Compared to curling against Marshall and his super-soft tee, his arm draped over the back of the chair and along my shoulders, it sucked.

Which was exactly why I needed to put space between us until I could follow my own rules. Commander and agent first, last, and always.

"You deserve to be happy." Vee's voice was almost as ephemeral as the breeze that had kicked up the dust devil, too low to be heard if you weren't standing right beside her.

"My *team* deserves better from me, to be secure in our performance and that I won't slack, putting my wants ahead of their needs. Even if that weren't the case, Oversight will never sign off on our adding anyone else to the team. That isn't your fault, or Stavros' fault, and I wouldn't ever want the two of you anywhere but alive, healthy, and with our siblings and Bruce, okay? That you came back makes me happy."

"Marshall."

I hated how the one word punched right through my defenses. "He has a life waiting for him, and I will be sure that at least means a secure job, and financial resources. That has to be enough."

Vee's eyes blazed silver. "That? That is basic. We've all been through too much to settle for surviving instead of really living. I will be the first to tell you existing without someone you love impacts your performance negatively. Fix this."

"There's nothing to fix." My temper spiked to match hers. "This is my team, and my compound. You don't need to like my decisions, but you are obligated to respect them."

$\mathcal{M}$arshall

MARSHALL EDGED out onto the narrow upper walkway, shading his eyes until they adjusted to the bright afternoon sun. Staying inside had made him claustrophobic, while at the same time the whole place felt empty without Liv in it. This time of day, Liv and the guys usually sparred in the sandy stretch of yard between the bench and gym. Even watching her from a distance was better than not seeing her at all.

Today, she and Vee faced each other, arms crossed. Attitude rolled off both of them.

"Ah, damn." Josh stepped out, seemed to think about retreating, before finally pausing by Marshall.

"What's wrong?" Something was, and this once, it wasn't because of him. Probably.

"They've been like this all their lives, pushing each other to be better, feeding off the competition. The positive kind, usually. Sometimes though, this." Josh discreetly pointed at the pair.

Matteo joined them, filling up the space. "There was this one time, somewhere around our fourth year, where they dragged out one of their not speaking to each other episodes so long that they both forgot what started their argument in the first place."

"Then they made up?" When silence met the question, he checked with Matteo, then Jace.

"Neither one of them is made for backing down."

"Kimi finally told them to knock it off, or else," Matteo said. "They united to face that potential threat. You do not want to really make Kimi mad." He shuddered, same time Jace said, "Truth," voice fervent.

Stavros did that creepy appearing out of nowhere thing. He took a look at the women, then muttered a string of Spanish. All Marshall really caught was something that sounded like he was asking God for help, or patience.

And "Come," directed at the other men, as Stavros took the narrow metal stairs, two rungs at a time.

Whatever Stavros' plan was, it involved more or less lining the four siblings up. Vee faced Matteo and Jace, while Liv faced Stavros.

Marshall understood, once Stavros tossed out the blunted knives Marshall had watched them practice with recently. As long as he didn't think of it being real, or there being anything attacking but another a teammate, a friend who didn't mean any harm past a few accidental bruises, he could finally appreciate the sight. All three were fast, and intense, and sure of themselves. But Liv—Liv shone. She moved like fighting was a dance.

Marshall rested his arms on the sun-heated metal rail, content to watch Liv. There'd never be a time he'd not want to.

The bout was a kaleidoscope of action and color, and it took a minute to pick groups apart. He'd seen one-on-one practices, and been crazy impressed. It must be a thing that C.O.s were that much better than anyone else, too, because Vee kept both the guys busy. Matteo was the first to step off to the side and out of the action, a rueful look when Vee slid between his and Jace's tag-team defense, whirled, came up behind him, and her fake knife rested across his throat.

Jace lasted longer, until he tried a punch probably meant as distraction, his knife snaking out underneath the blow. The distraction failed, Vee taking the punch although Marshall heard her grunt, and sucking in, avoiding the knife. She whirled under Jace's guard, her back hitting his chest, and tapped the bend of his elbow with her blade. Jace's hand spasmed open but Vee was already turned and tapping his other arm before his blade even hit the ground.

He shook his arms out, like he was trying to get the feeling back. Vee picked up his lost knife and handed it back. She wasn't sweating like the guys, but Marshall watched her chest heaving like she was sucking in oxygen. She glanced at the sky, another sunny Arizona day.

Stavros and Liv's bout was still going. Stavros—he was better than Jace and Matteo together. Maybe better than Vee. Liv though, she'd been amazing when she practiced with the guys. Going by how she wove in and out, avoiding Stavros and herding him at the same time, she'd also been holding back. Now, she moved quick enough it was difficult to keep track, constantly in motion. Body moving one way, then knife slashing out at an unguarded body part.

Marshall watched as Stavros ended up back to the gym wall. A dangerous place to be, and the soldier used the wall as a brace, and shoved off fast enough Marshall started. Launching at Liv. She stumbled and even though it was practice, Marshall's fingers vised around the rail.

She turned the stumble into a graceful fall, but Stavros raised a foot to stomp, on her arm or hand. She rolled under the kick, slicing her knife along the back of the leg supporting all his weight. And was up like she had springs in her legs and the tip of her knife lodged where Stavros' skull meet his neck.

He held both hands out, and when Liv stepped away, bowed to her. Whatever Stavros said, too far away for Marshall to make out, victory and happiness lightened her face, and she answered, smiling. A second later Stavros spoke and put his back to the house, putting himself between it and Liv. Or between Marshall and Liv, because Liv's attention shifted, and she looked over the agent's shoulder, right at Marshall. Her smile vanished.

He didn't need to hear the conversation to understand that Liv wasn't happy. Stavros' stern *'Do not blaspheme, Olivia'* carried clearly.

So did Vee's voice. "If Stavros isn't getting it done for you, let's go." She shouldered in, hard enough Stavros took an unbalanced step sideways.

The whole set of Liv's body altered, going from that readiness she always held, to all but vibrating. Vee tilted her head, doing that weird thing like in his room, like she was sniffing the air or Liv.

"Go big or go home," Vee said. Okay, more taunted than said. Her hands moved and metal caught and reflected the sun, causing Marshall to squint. Vee'd flipped a knife out.

Unease slithered down Marshall's spine. Fine, he'd been here less than two months, but he'd never seen anyone on the team use a real knife while practicing and sparring.

Liv snapped her fingers, and Vee tossed the blade. Liv snatched it out of the air, but Vee produced another from somewhere in her tactical pants. She flipped hers end over end, the weapon shimmering like strobe lighting. At the last second, Vee plucked the falling blade out of the air.

Liv lunged, arm straight and flat, aiming for Vee's chest.

Vee's elbow slammed down, where Liv's head had been a split second earlier.

This was a *fight*. Liv and Vee flowed around the yard, slashes and lunges coming fast. Trading places, never stopping, fancy flips mixed with what had to be ugly street moves. A thin red line opened on Liv's calf. A heartbeat later, Vee had a matching one along her bicep.

Marshall couldn't look away from the fight, but he caught motion on the edges. Stavros leaving his spot, Jace and Matteo nodding to him then separating. The three formed a triangle around the battle.

Sweat ran down Liv's forehead. Her tee was plastered to her body, not a patch dry enough to wipe her face against, even if she'd been able to take her eyes off Vee.

Her sister had a line of sweat down her spine, but nothing like Liv. Vee had slowed though. Enough Marshall noticed, and if he noticed—she had to be exhausted.

Like she was making a last Hail Mary play, Vee flipped the knife, holding it by the very end of the handle like he'd never seen done. He only understood when she feinted right, but her arm snapped straight, angled up, aiming for Liv's throat. She was giving herself extra reach, compensating for Liv's height and longer arms.

Liv jerked, head whipped back in surprise. She threw her arm up trying to shield her face and throat, and dropped her knife. But then she followed, knees hitting the sand, Vee's blade passing over Liv's head, catching hair. And Liv grabbed the falling knife in her left hand, the whole falling thing a ploy, bringing it up. Stabbing into Vee's stomach, blade sliding through shirt and skin.

Liv dropped her knife for real as Vee slapped both hands

over the wound, red already staining through the shirt. Vee's eyes widened, and she hissed.

Marshall let go of the rail, aiming for the steps. His knee banged metal, and the echo from the hollow railing spread across the yard. Vee whipped around, ponytail snapping. Staring up at Marshall, her warm coffee eyes blazing a flat silver, her face thinned until it was skin stretched over bone, a corpse face, not a real one.

Stavros was beside her between blinks. His eyes flickered silver, not as bright as hers. He caught her chin, turning her face into his chest. Hiding her face and eyes.

The same silver as at the hotel kitchen, that same see-through corpse face, like his old boss and his helper. The vampires.

Marshall hadn't had a clue what they were until they'd attacked, transforming from intimidating hotel owner, and pretentious chauffeur, to monsters. Even Liv and Matteo had had to use the scanner thing at first, to see if Marshall was human or vampire.

Liv's face had gone ashy, and the guys seemed frozen, staring. Shocked.

They hadn't known. That her sister wasn't human anymore. Matteo had said it—that they hadn't seen Vee and her team in months. Somehow during that time, they'd changed. Gotten infected.

Now they were here, inside the compound, fooling all the sensors and testing, because of course they'd know how to, after being agents once. Sneaking inside and waiting for—something, and that something had to be horrible. Turning other agents into vampires, or tricking Liv to taking them into HQ, and them killing or infecting all those kids.

And now Matteo and Jace, his friends, were standing yards from a pair of vampires. *Liv* was down there, even closer to what had been her sister. The guys only had useless blunt practice weapons. Liv had dropped her knife when she thought she'd hurt her sister, and she was still looking at Vee, as shocked as the guys, not fighting back yet, because it was her family that'd become a monster, messing with Liv's head, making her hesitate. If she waited much longer—

Marshall hadn't been in the armory. He didn't have to, to know what it contained, having heard Liv muttering about requisition orders for the anti-cryptid chem and bullets as she worked in the kitchen. Plus having seen all three agents coming back from it with handguns and rifles and knives when the mission call-out happened.

The armory was also only yards away. Marshall had seen how fast his boss had moved, though. Freaky, inhumanly fast, and as good as Jace and Matteo were, as fast as Jace was, they wouldn't make it before the vampires got at least one of them. And Liv was even further away from the building.

They need a distraction. Something to draw vampire attention long enough. Something to draw it *and* keep it.

When the chauffeur vampire had been wounded during the raid, Marshall had only had a couple of scrapes, but that weak smell of blood—the vampire had gone straight for Marshall, fixated enough it had ignored the soldiers and surroundings.

Marshall scanned the stupid walkway for options. All that was up here was old but well-kept metal, no rusted spots or sharp metal edges. That, and the sides of the house.

Sides covered in the adobe, surface bumpy and rough. Marshall lunged for the wall and slapped his forearm against the finish. Putting all his weight behind it, he dragged the underside of his arm against the wall. Then switched and dragged the other way, then back again, like the house was a grater.

Pain shot through his arm, skin peeling. Blood decorated the yellow-brown finish, left behind when he quit.

He hit the rail, bent as far over as he could and swung his arm in an arc, sending whatever blood was dripping from the gouges out and over the yard.

"The armory. Go," he bellowed and waved his arm again. Praying that the wind was going the right way, that the vampires could smell his blood. That going without blood for the almost two days they'd been here meant they were hungry.

Liv moved. But the wrong way, coming for him, the guys right behind her. Probably in shock over her sister, and making mistakes because of him, thinking about civilians instead of guns. "No, Liv, the weapons." He headed for the steps, arm out.

A flash of gray camo streaked straight up from the yard, defying physics. Landing right in front of him, Vee crouched between him and the stairs.

Which also meant between him and Liv, Vee distracted by his blood. Now his friends had time to get to the armory. He shoved his arm at the vampire, right in her face, braced for the bite or attack.

Vee rose. And stood there with her hands palm up, held out to the side. Her face angled slightly away so that she wasn't looking directly at him. "Marshall."

"Do it. Here, look. I'm not fighting you or running." He reached forward.

Vee took a step back. He tried again, and Vee retreated further.

Stair treads rattled under boots. Hopefully, Jace had figured Marshall's plan out, grabbed guns, and was already back. Marshall hoped like he never had before that was what was happening.

Vee, the vampire, spoke again. "Marshall, listen."

"Do whatever you want. I'm. Right. Here," he snapped at her, despite his head screaming to run, panic darkening the edges of the yard. He hadn't been able to stomach the thought of Liv hurt, when he first got to know her, during the ghoul attack. Now, nothing bad could happen to her. Didn't matter what it cost him, as long as she was safe. Safer, anyway, and had a real chance to fight back and survive. Liv was one of the few good things in the world, and he wasn't letting her get hurt, made food for a vampire. He couldn't fall into that pit until he knew she and the guys had a chance to defend themselves.

Vee caught his arm. He didn't struggle, pulse screaming at him, adrenaline turning him queasy. He stayed put though, for Liv.

Vee walked into him, folded his torn-up arm into his chest, the scraped side against his shirt. "Yes, I'm a vampire. I can get in your head enough to calm you, for a couple of minutes. But I'm not going to do that."

She backed away, her hands tucked behind her, until she was squashed against the rail, no way to go further. "I'm a vampire. So is Stavros." She looked down, and Marshall risked glancing where she did—to the guys and Liv, all bolting up steps, Liv in front.

Then Liv was there, slipping past Vee. Putting herself in Marshall's space, eyes worried.

Behind her, Vee's voice carried on. "I'm also Vee—Victoria. Liv's sister, an agent who freaking loves her family and job, and has a bossy fiancé, and is occasionally guilty of not thinking ideas through and doing really stupid things." He caught her jerking her hair where it must've caught as she blurred up here. The move popped the chain and diamond ring from under her shirt, the sun refracting from the jewel. She pulled the tie out of her hair in frustration, exactly like Liv did.

"Marshall." Liv reached for him.

He hated not touching her, but held his hand out, keeping

her at arm's length in case he needed a Plan B, getting her from under a vampire mind whammy. "How do you feel? Fuzzy? Are you under her—its—control?"

"No. It's very—I owe you an explanation, because this is—"

"Did you know? That she's a vampire? That they both are?" He tried making her think, work through the problem, because Liv was smart, and she'd see what was happening was wrong, that the vampires were messing with her head. That she needed to pay attention to the thing behind her, kill it before it got her.

Liv closed her eyes for a second. And he knew.

He knew what was coming next. It couldn't be true, but it was.

She opened her eyes, meeting his. "I did. There was a terrible accident, and neither Stavros or Vee ever wanted to become vampires. That was almost two years ago for her, and they are dedicated agents."

"We don't harm humans," Vee said from behind. "I swear, we never have. We're still agents and we live to protect civilians."

Liv tipped her head, agreeing.

"You knew. After all the lectures about monsters and people being more important. You didn't warn—didn't bother telling me, when they walked into the house we share. You lied," he said.

"I am so sorry about all of this. Truly." Vee wiggled out and Marshall tensed. All she did was walk slowly down the steps, and join the other vampire. Stavros. Who Liv had also known about. Jace and Matteo stepped up to the walkway.

Jace spoke. "This is—fucking complicated is an understatement. Look man, I get how this is hard to wrap your head around. Let's go in, grab a beer, or hell, hot chocolate, and talk this shit out."

Calm and ready for a beer, because sure, Jace and Matteo had known too, Matteo dropping his guilty as hell gaze to his boots.

Fire blazed up Marshall's face, anger propelling it until he wondered if the top of his head would blow off, like in cartoons. He stared at Liv. "Are you a vampire? Were all of you, this whole time?"

She shook her head.

"Are you lying to me now because I'm too stupid to know better?"

Liv made a noise and reached for him. Whatever his face showed, she dropped her hand. "No, I promise. Only a very few people know about Vee and Stavros—us, and a special section of the Company—"

"Why bother explaining to me now?" He went past Liv, not able to look at her now. Straight at the other two soldiers, both of whom melted out of Marshall's way.

"M'sorry, Marshall," Matteo said, still not meeting his eyes.

Marshall kept going, down the stairs and...out. Anywhere that wasn't near the people he'd been stupid enough to trust, who he'd been fool enough to believe respected him, at least a little.

"You can't leave yet," Liv said.

His laugh scoured his throat. "Right. I know the rules."

CHAPTER 42

iv

As the late afternoon shadows got longer, I dropped the sets of grappling gloves on the gym's table, checking with Vee as she and Stavros appeared, back from their emergency blood fuel-up in the desert. "Better now?"

I was surprised there were any chupacabra left anywhere in a ten square mile radius of the compound, thanks to their status as vampire snacks over the last year and a half. The cryptid pests didn't give Vee and Stavros the same strength as feeding on vampire blood, but they were a decent stop-gap until there was another call-out.

"Yes. Gross mission accomplished." She hovered in the propped open gym doorway, where I'd dragged the table, needing any kind of busy work but also needing to make sure Marshall didn't attempt to leave—dig under the fence to freedom, spell out an SOS message for passing planes, or steal the SUV and mow us down as he left, final commentary on our lying.

I'd also suspended his ability to call or text, since anything he did on his phone would show up on HQ records, standard practice. I was an awful person, more concerned with making sure my and Vee's epic mistake didn't endanger both our teams, than Marshall's potential need for contact with anyone other than us. He'd finally gone indoors, without acknowledging I was alive.

"Really you're okay? You'd had that windigo horde to clean out before you ever arrived here." I shaded my eyes, double-checking that Vee looked normal.

She pulled up the hem of her turtleneck—back to high necklines and long sleeves, to protect from the sun, showing me only a fading pinkish scab where I'd stabbed my sister. The fact that it was an accident, because I'd assumed she'd be out of blade range the second the tip of the stupid chem-coated knife pricked her skin, didn't matter. I'd hurt her.

"I'm so, so sorry. I wasn't thinking about how much of your power you'd burned off fighting under the sun, and that you'd had to had to slow down to conserve the energy you had left." Tears burned behind my eyes.

"No, it's *totally* my fault." She launched and tackle-hugged me. "Hello? Like I haven't heard a thousand lectures on not wasting our reserves, and pacing myself."

A *hrmph* sounded behind us, Stavros opinion of both our behavior.

"Okay, a hundred and one now." She sniffled, eyes as shiny as mine when she let go.

Assured our argument was over, Stavros strode toward the house. "Ay, niñas. You will be the death of me well before any demon can."

Vee let go and ducked inside, while I watched Stavros' stern figure disappear to the house. "Our papá is being—"

"Unnervingly calm about us outing ourselves at all, and to a civilian? Noticed." She came back out with arms full of the protective pads we used when training and dumped them against the table, then went back, still talking. "He only lectured me for the first twenty minutes of our hike, and helped dig out the burrows, too."

"Should we worry?" Stavros really wouldn't harm a human, and he'd completely lost the scary as heck father-vampire protective vibe. Still.

Vee dragged a chair out and shoved it beside mine, grabbing a rag and cleaning balm, starting in scrubbing a big rectangular pad. "Only about lectures. Like I said, I got mine earlier."

"Fatherly lecture, and digging up 'chup burrows. Insult to injury." I dropped into my chair, and went back to cleaning and conditioning the gloves. Basically, our penance work, because, sweaty leather used by multiple people every week equaled not especially great smells.

"Right? I truly am sorry," Vee said.

"We're going to have to split the blame. I didn't have to accept your challenge. I have no excuses, aside from being frustrated, and allowing emotion to lead me. You had every right to express your opinion yesterday and today."

"Have you spoken with Marshall?" She put effort into polishing the pad, staring at it like it might go AWOL if she didn't.

"Add being a complete coward to my list of crimes today."

"Like you said, shared blame. Chem-treated knives? Not a well thought out move on my part."

"What were you thinking?" Vee was impulsive, but she wasn't undisciplined and never took her role as C.O. lightly.

"You be honest and I will, too." She dared a look at me. "It was one thing when you were all twisted up about Marshall in a general sense. Like, hey, maybe Liv is taking a brief detour on the civi side, which is unusual, but only a passing, academic interest. Then I spent time with him and I *get it* now. He's so sweet and kind and—"

"And so Marshall."

She nodded, ponytail bobbing. "Talking with him this morning nearly broke my heart. Relocating him to some random city and generic job and him being all alone, it wasn't working for me."

"Did you do it on purpose?" I didn't need to specify what *it* was. She had been injured far worse on missions, including those in areas where a civilian might stumble in, and had never done the eyes and losing control thing despite some serious provocations.

"No. Maybe no?" She dropped the cleaning rag. "I couldn't miss how much he already means to you—and to the guys, who are treating him like one of them—and how much Marshall cares about all of you, so maybe not *consciously* on purpose, but maybe unconsciously on purpose? Like, I'd considered our nominating him for a permanent Asset position, preferably here, or if not and they felt he needed more training first, at HQ. But I also kept thinking about how you didn't like that much distance between you, and if it was me and B, and even if we were only friends and not together-together, I wouldn't either, and then subconsciously my brain was working on what circumstances would allow him to join the team without Oversight totally freaking and nuking us, and sometimes my newbie vampire brain gets fixated—"

"First, breathe. Second, you thought of accidentally letting him see what you and Stavros were, and since he was already a temporary Asset, there was a plausible reason for Oversight to agree, in order to keep our secret all in the family." Our precarious position aside, and our shock at

Oversight's Assessors originally suspecting us all when Vee returned—HQ and the Assessors were meant to be agent support, to help us, not to punish us. That role and avenue to turn to for aid was deeply ingrained in all of us.

She gave in, shredding a cuticle even as she made a face at getting a taste of cleaning compound. "Yes." She did the corner of the eye thing, no longer looking at me straight on. "Plus, he made you—you were more content, in a way that…" She trailed off, neither of us ready to face things like why I was now a C.O., and why her subconscious felt the need to do what she did.

I quit pretending to clean, and admitted the truth I'd refused to verbalize. "I'd prefer he be part of the Company, too, and if the situation was reversed, I'd do some version of the same thing for you and Bruce. I'm not sure it's fair to ask Marshall to belong to something he doesn't believe in, and that's inherently risky and violent, and it isn't as if we'd discussed whether he could or would deal with our lifestyle. Although I doubt Marshall is even willing to speak to me now, so, there's that. Which leaves what options?"

"Begging for forgiveness? You were trying to protect him by not telling the truth, and I had no idea how my springing the whole 'Hey, Vee's a vampire' reveal would come across, how deeply feeling as if he wasn't worth being trusted would wound him."

I sank lower in my seat. "I harped so hard on how people are always more important than cryptids, how vicious cryptids are, and that it was vital he understand the difference and that we, the Company, were in the right."

"B forgave me for being dead for a year. In comparison, your situational ethics are a tiny infraction." She held two fingers a centimeter apart. "Infinitesimal. Plus, you aren't coming back as, say, a vampire. It's all about context."

"You and Bruce were sleeping together and in a relationship. He had already bought a ring. That's a far greater emotional investment."

Vee drummed her fingers on the table for a second, forehead scrunched, searching for alternate plans, exactly the way we once brainstormed mission plans. "Fair point. Marshall has fewer options though. It is an ugly way to look at it, but true. Forgive you or…"

Or go back to HQ, which he hated but would probably prefer to being in the same house with me. HQ was kind of out for other reasons, too.

"Is it also abnormal that neither of us is acting as if Marshall reporting us to HQ is a realistic worry?" I asked.

"It should be? But he didn't think, didn't care about the danger earlier, just threw himself between me and you guys. All he cared about was you and giving you a chance to get to safety. That was—amazing." Vee went all dreamy.

Amazing and terrifying. That Marshall still didn't see himself as important wasn't healthy, especially around cryptids. "I agree. He has every right to hate us, and he may, but I don't think turning us in out of anger or revenge would ever cross his mind."

"exactly. Marshall is worth some groveling," she continued. "I would, if it wouldn't freak him out worse."

"I know."

"I'll finish these, then Stavros and I will pack. That might help, too."

I peeled myself out of the chair. Realistically, forgiveness wasn't on the menu. That didn't excuse me from assuring Marshall that going forward we would respect his boundaries, let him know Vee was leaving, and offer him the option of returning to HQ. I didn't get to act selfish and keep my dignity.

I owed Marshall at least that much as far as making him feel comfortable until he could leave us in his rearview. If yelling at me in detail about how awful I was helped, I owed him that, too.

Taking a deep breath, more nervous then when walking into HQ to petition to leave my old team, I rapped lightly on his closed door. "It's Liv."

Absolute silence answered me, no guitar and metal power ballads tonight.

"Can I see that you're all right? Physically all right? I take responsibility for what happened today, and understand that my actions hurt you, and I'm not asking for anything other than a check-in. Then I will go and leave you in peace."

The crack of pool balls signaled that the rest of the team was inside now. Vee's head inched around the edge of the entry, peering into the hall. She tilted her head in a *'Yes or no?'* question. I shrugged and shook my head. She bit her lip and disappeared back to the game.

For a cowardly moment, I toyed with having Jace come ask. He was go-to crowd control for a reason. He wasn't the leader, though. My decision, my fallout.

I pulled in a deep breath and determination. "There are a couple of things I need you to know, then you can yell at me." I paused, in case he opened the door.

When the view remained the same, I continued. "Vee is my sister. The Company was her life, the same as it's mine. It's who we are. Then, we thought she'd been killed. She died alone, and we weren't there, and it was awful. Then a year later, she comes back, but infected. It was my duty to terminate her, the way it would have been hers had I been the one infected. And I failed in my duty. I couldn't do it, and I couldn't give the order for our brother Josh to do it."

I slid down the wall, arms wrapped around my knees,

swamped by the grief and fear I'd thought was under control. Jace had been right about being blindsided. "Vee stayed away until she learned control. Stavros trained her. Then she came back, and basically said decide. Was she an agent, or was she dead. I can't count the people she and Stavros have saved."

This would be a good stopping point. Something in me wanted Marshall to at least understand what I was willing to sacrifice our friendship over. My throat hurt at the loss. I squeezed words out anyway. "Vee's team specializes in eliminating vampires. She hates them, more so now than before she was infected. She and Stavros can get into places we can't, do things that had been beyond any agent's abilities. Her entire team is under constant surveillance and there are a ton of unbreakable rules for their continued survival. I'm a double agent, reporting on Vee to our superiors. I suppose triple agent, since I'm only feeding them whatever will keep our teams alive."

The door stayed firmly closed. For all I knew, Marshall had his earbuds in, and hadn't even heard me. Since it was just me, I admitted my weakness aloud for the first time. "I decided to lie to the world, and not because Vee and Stavros are an unparalleled weapon for good, but because she's my sister and I love her."

Using the wall, I stood. My let's-talk-to-Marshall experiment could now officially go down as yet another mistake on my part. "We'll all stay out of the kitchen. It's clear whenever you want to grab something. There's even leftover pizza someone brought in." More like Matteo picked up Marshall's favorite, and then carefully put the entire thing in the fridge, shoving other food aside so the box was conspicuously visible.

Marshall's door opened, enough to glimpse bed and footlocker. I froze—was he expecting me to already be gone, or still be here so he could tell me how crappy I was?

Before I landed on choice A or choice B, the door swung wide, Marshall filling the doorway. I couldn't interpret his expression, which was bad, but he was wearing the blue hoodie, which might be good. That or he'd tossed the old one and this was the only one available, and it meant nothing.

"I'm leaving." I inched to the right, aimed at the exit.

He gave a small shake of his head, expression not altering.

I tucked my hands behind me and leaned back against the wall, giving him space.

His clear, blue gaze drilled into me. "Apologizing by explaining isn't an apology."

"I know," I whispered. "For what little it's worth, I'm sorry about acting childish, arguing with Vee and fighting like we were brainless first year cadets, especially around you."

"But you're not sorry for lying."

I scuffed my toe along the worn floor, the aged oak undoubtedly witness to hundreds of dramatic moments over its centuries. "What you asked earlier, outside? My not telling you our sister and father were vampires, even as I brought them into a house with you, wasn't because I didn't think you were smart, or because I didn't trust you. Partially, it was to keep you safer since in this case, the less you knew meant a greater layer of protection, and partially it was duty and keeping my sisters and brother secure by obeying rules. I left that team and them but...I can't lose them."

Marshall shoved his hands in his pockets, but crossed the hall and mirrored me, back to the wall. He seemed entranced by the toes of his battered kicks instead of the floor. "My head is telling me it wasn't your secret to share. The rest of me—half is mad. Furious. Half thinks it's cool that you protect everybody you care about, no matter what crap life throws at you. Then there's the half that's freaked that vampires are in our compound, and they ate my pie."

He braced his heel against the wall, and all the icy fury

vanished, back to being my too-kind Marshall. "Half plus half plus half is more parts than there should be. So maybe it's thirds of me that're conflicted, instead of halves."

I bit the inside of my cheek hard. A borderline hysterical snort-giggle still escaped, partially fueled by punchy-silly relief that he didn't hate me. I was acting inappropriately, but sometimes—rarely, and at *the worst* times—my body decided laughing was the best way to go.

Marshall jerked his gaze to my face, shocked I'd laughed. Righteous. Indignant. Judgmental. Which was also thirds. Another snort escaped, despite my trying to keep a repentant look plastered on my face. Repentant-ier, anyway, which, also not a word, or appropriate.

"Seriously, Liv?" He scowled, an impressive one when backed by his size. But then there was the cartoon tee peeking from under his hoodie, and the curl that refused to stay confined by bandanna or gravity.

"Sorry! Sorry. You sounded—Josh used to do that every time Kimi tricked him out of his chocolate milk when we were kids." Cartoon tee and all, Marshall glared and crossed his big arms, sleeves tightening around his biceps. It was awesome. "Exactly like Josh. He was five or six."

"Little kids can't bake ham frittatas." He looked down his nose at me. "Think about that."

His playfulness sliced the last of the cord of worry knotted around my heart. Vee had been right. In attempting to ignore the truth, I'd gone too far, pushing Marshall away. As far as he was concerned, we were friends and for no reason, I had turned into a jerk overnight.

"Point taken. One-hundred-percent. Definitely not laughing. Speaking of food, are you hungry? Even if you aren't, we should dispose of leftovers on principle, before Jace discovers their existence." Cold pizza was an excellent way to get back in our friend zone, on my part. There was nothing confusing or amorous about congealed cheese.

"Wait." I stopped before I really started moving, reminded of my promise. "Vee and Stavros are still here."

"The gate notice never sounded, so I kinda guessed they were."

"I can lock them in their rooms, or bring pizza here. Impromptu pizza picnic on the floor?"

Marshall's fingers flexed, running through scales on an invisible guitar. "Stavros is…"

I helped Marshall out. "To all appearances, a moderately stuffy and highly stern killjoy? Then underneath that, the kind of unsettlingly scary four-hundred-years cultivates?"

"Um…"

"Let's call that a yes."

"Vee was—I liked her, you know? I feel like I oughta apologize or something. How do you apologize for assuming someone wanted to snap your neck and suck all your blood? Or maybe recruit you into a trafficking ring?"

"A Death By Chocolate cake, with 'Oops, sorry' written in edible gold? There's a patisserie downtown that will totally do that. They expect odd orders from us, and roll with it." When he gave me a long-suffering sigh, very similar to Stavros', I nudged Marshall's arm. "I promise, she isn't mad or offended. She is also deeply sorry about earlier, and going all creepy vampire."

Marshall rolled his head, neck popping, and unzipped the hoodie, tossing it into his room. He headed us toward the main part of the house. "I dunno. What about—"

The fridge door slammed as we turned into the kitchen. Vee straightened and we shared a silent *'oh, crap'* moment.

"Just leaving," she mumbled around the spoon stuck in her mouth, and backed away, keeping the table between her and us.

"You should stay." His chest expanded on a deep inhale. "There's hot chocolate to go with your snack. There can be, if you want a mug, because even if she hasn't said it, Liv does, and she mentioned you like chocolate, too."

"To be clear, we're talking real chocolate, with real milk and copious amounts of sugar?" Vee asked around the spoon.

I shouldered my way into the no-man's-land between them. "Marshall does not subject people to the low fat, low sugar, lower tastiness version that Bruce insists—" I narrowed my eyes, train of thought derailed by outrage. "Oh. My. God. Is that *my* pie? That is my pie," I answered myself.

Vee twisted the plastic-sealed dessert plate behind her back. "Nope. No pie."

"You put that slice back *for me*, and now you're stealing it?"

"Crud." She produced the contraband and set it on the table, along with the spoon. "Sorry, Marshall."

He stared at her for a beat, then his face pinked.

"Yes, vampires have excellent hearing. However, she was an eves-dropper long before she was a pie-thieving vampire." I pulled cocoa supplies out. "She does *not* get cocoa."

"I didn't mean that, about you eating my pie. I'll make another for everyone, whatever kind you prefer." Marshall circled around me to Vee, brow crinkled. "You were wounded today, and you need to heal—needed to," he stumbled on. "I've worked in lots of traditional restaurants. I can make a blood sausage or a blood pudding, if it will help you. Both of you," he added as Stavros halted in the doorway, examining Marshall, head cocked. Marshall didn't flinch or hesitate at the influx of vampires.

Vee's expression went full-on romantic, meet-cute dreamy. Which mirrored mine, in all honesty.

"It is kind of you to offer, and very appreciated." Relaxed

wasn't in Stavros' vocabulary, but for the first time since he arrived, his watchfulness was gone, peace in its place. "However, our needs have been adequately met for now."

Yeah, like that would deter Vee, or Marshall. I hopped onto the bar counter and got comfy, waiting for the fun. Letting my legs swing, calf brushing against Marshall.

"If cooking ruins the blood, I'll pick up fresh from the butcher tomorrow." Marshall pulled out his phone, already making his version of notes. "Pork or beef? Wild game?"

Vee touched the back of his free hand. When he only waited for her answer, finger suspended over the phone screen, Vee clasped his hand and smiled. "We seriously appreciate the offer, but animal blood isn't on our menu any more than human blood."

So much for Stavros' peace. He attempted to contain the emerging situation, and my sister. "Niña, think—"

Vee talked over him. "We don't touch humans or animals because we live solely off other cryptids, primarily vampires."

Stavros threw up his hands and stalked out, muttering about non-secret secrets, and something about life having been safer facing conquistadors than living with us.

He understood what Vee telling Marshall meant. She'd adopted Marshall. Despite the mild theatrics, Stavros agreed with her decision. Otherwise, he'd either have hauled her outdoors before she'd had a chance to finish the first word, or still be in here, vampiric hunting face on, threatening Marshall as he'd once done with Bruce.

Marshall cleared his throat, and I tensed to intervene if mentioning blood and drinking in the same though went too far for his acceptance. "That's why you can be in the sun and don't set off scans, and can carry chem-weapons."

"There's a few more parameters involved as far as gaining our abilities, but yes." Vee's smile morphed into a naughty grin. "It allows us to do a number of things we shouldn't be capable of."

Marshall took over snack prep, grabbing the chocolate and shaving flakes off into a pot. "Feeding—" He glanced at Vee and she nodded. "—feeding off other vampires makes you sharper and stronger. That's why you're better now at finding and killing them then Liv."

I said, "As if," at the same time Vee said, "I was better than her *way* before being infected."

Vee ignored my eye roll and kept talking. "The blood is part of the boost Stavros and I use. It's also a secret that would bring every super-old vampire down on our heads. Only a few ancient ones even know it's possible, and they brutally obliterate any hints or rumors. Stavros and I don't exist as far as vampire-dom is concerned. We can't."

"That information would create anarchy." Marshall sat the pan on a burner, reached for something, and frowned when he didn't find his objective. He transferred the frown to me. "Milk, Liv."

Vee snickered and re-appropriated the pie, pulling out a chair at the table. "Yeah, Liv. Quit slacking."

There would so be payback coming Vee's way. She took a bite of my pie, then obnoxiously licked the back of the spoon, smiling at me.

So much payback.

She and Marshall carried on with cryptid political theory while I acted as kitchen drudge. Who knew comics prepared you for acceptance of vampire dietary needs, and cryptid social structures?

I mentally played around with the logistics of Vee's bring-Marshall-in scheme, twisting it into different configurations. A position at HQ might work, only a matter of an interview and moving his designation from temporary Asset to permanent, and wouldn't require revealing he knew what Vee and Stavros were. We went in monthly for DNA and blood samples, part of the agreement to monitor us and prove Stavros wasn't building a Company-trained vampire army. HQ was also far safer, its size and number of Instructors and agents insulating it from attack in a way team compounds couldn't be.

Although Marshall might never be comfortable there, even after getting to know us as people instead of soldiers. HQ felt far away now, in a manner it never had before.

Our compound had plenty of room, and we were well protected with security devices created specifically to hold off cryptids. Those devices weren't infallible though. They could theoretically be overwhelmed by sheer numbers if vampires or other species attacked en-mass. That hadn't happened since modern weapons and scientific break-throughs had given us the advantage, but it was still possible. No compound was ever safe in the civilian sense.

The fact he'd thrown himself between us and cryptids was a huge issue. Part of my lectures had stuck, just not the most important one. He refused to believe he wasn't expend-able. The sick feeling when he'd basically shoved his wrist into Vee's mouth, his first instinct to sacrifice himself as freaking food for a cryptid, settled into my stomach again.

If he found a job in Scottsdale or Phoenix, I could see him any time he felt sociable. Which skirted our rule not to be memorable, and not to draw attention. We spread our needs out among stores, restaurants, gas stations, even karaoke bars and pizza places. We couldn't truly have a favorite anything. The same with a set routine. We varied days, and times of day, to shop or patrol. Real outside friendships were a no-go for the same reason. Cryptids would memorize a routine. They'd do the same for any spot we hit constantly.

Seeing Marshall as often as I wanted risked bringing cryptids straight to his door. One that didn't have agents in residence to protect it.

Perhaps even more dire, either of the latter options meant him officially knowing who and what Vee and Stavros were. I hadn't even touched on their position as an off-books strike team, which Oversight would disavow knowledge of should things go wrong. Nor had I mentioned all the rules we now lived under, the reality of half Vee's team being implanted with kill switches. Joining us, or becoming involved as a long-term Asset with me, put Marshall in the same precarious position as Vee's and my teams.

Vee's certainty that Oversight would ever allow anyone to join us, that simply asking permission, or reporting that Marshall had discovered what Vee was, wouldn't violate our agreement in the eyes of Oversight was naïve at best. Delusional at worst.

Another far more realistic possibility was that Marshall might like us, but not enough to want us around once he got back into the real world. None of Vee's schemes, or my half-baked daydreams, would matter in that case.

As a reminder of how complicated the real world was, the security system came to life in a flash of color, and the front gate opening.

At least one inhabitant of the vehicle would veto any such plan. Loudly, and violently. While the scan completed, and *Approved Occupants* and their names flowed across the screen, I mouthed, "Does he know?" at Vee.

She shook her head, and worried at a cuticle. Thanks to the official request filed at HQ and granted, he knew Marshall was here. The rest…

Marshall hesitated mid-stir, melting chocolate clinging to the whisk he held, and he looked at me.

"This is the rest of Vee's crew. Our sister Kimi, our

brother Josh, and Bruce, Vee's fiancée and the chef we mentioned. Jace and Josh are twins, so brace yourself." I hoped my smile came across as reassuring.

"Whoa. B set a new record. I didn't expect him until close to dawn." Vee abandoned her dessert spoils, and headed for the garage.

"That's why I'm the smarter sister," I caroled at her retreating form. "You are so busted." I went back to swinging my legs, an outlet for the hit of nervous energy. My calf brushed Marshall again, and I hitched an inch closer as reassurance for us both.

He sort of shook himself, and went back to stirring. "How come Vee's in trouble?"

"She came straight here from her last call-out, instead of returning to the temporary base, then coming here. Bruce gets antsy when they don't come home, even knowing they weren't injured. On top of that, he had a job that didn't wrap up until tonight, and he couldn't come yell at her in person any sooner." Hopefully, he'd get the worst of his venting out in the garage, chewing out Vee and Stavros. Then once he'd calmed and been here long enough to really get to know Marshall, Vee and I could admit to our crime without Bruce freaking.

I stole a stray curl of milk chocolate and nibbled. Fortifying myself for the coming event. Bruce had an attitude, an extensive vocabulary, and wasn't intimidated by anyone, including Vee. Plus, he lived every day on the precarious line we all walked, and with Vee's tendency for out-of-the-box plans and solutions. Add on what amounted to a pre-teen's emotions and reasoning, which Vee was in vampire years, and he had every reason to be slightly enraged and highly worried.

Our unspoken agreement had always been him showing us there were more options than automatically sacrificing ourselves in the line of duty, and my remaining realistic and acting as the voice of logic and rules. Between us, we protected the team, even if that played out as protecting them from themselves. From the outside, to him, it now looked as if I'd flaked on my side of the checks and balances. Despite his bluster and tenacity, Bruce felt everything deeply, including the experience of losing Vee once.

"Are they vampires?" Marshall asked, barely audible over swish and clink of the whisk through liquid, seeming more curious than concerned

"All human." I twisted so he and I were in our own private bubble. "Be straight with me. Is having Vee and Stavros here too much? The only reason she didn't leave immediately was because her team was already on the road. They intended to meet here and go on to their primary compound. Vee will leave first thing in the morning as planned, if you say the word."

"Milk."

I opened the carton and leaned to pour it into the pan as he kept the whisk in motion.

Marshall shifted so my leg was back in contact, butted firmly against his hip. "They're your family and you guys are glad to see them. They shouldn't leave."

"That's not what I asked. Your opinion is as valid as Matteo or Jace's, and you get a say in who stays or goes."

He stared at me like he was trying to see through me, and his hand slowed. Hot milk and chocolate popped, threatening to boil over. Marshall lifted the pan and I shoved mugs under, already well trained. "Vee is—awesome runs in your family, so meeting your other brother and sister is cool. Stavros is okay, too," Marshall said, dividing the drink between the three mugs.

"Once he knows you, his real personality comes out. He's pretty awesome all on his own."

"Should I make enough for three more?" He tilted the empty pot at me.

"Another for Kimi, definitely. She will be all over this. Oh, she can hear, but she speaks in ASL, American Sign Language, with some custom Company additions." She'd jot notes as needed for newbies, but I needed to let her know that wasn't an option. "She'll let you lip read until you learn, and I'll help. There's probably an old tablet here with her favorite text to voice app, too," I added, stealing the mug with the most whipped cream, taking a sip before the crowd descended.

Mouth full, I hopped down to grab another carton of milk from the fridge.

"You've got—" Marshall pointed at his upper lip.

Instead of noticing yet again that he had great lips, I concentrated on swiping at mine.

"You missed. C'mere." He shook out the all-purpose towel he'd used as a mitt. Bracing his thumb under my lower lip, he wiped a spot closer to my chin. His thumb swept back and forth, a soft caress that sent a shiver through me. "There. Better."

I caught the edge of the towel, linking us together, and nodded at the bandage covering his forearm. "What about that?"

"It's fine." Instead of letting go of the towel, he rolled the slack around his finger.

I followed the tug closer. Enough that the heat I felt was from him, not the range. "It didn't look fine. I can never make up for this afternoon, and I don't expect you to forgive me. It doesn't need to be one of us cleaning those wounds. There's a twenty-four hour walk-in clinic in town. If you don't want stuck in a car with me, Matteo will go along as shotgun in a heartbeat. Kimi too. You already know each other from the gamer nights. Please."

Marshall twisted the towel again, and his fingers touched mine, then slid up and caught my hand. His thumb ran back and forth over my knuckles in the same way he'd touched my chin. "I'm not mad at you or Matteo or Jace. I've processed it all. This secret was about more than you or even the team, and you had to protect the people you love."

"All the people I truly care about, the ones who would leave a gaping hole in my heart if anything happened to them, are under this roof tonight." I caught his hand in both of mine. "So please pick a bodyguard and go to the clinic. You've been a hero once today, and that is plenty."

Marshall's other hand curved around our joined fingers. "I'd go anywhere with you, for real. I don't need a doctor though. See?" He peeled the non-stick pad back, exposing skin. "I took a shower to help cool off, and dumped a bottle of peroxide over it."

Scratches patterned his arm, some shallow and already scabbing, others deeper. I settled for, "You've had a rough day," and smoothed the bandage to cover the evidence that I kind of sucked. "There's only one remedy for rough days."

"What is it?" His fingertips rested where I'd rearranged the bandage, then dropped.

I opened the fridge and pointed. My solution wasn't much, but all I had for now.

"Pizza? Pizza and chocolate?" His auburn brows went up.

I shoved the red and white box at him and he grabbed the corners while I went for the milk that had been my original goal. "How could you, as a chef, not know pizza and chocolate go with everything? They're highly medicinal. And this is our last chance for at least forty-eight hours," I said, as barked questions and demands bounced and echoed through the breezeway, heralding Bruce's arrival.

Marshall turned toward the commotion, then checked back with me. "Is something wrong?"

"Nope. That is peak Bruce. Why speak in a well-modulated tone when you can yell? Also, healthy eating tyrant. It's all farm to table, seasonal and organic only, blah, blah."

I hit the button on the microwave, popping open the door. "Hurry before he confiscates all the good stuff."

CHAPTER 43

Marshall

IT TOOK Marshall a few seconds to understand Liv wasn't kidding.

She sighed and slouched against the counter, tucking the full mugs behind her back and out of sight, as people filled the kitchen. Only three extra, but the room shrank a little around the edges. He only needed to remind his brain that these were Liv's family, and everyone he'd met from it had been like Liv. Good. Patient. Not annoyed or freaked when he didn't act like other people.

The tall, pretty guy in front was easy. Not Jace's identical twin, but close enough. Same open, easy smile, and he sketched a wave in Marshall's direction. Then grunted as the person behind him shoved, moving him along bodily. "Dang, Kimi." When he didn't move fast enough, the woman gave up and ducked under his arm.

Kimi, the third sister, was reassuringly familiar too,

between Liv and Vee's size, skin more golden than their dark brown. Instead of Liv's waves or Vee's silky straightness, she had long, copper-tinted spirals. Her elegant hands moved fast in the sign language Liv mentioned.

Whatever she said, Liv sighed. "He's wound up, of course. Sorry you and Josh had to listen to him for six hours."

Kimi reached into a BDU pocket, came out with an earbud case she flashed, then tucked it back away. She cocked her head, and despite Liv's claiming she was all-human, zoned in like she had vampire senses, reaching around Liv and coming out with a mug. She propped beside Liv, shoulder to shoulder and they tipped their heads so that they touched in welcome for a minute. She wiggled, getting comfortable, completely at home.

She was an agent, and Liv's sister, and had every right to be here. Like she saw inside his head the way Liv did, Kimi turned her attention to him, and slowly mouthed, "Nice to meet IRL," and yeah, the reminder that they already knew each other made it easier to relax with her, same as with Vee now.

The comfortable atmosphere lasted two seconds.

"Where the hell is Stavros? Four-fucking-hundred-years and he still can't adhere to a simple protocol." The voice bounced ahead of the speaker thanks to the breezeway's acoustics. He stomped in, Vee right behind him.

Marshall missed whatever Vee or Liz replied, the blood drumming in his temples drowning out conversation. Liv's comments about her friend and handmade pasta and being on TV gelled. Vee's fiancé, the cook who she and Liv mentioned so offhand, looked the same as in every publicity shot. The same as when he'd chewed out the whole kitchen that one afternoon, the one where the owner fired them all on the spot, Marshall's first day on the job.

The guy folded his arms, the full-sleeve tattoos bright

JANET WALDEN-WEST

under the overhead lighting. Despite being only inches taller
than Vee, which made him one of the two shortest people in
the compound, he controlled the room. He glared through
black rimmed glasses, taking them all in.

His flinty brown-eyed gaze slid over Marshall without a
flicker of recognition, then stopped on the pizza box in
Marshall's hands. Framed by a dark goatee, its precise lines
sharp enough to cut someone, the guy's lip lifted off one
tooth, his opinion clear.

Without looking back, he demanded, "You've been eating
this trash?"

Behind him, Vee rolled her eyes, and made a slashing
motion in front of her throat.

Liv pushed her mug to safety on the counter. "Not just
pizza. Probably tiny doughnuts and weird sport's drinks too,
although I can't confirm—you know how they are about
subterfuge. But definitely pie. Rhubarb. She loves the stuff."
Her smile was all teeth and satisfaction.

Vee's eyes narrowed. Way scarier than when they'd
glowed vampire silver. A gravelly snicker escaped Kimi.
Sisters played *rough* here.

"I fucking well believe all of you have chemical-soaked
junk food squirreled away here, except squirrels have more
sense than to touch that garbage. Since when do you like
rhubarb?" He glared over his shoulder at Vee.

Whose *I-will-get-you-back* expression morphed to innocent confusion. "Hm?"

"Since this week. There was something about it being the
best pie she ever ate, too," Liv added.

Vee mouthed a believable death threat from behind her
fiancé, but Liv only pushed off the counter and stopped in
front of one of the most notorious cult-celebrity chefs in the
country, and slapped Bruce 'The Bastard' Kantor's thick
wrists.

He dropped his arms and reeled Liv in, hugging hard enough muscles stood out, as she said, "Missed you, grumpy guts."

"Changing the subject won't fucking work." Despite the warning, he hung on for a minute, then mostly let go, an arm around her shoulder, giving one last squeeze, like he was reassuring her.

The look they exchanged held some kind of silent, coded conversation. She nodded, and after a second, a degree of the aggression he'd come in with fell away. However it had happened, it was easy to see he meant as much to Liv as her sisters and the rest of her family did.

Liv stepped from under her future brother's grip as boots thumped on tile and the other three soldiers quit the den and thundered into the room. Or two did, Stavros bringing up the rear, his entry silent and intimidating. Hugs were handed out left and right, even to the fiancé. If Marshall only though of him as Vee's fiancé, it created a layer of protection between him and the arrogant, powerful chef.

Marshall felt a different distance open between him and the team. Unless it had always been there, and he was only now noticing. He was the only one not at home, because this *wasn't* his. He was a short-term friend, not part of the loud, tight family. He inched back, looking for a space to slip through and go, to leave Liv and the rest alone to enjoy each other. His shoulders bumped the slick metal of the fridge instead.

Like she sensed his retreat, Liv veered around his way, between him and the crowd. "Guys, this is Marshall. Marshall, the rest of the crew—Bruce, Josh, and Kimi."

"Man, you lit that last game charge up. You nearly ended us," Josh said. "Props."

Matteo bulled through and thumped an arm around Marshall's shoulders. "We got our own chef, yo." Despite his

329

size, Matteo glanced sideways at Marshall, his dark eyes uncertain, and hopeful.

The implication would've staggered Marshall if he wasn't caught between an immovable appliance and over two-hundred pounds of nearly as immovable agent. Matteo was asking for forgiveness. For Marshall not to be angry at him.

Jace watched them, and Marshall caught a quieter, but equally clear version of Matteo's question on the other agent's face. What Marshall thought mattered to the team. They cared if he was pissed, or disappointed with them.

He set the pizza on the counter with Liv's mug and nodded to the room. "Hey. Glad you got here okay."

A polite touch on his elbow registered. When he checked, Kimi raised her mug in a clear toast.

Heat prickled along his skin, a little nervous, a little embarrassed, but he managed, "Thanks. I'll make more whenever you want."

That earned him a smile, one that created a dimple in Kimi's heart-shaped face. Along with a low growl from the other side of the room.

"You for real have to feed these two?" Josh shoved his twin, and got a shove in return, obviously an old game. "Say the word, man, and I'll lay down cover fire and get you outta here."

Careful not to look at the chef glaring a hole through him, Marshall shrugged. "They aren't bad. Pretty easy to cook for."

"Move your equipment, and keep your knives out of my way." Vee's angry fiancé shrugged a strap off his shoulder, and carefully laid the double-sized leather and canvas case on the island, the logo of the most prestigious culinary award in the U.S. stamped on the leather. "I need space."

The prickles turned to an inferno, and Marshall's face burned at the question, because, yeah, real chef's had knives.

Liv stretched then slid between him and Kimi, picking up a mug. "The vampires, or at least their human associates, destroyed Marshall's apartment. He literally came out with what he was wearing that night."

The chef's eyes narrowed, weirdly magnified behind the glasses' lens. "I thought the raid went down in a hotel kitchen."

"Several of the targets evaded us, and tracked Marshall home," Liv said, her expression the one where she was blaming herself. "They trashed his possessions and equipment."

The guy looked Marshall over, expression calling bullshit. "He looks pretty damn well dressed to me."

"Slowly replacing necessities. Clothes before knives," Liv said, still acting like Marshall was important enough to own real tools.

"I thought I taught you better." The chef's tone pretty much said he knew Liv was lying and there was no way Marshall was legit.

"Your time is better spent unloading." Stavros' voice rolled across the room like smoke, spreading calm. "We've compared notes with Olivia, as well as Terrance, and the results bear discussing."

"Exactly. Come on. I'll help." Vee steered her fiancé, hand twisted in his sleeve, heading him back at the garage.

"Comparing notes sounds like work for C.O.'s, which we're not." Jace whistled and made a circular motion. "Move out. We got CoW on pause, and a game to win."

Matteo sprinted for the den. "Shotgun."

"You can't call shotgun on the good chairs," Josh yelled from the breezeway, and abandoned unloading gear in favor of racing the other agent to the game room.

Marshall eased around, headed the opposite direction. Liv and her sisters had their hot chocolate. No use

331

pretending that if people got hungry later they'd want him to cook, not with Kantor here.

"Marsh, man, let's hit it," Jace said, stopping him.

Behind Marshall, Kimi poked at him, her elbows plenty pointy. She jerked her head toward the guys' high-decibel argument, then poked harder, herding him along.

So much for innocent dimples. In real life, she was as bossy as during their online bouts. Marshall sighed and did Kimi's bidding.

CHAPTER 44

L iv

OUT OF MARSHALL'S SIGHT, Kimi signed, "I'll keep them distracted," before she turned the corner to the den.

Under no illusions as to what Kimi was distracting them from, I put the pizza away, then took a chair.

Stavros took the one to my right, back as ramrod straight as always, crossing an ankle over his knee. His order rumbled out, seemingly to the room. "Cease baiting the boy."

Bruce stomped into view with his duffle over one shoulder, and Vee's she'd left at the base in her rush to get here, over the other. "He's a grown-assed adult, and a problem. We'll be discussing your damn role in this security breach next."

When Bruce reappeared after dumping the supplies in his and Vee's room, Stavros picked up the conversation. "Soldiers though you are, you're all children to me. You are certainly acting more akin to a child in the throes of a tantrum than an adult."

He gave me a pointed look, then transferred it to Vee as she slunk in, probably already having picked up on Stavros' less than pleased aura, that hive bond thing the virus created between related vampires. "I've had enough of tantrums for one day, as has Marshall."

Vee winced, and we shared a look.

Bruce jerked the fridge open, coming close to cracking Stavros in the shin. "All that walking complication has done is make a mess in my kitchen. I don't count that as exhausting physical or emotional labor."

Silently, I checked with Vee, because Stavros sounded like he was about to spill *everything*. *'He isn't. Is he?'*

She shook her head, but more a super wishful *'Probably not?'* than a real statement.

Stavros gave the two of us measured looks.

He was. He so was. Stavros was outing us, Vee's and my pettiness, and by extension, Marshall.

Stavros rarely interfered, unless it was for a life lesson we had yet to experience, and he deemed it vital. Those lessons were never pleasant.

Vee went for a cuticle as Stavros continued. "He's faced down a vampire in order to give Olivia and her team a window to retreat to safety or arm themselves more appropriately. Leave him be."

Stavros now trusted Marshall, and Stavros trusted no one outside our family. Meaning he'd not only accepted Marshall, but considered him one of us and worth fighting for. His support blunted a little of the dread of what was coming next.

Bruce jerked out of the depths of the SubZero, gaze hitting Vee, then bouncing to me and sticking. "There was a call out today, that I'm only now hearing about? One serious enough that the entire team went through its primary and backup ammunition. Son of a—"

This was my base, Marshall being here had been my decision, and today's pettiness was half my fault. I accepted responsibility. "There wasn't a call-out or mission. Aside from Mattaeo picking up pizza, we never left the compound."

The tension in the room ratcheted up until it should have hit the visible spectrum.

Bruce straightened. He removed his glasses, and polished them on his polo as his face went from stroke-red to deathly pale, harbinger of the storm about to sweep the room.

Deceptively calm, he put his glasses back on. "You fucking told an outsider. What. Vee. Is." He bit the last word off, and braced his fists on the table, head bent. "You don't fuck up, Liv. You sure as fuck don't bend rules, not for random damn civilians, and never at the expense of your sister's and brother's lives."

The accusations stung like salt pelting exposed nerves. I'd never betrayed the pact we'd made, the trust between us before.

"This wasn't—" Vee tried mediating.

I cut her off. "It wasn't planned, although yes, I am culpable. I was careless while training, the situation escalated, and Marshall was unfortunately in a position where he observed it all."

"You exposed—" Bruce stopped, but only because he was too angry to pick a response.

Vee circled around us to get to him.

"This certainly wasn't anything I'd purposely sanction," I admitted. "However, Marshall isn't a threat. *I* am telling you Marshall isn't a danger to Vee or any other member of our teams. And lower your voice."

Bruce wound up for another tirade. Stavros hand sliced

down, vampire force and speed behind it, and the air whistled, one painfully shrill blast that left all of us flinching, ears popping. "Olivia is correct. He offered himself as a sacrifice to protect her and the team, without hesitation, with no regard for his own life. There's no subterfuge in him, but there is loyalty and bravery."

Bruce met Stavros glare for glare. "All you have are fucking opinions, with nothing to back them up but *feelings.* If you are that damn stupid, feel fucking free to risk your life. Hell, maybe you are so damn old you don't care anymore and are looking for an end and a way out. But that isn't enough reason to risk Vee and Josh's lives. I don't like this and I don't like him."

"I did not like you when I first met you, nor did I want you near my daughter," Stavros countered, face thinning for an instant, the ancient predator in him that the virus had created coming to the fore. "You had done nothing to earn trust or forgiveness. Marshall has faced down his nightmares to protect one of my daughters."

I squeezed Stavros' hand. Every time I thought I understood how much he cared, he raised the bar. Still unaccustomed to having people who loved him, after a moment of amazed hesitation on his part, he squeezed back, lending me his support.

Bruce responded best to facts, and I had plenty. "Marshall saw murderous legends come to life right in front of him, in the middle of a firefight, but put himself between them and a room full of terrified prisoners, who he sent out to safety. He took on a ghoul, bare-handed, to protect a street kid he didn't even know. He is a civilian and terrified in a way you or I can't truly understand, but he has held up again and again because he's more concerned with other people than himself. No longer than he's known the team, that concern is tripled when it involves one of us."

"This breach puts all of you at risk." Bruce lost his fire and rage. This was the real Bruce, under the arrogance and noise, and my chest ached, a ghost of the terror and grief from the year he was so sick, then the year Vee was presumed dead. He closed his eyes. "I stand to lose all of you."

I hated, *hated,* plunging him and Vee back into that nightmare.

The lines from heartbreak and despair carved his face, way too much like when he was dying and made me swear to keep Vee going after. "I'm having a hard time not picking up a cleaver and ending him right now, bleeding him out on the pool table, and telling HQ he got in the middle of a call-out and didn't make it."

Vee walked into Bruce and he spread his arms and hauled her in tight enough to bruise ribs. She nuzzled into the corner of his jaw and whispered, "Marshall would die before he'd give up a friend. I think Liv, the guys, and I are the only ones he has."

Bruce closed his eyes again and held on to her. "What the hell is it about this guy that's caused all of you to lose your damn minds?"

They all looked at me.

I focused on the patch of table in front of me, and the ragged gouge marring the wood, skimming my thumb over the damage. I couldn't erase that scar. I couldn't erase whatever it was inside me that wished Marshall could remain a part of our lives. I didn't know how to put into words who Marshall was. What he meant to me.

Stavros pushed past his comfort zone, a scarred, callused palm running over my crown and down my hair, his compassion cradling me.

* * *

I TIPPED the kitchen chair back precariously on two legs. Precarious seemed to be my motto now. Vee and Stavros were gone, Vee to join in the gaming, or at least the trash talk portion. Stavros was guaranteed outside on the roof, reading either his bible or yet another history of some saint. He'd gotten more acclimated to us and our emotions, but tonight was emotion cranked all the way up to eleven.

Bruce prowled the kitchen, poking and scowling, burning off a tiny measure of frustration and dread.

"Say it." I let all four chair legs hit the old floor, the crack traveling up my spine.

Bruce kept his back to me. "It's supposed to be you and me. We keep them on track. I veto all the fucked up martyr-hero plans, I show you life and all the fascinating parts of it you've all missed out on so that you might hesitate for one damn second when you get a call-out, remember there are things you've yet to experience, and possibly be that ounce more careful of your own lives. You force them to think logically, instead of relying on emotion and programming. We keep them safe from themselves. Why the hell didn't you this time?"

"It was a confluence of events I hadn't predicted." Which was a cruddy answer.

He scrubbed his hands over his face and finally turned to me. "*We* protect them."

Bruce was always intense. Full-throttle was his only setting. But the fire burning in his eyes now bordered on fanatical. "Oversight made it fucking clear that they don't have the teams' best interest at heart, which leaves it *our* mission to keep them alive, and what? Poof, fuck it, now it doesn't matter if those Company vultures tap a button that will shred your brother's heart inside his chest, and sever your sister's brain stem?"

I couldn't even get angry. Bruce was scared, and I understood that fear. It had become a part of our DNA. "My mission, all of ours, is also to protect humanity. That is exactly what I'm doing. None of this is Marshall's fault, if you're looking to place blame. I understand Oversight and their thought process better than you think. I don't trust them the way I once did, because yes, how they view my family now is different than how I do. However, we—Vee, Kimi, Josh, Jace, Matteo—we will also fulfill our duty, our first and most important mandate to protect innocent civilians, no matter the personal cost."

"You and I are the realists. The moment Oversight learned of my insurance cache, they begun putting counter measures into action. Given time, they'll also find and destroy, or neutralize, every copy."

"I'm aware." He had created a packet, complete with mission reports, gory call-out photos, what information he could mine from Vee's laptop on how the Company used Assets to manipulate everything from traffic lights to new laws in our favor. He'd entrusted the thumb drive to me, as well as a few of his many media contacts. It was leverage in case the Company abused us, or we ever wanted to leave. He'd utilized the threat to ensure Assessors didn't execute all of us on the spot when they had learned what Vee was now.

Bruce wasn't done yet. "We look at situations and react with clear-eyed logic instead of emotion and bullshit, reckless, heroics."

"This isn't reckless. It is reality. I need you to believe me when I say that Marshall isn't a danger to Vee and Josh. He won't be a problem, because I will be keeping eyes on him once he's cut loose."

Bruce's tone went from angry to exhausted. "I fucking need you to think. To envision what it's going to look like to see your sisters and brothers dead. Really, for the final time, no magically coming back, dead. Then, do what you should have from the beginning. Have Stavros get over his outdated ideals and fucking drain this idiot until he's nearly dead, then wipe every damn memory of us from this guy's brain, and I don't give a flying fuck if it leaves his brain completely scrambled. Either that, or drop him in the desert. Drop him across the border and let him take his chances. If you don't, I swear to God, I will." His voice held the final ring of a guillotine's blade falling. Bruce tossed the towel Marshall and I had used on top of the gleaming knives, and walked out.

I slid down in my seat, back of my head banging over each of the planks making up the chair's back. What Bruce really meant, underneath all the threats, was saving me from myself. He'd switched me from Company, but logical enough to assess first, to *the hero who doesn't have the sense to live* category.

Bruce was a harsh reminder of reality, that every action I took had consequences, good or bad, involving more than just myself.

He wouldn't act on the threats. I had no doubts Bruce would harm another person if it meant saving one of us, despite his religious convictions. It would only be in the heat of a fight though. Whether he admitted it or not, he had too much hero and morality in him to kill in cold blood.

As old as he was, and powerful from utilizing other vampire's blood, even Stavros couldn't permanently alter human memories or desires. Whatever allowed vampires to mesmerize prey was biologically based and faded quickly.

Basically, there was no going back, no scenario where Marshall didn't know about my sister and Stavros.

I wasn't throwing Vee and her vampire-reveal decision to the wolves, and informing Bruce what really happened either, how Marshall discovered what Vee and Stavros were.

Vee was an excellent C.O.. She was also the definition of thinking outside the box, often also known as rule-breaking. I knew that. I hadn't warned her to dial back the challenge and attitude. I hadn't pulled punches any more than she had.

Because deep down? I liked Marshall being here, sharing my space.

My sister was accustomed to taking any measures required to make each member of her team happy. She'd understood before I did that Marshall made me happy.

The increasingly familiar squeak of rubber soles on old flooring sounded. I opened one eye and rolled my head sideways.

Marshall waited in the no man's land between the den and kitchen. He shoved his hands in his pockets, and tilted his head in clear apology. "I didn't mean to disturb you."

"Disturb away. My headache is lousy company. Did the game-fest end?" Kimi had bailed earlier, informing me that the kids were all playing nicely together, stealing several pieces from Marshall's pizza on her way through.

"I kinda thought they could use the time to catch up."

"Ah."

"I thought you'd be doing the same with—" He cleared his throat, then committed "—with your sisters and brother."

"They're all beat. Kimi and Josh packed, then hit a last patrol of the area they were leaving, Bruce closed out some month long high-concept pop-up thing last night, then the drive here."

Marshall toed the edge of the baseboard. "There are things you can't share and things you probably have to lie about. I get that, and maybe it sucks for you as much as for the people you've gotta lie to." He looked up, eyes clear and intent. "But don't lie to me about the other stuff."

I added convincing liar to my list of sub-par abilities. Hooking the chair beside me, I shoved it away from the table.

Marshall crossed and sat, elbows on his knees.

"Ask whatever pops into your head and I'll answer if I can. You've earned some transparency," I said.

Marshall ran his thumbnail back and forth along the seam of his jeans.

I sat and let him think.

"You're in here alone, and with a headache, over me." Marshall didn't phrase it as a question. "Kantor doesn't want me here and you love him and—why am I still here? Because it sounds like you even bringing me here was dangerous for Vee, and you too."

I tried coming up with a reply, but Marshall wasn't finished. "There's HQ. That's where I'm really supposed to be anyway. You know I'll never tell about Vee."

Marshall repaid the earlier favor, sitting patiently while I ran through ideas and explanations. "You already know about the restrictions and safeguards on Vee's team and us."

Marshall dipped his chin in agreement.

"Vee, and the guys, are thinking that they'll save enough people, perform so brilliantly that Oversight will recognize their value and loyalty. Which is true. They don't really grasp that that may not be enough though. If vampires discover what Vee and Stavros are, every Master in the Americas will come for them. Even the Company can't field enough of a force to stop that war. So they will either toss us to our fates, or quietly eliminate us first, to save every other agent, cadet, and Asset. And I can't blame them."

I rubbed at dry, tired eyes. "Unlike them, Bruce does see that fact. He's terrified of losing Vee again."

Marshall didn't stir and didn't take his attention off me. That level of single-minded focus should've creeped me out. Instead, with only the two of us, and the quiet house heavy with the comforting history of generations of us, my tongue loosened. "Losing people you care about is awful. It's a simple fact that agents are killed, and sometimes civilians, if tips on potential attacks come in too late for us to act on. That has happened multiple times in the last couple of year alone, with people from our year group, who we've known all our lives. I believed that I knew what death and loss was.

"Then, Vee was…gone. No body to mourn over. Gone." I tilted my face up, gravity helping keep tears at bay. "The point being, the way we thought she'd died affected Bruce deeply. The bond between him and Vee is unreal. He is fanatical about protecting her and the team, and he sees you as a potential leak, thus a threat."

Marshall nodded. Instead of arguing or leaving, he scooted his chair corner to corner with mine, and gripped my knee, hand easily spanning it. His forehead crinkled. "Losing Vee tore you up, too."

"Not the same—"

He squeezed my knee, not hard, but calling me out. I quit trying to pretend. "Do you want to hear the most illogical thing ever?"

"Yeah. Always."

"We've been injured repeatedly. We hadn't even come close to graduations yet when the ghoul ripped into Kimi. Yet it didn't sink in that we weren't immortal until I walked up on the truck, its doors and roof torn away, and Vee's blood everywhere." I ran my fingers under my eyes, done. "Which is a long way of saying Bruce's dislike isn't personal."

Marshal straightened and let go of me. "Take me back to HQ tomorrow." Steel resolve braided his voice. "I'll never talk. What Vee said—she's right. You guys are the only friends I have worth the name. I didn't mean to eavesdrop. I came to make popcorn for Matteo and heard."

My stomach bottomed out, like I was in a free fall. "Marshall."

"Take me to HQ in the morning. It's too late tonight, all of you are tired, and I don't want you on the roads like that.

343

None of this happened. All I know is that Vee and Stavros are agents. I never saw her turn into a vampire. The only vampires I've ever seen are the ones you killed at the hotel. My DNA profile thing is at HQ. They'll see I'm still human when I go back in. All of you will be safe."

I squeezed my eyes shut. Marshall was amazing and self-less, and I hated it. "No."

He eyed me, utterly implacable. "You know I won't talk. Tell Kantor what I do and how I shut down and can't get a sentence out when it gets bad. I wouldn't be able to tell any human or vampire that found me about Vee's team and you guys."

The plan would mollify Bruce, not alienate him further. Which was my problem, not Marshall's. He was brave enough to announce his secrets if it meant helping. My actions affected him, too and he deserved better. "No."

"Liv, come on. They're your family, and that means something to you."

I stood and rammed my chair under the table hard enough it bounced back, smacking me in the shin. "You're our friend and our chef. Matteo, Jace, and I trust you. You're staying."

"No. I'm right about this." Marshall rose way more calmly, and crossed his arms, taking a stab at staring me down, glaring from his height advantage. "I'm going back to HQ."

"Yes, and *stop*. Stop thinking you aren't as important as the rest of us, because you are. Quit being noble and sacrificial. Given time, Bruce will get over his paranoia. Vee and Stavros trust you, and Stavros doesn't give his trust easily."

Marshall shoved a hand through his hair, sending curls springing out like a halo. "I told you to stop saying things like that."

"You told me not to lie. This is the result."

"Liv—" Marshall caught me around the shoulders. Like he

might prefer to shake me. Then he tugged, gentle as always, asking me to come closer.

I went with the pull. He hugged me, big enough to envelope me, arms around me and holding me snug. "I don't know why you say those things, but I'll live up to them."

arshall

ARM CURLED UNDER HIS HEAD, Marshall drifted in that between place, awake, but not here-awake. The place he went to pull out memories, or work the day into a manageable shape and understand.

There weren't enough hours in the night to process the last twenty-four.

Vampires slept a hall away. They weren't all monsters, and they ate pie, not people. One was engaged, to culinary royalty who hated Marshall on sight.

All he kept coming back to was Liv. The way she defended him, to her family and to him, refusing to back down to any of them. The way she fit against him, the rise and fall of her chest against his.

She was strong, and the leader, and it still felt like she'd accepted comfort from him.

She'd stayed wrapped in his arms, hugging back, with her

head on his shoulder. She'd only let go when her phone chimed with a text. She didn't look at the phone until she'd gotten a promise out of him not to mention HQ again.

The promise led to a new topic. Liv's family was okay with him. Even the stern vampire. Which only left one unfriendly chef, soon to be Liv's brother-in-law. Every chef expected warm bodies to magically appear in the kitchen, there for the scut work.

Marshall excelled at that. He'd keep his hands off meal planning, and take whatever crap the guy doled out, and do every menial task thrown at him. Anything to get on the guy's better side—he didn't have a *good* side, at least not where Marshall was concerned—and take some pressure off Liv.

He couldn't truly stay, but he'd do his part while he was sorta part of the team, and protect Liv in his own way.

$\mathcal{M}$arshall

MARSHALL STEPPED from the steamy communal shower room into the cooler hall, juggling his shower case contents, and ran into Liv. Literally.

She grunted from the impact, and his case clattered to the floor as he grabbed her shoulders to keep her from ping-ponging around the hall from bouncing off his bulk. "Nobody is ever up this early, or if you are, you're outdoors. Sorry."

Liv only wheezed and smacked his arm, then bent to retrieve his case and its scattered supplies.

"There's a reason no one is up at this hour. It totally sucks." Josh strode past them, no fonder of early than his brother.

That fact that despite the complaint, Josh was dressed registered. Liv stood, all his stuff neatly back in the bag, and she had on the splotchy black and gray urban camo they wore for missions. Dread unfurled and wove cold tendrils up Marshall's backbone. "A mission?"

"I got some chatter last night. It checked out with HQ. Whatever has our cryptids off their normal schedule seems to be spreading. Allegedly, this involves ghouls and another, unspecified cryptid. Ghouls don't socialize with other creatures. They either avoid them or eat them." She scowled, like the monsters' behavior was a personal insult.

He swallowed, keeping his vow of helping Liv front and center, even if he was the only one who knew. He took his junk from her and crossed to toss it into his room. "You need breakfast, and coffee."

The faint lines bracketing her lips faded and she fell in step beside him. Which was good, but only a start. "You've been up all night. I'll make you an extra travel mug to go."

Banging echoed back from the kitchen, followed by the whir of their coffee grinder.

Kantor. Of course he was already in there. Marshall inhaled, silently pep-talking his wobbly resolve.

Liv bumped against him, reading him like nobody ever had. "Bruce is a good person under all the grumpy camouflage. Talk food. You two have common ground."

Liv was uncannily perceptive at times. And clueless at others. "He's like a culinary rock star, okay? The ones that trash rooms, stomp off stage, and punch photographers. I'm a nobody line cook. I'll wash pans, set up the prep areas, and I won't piss him off." At least, he'd try not to, beyond what the guy came pre-loaded with.

Liv swung in front of Marshall, blocking the last step into the kitchen. "Bruce is wonderful, yes. However, you are also talented. Go dazzle Bruce with your muffin mojo. If he has a weaker spot, it's baking."

"I'll stay out of his way in the kitchen."

"Unacceptable." She linked her arm through his. "I'm expecting muffins when I walk back in here. As a matter of fact, an entire rainbow of muffin choices." She bumped against him again, and gave him that smile, the conspiratorial one that said he was part of the in-group.

"Yeah, I can do that." He bumped her back, more carefully, and finished their trek to the kitchen.

Just in time for Kantor to turn and catch them. The glare from behind his glasses froze Marshall out.

The drip of coffee and the pan sitting on the island were evidence Marshall sucked at his one purpose.

Kantor only snapped the towel, the one he'd used to move the skillet, in Liv and Josh's direction. "Get weaponed up and get back in here before this is inedible."

Liv didn't move, although tension vibrated through her where they touched. She and Kantor had their own version of silent communication, and this conversation didn't look especially pleasant.

Take the guy's crap, for Liv. Marshall unhooked his arm from hers, acting like this wasn't a big deal. "I'll fix your coffee while you get ready." He kept up the charade until the air pressure changed, outer door opening then closing.

The air seemed to grow mass and in press in with her gone. He grabbed the milk that was already on the counter, a regular mug, and the best of the dinged-up travel mugs.

"Liv takes her coffee black."

Marshall kept his head down and measured. "She's trying something new. Foamed milk." He loaded the machine and pretended it was any other morning.

"Liv's trying a lot of shit lately that isn't good for her." The crash of cast iron on stainless steel racks punctuated the comment.

Marshall heated and mixed, careful to keep foam and

coffee separated, and sealed the insulated mug. He sat it on the bar, in Liv's working spot where she wouldn't miss it on the way out. Then he fell into his work mode, second nature by now, and pulled out plates and silverware. He let the snapping and orders about portion size and plating flow over him, all familiar enough, and grounding.

He only veered off-course when Liv reappeared, finishing her cup and handing it to her. She sipped, then gave him a thumbs up.

He passed out plates, and once everyone had food, Jace shoved out a chair for Marshall—the one it looked like Jace had saved, between him and Matteo.

Which was cool, even if it earned Marshall another ball-shriveling glare from Vee's fiancé. Thinking of Kantor that way made it easier. Vee was awesome, she loved this guy for some reason, so Marshall would work around the dislike and snarls, same as he was doing for Liv.

He grabbed up empties as they all finished, letting the teams go over the mission. The fiancé stayed involved, like he knew exactly what they were talking about. Marshall eyed the matt black weapons lined up on the counter, too bulky or large to fit in holsters.

Matteo had his seat pushed out from the table, looking over a shotgun by his elbow as Liv and Vee double-checked something with Stavros. With half the crew busy, Marshall leaned to Matteo, keeping his voice low. "Liv said this was a weird mission, because of ghouls."

"Among other things. Ghouls are solitary, except this is multiple ghouls in one spot. I'm betting on a fighting ring." Matteo's hand flexed, like he was already driving a knife into a creature.

"Like a cage fight?"

A glance at the still occupied C.O.'s, and Matteo signaled

Jace, who angled in toward them. "More like a dog fight, run by vampires, or some of their human employees."

Multi-tasking, Kimi tapped something into a tablet, and spoke slowly for Marshall's benefit. "It's usually windigos fighting. Occasionally a human, rarer cryptid, or vampire that's crossed its Master. Vicious, low-rent gladiator games, lots of betting and cash or favors involved."

"These vampires are all like the traffickers? Not good like Vee?"

The table shuddered and skidded several inches, propelled by inhuman force. Marshall and the guys jerked back.

"There is no such distinction as good or bad among demons." Stavros towered over the seated crowd, an unsettling silver ring around his brown pupils. "They are purest evil."

Kimi laid her hand on top of the old vampire's.

"The boy deserves the truth." He fixed those glowing eyes on Marshall. "For whatever unknowable reason, God has seen fit to utilize me as his scourge. Victoria is a product of my weakness, one I will answer for at Judgment. God has also seen fit to hold us outside our sins for so long as we serve Him in eradicating others of our kind. Do not make the mistake of believing others are as we are. To do so puts your soul at risk as surely as your life." He patted Kimi's hand. She stood and joined him as he strode out to the garage,

"Get loaded and quit wasting sunlight on bullshit questions." Kantor gave Marshall a look usually reserved for the family dog when it forgot it was housebroken, right in the middle of a holiday dinner.

"Queue up some pure B-movie awesomeness for tonight," Jace said.

Matteo gave Marshall the expected good-natured slap. "Yeah, man. The seventh shark and tornado one is out."

The crowd thinned, all three men picking up weapons and heading out. Leaving Vee and her fiancé. She wrapped around him, whispering something against the resolute set of his clenched jaw. Marshall spun to face the breezeway, so he didn't see more. Thinking of the guy as terrified messed with Marshall.

Liv jumped at Marshall's sudden movement, her attention pulled away from the pair. He and Liv both pretended they hadn't been watching the couple.

Marshall scooted the mug across the bar to Liv. She reached, and their fingers touched. A shock bounced through Marshall, not physical, but still real. Liv left her fingers over his, Marshall's caught between the cool metal and her heat.

"Bruce has the drill down pat. He'll keep HQ updated, or if anything more serious happens," she said.

Liv turned her hand palm up, and Marshall worked their fingers together. "Be as careful as you can. You and the guys."

"Muffins?"

He accepted that as agreement, developing their own shorthand. "A rainbow of them, plus extra chocolate chip."

He squeezed her fingers then let go. As soon as she turned, so did he. He'd heard once that watching someone walk away was unlucky. Superstitious or not, Marshall refused to take any chances.

Time to bake, and not think about rubbery-skinned sharks with legs, and gladiator rings full of people.

The fiancé's lean frame blocked the way between the island and table.

Marshall backtracked the long way around the pantry. He came out loaded with ingredients. He separated out batches—chocolate, chocolate plus cinnamon and cayenne, lemon. Pumpkin spice, because it was a thing, so why not?

"What the hell are you doing?"

Marshall concentrated on chili amounts. "Baking. They like muffins."

"No one needs ten fucking dozen." The fiancé prowled the kitchen, getting closer with each pass.

"Jace prefers lemon, Matteo likes anything with heat, and Liv's favorite is chocolate." He dumped a handful of chips into a bowl, and turned the oven on.

"I don't like you in my kitchen."

"I'll stay out of your way."

"You could get the hell out, and out of this compound, while you're at it."

"Okay." Lemon first. Then pumpkin. Marshall loaded tins and tucked two into the oven, setting a timer. "After I make the muffins."

"I don't like people who won't argue back."

"Okay."

"Answer me this. Why are you hell bent on facing me down over a bakery's display case worth of baked goods?"

Marshall lifted one shoulder, and kept mixing.

"That isn't an answer."

The timer chimed, and Marshall switched out tins, setting the first aside to cool. The chocolate had melted and was ready, so the Mexican hot chocolate ones next.

"I'm not leaving this kitchen. You answering me is only a matter of time. Why?"

Fine. If it shut him up, so Marshall could really concentrate and not screw any steps up, he'd answer. "Because it's Liv and she always takes care of everybody else, and she should get the stuff she wants sometimes. This is the only thing she likes that I know how to do."

Wood scraped across flooring, then settled with a creak behind Marshall. When he turned and checked the oven, The Fiancé was in one of the chairs, dragged around to face the counters, his legs spread and arms crossed, gaze drilling into Marshall. "That's the most you've said since I arrived here."

"I guess I could've left it at 'because Liv likes muffins'."

A snort sounded from behind him. "I can almost respect a smartass."

Not able to tell if that was true, Marshall kept mixing.

"What's Liv to you?"

The walnuts Marshall was pouring hit the counter in a meaty rain. He swept them up and got them into the batter.

"Give me an answer and don't waste my time lying. I'm one lie away from knocking your ass out and dropping you in the desert near a chupacabra den."

Whatever a chupacabra was, it couldn't be worse than Kantor. A pulse of defiance rose, hotter than the cayenne. The guy already hated him, so Marshall didn't have much to lose. "Liv is fucking awesome. She helps people, even people who kind of suck." He dared a look at the fiancé. "And she's loyal to people who probably don't deserve it."

Another snort blasted, loud in the under populated house. "Fuck you, too."

"Liv and Jace and Matteo are what you think friends means, until you learn otherwise the hard way, and that ninety-percent of the population are really dicks. Liv's brave and smart and funny, and really damn scary, and she hates the cold, and loves embarrassing people in the clothes aisles."

"Son of a fucking bitch."

"Do whatever you're gonna, but you aren't doing it until I finish every last batch of muffins." Marshall jerked the baked muffins out, shoved the new ones in, and faced Kantor, chin up. The guy was a good six inches shorter, but he also had real muscles and scars that didn't come from kitchen prep.

The fiance took his glasses off, and polished the lenses on his shirt sleeve, but more like it was a habit than necessity.

"You poor, dumb fuck. There's nothing I can do to you worse than what you're doing to yourself."

After that announcement, the guy sat, a menacing statue.

Marshall switched baked food for unbaked, and sorted results into for now, and to freeze for later. He emptied the last pan, and checked his phone. Only three hours in.

"Get over watching a clock. All it will accomplish is making you crazy," Kantor said. "Make a pot of coffee, and use the beans I brought. Up over the other mugs," he said, as Marshall opened the usual cabinet. "Liv and Vee don't waste it on the day-to-day, since the rest of this bunch can't tell the difference."

Marshall followed orders, while the muffins cooled and coffee, the fancy small batch stuff you never saw in restaurants, brewed. When Marshall poured two cups, The fiancé kicked a chair more or less in Marshall's direction. "Sit." He pulled a deck of cards out of his pocket, and dealt.

After losing three consecutive hands, Marshall cashed in some of the goodwill he'd maybe built. "That thing about demons—"

"I'd strongly consider that Stavros had syphilis back in the day, and it ate holes in his pre-frontal cortex, well before he was ever infected with the vampire virus." Kantor raked in the cards and shuffled. "He views cryptids as pests. Dangerous yes, but pests. He won't be swayed from the concept that vampires are in a different category, Christian demons made of distilled evil." He tossed cards out in a practiced motion. "He's correct about the evil."

Marshall fiddled with his coffee, arranging the ideas in his head into something he had a chance of other people understanding. "Vee is a vampire. Stavros is a vampire."

The Fiancé slapped the undealt cards down, and pushed away from the table. Like he was going to need room. Tendons stood out in his neck, and for the first time,

Marshall got the same feel as when facing his ex-boss or the ghoul. Hairs on his arms rose in a wave.

"You don't want to go there." The guy enunciated it clearly, voice level. Which felt more serious, more dangerous than when he'd been barking orders, or yelling.

And again, the crap in Marshall's head hadn't translated right. "Not that. I'm saying they aren't evil. At all." Marshall didn't twitch, kept his hands where they were. Trying not to tip the balance, and trigger the violence coiled inside Kantor, waiting to explode. "They're like Liv."

The ugly potential riding the vanilla-scented air finally broke, like a storm blowing away, and the guy sat back. "Since Vee and Stavros aren't evil, logic dictates there's a reasonable chance that not all vampires are evil? Or at least not murderous fucks?"

"Yeah."

"It doesn't matter."

Marshall couldn't have heard that right. "But if—"

The crack of palms hitting the beat-up tabletop reverberated and Marshall jerked. Kantor stood, table between them, but his sheer fury pinning Marshall to the seat. "There are no exceptions. Hesitating, wondering if the vampire in front of you has a conscience, that will get agents killed. The theoretical few decent vampires or cryptids are acceptable collateral damage. This is the one place where the Company's damned brainwashing and I are in agreement."

Marshall sat, seconds ticking.

Kantor leaned on the table, looming over Marshall. "The Company creed is humans first. *Mine* is the team first. Vee, and even Stavros, are as human as you or I, in our eyes. They are also Company in their eyes and ours." There was no doubting Kantor's conviction, or the dread and what Marshall was pretty sure was fear, lurking in the guy's eyes.

He wasn't done, either. "Drop the empathy, because it is

worse than useless in this world. You'll end up dead, and the team along with you because they were protecting your ignorant ass. Decide now who is more important—Liv and the team, or some random cryptid. If you can't, I will take you out before you put her in danger."

The mug handle bit into Marshall's palm. *Collateral damage* and *acceptable losses*, which really meant murdering people. Because Vee and Stavros were vampires but people, too. All those other vampires, and ghouls, because they wore clothes and that had to signal they weren't straight-up animals...Horror swamped him. It was murder. Flat out murder.

Except when Marshall blinked, instead of Kantor's face, he saw Liv's. Liv asleep on his bed and using his chest as a pillow. Liv curled up with him, keeping nightmares at bay. Liv, putting herself between a meat locker full of women and his ex-boss. The women, who the vampires, and their human but evil crew, were selling like a prix fixe meal off a menu.

Who was more important?

Whether it made Marshall an accomplice or not, there was only one real answer.

A grunt brought Marshall back to the kitchen and reality. He blinked, but Kantor sat down like he was satisfied, gathered and reshuffled, flicking cards to each of them before laying the rest of the deck in the center.

The guy gave his a critical once-over, and discarded one. "What's your plan? Butter Liv up with custom meals and baked goods to get into her bed?"

"I'm not—"

"Ten dozen is way the hell over the top. Liv isn't high maintenance—no one Company is. She also has no problem with a quickie when she's in the mood. There's no such thing as a couple or romance, another quirk thanks to the Company's upbringing. It does promote sex positivity though.

According to Vee and Kimi, there was this one time after a mission when they all—"

"Don't." Marshall's voice rumbled, feeling like it was boulders crashing together, not plain vocal cords and lungs. "Don't talk about Liv that way. Don't talk about her sisters, either."

Marshall's fingers spasmed, forming a fist, cards crushed. His other hand clamped onto the table edge, hard enough his knuckles cramped, because if he let go... "Liv thinks you aren't a dick, and you're important to her—and to Vee and Kimi—and they are smart and I don't get why they still like an asshole, but they do. For your own good, just—stop talking."

"Fucking finally." The asshole, because Marshall had downgraded him from fiancé, snapped his fingers, whole demeanor altered, and pointed at the trashed pieces of cardboard in Marshall's hand. "Now we are getting somewhere."

Marshall shoved the cards across the table, and jerked his chair clear.

"Sit your melodramatic ass down and play poker, now that I've established a baseline as far as whether you're worth even a second of Liv's time. As opposed to this being your fulfilling some wet dream fantasy, then bolting on her afterward." The asshole stood and tossed the cards in the trash. "There's got to be one of Liv's marked decks around here."

Without the guy in his face, Marshall got his blood pressure back under control. Then he made the mistake of looking at the security screen, time displayed in its corner. He pulled his phone out, even though he didn't expect Liv to call. She'd given him the phone, and that made it—a talisman. His talisman.

He spun it in around on the table, the hypnotic, repetitive circle distracting the part of his brain inching toward older patterns. He didn't need one of the apps. Yet.

"What did I tell you about checking?" The asshole dropped into a chair, and sorted through a new deck he'd found, running his fingers along the edges of each card, then holding them up to the light and squinting. "They won't text, they won't call, or answer incoming calls. Theirs aren't even on. The phones are supposedly hack-proof, but Vee and Liv don't take chances. They'll make a call, under thirty seconds, to the Cleaners if needed."

Marshall slid his phone away, but only into his pocket. "Are you gonna be a dick?"

"Probably. It's an untreatable condition." Kantor gave up on inspecting the deck, and cut and shuffled. "Four years, and I haven't figured out Liv's system."

The asshole dealt cards again, and his body language altered, the challenging edge dropping. "When you are associated with the Company and a team, you spend a shit load of time in strange towns, in a string of more or less identical barracks, most lacking even the outdated, bare bones comforts of this place, waiting for people to return from missions. There's plenty of time to work on solitaire." He glanced at the rows of muffins. "Or whatever coping mechanism gets you through."

"Liv mentioned her friend sitting up and waiting and that she kind of missed it. You, I guess."

"That's why you started bake-a-thons?"

"I didn't know until afterwards. After a windigo call-out last week."

The asshole *hmd.* "No matter what you pick, waiting is one of the biggest mind-fucks I've ever encountered. You're waiting to see which one of them comes back torn up, and whether you have the skill to fucking patch them back together. If you are in public and at a job, you're calculating whether you can or should leave and get back to them.

Although the truly shitty alternative is not having one or all of them return at all."

The lines and hollows etching Kantor's face, a map of injuries and exhaustion and fear was too much for Marshall to look at. He concentrated on the red and black shapes in his lax hand, decoding the numbers. Liv would come back.

The asshole tapped the table, and Marshall randomly discarded, and drew another card. "Why are you telling me this?"

The ssshole folded up his cards and looked at Marshall, and his expression made Marshall's entire body clench. Compassion freaked him out way more than threats.

When the guy spoke, it didn't help. "You have feelings for Liv."

"She's—" his throat constricted, and he sucked in air before he could get more words out. "She's great. A great friend."

"I'm already aware of that, dipshit." The swearing lacked oomph. "You're feeling more than friendship for her."

Deny it. Tell him he's crazy off-base. Easier for Marshall to stop his blood from pumping. His body wouldn't allow him to utter the words, any more than it'd allow him to stop his own heart. "Don't tell her. You hate me, and that's fine, and you can bitch and yell, and point out in front of Liv all the things I do wrong. You can throw the plating station at me the way you did at that benefit dinner. I'll take it all. But don't tell her...any of this."

"You may not be an abject waste of space but I have no damn intention of cluing Liv in, and giving your cause any sort of boost."

Out of sight, Marshall jammed his knuckles against the edge of his seat, pain hopefully distracting his brain. Only a shaky agreement with a guy who'd threatened twice to kill him stood between Marshall and Liv finding out and it all blowing up in Marshall's face.

Kantor sighed. "Stop and listen to what I'm saying. Despite what they'll tell you, agents don't go *meet* danger. They chase it. They're adrenaline junkies and that's their fix. They're also indoctrinated to put everyone else's lives before their own. Sacrificing themselves has been trained into them. Now, think about sitting this way in some generic shitball base, in some random town, night after night, waiting for Liv to come home. Is that what you want out of life?"

"What's that have to do with me?"

The asshole held his arms wide, showcasing bright tattoos and his expensive-looking shirt, the glint of silver Marshall had glimpsed earlier turning out to be a Star of David as the chain it was on slid out. "The Company accepts civilians, under certain circumstances, if they fill a role beneficial to the team. Once you're in, you're in, though. There's no leaving. Not even if Liv goes down one day. Not even if the entire team is wiped out. HQ will sweep the barracks for usable bits and pieces, including you, tuck you into a SUV, and after a good debriefing, will reassign you."

"I'm not—I couldn't..." Marshall switched from knuckling the chair, to holding on, as possibilities whirled and twisted, colors and ideas swirling, fracturing, and rejoining in new shapes and shades. Except—"I'm not a fighter. With knives or guns."

"Neither was I. Then, I was."

"Why are you helping me?"

"You're distracted, but not stupid. You'd eventually look at me and my place on the team, then start wondering if you'd fit into that slot." The threat crept back into Kantor's voice, colder and more final than ever. "To be fucking clear, I'm not helping you. I don't give a shit about you and your ignorant ass. I am doing this because Vee thinks for some damn reason that you have the potential to make Liv happy. And Liv fucking well deserves to be. So this right now? I'm deciding if you're worth the investment, and if you pose a threat to her, or Vee and Kimi, and the rest of these other damn heroic martyrs."

When Marshall only stared, the asshole scrubbed a hand over his neat beard, calculation replacing the threat. Sort of. "I know damn well Vee has already left you a bread crumb trail, if she hasn't outright put the idea of joining into your head. She's betting on me taking that trail and running with it while I'm stuck here with you."

Vee hadn't. Except, she'd sat in this kitchen, at the bar only feet away, quizzing him about future plans, and belonging. She'd given him a nickname.

"Exactly." The asshole answered, like he had x-ray vision, seeing through to the inside of Marshall's skull, and reading the ideas forming. "Now, listen while I tell you the things Vee didn't. Not because she's holding back, but because none of them have a frame of reference and thus can't see the problems."

A chime sounded from the fiancé's phone—Marshall had upgraded the guy's status again. Despite the lectures, Kantor silenced the alarm and checked the time. Then traded cards for the knife case, laying out his choices. "Grab the chicken and avocados for lunch."

Marshall wiped sweaty hands on his jeans, and followed orders. He fell into the rhythm, prepping, taking orders.

When the meal had sat for half an hour, and there was no sign of the team, it all went into the fridge. Marshall couldn't bring himself to touch the food. Kantor seemed to share Marshall's lack of an appetite, switching out coffee for mug after mug of lemony green tea. They went through more poker hands while Marshall worked out ideas and questions, because his current audience for sure didn't have the patience to wait or translate Marshall-speak in real time.

As Marshall once again acted as sous, this time for spareribs meant as dinner, the fiancé asked, "Where did I throw shit at you?"

The question fit in with the choppy rhythm of Marshall dicing onions. "Tempe."

"Did the place usually have a shit system?"

"It was my first night."

"You get fired?"

"Yeah."

That got another grunt. "When was this?"

"About—" Marshall counted "—about eighteen months ago."

The snick-snick of dicing and the hiss of heating oil served as conversation for a while.

"Vee hadn't been infected and a vampire long at that point." A pan slammed. "She'd been one, but—whatever. Long story that's none of your business. So, I was a bigger dick than usual."

"Was that an apology?"

A muffled snort, or a muffled laugh, sounded from closer to the range "No. That was me stating a fact."

"Liv said that Vee disappeared."

All motion to his right stopped. Marshall tucked his elbows in, making himself smaller. "It hurt her. Liv, I mean."

"Meaning?"

"I'm used to getting fired. I got another job."

Motion resumed, but Marshall kept his head down anyway. "Liv tells you the team's life story. Vee spills shit about the past and missions. You're a fucking walking confessional booth."

Since no plates flew at him, Marshall shrugged and kept

working. "Vee also said she met you when you were drunk in an alley, and saved you from a succubus lizard thing."

Marshall took a little pleasure from knowing that fact. A little more from it having been Vee telling him, and a shit ton more from the chef knowing *Vee* had told Marshall.

That got a satisfyingly testy, "I wasn't fucking drunk and it wasn't a—look, save the shit and ask what you're dying to know."

Marshall diced through all the potatoes before he figured out that Kantor meant that last statement. It took him through sautéing to frame his question. "What happened after Vee found you?"

"I said, ask what you really mean."

Marshall double-checked from the corner of his eye, but Kantor had closed the oven and was watching him, relaxed and waiting.

"What did you do, and how did you get to stay? With the Company and Vee?" The moment the first word left his mouth, the truth settled over Marshall. This was it, what he wanted, and been afraid to acknowledge. If he had one wish to use, it was staying with the team, and Liv. He'd live with the friend tag, because he'd be with her.

Minutes ticked away, the guy sizing Marshall up, before he finally spoke. "I'll tell you about rules and applications, but first you'll listen. Liv is more by the book than Vee ever was. A shit load of psychological factors go into putting teams together. One thing each has in common is that the C.O. and their lieutenant have an alpha streak, and an outsized sense of responsibility. They have to, in case a leader falls, and the other has to step in and reform the team, so they all survive. Liv got that, and it suited her. She couldn't go back, but she wouldn't tear her family apart fighting to remain. She elected to do the impossible, melding three remnants into one whole. She won't risk her commission, and she shouldn't have to."

Marshall rolled the speech around. Liv couldn't take on dead weight. Her career might rest on that. The whole team might. Marshall wouldn't ever risk any of them, no matter how bad he wanted to be here. But...he hadn't fucked up so far. "She said three was the minimum, but four or five was better."

"If you don't already think I'm a bastard, buckle your seat belt. Liv may want you here, but that doesn't mean you're good for her. Not if you drag her down, and split her concentration, or can't get it through your head that cryptids are the enemy. Liv cannot spend her energy and time constantly watching out for you."

"I can learn. I will." He would never put her or the guys in danger. He'd do anything he had to, to make sure he did his part to keep them safe.

Kantor sighed. "I'm telling you—Liv may not be able to be what you want. None of them, no one in the Company, had any clue about, or need for, any permanent relationship aside from their team. Liv has been exposed to it now, but that doesn't mean she wants anything romantic herself. Even if she felt more than friendship, there's every chance she'll put team before relationship. A whole damn lot of people are edgy over Vee and I being together publicly as well. Legal is looking at conduct rules in a new light."

"You said you wouldn't mention the other, the personal thing. I only need to be part of this," he pointed at the beat up old floor as a stand in for the kitchen, the compound, and the team. "That'll be enough."

"You may not feel that way after a few months and missions and jumping through HQ's never-fucking-ending hoops."

"You stayed. Did you have other options?"

"I did."

"Was it worth it?"

"When I'm with Vee, it's a hundred-percent worth the worry, the stress, and the lies. The rest of the time? Fifty-fifty, on a good day." He flipped the short ribs and gave them a vicious stab. They'd already sat too long, and gotten tough.

Marshall snuck a glance at the time. Not midnight yet. So it was still the same day. He could rationalize that Liv hadn't been gone too long.

He opened the fridge and without being told, made room for the dinner no one was here to eat, right beside the lunch. He finished and turned to Kantor. "What do I need to learn, to stay?"

CHAPTER 47

*M*arshall

BRUCE, because Marshall couldn't find a better name for the domineering asshole who'd maybe-hopefully offered Marshall everything Marshall had ever wanted, glared from across the expanse of the bar.

This glare wasn't any more judgmental than usual, more a default expression, but if Marshall was getting on Bruce's last nerve, the way Bruce was getting on his…

"This will cut you off from everyone in your old life. One way or another, you will always be lying to someone." Bruce had repeated the warning in one form or another, again and again.

The one thing on the list that Marshall *didn't* care about. Marshall repeated the shrug *he'd* given his grumpy lecturer, same as after every other repetition. "Okay."

"Don't fucking *okay* me." Bruce leaned in until hipster-ish glasses and bloodshot eyes filled Marshall's field of vision. At

368

least he'd quit slapping the table for punctuation. "I'm talking about people you work with, people on the street, your family, all of them. The ones who don't cut you off for being a flakey asshole and bailing on promises and shifts and weddings—hell, funerals, too—you are going to be lying to them with every breath. It creates a barrier. They'll feel it, and you will feel it."

Bruce's hand bunched into a fist, and Marshall held back the *okay*. "I get it."

"You *don't*."

Resentment he didn't know he held roared up, winning over irritation and hope. Marshall leaned and met the other man's gaze. "I don't have anybody I care enough about to mind lying to, or even disappearing on. They don't care enough about me to notice if I do disappear." A laugh sheared up his throat, leaving bitterness like unripe persimmons behind. "I'm already weird and borderline embarrassing. They won't notice any extra weirdness. Trust me on that."

Bruce's expression altered for a second.

Marshall didn't need pity. All he needed was information. The kind that allowed him to stay with the team. He sat back, away from the anger now popping off Bruce like hot grease, the sympathy gone as quickly as it'd arrived.

Marshall would take a punch. Except that risked permanently pissing off his one contact. "Sorry." He put in enough regret to hold off a fight, even if the regret was over potentially messing up a chance to get what he needed.

Bruce took his glasses off, and massaged the marks the sidepieces pressed into his temples. "You'll be replacing those normal relationships, however strained they may be, with people who don't bat a fucking eye at discussing the intricacies of decapitation methods over brunch. It's brutal and ugly, and the majority of the time they don't get why you're fucking skeeved-out and have lost your appetite."

"Okay."

Whatever Bruce barked at him was lost under the flash and hum of fence sensors, the security screen coming to life. The system recognized all seven truck occupants a beat later, their DNA matching and accepted.

Liv was back. Marshall's heart jumped out of rhythm from sheer relief.

Then a sharper, shrill note he'd never heard blared.

Bruce surged past him, the stool hitting the island and falling to its side. "You're about to put your opinion of what you can handle to the test."

Marshall untangled himself from his seat, and followed.

Bruce slowed enough to slap a panel on the room between garage and house, one Marshall hadn't ventured into. Doors *whoosed* open and lights flared, on gurneys and machines like in hospitals, their polished surfaces reflecting back the harsh fluorescent glare.

Marshall hung back, at the door. "What is that?"

"You'll learn that alarm code and it will be the soundtrack to your nightmares. Someone is down." Bruce hit the decontamination breezeway, the door bouncing from the impact as he straight-armed it.

It wasn't Liv. She was too fast and smart. It couldn't be Liv.

Thick fingers crushed Marshall's forearm, jerking him around. "Don't get in the way. If you're going to puke or pass out, do it in a corner." Bruce bit off the orders and let Marshall go without waiting for his agreement. That garage lift whirred.

Marshall held onto the chamber door, its chill metal lip biting into his palm. Liv was fine. She'd jump out of the truck and take over and be fine.

Bruce's string of curses shattered Marshall's fairytale. Scratches marred the truck's black finish. Claw marks had cut through paint to metal, and ran in jagged lines from the rear quarter panel down to the bumper, which was melted into a misshapen ball.

Marshall dared a glance at Bruce. Whose face was a bloodless-pale. He strode forward as the garage door sealed them in, jerking the rear driver's door open.

The stench rolled out, and Marshall choked on hot bile. Those small specialty restaurants he'd worked at did their own butchering. He'd never forgotten the cloying stink of mass quantities of blood left out too long, or the spilled intestine aroma of raw tripe they'd wash and prepare. The rotted-garbage reek of windigos rode over it all, and Marshall took shallow breaths.

Wide shoulders bulled their way free of the truck. Matteo bent back in, hauling Jace out, then Josh. The pair leaned on the truck, like bloodless ghosts, ashy-gray faces seeming to float against the dark clothes and black paint.

"Report." Bruce's order was muffled, interior upholstery dampening sound while he shoved the front seat up in a crash, making room to get in.

"It was a fucking slaughter house." Matteo's bass deepened until Marshall expected the walls to vibrate from the fury contained in those few words. "No rhyme, no reason, no stealth. We heard the screams a block out."

"Chupacabras running around like a stirred up anthill, and why the hell they were in an urban area, I don't get. More scrawny ghouls." Jace coughed, too wet and raspy. "Fucking freshy vampires, acting like they were high on something, and partying like I've never seen."

"Get them inside," Bruce ordered, now deep in the truck.

"Man, you're gonna need another set of hands," Matteo said.

"Go. If they pass out, they'll have to lay here."

Matteo sighed and fit a shoulder under each twin, huge muscles bunching and straining. The motion opened a gash along his hairline Marshall hadn't noticed. Blood trickled over the agent's ear, and down into the filthy shirt. He still looked better than Josh, whose eyes were closed, bruise already covering half his swollen face.

Marshall held the door wide for the trio. Matteo grunted thanks.

Jace turned his head. Bruises ringed his throat, and the shoulder visible through his torn shirt looked like someone had dragged him over gravel. "Go—" He coughed again and his breath whistled through swollen airways. "Go on inside."

"I'll help Liv first." Hearts probably couldn't really stop from fear, but his took a try at it, waiting. Wanting Jace or Matteo say *sure* and nod.

Jace licked his split lip, and Matteo answered. "You oughta come on in and let—Kimi and Bruce have got this."

Matteo grunted again then caught all of Josh's weight as the other agent sagged. Matteo hauled ass down the hall, Marshall forgotten.

Marshall let the door go. Somehow, he got from doorway to the truck.

Kimi reappeared with a board-thing. She popped levers and wheels dropped, the board an EMT-style gurney. Marshall swallowed, keeping his bile and fear from splattering the floor.

Kimi had tossed her outer shirt, leaving only a thin tank, and blood coated her arms up to her elbows, macabre scarlet gloves. She shook her head and elbowed him, easing him out of the way.

Bruce swore non-stop, words tumbling and linking together into one curse-prayer. Kimi repeated the pop-open thing with another gurney. Three people not accounted for.

Two gurneys.

"Liv?" Marshall didn't know if the question made it past his lips.

Bruce turned, blood streaking his polo, and lifted out a—person. It had to be a person but Marshall's brain couldn't process the raw, exposed muscle and bones, and turn them into what they should be.

"If you're staying, fucking hold this." Bruce kicked a gurney.

Marshall grabbed, bracing it as the other man rolled his burden onto the board. A head with short, black hair lolled sideways. Stavros. Most of the side of his face was gone, the other side a mass of ground meat. Like it had passed through a kitchen grinder. His sweater was a melted mess over one arm, a sharp, chemical stink rising from it.

Bruce dove back into the vehicle, Kimi cutting around to the other side, and jerking the door open.

"Wait. I can do it."

They all paused at the thick, raspy command.

Legs emerged from the truck. Bloody, pants torn, a tall boot split down the side so that the lining showed from calf to ankle. Kimi crawled straight through, and came up behind Vee, wrapping arms around her.

Claw marks scored Vee's face and arms, her jacket shredded until it hung by the shoulder seams.

Bruce's swearing ramped up, but he turned from Vee. Bending into the very back of the truck at an awkward angle, he grunted then backed out slowly, muscles in his arms bunching and standing out from the weight of whoever he'd grabbed. Bruce got his patient out and into the light.

Liv's blood was responsible for Kimi's gloves. Because there couldn't be any blood left in Liv. A gash went from her throat, ran down, then changed to rows from her chest to her stomach. Claw marks. Like something had braced a set of claws at her neck, and swiped with the other set, attempting to gut her. Pinkish-white things showed through the gashes, a white knob of rib visible.

Too many emotions balled together, catching on each other like they had barbs. Terror, grief, denial. They worked their way from what felt like his soul, coming out of his throat.

The noise brought Vee's attention to him. Her eyes shone flat silver, pupils lost.

"She's alive," Bruce said. Steady. Flat. Like he'd ground all the emotion away.

"She's—" Metal screeched as Vee braced her hand, and it slipped, her claws gouging new scars down the door. "She needs more. I didn't get enough in her on the way."

"You don't fucking have any more to give." Bruce jerked his head at Kimi. "Go drain Stavros."

"He can't."

Bruce didn't even glance at his fiancé. "He doesn't get a vote. He's older and he'll fucking survive. You be still and. Quit. Talking."

Kimi left in a swish and hiss of the breezeway opening and closing.

Blackness crept in on Marshall's vision, pouring from the corners and threatening to blanket him.

A clammy wetness smeared his chin. Something sharp pricked through, a bright pop of pain. He slung his head sideways and the blackness receded an inch. Blinking, the watercolor mass in front of him solidified into Vee. Her hand around his jaw, nails turned sharper, more like claws now, but barely out, only enough to prick him. Her other hand was wrapped around the SUV side mirror, holding them both upright.

"Marshall, stay with me," she said.

He followed the sound of her voice. "O—okay."

"Squeeze closer and breathe with me. Concentrate on my eyes and voice. If we're touching, I can try to make the fear and anxiety go away for a minute, long enough for you to go inside."

Bruce swore louder. Because his fiancé was bleeding like crazy, torn to shreds, and wasting energy on Marshall.

He was in one piece. They weren't. Part of him thrashed, and backed toward the dark corner, the familiar safe space in his head.

Liv hadn't been safe.

She still wasn't.

He tore his attention from inside his head, to the here, the garage. Focused over Vee's head to Liv's swollen face, her lips going blue. "No. Tell me what to do."

"Infirmary," Bruce barked, already past Marshall, the gurney aimed for the breezeway.

Marshall slid an arm around Vee, the exact way Kimi had. Vee's head didn't even come up to his shoulder. She couldn't weight more than the sacks of grain he'd routinely unloaded at jobs, and he carried two of those at a time. "I won't drop you," he promised her.

She nodded and more collapsed against him than leaned. Trusting him. Vee was fierce and a leader and believed he could help.

"Hang on." He bent enough to catch her under her knees, and scooped her up. He strode in, keeping the gurney and Liv's face in sight, as his touchstone.

The room constricted and pressed in when he entered, surrounded by wounds and hurt. Jace and Josh were slumped on one of the table things, crowded but obviously squashed there because they were basically propping each other up. Their shirts were off, gashes and bruises exposed. Strips of the white tape hung from the metal edge of the table, Matteo methodically pulling one off and using it to secure bandages over cleaned wounds.

Kimi stood over Stavros, what there was of him, one of

the hospital blood tubes stuck in his waxy gray arm, the one not coated in melted fabric. She pulled the partially filled tube free, laying it beside another full one. Her hands moved in a blur. When Bruce grunted and snatched the pair, Marshall interpreted it as those being all Stavros had to give.

"Table," Vee said softly, one hand on Marshall's chest. Her fingers trembled like leaves in a high wind, arm cooler than it should be where it pressed against him. "You're doing great."

Marshall sat her on the only empty table, the paper cover crinkling.

"You."

Marshall flinched at the whip-crack of Bruce's voice. "Go to Stavros' room. There's a metal case in the footlocker. Bring it." He bent over Liv with the tubes. "Stavros can get over this acting like blood supplies are contraband bullshit."

By the time Marshall came back, Liv and Josh were hooked to lines, clear liquid dripping from bags attached to poles and boxy red machines.

Bruce kept one eye on Vee, the other on the syringe in his hand, pushing thick red liquid into Liv's catheter thing.

Kimi signed, and Bruce passed her the syringe. He snatched the case from Marshall. "Go help Kimi."

Liv. Marshall held onto that one word, letting her name repeat in time to his pulse, and inched beside Kimi. She pointed at a pair of scissors with blunt ends.

"Cut that shirt off her," Bruce said.

Marshall picked up the shears on the second try, metal clattering, his hand shaking almost as hard as Vee's. Vee, who helped and gave and worried about others, even wounded and probably in pain.

Marshall inhaled, then let it out slow. Concentrated on his muscles, the way the scissors fit, and the force to cut through the heavy camo, then the stiff webbed belt and holster. Ignoring the bits of flesh and stuff splattered on Liv's clothes, some bits too grayish for human.

He slit the fabric the way he slit sausage casings. Peeled it off carefully, and worked her boots free next. Kimi moved between him and Liv, syringe gone and something antiseptic smelling in its place, the bite covering the organic smells.

He fumbled one handed for one of the squares folded in the cabinet by his elbow, because Liv hated the cold and he was pretty sure people who went into shock got cold. He shook the woven blanket out and draped it over her legs.

Keeping one hand on Liv's ankle, he dug for his phone. "Do we call the ambulance or the medical flight or—"

"No hospitals," Bruce said, with the finality of a casket closing.

"Josh is hurt. Liv is—can you not see how bad she is?" Something hazy-red washed over his vision in place of the customary numbing darkness. "She's going to the hospital."

"Agents don't go to civilian hospitals."

Keys. SUV keys were in the kitchen. Marshall pivoted for the door. "Liv is going."

Kimi stepped in front of him, guessing what he was after. She stopped him with a hand on his shoulder. Sympathy softened her features and she caught his balled up fist with her free hand.

"Liv needs emergency rooms and doctors and surgery—and all those are at the hospital," he said, head bent closer, keeping the conversation between the two of them. Liv's sister had to understand and agree, even if her dick of a future brother-in-law didn't.

Kimi pressed on his shoulder until he understood and he swung in a half-circle, facing the room and Liv, and God, if she was trying to tell him it was already too late for Liv—

Vee pointed. A new line was hooked to Liv, thick reddish stuff that wasn't human blood pumped through into the

377

catheter in her arm. "I gave her blood on the way, to basically keep organs functioning. Mine isn't strong enough to do more. This is Stavros' and his is very potent since he's been infected for centuries and the virus DNA has matured. Our blood will heal her and Josh. Promise."

His gaze went from bandages to IVs and oxygen, to the gaping wounds crisscrossing Liv's abdomen.

Vee's voice was soft from exhaustion. "The IVs and fluids help with blood pressure, while Stavros' DNA works on repairing the damage."

"You've got to trust us, man." Jace's voice was stronger, no coughing or rasp now. "Look."

Marshal shifted enough to check while still keeping Liv in view.

Jace tilted his head. Murky green bruises wreathed his neck, the ones on his shoulder faded to nothing. "This is after a ghoul tried snapping my neck. I couldn't walk right when Matteo dragged us back to the truck. Now all I need are a handful of ibuprofen, and time in the gym's hot tub."

"Liv will heal," Vee said.

Marshall met her gaze. Her eyes were all-human, soft brown like her sisters'. "It still weirds me out too, not to have a med flight and people headed to the HQ hospital wing. But we've done this before. She'll be okay, I promise."

There was something else under her factual statement, when she mentioned HQ. He felt the truth in her promise, though. "What—" he had to clear his throat "What do you need me to do? I know what you and Stavros said, but I've donated blood before." He opened his fist and twisted to Kimi, rotating his wrist softer side up. "You can draw blood. Donating is donating." Especially if his supplying Stavros his blood, and getting the guy healthier, meant there would then be more vampire DNA-whatever for Liv.

Kimi smiled and transferred the touch on his shoulder to a one-armed hug.

"Did you listen to one damn word I said today? This situation is the norm." Bruce's brows drew down, and he took a split second to glare at Marshall. "This is what Company life is. Of fucking course we're prepared."

"What B means is thank you, but Stavros and I carry a small amount of preserved vampire blood with us, for extreme emergencies. It doesn't work as well as fresh, but it's enough to keep us going." Vee gave him a tired smile.

Kimi used her hug as steering, aimed him at Liv, and turned him loose.

He moved to the off side, where he could watch everything Kimi did without getting in the way, and make sure Bruce didn't come near Liv.

Kimi held up a clip thing, and clamped it on the end of one of Liv's fingers, and pointed to the machine by Liv's head. Numbers and percentages flashed up on its tiny screen.

"That's a pulse-ox." Vee explained Kimi's actions. "It measures pulse rate and oxygen levels. As long as it stays over ninety-six, she's good."

Ninety-six. He burned it into his memory, working harder than he ever had to line the numbers up, then not flip them. The same when Kimi showed him the round pads stuck to Liv's chest, and how to feed the plastic IV lines into the boxy red machine, while Vee lectured along, about kinks and air bubbles.

Marshall focused, storing snapshots of the equipment and Kimi's movements in his head, the sound and rhythm of the monitors, the same as watching music being played or cooking demos. Burning it all in, his way, to join the oxygen information. To the extent he jumped when Kimi patted his cheek, one of her brows up. "Uh, sorry."

When he checked to see what all he'd missed, Matteo and

the guys were gone, nothing to mark their presence except a trash can full of gauze and empty tape rolls.

Kimi pointed to the door and raised her other brow.

"There are muffins, and the coffee maker is set and electric kettle full, if you want to make tea." Which was his job, and the rest of the team needed to refuel too, but his fingers tightened over Liv's covered knee. "Or salad and chicken in the top of the fridge."

"I know," Kimi mouthed. "You?"

"I'm staying with Liv."

She smiled again and rough-patted his cheek. This time, she signed, slow and in time with her lips. "If anything changes, or drops lower, come and get me. Okay?"

"Yeah. I will." He tried the okay sign. Kimi could hear, but putting in the same effort she was using on him only seemed right. Plus, doing it helped cement the sign in his brain.

Vee joined them, dark circles under her eyes, the arm that'd been chewed up in a sling, and she had on a clean tank top and baggy drawstring pants. "Come get me if you need anything, too. We'll all be sleeping, but just knock on any of our doors." She frowned. "Any but Stavros'."

When Marshall looked, the table their father had been on was also empty. Marshall hadn't noticed the vampire regaining consciousness or leaving, any more than he had the guys and Vee. Heat prickled his face, then stopped. He'd been busy, and with something way more important.

"Don't fuck anything up." Bruce filled the doorway, and tucked Vee in against his side when she joined him. "I'll do dinner when everyone wakes, but only this once. Don't think you're some delicate flower who gets a pass on working because you're up in your feelings."

"Okay."

"Fucking knock off that okay shit. Read a damn dictionary while you're sitting in here, and broaden your vocabulary," the guy bitched, already heading away.

"Okay." And yeah, this one was on purpose.

Kimi's—and Vee's—snort-giggles drowned out Bruce's swearing.

Marshall pulled the metal stool tucked under the counter that held the blankets and supplies his way, its wheels rolling without a squeak. Like it was used regularly and maintained. Bruce had said as much. Marshall hadn't understood until now, though.

He tugged the ugly green hospital gown Kimi had put on Liv up higher over Liv's chest, careful not to dislodge monitor pads, or catheters, or graze any wounds. The pulse thing climbed at a steady rate, the pattern of machine beeps already familiar.

More reassuring, Liv's lips had lost the bluish tint, chapped but pink again. Her breathing had smoothed out, the same rhythm as when she'd fallen asleep on him. The bruises on her face and arms faded. He didn't dare peel back any of the loosely taped pads to check underneath, although the scratches on her hands were now only faint pinkish lines.

He adjusted the blanket, tucking it better, then worked his hand under and found Liv's, the one without tubes and monitors. Marshall cupped her fingers between both of his, keeping that much of her warm.

The house's silence settled around him, that feeling like when everyone was asleep and safe. The reassuring beeps marking Liv's progress felt like the house's heartbeat.

For the first time, he really breathed. Exhaled, and all the dread and terror from twenty hours of not knowing escaped into the air. His gaze unfocused until it was him and Liv's warm skin, her regular resting-breaths.

He'd done it. He hadn't frozen. Hadn't gone into his head only to come out hours later after all the action was over. He hadn't freaked, or ruined anything, or gotten in the way and gotten anyone hurt.

Bruce thought day after day of routine, the nights waiting up, and call-outs, and worrying was a negative. It only meant Marshall had more chances to learn, for this to become his normal, to practice getting it right, perfecting how to help the team. Repeating over and over, learning his way.

He brushed loose hair off Liv's cheek, where Kimi had finished taking the half-destroyed bun down, leaving it loose. The enormity punched him in the chest and he tightened his grip on Liv's hand.

"I can do this," her whispered to her. "I'm always anxious, there's always the not so great voice in my brain, worrying about stuff, all the time. Nobody gets that. Here, I'll know why, and there's real stuff to do to make it better. I'd be more scared thinking of you guys out fighting but me being somewhere else, and not seeing you come back in, not taping up cuts and making muffins. You and the guys don't care that by everybody else's standards I'm messed up. Like you said, I've got work-arounds. I can be here for you. I'm *going* to be here, and you're going to wake up. Then I'm gonna find a way to convince you all that I can be your Bruce if I stay. Except not as big a bag of dicks and with less swearing. Less swearing, and more pizza."

After a few hours, people came and went, infirmary door whooshing with each trip. All his attention and energy committed to Liv, Marshall only marked who was who by how growly they sounded. None for Kimi, Vee, and Matteo, Matteo checking machines and adding or removing IV bags. Maximum growl for Kantor, who Marshall had zero problem ignoring.

A medium growl sounded, right beside Marshall. Medium meant Jace or his bother. "You need a break."

Reluctantly, Marshall focused. Jace was in front of the

gurney, waving a mug under Marshall's nose, coffee scented steam rising.

"I will, after Liv wakes up."

"Man, your ass has got to be numb."

"It's fine."

"It's been eighteen hours," Jace countered, and set the mug at the end of a line of other mugs, mismatched ceramic marching down the counter.

Marshall tensed, and locked his ankle around the stool leg. Jace could probably drag him away, but Marshall would damn well make him work for it.

"Hey, relax." Jace drew up a second stool, not bothering raising the seat height, instead propping elbows on his bent knees, resembling a weirdly attractive praying mantis, all legs and elbows.

"I can't leave until she's awake. I get it's stupid and my being here isn't some magic cure or whatever—"

"But you're staying." Jace squeezed Marshall's shoulder. "I feel you. I'm saying, we're all here and we'll step in for a few if you decide to grab a bite, or shower, or five minutes of fresh air."

Marshall bent his head, hiding how much the offer meant —the support part way more than the rest. "Thanks."

An explosive snort killed the moment. "For fuck's sake. You don't hold proprietary rights on worrying." From the doorway, Bruce glared at Marshall, then switched to Jace. "Quit feeding his ego."

"Yeah, having a team member with an ego. That would suck," Jace said, rolling his eyes.

"Fuck you and fuck your smart-assed brother, who I relieved of a case of chemical and dye-laden liquid sugar masquerading as a healthy drink, which he attempted to sneak from the damn truck to your room. Dinner is on." Bruce stomped out.

"Gotta love the guy." Jace stood and stretched. "Fair warning. There's one set of circumstances where Liv outperforms Bruce as far as sheer bad attitude. She hates people noticing she's sick or hurt. She's so bad that she's notorious in the HQ infirmary. Like, they draw straws to avoid being her doctor or nurse, because, whoa, is she a lousy patient."

"Good luck with that. She can yell at me all she wants. I don't care."

A smile transformed Jace's face, humor banishing the concern. "Give her hell. Bellow if you need reinforcements. I got your back."

iv

I LET the noises wash over me, like the tide when I was laying on the beach, drowsing to the sound of waves coming in, then receding. Now, every time noises ebbed, they took some of the disorienting grayness with them.

The noises finally transformed into voices. The voices, to individuals.

One thing to be said for vampire DNA-induced healing, waking was different, but easier, then coming out from under drugs. Since information made all of us more valuable, thus less incentive for HQ to end us, we'd all volunteered as lab animals. When injured now, DNA was our first line of E.R. treatment.

I swallowed a couple of times, getting tongue unstuck from the roof of my mouth, as grumbly-barks dominated the conversation around me. Bruce's, definitely. Followed by Jace's more level one, which was reassuring since he wouldn't sound so calm if anyone else was still seriously wounded.

Then Marshall's deeper, more mellow burr. Mellow Marshall.

I blamed Vee's blood for the warm, fuzzy feeling that hearing his voice produced. Clearly, engaged-couple romance germs were also carried by vampire DNA, and transmitted via blood transfusions. I should add that to the next medical report.

After the voices died out, I licked my chapped lips. "Why'm I yelling at you?"

Someone's breath hitched, and whatever was pressing my fingers together tightened. I blinked hard, ungluing eyelashes and dry eyeballs. A blur of white, with copper and blue smudges, sharpened into auburn curls and Marshall's face, inches from mine.

I tested my extremities. Toes curled against the woven blanket. Same for fingers. One set was toasty warm, wrapped in someone's hand.

"Do you need—never mind, you're still out of it. I'm getting Kimi or Matteo."

"*Oooh. That's* why I'm yelling at you." I blinked a couple more times, vision clearing more with each. "Bruce stuck you here as nurse for your initiation. He's sooo mean."

"Yeah, and you're so loopy. Be still."

I hadn't realized I was moving. I tried it on purpose, shifting an elbow, readying to push up.

"Liv, c'mon, don't." A strong arm encircled my shoulders.

A big chest was attached to the big arm. That was nice. I used the chest to brace and sit.

My entire abdomen roared awake, pain flaring from my middle out. Not nice. So not nice. I gagged, which hurt worse. Taking small sips of air, I stopped short of throwing up. Riding out the spasms and cramps. They finally eased up. Not gone, but bearable.

Okay, I'd taken some kind of gut wound…a ghoul. This was thanks to a ghoul. One that had acted like it was partnering with another, attacking as a pair. Which couldn't be right. Yet the one bent me backward, as if it was positioning me for the other to swipe at my stomach. That had been real.

"Lay back. Then I can go grab Kimi. And Vee," Marshall said.

When I opened my eyes again, he was half on the table, holding me, blue eyes worried. My hand still wrapped around his, where I'd latched on during the pain. I tried out a couple of deeper breaths. "I'm all right now."

Marshall's brows dipped. "Not true."

"Is too." I tried sounding more Commander-ish. "The muscles aren't a hundred-percent reknit yet."

"You think?"

I ignored Sarcastic Marshall. "Yes. Sitting is good, and necessary. The sooner I move around, the faster the DNA works. No idea why yet, but all our injury reports and data go to the Research division, so they'll eventually discover the reason. Backrest?"

I must've sounded more believable. Marshall didn't let go, keeping me close while reaching around to raise the headboard. "Where were we? Oh, yelling."

"Go ahead. It won't make a difference." He eased his arm from behind me. Free, he inspected the IV line and monitor like he knew precisely what he was doing.

Which was weird. While he fussed, I looked around. The bay was empty, other tables clean and neat, although I also remembered watching a ghoul try to break Jace in half, seconds before Kimi's shot took it out. Color drew my gaze. The majority of our mugs lined the counter under the gowns and linens. Some cups empty, some full of brown liquid. "They stuck you in here the entire time?"

"I wanted to be here."

That was—I couldn't process emotions yet, mine or his, and switched to facts. "How long?"

He checked his phone. "A day, about." He shrugged. "It's no worse than a double shift."

Sitting upright, talking, whatever the reason, the confusing grayness thinned further. "Except you didn't sleep the entire time we were gone, on top of staying in here for a day."

I flexed my hands, then elbows, and when moving didn't restart the spasms, rubbed at my eyes. "The excitement is over. Go on to bed."

"No." Marshall had the same implacable tone as when he was willing to go back to HQ, to protect us.

"Excuse me?" I dropped my hand, double-checking who I was speaking to.

"No. N.O. You can yell or whatever but you aren't moving, and I'm staying 'til—" He peered over me to the IV pump. "Until that last fluid bag is empty, when I then go get Kimi or Matteo. Probably both of them."

No hesitation or anxiety marred his stubborn posture. He looked prepared to sit here until doomsday. Possibly, sit on me, if required.

"Did Vee accidentally inoculate you with her blood? Because you've developed a sudden annoyingly familiar streak of know-it-all stubbornness. It isn't attractive." Except, it was. On a par with him sitting up for hours, in this uncomfortable room, so I wouldn't wake up alone.

Coppery brows lifted, almost haughty. "Maybe she did. And I'm a curly haired ginger who is extra pasty-white from never getting any sunlight, so attractive went out the window a long time ago."

Not true. Not even a little. Also, not the time for that argument.

"The crew is having dinner. Do you want something?" He frowned. "Nothing heavy, toast or soup. Bruce can make soup."

"Dang. Ordering Bruce around? I missed all the good stuff."

Pink tinted Marshall's ears, but he didn't blush anywhere near as bright as in the past. "What about toast?"

"Not yet. Sitting and breathing is good for now."

Marshall seemed to realize he was on the table, hip against mine, at the same time I did. He fidgeted, weighing whether to go or stay.

"You're warm, and nice." It was true, and my filter was still partially offline.

Marshall hitched further onto the table, lifting the blanket over my chest and shoulders, then staying, arm back around me. He braced the other, across my lap to the opposite side. "Sitting is good?"

I nodded, cheek grazing his shoulder. "It does take a bit for reality to re-center after being out of it while healing, or brain and body."

"Take as much time as you need. I'm not going anywhere."

I relaxed against him. His breathing, and the faded scent of our detergent and the fresher aroma of burnt coffee, helping me shake off the after effects. "You've done the medically impossible, as in, not annoying the snot out of me."

"Jace implied you weren't a very accommodating patient."

"Implied, huh?"

A grin slipped up on Marshall. "Implied strongly. But you're not so bad."

"Neither are you." Brain cells came back online. We'd been ambushed, vampires and ghouls pouring out of surrounding buildings and up through manholes. All of us were hurt, several of us seriously. Which equaled blood and gore, and we were currently sitting in the infirmary. Where Marshall had been for a day. Which…I laid my fingers on top of his. "You seem—"

"Not a freak show?"

I tightened my hold on his hand. "You are never, ever a freak show. Being confronted with mangled bodies is a shock, doubly so when they're people you know. Then all of it happening quickly and under the stress of a what's essentially an emergency room. That scenario isn't something most people are prepared for."

"You, the guys, you're all okay, so I'm okay."

Admiration joined the warm-fuzzy feeling. Marshall had the bandana on, but a curl had gone rogue anyway. I reached and Marshall lowered his head to make it easier, like he already knew what I meant to do. I tucked the curl back where it belonged. "Thanks for hanging out with me."

"You're welcome."

I stayed there, with Marshall's breath tickling the short hairs at my temple, stretching muscles group by group, under the blanket. Everything worked again, even if grudgingly. My dry throat burned every time I swallowed, and my abs ached like I'd done an hour-long plank. "Hey, that offer of food?"

"You're hungry?"

"Thirsty. Do you mind grabbing something with ice?"

Indecision flickered, but Marshall wasn't the scheming type. "Sure. I'll be quick."

I waited until the door hissed closed, then swung my legs over the edge of the table, and turned off the monitors. I peeled the sticky electrode pads off, pulled the catheter out, and tossed the whole mess into the trash.

I dropped the ugly gown on the table, and sorted through the cabinet for scrub pants and a tee, wincing as sore muscles pulled. The cold air raised goosebumps all over my body. Being nude still wasn't as bad as the gown. It felt vulnerable in a way that nudity didn't.

Wiggling into the clothes, I shoveled gown, blanket, and pillow into the laundry bin.

"Liv!"

I turned to check, then held my hand out for my drink, an oversized sports mug, complete with a straw. "Thanks."

"You can't—get back on the gurney."

"There's no need."

"There's need. Lots of it. I'm getting Vee. She can make you get back up there, and hook that IV back up."

I set the mug down, grabbing Marshall's wrist. "It was empty, see?" Letting go, I bunched the drained plastic. Then remembered I was talking to a civilian, whose exposure to experimental DNA treatments was non-existent.

Marshall spoke slowly, like I might understand if he enunciated clearly. "Your insides were on the outside. I don't know how much blood is in a person, but you lost most of yours."

He patted the bed, and held his hand out. "Lay down with your drink."

"I don't need to lie down. I need to drink this." I took a long swallow of unflavored and extra vile electrolytes. "Then write up a report, and think about a shower." Vee and Jace would've already submitted theirs, but I couldn't slack on mine.

"You can't be off the machines. How are we going to know if your pulse or oxygen is dropping? Or if you're bleeding from something we can't see?" The annoyed blush faded, leaving his handful of freckles standing out, and his jaw set. Stress lines cutting deep across his forehead and lips.

I shoved my drink away, to join the line of used mugs. "I'm the next thing to healed." I wadded up the shirt, exposing everything from under-boob down to the pant's drawstring. "Look."

I couldn't tell if I grabbed for him first, or he reached for me. His rough fingertips traced the parallel rows of bright pink scars running down my stomach, my fingers over his.

A ragged sigh rolled out. His voice wasn't much louder when he said, "When you came in—it was bad, Liv. I've never been that scared. Never. I know what Kimi and Vee said, but you were ripped open, and your lips going blue."

The confession tore at me. Marshall waded through fear daily, and somehow, I'd accidentally given him a new entry for his Top Ten Worst Memories list. "Fear can be good, and normal. Human. We're very pro-human here." I flattened his hand over the scars, pressing his palm in. Reminding us both the crisis was over.

"That wasn't it. I was scared for Jace, and Vee and everyone, but not the same way as for you. All I could think was that you had to make it. There couldn't be a world where you didn't, and weren't here." He touched my cheek, gentler than he'd ever been. "You had to be here."

I turned my face into his hand, and nudged closer.

Marshall made a noise somewhere between agreement and hurt. Then we were together, his head bent so that we were forehead to forehead, his curls mixing with my tangles. His other hand ran up and down my back, trying to sooth me, or maybe sooth us both.

I wanted to say...a lot of impossible things, things I'd never considered before. To promise I'd never scare him this way again. To tell him I'd always come home to him, and so would the rest of the team. For this to be home for him.

"I'm acting stupid, and that's the last thing you need to deal with after nearly dying, and still having reports to write about monsters acting weird." His apology tickled, lifting the hairs along my temple, his gruff tone rumbling through me where we touched.

"Between us?"

He nodded, those ridiculously curly lashes sweeping my forehead.

"I hate infirmaries, and medical personnel, primarily because I hate being ordered around."

"Sorry."

"Today wasn't so bad." I eased closer. "By not so bad, I mean waking up to you was—different. Comfortable, or comforting. I'm not clear which."

"I never thought I was good in an emergency. Probably I'm not, not really." Marshall's thumb ran along my jaw and up, to arc under my ear, then back again.

Waking a tingle that radiated through me. "You are good enough in an emergency situation to save bystanders. Twice. And to step in, and help Kimi with all of this. You've never even had crisis management training."

Forget propriety. Marshall wasn't shy about touching, and admitting he needed contact after life temporarily blowing up.

My right hand was still over his, his pressing against my stomach. Propriety wasn't an agent thing, anyway, and I'd already seen that the rules didn't always protect you, the way I'd once believed.

I rested my other hand on his side, taking advantage of our closeness, of us sharing the same space. "You're amazing." I let my admiration free, showing him how impressive he was.

Marshall closed the tiny gap between us, like my touch was permission to go for the rest of what he wanted. "I can learn. I can learn to be useful here."

My language center fritzed, overloaded processing what Marshall said, and what the words really meant. Because coming from anyone Company, his statement was a hint, suggesting he wanted to join a team.

His palm warmed my stomach and the achy muscles, heat spreading outward from his touch. "You're a fast learner," I agreed.

"Only when I'm motivated."

"You're motivated now?"

"Yeah." Marshall let go of my jaw, and cupped the back of my neck. Gentle, the way he did everything.

"Joining the guys and valiantly trying to best Kimi in online gaming is motivational?"

"They're awesome, and that part is cool. But not the thing that pushes me."

"Thing?"

"Person. The person who motivates me and makes me feel like I can do things I never dared, because I was scared I'd lock down and screw up."

"Now you can?"

"Now I want to try. Now that its maybe not the end if I need to ask for help or whatever."

"Yeah." My heart was perfectly fine post-injury, as evidenced by the way it sped up. "Teams are the key. That's what we're all about. We back each other, and each fill in pieces to create a whole."

I cut off my disjointed ramble, and shifted, embarrassed. Marshall moved as I did. My leg slid between his, like we were meant to interlock.

"I can fit in," Marshall added. He exerted a tiny bit of pressure, against the nape of my neck.

When I looked up, the blue of his eyes filled my vision, my entire world, for a single heartbeat. "Marshall..." I didn't know what to ask.

"Yes." His lips were right there, and brushed mine. More like a promise than a question.

The clatter of pans on an oven rack boomed, intruding as the infirmary door hissed open.

I jumped, and Marshall took a step back.

"Awesome. You got her moving," Vee said, letting the door close behind her. She stopped, head cocked, gaze traveling between me and Marshall. Her nostrils fluttered.

We were so implementing a strict no sniffing rule. I glared at her. "That isn't required, since obvs, I am up and fine."

Vee lounged against the door. Totally, purposefully, blocking it. She spoke to Marshall. "FYI, tolerating her testiness in a medical setting qualifies you for a hazardous duty stipend. Like, to use on noise-cancelling headphones and tequila. For real."

Marshall averted his face, and rolled the IV pump back to its spot against the far wall. Then placed each rolling stool in precise alignment under the counter. "She wasn't so bad."

"See? You guys all exaggerate." I pulled attention away from Marshall before she questioned his muted response. "Honestly, I'm a model patient."

"She unhooked lines, and snuck and got dressed." Marshall ratted me out. "Should one of you check her?"

"Neener-neener, Miss Model Patient." Despite the teasing, her soft expression gave her away. "She's absolutely fine, Marsh. Some residual bruising and soreness, but that will pass in a couple of days."

He paused, and his fingers flicked through what I recognized now as a complicated musical chord progression. "You can tell because of the blood you shared?"

"Sort of. Mostly, it's due to Stavros' contribution."

Marshall nodded, accepting the reassuring little white lie. Vee was confident thanks to our detailed accounts from past instances, and Kimi's private calculations on injury type, blood volume used, and healing rates. "I remember what you said before, but are you sure I can't make something to help you and Stavros? Blood pudding won't take long. Or liver. I can make a chicken liver mousse. With spinach, since spinach has iron, and probably that's important for vampires the same as for everyone else, since you're people, too."

She pushed off the door. When Marshall didn't shy away, she caught him in a hug, her head brushing his chin.

Marshall hugged her back.

Some reservation I hadn't acknowledged broke, the last hesitation draining out like water from a breached dam.

Vee let go and smiled. "Anything with loads of sugary goodness, and butter, works miracles in perking up Company agents. Also, bacon."

Marshall slanted me a look, fighting not to show his amusement but the edges of his lips angling up anyway.

"It's probably true. Butter is fat and bacon is protein, both of which we burn while repairing tissue."

"Sugar?" He quit pretending not to smile.

"It makes us nicer? Which qualifies as improving mental health, thus, also medicinal."

"Points if you can pull it off under B's nose," Vee added.

Marshall's laugh filled the room. "Yeah, I can do that." He gathered the mugs into two iffy towers, and as Vee held the door open, walked out, his shoulders relaxed.

I had to do my report. I also had to hit the shower, and scrub ook off.

Instead, I grabbed Vee's wrist and pulled her with me, out of the infirmary and to the y-split between halls, out of sight and hearing range of the guys. "Get Kimi."

Vee aimed for the ladder and the roof, while I headed for my suite. I had official things to do, but right now, I *needed* my sisters.

By the time I came out of the shower, Kimi was curled in

my comfy chair, and Vee was in one of the beanbag chairs she'd appropriated from the den.

"Marshall?" Kimi signed.

Of course she knew, and of course she could sum up a multi-layered situation in one word.

"I adore him," Vee said.

"Same," Kimi signed. "Josh, too. Even before Jace and Matteo filled him in. Papá respects him."

"There was no bloodshed while we were out on the mission. So, B doesn't hate him." Vee wiggled deeper into the squishy beanbag. "Okay, doesn't *totally* hate him. Plus, he has shelved the whole drop Marshall in the desert thing."

I propped my leg on the edge of the bed, slathering cocoa butter on, then switching, finishing with the itchy new scars on my torso. We'd already established that Marshall fit in here, as well as the fact that I wanted him here.

Then there was the fact that he also evoked different emotions than with any agent I'd ever slept with.

It hadn't been a kiss in the infirmary. But it could have been. Vee's questions when she first arrived surfaced. *I think maybe you don't just want him close by because he's a friend. You feel more than that. Kinda like I did with Bruce?*

"Say that I'm interested in Marshall."

"Romantically," Vee said.

"Consider it said," Kimi signed.

"When you were sniffing away a few minutes ago?" I pinned Vee with my gaze.

"He is interested."

"There's no chance you misread? Marshall is so contained. He's difficult to read. Sure, he's grateful to us. I'm not arguing that he likes us. But what if I'm wrong, and it comes across as my expecting payment for keeping him safe, or as harassment?" I sank onto the bed, legs folded.

Kimi shook her head, curls bouncing. "The moment we

got everyone else stabilized yesterday, all Marshall saw was you," she signed.

Vee sat straight, her tone reverent. "Wow, was he terrified. The emotions coming off him threatened to lay me out. I had to pull on Stavros' aura to stay upright. Marshall refused to give in, though. Somehow, he fought his way through, all to help us and watch over you. And just now? He wants you so badly I'm hurting from the sexual tension. I don't *know-know*, but I think that's why Stavros has been reclusive the entire visit."

"Marshall leaving is…I hate the idea."

"Jace and Matteo aren't on board with that plan, either," Kimi signed.

At my look, she gave me two thumbs down. "We had hours to kill while you were recuperating, and Marshall wouldn't leave your side. They brought it up, not me."

She and Vee shared a look, and Vee seemed to be nominated spokesperson. "Sooo. Marshall has it bad for you, true, but I didn't get straight lust off him. The attraction part is all tangled in with these other emotions. Aside from saying he cares, which, duh, I can't be more specific. Stavros could. I guess asking him is an option?"

This time, our shared look was universal, and Kimi shuddered. No, we would not be asking Stavros how sexually attracted or frustrated Marshall might or might not be, in conjunction with whether he held other feelings for me. Stavros did *not* react well to topics in that vein, way worse than regular civilians.

"There are three issues in play here," Kimi signed. "One—Asset career positions, and whether that means at HQ, here, or as a floating Asset, if Marshall prefers civilian jobs. Part One-A—Oversight's reaction to an addition to your team, and our dual-team rules. Two—sexual attraction. That one is mutual, and settled. Three—bonds outside of sex. Way iffier."

I grabbed and hugged a pillow to me. "I have no idea where he stands on staying. He's not sold on the morality of our actions, no matter how much he likes us personally."

"We heard," Kimi signed. "Stavros, and Bruce."

"I think B came down on him like a ton of loud, judgmental bricks while he had the chance." Vee looked guilty, although, not even she had a chance in deterring Bruce from his opinions and actions.

My stomach knotted, and not from healing and side effects. "Marshall has talked about his panic and anxiety, among other things. No one ever helped him, or addressed it as neurodivergent, and not a defect."

Even if the Company was guilty of some of the faults Bruce claimed, no one, ever, fell through the cracks, or was made to feel lesser. "I don't get how he came out so kind and compassionate, to the extent that he can think cryptids might be redeemable, in the face of being raised by people who didn't even think their child merited help."

"Speaking of amazing things." Vee sat straight. "Putting aside the question of career choices, let's get back to Marshall, you, and potentially, cruddy one-off sexual encounters."

"I think that's called loading the question." Under her and Kimi's hard stares, I flopped backward on the bed. "Fine. I don't think Marshall is built for our kind of casual. We've established that I'm attracted to him and invested in his happiness. So, transitioning to that civi friends with benefits thing is logical." I ignored the analytical voice in my head reminding me of a similar conversation we'd once had with Vee when Bruce was only here until a cryptid threat was eliminated.

As if it was reading my thoughts, the engagement ring hanging from the necklace around Vee's neck caught the lamplight and seemed to wink back at me.

I yelped and ducked as a paperback winged my way and whacked me in the knee. Sitting up, I glared at the slot the book should've been in, on the bookcase between my sisters. Since both looked irritated, I wasn't sure of the culprit. "Quit abusing my books."

"Quit being such a weenie. Stop using logic, rules, and percentage strategies to put up a barrier between you and what you really want—you and Marshall." A thin ring of silver circled Vee's irises, her annoyance rising.

"Not everyone is ruled by their emotions, or want the same thing as you and Bruce. Tell me you want a civi, romantic relationship with someone?" I turned to Kimi.

"Who knows? The point is that you do," she signed.

I rolled off the bed, pacing a short arc around it.

Vee bolted to her feet, and blocked my path. "Say it. Even if this is the only time, quit thinking about duty, and say. What. You. Feel." Her voice rose with each demand.

I matched her volume. "No, Marshall isn't convenient sex, and I'm pretty sure you don't go to sleep kind of wishing someone who is only a friend was sharing your pillow."

"Right? Don't you feel better now," Vee asked.

"Not even a little. Granted, as far as romantic unions, you and Bruce—"

"And Ridge and McKenna," Kimi signed, and didn't even bother trying to look innocent or neutral.

"McKenna is at least government, and military-adjacent, and *back to my point*. The four of you are it for examples or role models. I'm not certain that I'm up to that level of commitment, because when—" I stopped there. When Bruce thought she was dead, he might as well have been, too. Reminding Vee of that would hurt her, and I wasn't going there.

I tried again, hugging myself, mashing sore ribs and sorer muscles. "The idea of giving up that much of myself is terrifying. I don't know if I can let someone else in, give them space in my life and heart, and survive if they chose another life or another person."

This was why teams were supposed to be closed units. They were the people we grew up with, the people we trusted and loved, and spent our life with. Teams removed that awful uncertainty that civilians lived with.

Kimi abandoned the chair, hugging me. She let go to sign, but stayed beside me. "I would be the same way. Absolute control isn't possible though. Four-hundred-years of it, and Stavros wasn't really alive or happy until he traded a measure of control for messy, unpredictable ties with messy, unpredictable people. I guess it's about which you need more—control or the relationship?"

"Seriously, Liv. What's adding one more person to the list of people you're responsible for and love? You're responsible for Jace and Matteo every second, and responsible for all of us thanks to the Oversight thing. You took responsibility for me, Josh, and Kimi, then Bruce, long before you were my Lieutenant or a Commander. It's your lifeblood the same as it is mine."

I sighed, because no, there was no refuting facts.

"Exactly." Vee crossed to the door, and opened it. "So what's adding one more person to the list of people you protect and love? A real relationship has all those drawbacks, but the return you get—it's the best thing in the world."

If plans went perfectly, maybe so. If you had already lost everything once? I didn't know the number of times a person could break and put themselves back together before there were too many pieces missing to make repair possible.

iv

THUMPS, bickering that wasn't really bickering, and laughter echoed down the hall and into my room through the open door. It was the usual routine. A little louder and more exuberant, which in my world, rocked. The compound felt like home right now.

I'd grown up with a larger group, and even the Company preferred at least four to a team. Meaning there was plenty of room for Marshall. I bent over, finger combing my hair, which had dried overnight into waves, and pulling it back. I rolled the band off my wrist, and secured the neat ponytail. Which constituted my last procrastination option.

Getting gutted by a cryptid only bought me so much time, and breakfast had been in full swing for thirteen minutes. Fifteen was the max, before someone came looking. Plus, as an agent responsible for eliminating predators, and directing a team, hiding from a single, unarmed human with a penchant for cartoon shirts was beneath me. Theoretically.

What Marshall wanted in a career, what he wanted from me, what I wanted, versus newly formed teams, Oversight demands, and my sisters' barbed but welcome insights churned and brewed inside me, using me as a human pressure cooker. I still didn't know what the final product would look like when done.

I kicked my door closed, striding into the kitchen. Bruce held center court, barking at his diners and sous indiscriminately. I moved to intercept Bruce, until from her spot sitting on the bar counter, Kimi flashed me the all-clear sign. She'd been strategic, her seat inches from Marshall's station, prepared to referee.

She and I needed a night out, soon. After Vee bailed, Kimi and I had stayed up until past midnight talking, long, rambling conversations, about everything from cryptid theories to the latest season of our favorite telenovela. We hadn't touched on Marshall though, aside from her stating we needed to show Oversight that Marshall had an indispensable talent. Basically, buying his way past their restrictions. Where Vee dropped bombshells into team life, Kimi preferred surgically precise strikes.

The object of our three-way sister drama turned in my direction, as if he'd sensed me before the teams did. He gave me a quick smile, but his eyes didn't match, a tentative question swimming in them.

At least I learned from my mistakes. No freezing him out just because I was a big baby-woman.

"Coffee." I stopped beside him, reaching for the mug cabinet over our heads.

"There's a glass of juice and protein powder by the fridge, with your name on it," Bruce ordered.

Bruce's concoction, and the slime he obtained from

macerating kale and insisted on calling juice, was one thing I hadn't missed. "Coffee," I countered, and rattled the cabinet door for emphasis.

"Coffee is a diuretic, and you need fluids because you lost blood volume, plus to hydrate," Marshall said.

"First, coffee is the foundation of all happiness, and second, you've joined forces with the dark side? With what's essentially the dark side's cruel emperor?" I snatched a mug and waved it at Bruce. Marshall wasn't a medic before Bruce and his influence arrived.

"Should she have coffee?" Marshall turned from me to check with Vee.

"Juice and protein." Vee pasted on a fake apologetic expression. Then out of the guys' sight, signed *"Payback."*

"You can't have coffee." Marshall went back to flipping sizzling meat from a pan to plates.

"Why do Josh and Jace get coffee?" Since they were kicked back, empty coffee mugs in front of them, I threw them under the bus without a single qualm.

"Because they drank the damn juice instead of whining and moaning like Essie when she has to clean her room," Bruce said, pointing a serving spoon at me.

I hoped he was nicer to the nine-year-old niece in question.

"Drink the juice, then I'll make you coffee." Marshall took the mug from me, his fingers brushing the back of my hand a beat longer than necessary.

"Worst. Day. Ever." I drained the chalky green sludge.

Marshall patted me on the head. "All done, see? You survived and everything."

I curled my lip off a tooth as warning. He only smiled and handed me a plate. I blamed the funny dance my stomach did on the kale, not on how much I enjoyed his ease with my family, and his new teasing.

The plate was piled with eggs, cheese, and the kinds of veggies people actually liked. "You are partially forgiven for falling in with a bad crowd, and heeding even worse advice." I thwacked Marshall with my elbow, directing him to the table.

"I made this damn breakfast," Bruce said.

"All I know is that you forced me to drink leaf cuttings, while Marshall is feeding me turkey bacon and cheesy eggs." I took the middle seat among the three chairs left. Bruce dropped into the one on my right, beside Vee.

He gave me a once over, cataloguing how I moved, judging how far along my recovery really was, brow scrunched in his default frown. He'd have already done the same with the guys. I kicked his chair leg, and offered him our version of *I'm fine* and *love you, too*. "What do you want for your birthday?"

He replied with the same answer as every year. "For the three of you to have nothing to do with it."

At the table now, Kimi gave him an angelic smile, while I leaned around him to ask Vee, "Did you order that thing we saw in that really cool place? Because it was *awesome*."

Bruce swore into his coffee.

"Of course. This year calls for—hmm"

"Something more? Go big or go home?" Kimi signed.

"Exactly," we chorused all together.

"I told you to put a lid on them." Bruce glowered at Josh.

"They're sneaky. And they blackmail," Josh whined, glaring at Kimi. "You're on your own, man."

"You should change your password more frequently," Kimi signed.

"It should be beneath the team's intel specialist to blackmail her brother."

"You'd think so, wouldn't you?"

Head swiveling between us like an avid tennis spectator,

Marshall sat a glass of orange juice by my plate as he took the last chair. "Eat." He absently tapped my plate, still following the argument, Kimi pairing signing and lip reading for his benefit.

Bruce's degree of grump lessened microscopically, at the juice and Marshall's mother-hening. Which bore a strong resemblance to Bruce's, without the volume and overt bullying.

I took a bite and raised a brow, holding a silent discussion. *See? Marshall is solid. Are we cool?*

He grunted. *I don't like it. But maybe.*

Interpreting our conversation, Vee gave him a ninja-surprise kiss and grabbed her fork. Bruce angled into her, not touching Vee, but aligning his body to hers. He inhaled, like she was his oxygen, neither seeming aware of what they were doing as they continued breakfast.

For the first time, I wasn't comfortable watching people in love, so concentrated on my plate and putting a dent in the mountain of food. When I stopped for coffee, Marshall side-eyed me. "I'm eating, I'm eating."

"Okay. Keep going."

I snaked my leg out, bumping my ankle against Marshall's. Somehow, he kept his firmly against mine yet shifted so his knee also rested against me.

It's the best thing in the world. My sister's parting shot from the evening before surfaced, and wove intricate patterns through my brain. Curving around images of Marshall waiting for us, muffins as far as the eye could see. The sensation of waking up, my head pillowed on his chest. The look in his eyes when we stood in this kitchen, only days before, and the growl in his voice as he pressed me in tight against him.

Immune to any sort of romantic undercurrents, Jace and Matteo squabbled over the last of the casserole Kimi had put to the side. Jace reached, betting on speed, but Matteo body blocked him. The table rocked at the impact and sent a cup of juice sideways, headed for a quick death against the tile floor.

Stavros caught the glass, so fast I couldn't really register him even moving. He gave the guys a *look*, which he had to have picked up from Bruce, and they settled down immediately.

Watching them, being so tuned in to their behavior that I could anticipate issues, was supposed to be my job.

We were good. Really damn good. Yet clearly not as in synch as we needed to be.

If I ever got involved with a partner, it would be because I'd found what Vee and Bruce had. It just couldn't be right now. Even if this was my only chance, even if I suspected my person was sitting right beside me.

I couldn't have both that total dedication to one person, and to building my team into a unit that functioned like we'd been together the last fifteen years despite it being less than one. I couldn't split my energy and focus.

We were working to replace the old patterns and responses that were as natural as breathing, geared toward the strengths and weaknesses of team members we no longer served with. Not getting civilians or Jace and Matteo killed while we learned was paramount.

I closed my eyes, as if I could blank out this reality. I had a commitment to fulfill. I also had things to prove to myself. That I was qualified to head a team. That this was *real*, that we were a unit, and we were the one thing none of us could survive without—a family. My potential love life couldn't trump Matteo and Jace's needs.

Fitting Marshall in as a teammate, if he was interested, and if he'd absorbed that cryptids were the enemy, would be challenge enough. Fitting him, and myself, into a relationship at the same time, an area I had zero experience or training in… It wasn't fair to him, or to myself.

I opened my eyes to Stavros watching me, sadness deepening the lines and hollows of his square face, the marks from the experiences he'd endured. They gave him an aura of authority owing nothing to viruses and mutations. He spoke to the group, the weight of his life experiences in his voice. "I've no wish to leave, yet we have a schedule to maintain."

He'd picked up on my internal debate, his regret clear. He understood duty first, and agreed. I was an agent and C.O. before I was a person. I rose, coffee in hand, hoping another gulp of the scalding beverage would drown my resentment. "I'm grateful that we had this time together."

Marshall pointed at the glass of orange juice to my left, half remaining. I clutched my mug to my chest. "I'll have it for lunch, because caffeine withdrawal is an ugly, ugly thing."

Marshall sighed, sounding more and more like Stavros. "It's going to be a whole glass at lunch."

Vee stood, hands on her hips, and glared at me. "You should listen to Marshall more often. He understands helping his team."

I guess my sister had finally picked up on the same emotions Stavros recognized. Instead of engaging, I made the circuit, gathering up plates and utensils. Kimi hopped up, herding everyone around, creating a distraction.

It didn't take long to run out of busy work. Marshall closed the dishwasher, and flicked me with his towel-oven mitt hybrid. "Go on and help your family. That's more important than crumbs on the counter."

Kimi had done her best, but Vee was lying in wait at the hallway intersection. I held my hand up. "Don't."

Of course she did anyway. "*Oh, my God.* You really are bailing on the guy that is in the kitchen right now, hand squeezing fresh juice for you?"

Kimi paused on her way through. She shrugged her duffle out of the way, and signed. "Do I need to referee? Because you two clearly jump first, think second."

Vee and I both cringed.

"Papá?" I asked.

"He told me what really happened with the knife fight, not that I hadn't already started piecing the picture together."

"I'm merely trying to understand why our sister is making decisions that aren't in her best interest. At. All." Vee crossed her arms, aiming to win Kimi's vote.

"Name one reason that justifies my risking the civilians in my Division, much less Jace and Matteo, all because I'm a little—whatever this is. Can you picture Josh if he gets the call that Jace is dead? Because I can. I *lived it* with him and Kimi. The guys have already lost too much, too."

The fire in Vee's eyes banked, and she hesitated. "You don't know that spending time with Marshall will impact your performance."

"No, but I also don't know that it won't. You'd always been leader, and the team was at its peak when you met Bruce. That isn't my situation."

"Tell me you won't freeze him out? That you'll seriously consider the other part, him joining the team?"

My chest hurt a little at the questions, because it meant she recognized I was right. Unwillingly, but she did. "I won't alienate him. Marshall is our friend. As for joining, I need to think, then speak with Jace and Matteo. None of our planning or what we want will matter if I can't convince Marshall he isn't expendable, and if we can't come up with a stronger reason that will make him indispensable in Oversight's eyes."

"You also need to speak to Marshall. It's not your right to make decisions for him." Vee's lips thinned out. Stavros made a decision for her, infecting her without asking. Their relationship wasn't much of one for the first months of her change.

"I hear you. However, I'm familiar with what being Company entails. Marshall isn't. That comes into consideration. That's it. That's all I can promise you," I told her and Kimi. It was all I could promise myself, either.

CHAPTER 50

$\mathcal{M}$arshall

MARSHALL STOOD out of the way, as much as possible with a pair of SUVs and nine people crammed into the garage, while duffle bags were tossed into Vee's team's ride. He kept his gaze off the dents and scraps in the truck, and the patched-up bumper. It was much wiser for him to watch Jace and Josh put each other in headlocks than think of them bleeding on the garage's concrete floor.

A jab on his shoulder announced Kimi and her intentions. She side-armed him into a hug. When she let go, he signed what he hoped was 'thank you'. The signs stuck in his head the way chords did, not mixing up like written words, but he hadn't had much practice, Kimi disappearing the night before. And, okay, he didn't need to sign, but it felt like he should show her that he was putting in the effort and work, the way she did for him, signing slowly and mouthing the words.

Kimi caught both of his hands and squeezed them, smiling. "Perfect, doll," she mouthed.

His cheeks heated, but that was cool.

Vee cocked her head and waited to see what Marshall was comfortable with. Bruce caught the by-play and glared. Liv had rubbed off on Marshall though, and he took the dare, holding his arms open. "Hugs all around?"

Vee squealed and dived in, squeezing and air *oofed* out of him at her vigorous tackle.

"Don't break him, please and thank you. I don't want to spend my afternoon filling out an incident report," Liv said from somewhere in the middle of the pack.

"As if." Vee did let go, stepping back enough to look him in the eye without craning her neck. "You've got my number. Call if you need anything, any time. I mean that. Got me?"

"Okay. Thank you."

"You are welcome should you ever find yourself requiring sanctuary." Stavros ghosted in, appearing in front of Vee, which was still a little eerie and the guy was too grave and formal among the exuberant goodbyes. He held his hand out, and Marshall shook it. He was shaking the hand of a four-hundred-year-old vampire-father guy.

"Get in the damn car already." Bruce tucked his knife case between the driver and passenger seats. "Hit me up if you need a job or recommendation."

The driver's door slammed, and Marshall blinked at his faded reflection in the smoked glass window. No idea if that was Kantor wishing Marshall good luck, or an acknowledgement that Marshall didn't have a chance at remaining here.

Likely, he didn't, but this time, he was going for the impossible.

"Ah, glorious peace and quiet." As the gate closed on red taillights, Jace stretched and slung his arms in a backward arch.

"Wanna hit the firing range? There are those new mini-grenade prototypes we haven't tried out yet." Matteo ambled past them.

"Hells yeah."

Liv did that goofy snort-laugh, and Marshall's heart melted a little more, because damn—cute Liv.

She fell in beside Marshall. "I love them, but their verbal comprehension skills leave something to be desired. Are you getting in on the cheering them on as they blow stuff up action?"

While the sisters had disappeared for a couple hours the night before, Marshall had basically cornered Bruce, getting a terse rundown on day-to-day things the team needed but Company rules didn't address, and things the Company did and that Bruce had improved on.

Those suggestions fresh, Marshall said, "Thought I'd go over everyone's rooms, then clean the infirmary some." And check the list he'd recorded as Bruce issued a list of items they had used patching the team up, then record how many Liv should order to replace them.

Liv held her arm out and across the breezeway door, blocking him. "We all clean up after ourselves, doubly so when we're going between compounds or visiting another's. I promise, the rooms will be immaculate."

"Can't hurt to double check." He pressed down hard on the old tang of fear, and kept it casual. "Everyone was pretty beat up and tired, so they might've missed a spot. I'll toss in the laundry from the infirmary. I saw where the scrubs and blankets go."

"Matteo takes care of the infirmary. There's no reason for you to deal with bloody clothing."

She did think Marshall couldn't handle the reality of her job. He caught her elbow, the one blocking the way. "If I think of it as no different than kitchen prep, the blood

413

doesn't bother me. I've worked lots of places where they did their own butchering."

"Why are you doing all of this?" Liv watched him, those bottomless dark eyes probing.

"Because I can, and it helps you guys." He stiffened the backbone Kantor had snapped at him to grow. "Maybe enjoying organizing the compound, meal planning, and cooking sounds stupid, but I'm good at it. I enjoy helping you."

Liv folded against the doorframe, studying him. She didn't pull her elbow free, though. "Playing Responsible Adult to a bunch of loud, occasionally juvenile, and semi-nomadic soldiers that don't technically exist is your idea of enjoyable? Just so we're clear on what I need to tell Doctor Jill, the HQ psychiatrist, when she asks."

He joined Liv on the wall, and shoulder-bumped her the way she did with her family. "You're better than my last employer. Guess that's a pretty low bar, though."

Her laugh wrapped around him. "Going forward, I'm not leaving you around Bruce unsupervised. You're picking up his lack of respect for chain of command."

"I found out how he makes that agnolotti and ragu."

"Dang." Liv whistled, and bumped him back. "Let's keep it between us that I'll tolerate all sorts of insubordination in exchange for fresh pasta. Need any pointers on getting blood stains out?"

His heartbeat picked up. "I've got some solid techniques."

Liv pushed off the wall and waved him inside. "Have at it. I'll be outside, supervising blowing stuff up."

* * *

MARSHALL SPENT the afternoon taking photos of the infirmary shelves and supplies to study, and the arrangement of the machines and tanks. First, memorize where they all went. Then learn what they all were. And eventually, how they were used. Step by step, hands on, so he'd remember.

A tap on his shoulder out of nowhere and he jerked, fumbling and barely keeping his phone from hitting oxygen tanks. He turned, coming nose to eyeball with Liv.

"You in there?" A grin curved her lips up.

The embarrassment heating his neck was worth it, to see Liv happy. "You need to make good on our deal." He headed for the kitchen. He laid his phone down to grab a cup, then the carafe he'd stashed on the top shelf.

Liv had followed him, and was staring at his phone screen, which was still open to the shots of the infirmary.

"You promised." He held the orange juice out to her.

She stared at the glass the way she had the phone, before taking it. "Did you squeeze this?"

The question sounded more important than fresh juice versus store bought. He couldn't translate whether that was good or bad. "We had those oranges I'd bought to make a marmalade, and fresh juice has gotta be more nutritious. There's some for Jace, too."

When he closed the fridge door after replacing the carafe, the kitchen was empty. So was the glass, drained down to bits of pulp.

When Liv only tagged into the conversation here and there during lunch, and drank more juice in place of having a meal, Marshall kept his mouth shut. She had every reason to be quieter. Nearly dying had to leave after-effects. He'd glimpsed the scars when she twisted side to side after whatever workout left her dripping sweat. Bruises still shaded the injuries, like dirty smudges.

At least by dinner she was eating again, and arguing with Matteo over movie choices. Marshall made popcorn, commandeering the den love seat and kept control of the bowl once the movie started. Liv took the opposite end like usual, but there was no snuggling or afghans or joking around tonight. Since he wasn't paying attention to the movie, he noticed when Liv didn't either, instead watching the guys and him.

He didn't care that she wasn't talkative, as long as she was in the same room with him. Once she'd left with her sisters the night before, he hadn't seen her again. Despite Vee's reassurances when she came from whatever had occupied the three, he couldn't stop worrying. Whether Liv was still in pain, whether she needed something and he had no way of knowing. It sucked out loud, and the only thing keeping him from Liv's door was that Kimi was still with her.

Liv unfolded from the couch and left, with only a simple, "goodnight," directed at the room.

"Popcorn?" Matteo nodded at the mostly full bowl.

Marshall passed it over, and double-checked that Liv was gone. "Is she okay? For real?"

"Going by how she dusted my ass on the obstacle course, I'd say she's back to at least ninety-five-percent."

"But something's not right?"

Jace raised the volume on an already loud scene of killer robots, and he and Matteo crowded closer.

"That fucking vampire party." Jace's layer of affability drained away, leaving him hard. Almost vicious.

Marshall had heard enough when the rest of the team discussed it the night before. Vampires partying like they didn't care who heard them or stumbled in. Caged humans, ghouls chained in the corners then released like attack dogs. All the cryptids fighting like they really didn't have any survival instinct. Throwing themselves against Vee and Stavros' machetes, and ignoring the barrels of guns, as long as they could hurt the humans in the process.

The mess was the reason Vee's team left, to present an in-person analysis at HQ. Probably to the Oversight that was really their bosses. The ones who had put tiny bombs in Vee, and were full-on assholes.

Marshall leaned in. "That thing last night with her and Vee was about more than sisters."

"Odds are yes," Jace said. "It's only been Division C.O.'s in the last couple of meetings, but it's not like they're hush-hush. There's been talk of shifting some of HQ's private force, and auxiliary teams. Assuming there are any to spare, which is a bad bet. With losing entire teams—" Jace stopped, like he needed a minute "—with teams gone, the few floating auxiliary teams have officially been assigned those Divisions. Shit like this is why I'm happy not being Commander."

Matteo grunted agreement. "Word is that it's the same in every Region from the Northwest down to Southern South America. Hope to hell there are a few teams available. I'm not voting for frosh stepping in."

Marshall checked with Jace for a translation.

"The Cadet teams that are on our version of an externship. They are sent to back up Division teams, see what else besides classroom and field mission work goes into being assigned an area, how to actively deal with civis, law enforcement, our Assets. They also learn that cryptids don't always follow the rules cadets learn in Academy, and when to call for support from other teams."

"This shit, these mutants, it isn't for those kids. They'd get shredded." Matteo's voice throbbed, sub-vocal fury embedded in the few words. "Liv'd never let HQ do that even if they'd trust us with cadets."

"But you guys need more people?" Marshall kind of hated himself for hoping a crisis gave him an in.

"Technically, we're bare-bones, but we're fucking *good*." Matteo lost some of the harshness.

"No ego, but he's right," Jace said, and got a fist bump. "We're tight, and we'll only get better."

Marshall wasn't a fighter. This once, it might work in his favor. Vee and the guys were great soldiers. They had access to another full team when they needed an assist, maybe two, since Liv spent a lot of time talking to the Texas C.O. and they seemed to agree on everything. Plus, she had access to healing vampire DNA.

Marshall was like a support crew, the one thing this team didn't have.

He left the guys arguing the merits of sports versus cheesy nineties flicks. Liv wasn't in her room or office when he checked. On a hunch, he climbed the thick inset beams that made up the stairs, and opened the trap door to the roof.

The platform swing moved in a soft creak of heavy chains. That and the breeze swirling around the buildings were the only sounds.

"You're welcome to stay," the Liv-shaped shadow on the swing said.

Marshall braced the hatch he'd been prepared to close. "I only wanted to check. Jace and Matteo said you were fine, but I guess I never listen."

"Always the cadet who has to poke the firebug before he believes they breathe fire?"

He didn't know what a firebug was, but otherwise, Liv had it right. "Yeah, that's me."

"Join the crowd." Liv braced her heel against one of the frame's posts and stopped the swing.

Marshall climbed out, letting the hatch bang closed, and backed onto the swing. Still half-waiting for it the wood to crack and dump him on his butt.

Liv pushed them back into motion. Not looking at him, but seeming mesmerized by the plantings around the bird bath in the yard, or the far off mountains. She rested in the corner, against the raised x-shaped backrest, one leg straight, the other bent and her arm propped on it.

She didn't seem inclined to nap this time, or do anything besides absorb the view. As the mauve and pink shaded to deeper purple on the horizon, his mouth took over. "We should plant lemon and orange trees. The dwarf ones, not anything a cryptid could climb. Bruce mentioned they did those at their compound. And some beds of herbs and basic vegetables, the ones that do the slow absorption, so they'll survive when we're rotating bases."

"Bruce infected you with his sustainable, all-natural crusade. He's shedding his influence like a virus."

"His ideas are good. Mostly."

Liv did a sharp turn, sending the conversation in another direction. "It doesn't bother you to talk about drought resistant plants, and traveling, randomly switching bases and cities, following cryptids? From what I've observed, it's not a settled life like what civilians seem to prefer." None of her earlier teasing came through.

Respecting her seriousness, he though his answer through. "I've never had—" not a home "—a long term place. I always moved as jobs dried up. It never mattered. Like, I didn't have some career plan, so one place was as good as another."

"Was."

The word hung in the evening air.

Tell her it was a word slip. No big deal. His mouth stayed stubbornly closed now that he *needed* it to run.

Liv tilted her head back, watching the stars over them appear and brighten. "Can I infer your use of 'was' means you're considering a different lifestyle now?"

One of the resident crows that Bruce seemed to have a grudge against swooped in front of them. Joining a flock lined up in uneven clumps on the walkway railing. Witnesses to whatever event unfolded here. Marshall couldn't put a name to it, any more than the universe had with the event horizon that created it.

"I don't mind traveling. I'd stay in the Southwest though. The rest..." He let his hand do its thing, flicking through musical notes, and went for it. He motioned at the birds. "The idea of sticking around, seeing the same people every day and being part of something, like that flock? It sounds good now."

"This week didn't sour you on extreme group togetherness?"

Now his mouth got back in the game. "Bruce is a jerk, and Stavros is borderline creepy-intimidating, and I don't think Kimi understands privacy laws, and this week was awesome."

"Yes, it was."

The hour, and feeling this was a time Liv needed privacy, finally drove Marshall in. Then, not able to stop himself, he grabbed his hoodie, climbed back up, and draped the over-sized jacket over Liv without asking.

Liv stayed, silent and still, a guardian watching her land.

CHAPTER 51

*M*arshall

MARSHALL STOLE the few minutes of quiet before the team descended on the kitchen for breakfast, swiping his phone to life and scrolling through photos of the compound. He'd added shots of gym equipment and showers, and the garage setup.

He flipped back to the infirmary, pushing the queasy spike of adrenaline aside. He'd already handled wounded people. He could do it again.

Kantor was a dick, but he'd also sent Marshall links to irrigation systems. Anywhere a small tweak could make the compound more self-sustaining translated into fewer outside trips, which translated to less exposure and more safety for the team.

Marshall rolled that argument around in his head, slotting it where it belonged on his mental list. When the time was right, he'd go to Liv and lay out why he should stay, what he could do, the way's he'd make their lives easier. He could take over all the domestic stuff they'd been dividing up, leaving them more time to focus on agent concerns. And more energy to train, and for missions. He moved that to the top of his list.

Liv didn't have as many agents as the other teams, so the three of them had to do more. They shouldn't waste energy on non-agent tasks. That was another important point. Vee's comment about how being off even one or two-percent potentially changed a fight from in the team's favor, to into the monsters, felt like it was tattooed on his brain now.

He wanted to stay, but more importantly, maybe the team really needed him. He gripped the island edge, the cool tile under his sweaty palms helping to settle him. Matteo or Jace couldn't get hurt because they'd spent an hour cleaning when they should've been training or sleeping.

Liv couldn't. Nothing bad could happen to Liv. She had to be all right, striding through the world, ponytail swinging, saving people who didn't have anybody else to protect them, refereeing Jace and Matteo's arguments, and reading comics Marshall picked out for her.

"Man, you are the most beautiful thing I've seen this morning." Matteo's voice boomed and Marshall startled, hand bumping one of the glasses he'd set out, the cup rolling towards the edge of the island.

He grabbed. Liv beat him to it. She caught the glass, and his hand caught hers, wrapping around it and the cup.

"If you're thinking of filling this with juice, then spiking it with that foul protein powder—" Liv raised a brow, and loosened a finger, glass tilting again.

"No." And because honesty mattered, "Only because Bruce took it all with him."

"Good answer." Liv straightened and moved closer, mainly because the guys fell on the food like they hadn't eaten in days, not the six hours since midnight snacks. They hadn't even waited like usual, grabbing plates from the stack and scooping food from the pans on the counter.

She twisted her hand, leaving the glass in Marshall's and shook her head at the guys. "Save me something edible." Her ponytail swayed as she walked away.

"You are for real a lifesaver," Matteo said around a mouthful of chorizo and eggs, chewing as he walked to the table.

"I though you all were still getting up and getting ready."

Jace snorted, and refilled the cup he'd already emptied once. "Early PT."

"Liv's got a bug up her butt over the Lab's report that came in on those last cryptids," Matteo said, dropping to a seat, chair creaking.

"A justified bug." Jace overfilled his plate and sat beside his partner.

Marshall went through the motions, putting away a plate for Liv, and making coffee. When the guys finished and she hadn't returned, Marshall joined the pair. "Whatever is making all these cryptids act off and band together is serious?"

The two soldiers exchanged a look.

Despite twin mountains of sweaty agent, Marshall scooted in and caught Jace's eye. "I'm not gonna freak out."

When Matteo nodded, Jace wiped his mouth. "Shit is getting real. Liv's already on it. This is what she does when she's weighing a major decision." He plucked the sweaty tee an inch off his body.

Marshall revised plans. Liv had to be planning on bringing the team up to strength somehow. She had looked calmer after Vee left, and adding to the team was the kind of thing she'd discuss with her sister. He already knew that, like he knew his name.

If Liv filled the empty team slots with fighters, he'd be gone.

His timeline just got moved up.

* * *

LIV NEVER CAME BACK for breakfast. She got as far as the kitchen entry before the chime of an incoming call echoed down the hall. After, her jaw was set, and she motioned the team outside. Lunch was them changing out soaked clothes for dry, chugging water and sports drink. None of them looked in the mood for conversation, only grunting please and thanks, and disappearing outdoors again. The sound of gunfire from the range carried clearly.

Marshall alternated going over his photo version of a cheat sheet, and practicing his hire-me speech. The empty house gave him the privacy to mumble lines to the non-judgmental backsplash while he prepped.

"You say something?" Matteo paused in the entry arch.

Marshall had been too lost in his own world to notice doors opening.

"Double checking ingredients," Marshall improvised, ignoring the automatic spurt of shame. The team already knew he recorded important stuff, and nobody here acted like it was a big deal.

Jace stopped behind Matteo, peering in. "Whatever it is, it smells freaking amazing."

Maybe Marshall had gone overboard with three courses, and replicating Bruce's agnolotti recipe. "It'll be a couple of hours before dinner is ready."

"Score. We've got time for a CoW quickie," Jace said, and both headed for the showers.

Marshall pulled in a slow breath and went back to work. Finish the food, put Liv in a good mood, then not freeze or turn in a gibbering mess. He hadn't planned that part out as precisely. Maybe pitch to Liv in here over dessert with the team, one of those 'Hey, I had an idea' conversations. Or catch her on the roof swing. That would be even better. Lowkey and relaxed, and in the dark, meaning way less pressure.

"Gaming break?" Jace ambled in, hair still damp from the shower.

"Later." Liv answered for him, breezing past. "Grab Matteo and be in my office in five for a team meeting.

Jace's face clouded over. He backtracked without a word.

Shaved parmesan floated down on the pasta and island like snow where he'd twitched. Marshall forced himself to set the rind and grater away. If Liv couldn't talk to the guys in here over a beer or dessert, not minding Marshall in the background, it meant something big.

Right. This was his shot. Jace and Matteo were cool. They might back him when he brought the topic up. They liked regular meals, especially ones they didn't have to prepare.

Except they had made it nearly a year without Marshall here cooking or working. Clean grout and a cheesecake that didn't crack were at the bottom of their list of concerns. Even Bruce knew how to fight, handle weapons and explosives, as the guy had pointed out with brutal honesty. He could also read a list without it taking all day, and his brain didn't overheat and forget how to react to threats. For sure, he didn't mistake a monster in an alley for a person.

Maybe Marshall didn't have a chance at making his dream reality, but he didn't have anything to lose by trying except pride. He'd been embarrassed often enough, humiliated himself, and for no real purpose. Once more, for Liv, wasn't too much to endure.

He kept one eye on the clock, one on the hallway. Nobody came out for a game, or dinner. The house stayed dead quiet.

He'd put his playlist on, but couldn't keep music and his pitch in his head at the same time, the music edging out the list in bright pops of color.

Which didn't bode well for him managing important stuff like patching people up and—

The boom of a door slamming, then the thud of footsteps knocked him out of his loop. He whirled, dropping pasta in sauce. "I'm nearly done."

"Thanks."

Marshall waited but Matteo's was the only reply. He plated food and checked over his shoulder. Only Matteo and Jace sat at the table. "One of you go let Liv know dinner is on."

"Liv…" Jace didn't seem to know what else to say, muscle in his jaw standing out as he clenched his teeth. Easy to guess he was the source of the slammed door.

"She'll be late." Matteo didn't sound any happier.

"More problems with cryptids?"

"Uh, sure." Matteo practically buried his face in his plate.

Matteo sucked at lying. Jace agreed, glaring at the top of his teammate's head. Although he dropped his gaze even faster when Marshall approached.

Don't freak. He kept his voice matter of fact. "Leave some room for dessert. I experimented with a new torte thing. There's a lemon sauce for your part."

Jace winced and rubbed the back of his neck. "Thanks."

Marshall concentrated on separating the food out, one portion in case Liv showed, the rest for the fridge.

"Hey, come eat." Matteo paused in shoveling pasta in, forehead scrunched, eyes sad brown pools.

"I'm good."

"You should go ahead and eat with us," Jace said. "You know how she gets about that."

The compassion almost dropped him, worse than insults ever had. "I'm not all that hungry."

The skin around Jace's eyes tightened. "Sure. I mean, you get to choose." He said it like there was a lot more involved than the few words covered, or like it was an argument he'd lost.

They made it through the meal without any other conversation, joking, or shop talk. The sounds of chewing, and the imaginary creak of an axe about to fall, their backdrop.

Matteo bounded up, gathering plates, snatching Jace's, and practically bulldozing Marshall.

"I've got it." Marshall took the wobbly stack.

"I'll help, then we can get to CoW faster."

Matteo knew. He knew, and was trying to blunt the news in his own way, expression earnest.

Marshall almost asked. *How soon did he have to leave?*

The guys were his friends. And Liv's, and she was their leader. He bit down on the question. He wasn't doing that, putting them between duty and friendship.

Jace's phone sounded and he glared at the screen. "Marshall, Liv's asked me to send you to the office when you get a minute."

Marshall kept his back to the room. "Sure. Let me finish."

This wasn't the last time. Even if he had to leave for HQ to make room for new team members, he'd still make breakfast tomorrow, and put the kitchen he'd sorta thought of as his to rights. Because the edges of the room darkened at the idea of right now being the end.

He needed tonight to get leaving set in place, to put all the feelings in order first. Then put his walls back up.

Marshall rocked from Matteo's sneak-back slap, ending in a hard grip on his shoulder. "We'll hold up on the game and wait for you."

More practical, Jace said, "Come play if you're in the mood after. If you want to grab a drink in town instead, we're up for getting out of here, too."

Marshall nodded, holding on hard to the illusion of normal. At least, until Liv annihilated it.

iv

I SENT the cursor back over the photos, as if one more pass would change their content. The mission my and Vee's teams had been caught in only days before had been a vampire-led bloodbath. We'd had access to mutated DNA with healing capabilities and survived.

The northern Oklahoma team hadn't. They had lost one member at the scene. The rest of the six-person team was in ICU, or still in surgery. The Cleaner's summary and photos were horrific.

Terrence had messaged privately that one of the teams on his eastern border had gone on a call-out the day before. It had been close to forty-eight hours, and they hadn't reported in. We both expected to receive a grim official notice from HQ soon, reporting the missing team was in the same shape as Oklahoma's, or worse.

Whatever we'd landed in the middle of wasn't a one time or localized phenomenon.

I pulled the band from my hair and massaged my scalp, my headache an echo of the ache lingering above my belly button, muscles still sore. I thought I had a plan as far as what to do about Marshall, because after his comments last night, there was no doubt he wanted to join us and that he was ready to address the possibility directly. When he'd said he wanted to be part of something—the same rush as a shot of mescal had sizzled through me. Followed by a quieter, warmer one when without saying a word, he'd returned and bundled me in his hoodie.

This day had begun on a bad note, with the emergency meeting and then news of wounded and lost agents, and was potentially ending on a worse one.

On the personal front, my day had taken an equally awful turn. My Lieutenant was furious with me. My second team-mate equally unhappy. They both were impressed with how Marshall handled saving the street kid, and his quick thinking and loyalty when he believed vampires had infil-trated the compound. Plus, he was their friend, not some-thing that happened often with agents.

And now I had to somehow inform Marshall that this couldn't be his home.

The pain under my breastbone was all emotional, not physical. I wanted, badly, to have Marshall as a part of the team's daily life. After the Oklahoma and Terrence's message, there was no denying the cryptid situation had altered. We weren't simply following protocol with planned missions interspersed with emergency call-outs. It might not happen this week, or the next, or this year, but facts were inescapable. We were headed toward a full-on war.

I couldn't stop superimposing Marshall's face over those of the dead civilians in the gory photos, and for the first time in my life, almost threw up over crime scene images. Marshall couldn't be part of what we were preparing to jump into. Honestly, he should be headed to HQ immediately.

First, I was speaking with Food Services to have a position waiting for him, and with the Domestic division to also ensure he had a private room. He wasn't going back into the nebulous, anxiety-inducing situation with no role, and forced to bunk with cadets. I should've been on the phone already.

One heartbreak per day was my limit though, and I'd already racked up today's. At least I had a few minutes to collect myself, while everyone ate.

Or not. A knock filtered through the thick office door, and I checked the clock. Dinner was long over, and so was my reprieve. "Come in."

For a moment, Marshall was backlit by the hall lights, a wide-shouldered silhouette haloed in soft gold. Like one of Stavros' warrior angels.

Marshall stepped inside, pulling the door closed behind him, and the illusion dropped. Back to my Marshall, bandana still losing the fight to control his riot of curls, a scattering of freckles over the bridge of his nose, and in another red and blue superhero tee. "Jace said you needed me?"

The simple statement slammed into me. Needed. Wanted. Flip sides of the same coin. I wanted to brush my fingers over his face and erase the worry he was so good at concealing, unless you knew him. I wanted another of his hugs, to bask in his determination and easy calm.

I needed to make the decision that was best for him and for my team. I forced joints that preferred to lock and delay what came next to bend, and stood. Circling my desk to get close to him was another want, one I could indulge for a bit longer "Do you have a few minutes to talk?"

"I'll always have time for you."

Squeezing words out past a constricted throat, I said, "We should finish the discussion we started a few days ago, that Vee's arrival sidelined."

He shoved his hands in his pockets, then blew out a deep breath like he was about to plunge off a cliff. "You've probably already talked to Bruce. Or he talked to Vee, and she talked to you."

"No, not really. I—"

He gave me a level look. "Whether you did or not, you're smart and know what I'm going to ask. I know you've already made up your mind and told the guys, but I'm gonna say this anyway."

I owed him the chance to express himself. I stuck with nodding.

"This whole weirdness with cryptids has gotten worse, and you need people. You can't break up other teams to add to yours, and Matteo says it's too dangerous for those new externship people, the ones who haven't really graduated, and if he says so, you for sure will because you'd never put kids at risk. And those cadets I roomed with, they said they were almost agents, so the ones that've just graduated can't be much older, and no matter what title they have—they're still kids."

He jerked forward a step, passionate and direct. "Even if they weren't, bringing anybody new in risks messing with the team. But I'm already here, and we—you guys—are still working the way you should. I get that I'm not a fighter, but I can give you extra energy. Not *give*, but I can do all the everyday work, the stuff we talked about that even superheroes don't get to skip. That way, you guys won't waste time and focus, and will have more for training and missions."

I held on hard to facts. They were cold and unchanging and safe. I protected my team and civilians, and made the hard decisions. "I realize you and Bruce had several conversations. However, he didn't mean—"

"He hates me. Not as much now, but he does, and he *did* mean that I could learn to help. Sure, mostly because this is an emergency situation and you don't have other choices. I fit in here okay though. You know I do." He shoved his hand through his curls, accidentally catching the bandanna. He jerked it off and out of his way. "Jace and Matteo don't mind my being here, and I'll quit distracting them by staying and gaming, and you don't need to waste time checking on me anymore. I've always figured stuff out on my own, and I will here, too."

A spark flared, like touching a lighter to det cord on an explosive. I was the explosive. Marshall hit the tip of that cord, the bit I couldn't tuck out of sight and pretend didn't exist, woven of people assuming you'd fail, of Marshall's family neglecting him, and employers using him, and his absolute belief that he wasn't important.

He plowed on. "Give me a chance, that's all. A probation period."

He took my gritting my teeth, attempting to keep everything safely inside, as imminent refusal and for the first time, raised his voice. "You don't have to pay me until later, after the probation. And then I'll work for half of whatever they pay real team members. Less than half since I'm not vital the way you guys or Stavros or Bruce are, and—"

That spark inside hit the primer, and blew. "Enough." I slammed my fist against the desk surface, laptop jumping, the Dracula pencil holder tipping over, and pencils and odds and ends rolling off the desk edge as if they were trying to escape. "*Don't* say you aren't important. *Stop* apologizing, *stop* undervaluing yourself, *stop* allowing horrible people to convince you that you aren't valuable."

The echo of the last word died, sucked in and drowned by heavy beams, ancient wood, and worn leather and canvas.

My temper died with it, in the appalled silence.

Marshall's laugh was ugly and raw. "You aren't doing great with that promise about not lying. If I wasn't useless, I would've made enough of a difference here that you noticed."

He averted his face, preferring staring at decades of thumbtack holes in the far wall. "The worst part isn't that I'll have to go. The worst is knowing you and Jace and Matteo need help and support but I'm not able to give any, and if there's something worse than the guys or you getting hurt, I don't know what it is."

I had worried about Marshall being gutted, injured horribly by some creature. In my obliviousness, I'd done at least as a lethal a job as any cryptid we battled. For him, leaving was more dangerous than staying. "Damn it."

He turned for the door, slow, like he was suddenly carrying an unimaginable burden. "I'll pack."

I lunged, and managed to grab his sleeve, leaving us a tangle of limbs. He could have shaken me off, at least long enough to get out of the room. Instead, he slammed to a halt, and his other arm shot out, ready to catch me if I stumbled.

"Jace and Matteo voted for you to join the team." Which wasn't at all what I meant.

"You didn't." His answer held a cold finality.

I knotted fleecy-soft shirt around my fist. "I haven't cast mine. Officially. I'm realizing there are more implications to consider than I first though."

He inched enough to face me, sleeve still in my grasp, and stretching the neck of the tee out of shape. "What does that mean?"

"Can you honestly stand here, right now, and tell me you'd rather risk serious injury or death doing what basically amounts to chaperoning us, instead of being free to pick or quit jobs, and set your own schedule? Even—even have the ability to get in a car and go to the store without considering whether something might be out there waiting for you to drop your guard, and plotting different routes home so you don't have a set, predictable pattern, and making sure even then that you pick roads and streets that allow you to watch for a tail? Every. Time."

"I didn't choose my life. I let it happen to me and went along because I didn't care. What you guys do, it matters. You make a difference, whether the people you're protecting know or not. You see planning decent meals, and restocking the infirmary, and all-night muffin baking, but I see the first important thing I've ever done."

"You didn't choose to be exploited by a cryptid-led human trafficking ring or forced to hide with a secretive group of soldiers. For civilians, that's a nightmare, not a decision." I couldn't stop, going into forbidden territory, the secret thing I was afraid of and hadn't acknowledged. "We both know you didn't want any part of this life—cryptids, the Company, and agents."

"I'm choosing now. Because most of what I first thought about you wasn't ever true. Now, I have all the information. This is an educated decision."

I wrapped my arms around myself. Wanting to believe, and afraid to. "You said you couldn't think of anything more awful than seeing one of us harmed in the line of duty. That is exactly, and I mean exactly, how I feel about you being injured, except if that happens, it will be *my fault*, because I knowingly brought you in."

"I know the risks. I've been face to face with vampires and ghouls, and cleaned my friends' blood from tables." Steel laced his voice. "This is what I want."

If Jace or Matteo used that tone, I would respect their convictions and intelligence. Then give them the chance at what they were passionate enough about to argue for. We were partners, and I trusted them because they'd earned it. The same as Marshall had, again and again.

I forced myself to stop huddling, and hiding, and did the only thing I could in good conscience. "All right."

Marshall frowned. His fingers twitched to life, the intricate beat they did when he was thinking. "All right. Do you mean all right, you vote yes? On the team part?"

"Bruce set a precedent, but that doesn't mean automatic approval. Plus, there's the complication of our and Vee's team's position. You'll be required to learn all of our protocols and rules, medic training, and cryptid behavior. Then an Assessor will observe our performance for at least twenty-four hours."

His face lost some color, but his voice stayed firm. "I can learn. I will."

He caught my shoulders, hands covering them, nearly meeting in the middle of my collarbone. "I won't freeze and let you bleed out. Not Matteo or Jace, either."

"I knew that even before Kimi told me what you did and what you offered the day we were ambushed. She didn't realize that waking up to you in the infirmary told me everything I needed to know. You don't let pride get in the way when it comes to your people. If a situation is beyond your skillset, you do whatever is necessary to get us what we need."

Passion and conviction carved his face into new planes and angles. Promising that it wouldn't go well for any creature or obstacle that came between Marshall and his duty. "I'll take care of you."

"Once you become part of the Company, you can't leave. It is a lifetime commitment." My heart drummed too hard, examining Marshall's body language, his breathing, and afraid of seeing hesitation.

Marshall used his hold to draw me closer. Blue eyes, the sharpness of bay leaf and mellowness of smoke from dinner, blotted out the rest of the world. "There's no way I'd ever leave. You found me, then I found my home."

My hands inched up his chest, feeling the reassuring beat of his heart. "I will find a way to get Oversight to agree, somehow. Kimi is helping, too. As for the tests, we can request them in whatever format works for you—questions read out by an app or program, your answers recorded as audio. We will research resources designed for your type of dyslexia, all of the things you should've had from the beginning. Whatever you need."

There was that word again. Need. I'd looked at our situation incorrectly. Sometimes, what you wanted and what you needed were the same thing. Marshall needed us. We needed Marshall.

"I'm a lot of trouble."

I heard the echo of other people's criticisms and judgments coming out of Marshall's mouth. "We don't think so. And as your almost-C.O., what I say goes." I didn't get the smile I expected.

"I've gotta ask this." His voice rumbled through me. "Do you really want me here? Liv-you, not C.O. Liv, being a leader and democratic and all. Staying here is to help you guys. So if all this is stressing you out, that's the opposite of helping. Nothing will ever be worth me making it harder on you."

"You've never caused me that sort of stress."

"Yeah?" His head dipped, curls tickling my forehead, lips close to mine.

A meaty thump rattled the thick door. Marshall put space between us, letting go.

I cut around him and jerked the door open. Matteo slapped his big mitt on the doorjamb, barely keeping from tumbling in. "Worst. Evesdroppers. Ever. This? This is one-hundred-percent the reason you aren't ever assigned intel gathering duty."

Jace leaned around his partner in crime, grin plastered on his face. "Yo, boss. Can Marshall come out and play?"

I swept my arm wide, motioning Marshall out, then propped against the jam and waited.

The instant Marshall cleared the entry, Matteo whooped. Jace got there first, hauling Marshall into a loose headlock. "Welcome to the team, brother."

Matteo's hearty love tap knocked Marshall free of the half-Nelson. "Yeah, man. About time."

Marshall's face flared ruby, but he shoved back, the largest grin he'd ever given us lighting him up. The guys rolled him back and forth, like a couple of eager, oversized puppies.

I gave it a minute. That, and basked in the atmosphere of pure happiness, a huge improvement over our time before Marshall, and Jace's earlier cold shoulder. I owed him an apology, as well.

"All right, break it up. Deadly serious about my dislike of writing up incident reports." I poked the nearest participants. After a couple more shoves they all more or less laid off, Marshall's bandana gone and hair wilder than ever.

I lifted a brow. "You're still positive you want in on this barely contained chaos?"

Marshall spotted his bandana in a corner and grabbed it, tucking it in his back pocket, and running a seriously ineffective hand through his hair. "I'm in. All in, always."

I felt the shift in Jace, a bit of his well-camouflaged seriousness surfacing. "All goofing aside, we're glad you signed on. Me and Matteo are up for study duty, twenty-four-seven."

Matteo dropped an arm around Marshall's shoulders.

"We talked it over. We're taking turns reading off the rules, and recording them for you. Jace'll do regs, I'll do species classifications. Safety we can do hands-on all around the compound and stations, so it'll make sense."

Marshall frowned at them. "You can't waste time on me."

Out of Marshall's sight, Matteo's expression turned vicious.

I caught his eye, and tilted my head in agreement. We were sharing a highly inappropriate vision of a strike team, made up of the two of us, showing up on the doorsteps of the people who'd failed Marshall.

"We don't have more important duties. Getting a teammate up to speed is always priority one," Jace said. "That's what team life is, man. We've got that part covered, while Liv twists rules into doing her bidding and develops some brilliant plan that'll have Oversight begging you to join."

Marshall cleared his throat but didn't blow the guys off. "Thanks. For real."

A chime from my phone ended the moment.

"A mission?" Marshall checked with me.

"Brainstorming session between all the Southwest Division C.O.'s."

Jace pulled the door to give me privacy. I stopped its arc long enough to warn Marshall. "No more sugar for them tonight. Or caffeine. You can see how that could lead to continued shenanigans. Call that my first order."

"Call her ma'am," Matteo stage whispered. "She loves that shit almost as much as kissing movies."

"Got it." Marshall's lips curved up, and he turned from the guys to me. "Okay, ma'am."

I closed the door, leaving them to celebrate. Now I needed to make good on my promise, and find a means of convincing Oversight to both not eliminate us all, and to allow Marshall into the Company.

iv

THE MUTED BUZZ of virtual gunfire and live trash talk filtered from the den as I left the office. The guys and Marshall bonding further, and burning off adrenaline. They could light up the real firing range right now, and I'd give them a pass. I loved them both for their plan to help Marshall, one they'd hatched on their own.

My stomach rumbled. Heating anything, even slapping a sandwich together, felt like serious effort. Three hours of hashing out issues and potential solutions sapped me more than a mission. There were too many *what ifs* and *maybe thens*. There hadn't been any update on the missing team, either.

I slipped down the hall and closed my suite door on the crew. Time enough tomorrow to drag them back down to earth. I shed boots and BDUs, and rolled a drawer open, reaching for my usual tank and shorts.

The set of pjs I'd dared Marshall to choose for me sat in the corner. I pulled the tee on, the red spider emblem centered on my chest, and wiggled into the black shorts.

I hit my playlist, killing the bright overheads, then tapped the bedside lamp to life. Amber light shown through its leaded glass, and cast a cozy oval on my bed. I crawled on and pulled the e-reader over.

Nothing on it held my attention. I flipped to the store option, and went on a search, and...bingo. Comics and graphic novels were also digital. Finding the titles I wanted, I clicked the buy option.

A soft rap mixed with the mournful notes of a power ballad, a whisky-rough voice, and images of neon signs reflecting off oily puddles and broken glass. The suite door wasn't as thick as the offices, not requiring a raised voice. "I'm up."

Marshall peered around the cracked open door. "Am I bothering you?"

"Nope. Need to talk?"

He pushed into the room, revealing a plate and bottle of water. "No, but you need to eat."

"Really?" Not point in attempting to keep the smile in check.

"I have a job now, and part of that job is taking care of you guys. Bruce is a jerk, but he's a jerk who's right about you all not being very good at that on your own." He gave me a new look, bordering on authoritarian, and waggled the plate at me. "So, agnolotti."

"I don't hate the sound of that." Not the dinner, or the warmth that sprang up under my breastbone at his caring.

I moved the tablet to the nightstand. Marshall sat the dinner on my bed, and backed off. His gazed darted around, from the *I like kissing books plaque* and the book character scented candle—this month's theme British Detective and allegedly scented with moss, leather, and opium poppy—to the paintings and odd bits and pieces draped or displayed everywhere.

"Your C.O. is a packrat, according to Jace, Josh, and Matteo." I took a bite of pasta. It wasn't exactly like Bruce's, Marshall adding his on touch. Layers of richness dissolved one by one, with a hint of sweetness. I loved it.

"It's cool," Marshall said. "Having interests and favorite things."

Like his guitar and comics. Plus, I really didn't want him to leave yet. "Feel free to explore."

He double-checked my sincerity, then started small, touching the tablet and when I nodded, pulling it around to check my reading material. "Comics?" Wonder and pleasure laced his voice, and turned it into something it felt as if I could wrap around me, luxuriously fluffy and indulgent, and pet.

"I bought the first five issues, to catch up," I said between bites.

Marshall moved from the nightstand to my dresser. A gift shop's worth of frames lined it. He inspected each one. I caught a tiny smile at the one of twelve-year-old me, Kimi, and Vee draped over each other, in the midst of a hair color craze. Each of ours was streaked with a different primary color, the temporary spray on kind so that we didn't get detention.

He trailed a finger over a silver frame, the one of me and my old team in Santa hats and swim wear on the beach. He paused the longest at the newest, another of my old life, all of us hugged together against a backdrop of tiny golden lights and masses of flowers.

"Vee and Bruce's engagement. In true Bruce fashion, he hauled us out to a friend's restaurant after hours, and proposed in front of all of us."

"That's brave." Marshall's finger rested on the sharp corner of the photo.

"He said we did everything else together, so why not a proposal. I think he knew we needed a fairytale moment."

Marshall faced me. "Something bad happened. More than with Vee and the becoming a vampire thing."

Half of the decadent pasta remained, but I pushed the plate away. Even now, the antiseptic smell of medical corridors, and the fake-vanilla reek of protein drinks gagged me. "Bruce had been seriously ill. Anyway, after all the Vee and Bruce drama—group engagement."

"Then you had to leave." He stepped closer, stopping outside the ring of lamp light.

I settled for a shrug and grabbing the water bottle.

He didn't call me out on avoidance, instead returning to inventorying my room. He was as serious and thorough as if it was part of the rules he was required to memorize.

He was memorizing *me.* I waited for the surge anger at the of violation of my privacy. It had been months before Jace dared stick even his head in. When the feeling didn't come, I drew a knee up, and watched Marshall.

He stopped in front of the enormous canvas taking up one wall.

"Kimi paints."

He pressed closer and touched the ombre surface, tracing the curving sweeps of color, glossy steel gray shading to blue, then purple, and a wild mix of yellow and orange in the center. "This is you. Kimi painted you," he said, caught up in the swirls.

"So she said." No wonder she'd come down on the pro-Marshall side.

He finished where he began, by the bedside table, staring at the colorful pool of glass and plastic beads and fake gold trinkets looped around the lamp base. "You went to Mardi Gras?"

"Sort of. That is one of several all-agents-on-deck type of civilian events. The guys and I tagged in with the NOLA team as our final test before HQ signed off on us. We threw our own graduation party after." Three days of dancing, drinking, goofing, sleeping it off, and repeating. Our celebration that we might yet turn into a unit, the three orphaned agents, starting over under the watchful eyes of a Company fearing we would fail.

The playlist segued into another ballad, slower, more mournful blues notes mixing with the power chords.

Marshall full-on studied me.

I sat and let him.

"You kind of lost your whole life. Now you're rebuilding from the ground up." He finally broke the silence as the last note throbbed and faded. "So are the guys. This is—" he frowned, possibly sorting words "—not important. Bigger than that. Vital. It's vital to you."

I dropped my chin on my raised knee, silent agreement. "The Company, the team, it isn't what I do. It's who and what I am, my whole world. The same is true of Matteo and Jace."

Marshall knelt in front of me, a hand on the mattress as balance. "I won't get in the way or mess up what you're building. I screw things up, a lot, but I won't here. I promise, Liv."

I studied Marshall. He knelt, patient, waiting. Because that was Marshall. He fit in the kitchen, he fit into the gaming battles with the guys, he fit in with Kimi and Vee. He fit in, period. Like there had always been a Marshall-shaped slot, waiting for him to show up and claim it.

I gave in to the desire I'd resisted in my office, stroking over his face, along his jaw. "You are part of what we're building. A crack team isn't enough. We want the kind of family we were raised to belong in. I wasn't sure we'd ever get there again. Somehow, you've pushed us further that way in the last two months than we've managed in nearly a year. It's everything—ensuring there are real meals, goofing around after hours, and staying up twenty-four-hours straight so that you and those muffins are the first thing we see. You've pulled all our single threads together into one, because this feels more and more like our true home."

Marshall leaned, pressing as close as the barrier of bed frame allowed. Closer to me. Marshall, who had every reason to hesitate and hide, but who put his raw emotions into the harsh spotlight, because he cared, and was afraid but brave enough to try for what he most wanted.

"When you asked if I wanted you here? I want you here because you finish uniting our team." I spread my hand on his cheek, nearly invisible stubble scratching my palm. "As plain Liv, I want you here, too."

He tipped his head so it filled my palm. "Why?"

The rational part of me, that calculated odds, and understood probabilities tried taking over. "First, tell me that you understand you aren't expected to do anything beyond what's outlined in your job description, or anything that makes you uncomfortable."

His brows scrunched together. "Like what?"

"This. Like this." I ran my thumb along his chin, then let go. "You are all about making us happy. I need you to understand there are lines you do not have to cross, unless that's what you want. To be clear—I'm the team leader, similar to one of your civilian bosses. Am I—is this taking advantage of you?"

Marshall swallowed, but his gaze was steady. "When I said staying was all that I wanted, I wasn't telling the truth."

The pasta formed a lump, threatening to come back up. I wrapped my arms around my knees, pulling away.

"Hey, no." He pried my fingers from my knee, and pressed my hand back to his cheek. "This is the rest of what I want. Really being with you. If I'm not understanding right and you don't mean us, together, then okay. I won't ever mention it again, and I'll be careful about getting too close or whatever. I'll be okay as long as I'm here at all."

"I'm at a loss as how to convince you that you get to be happy, too."

His new determination surfaced again. "Telling me why it's important to you that I stay will make me happy."

His stubborn resolve tugged me from behind my C.O. mask. "Let's start with the obvious."

"I make okay agnolotti, and great cocoa." He gave me a crooked grin.

I pointed a warning finger at him, and he tried putting on an innocent expression. "You are hands down the kindest person I've ever met. You're smart and a survivor. You're interesting and great to talk to, and equally good to be quiet with. And brave. Wow, are you brave."

Everything in me wanted to touch him again, both to explore and to borrow some of his courage. Starting small, I touched his sleeve, moving across his shoulder to his chest and tracing the top half of the diamond-shaped emblem.

Marshall followed my every move, like he was mesmerized. Then sort of shook himself. "Is that all?"

"No. I like walking in while you're in the kitchen humming to my playlist, watching the way you get lost in a project, hanging out on the couch and dissecting bad movies, on the roof watching the stars come out, and—" I couldn't miss his heartbeat speeding up. A match to mine.

Knowing what I needed, which was one of *his* superpowers, he tangled our fingers together, his thumb running back and forth over my hand, so I could continue. "I especially enjoy any activity where we're touching."

"Yeah?"

"Yes." My hand had moved all on its own from his chest, up his neck, creeping into his hair.

"What else?" His fingers tightened around mine.

His *I'm all in* echoed in time with my heart. Marshall deserved to hear that, too. *I* wanted to say it. I nudged and he rose, lifting me with him. "I want to kiss you, for a start."

He widened his stance, pulling me in, my bare knee sliding between his. His hand curled around the back of my neck, and he bent that little bit so that his lips were on mine. The kiss was sweet and soft, minty toothpaste eclipsing what Marshall really tasted like.

I looped my arms around his neck, and his curls tickled my hand, like the silky loops were alive. Caught between the sensation of his tongue tracing along my lips, and the unexpected erection pressing against my stomach, I clenched, accidentally catching and pulling.

Marshall groaned, grip on my neck tightening, more possessive, and a hand slid down, just above my ass, pressing me into him. I opened up to him. Sweet turned into demanding, and his tongue tangling with mine.

His hand dropped lower, flirting with the hem of my shirt, continuing on to cup my ass. He pressed his lips against my throat, right under my ear. "You said a kiss was what you wanted for a start. What else is on your list?" There was a growl under the question.

I squirmed as it vibrated against my neck and kept going. "Selfish things." I turned my face into the spot between his jaw and throat at the admission. "I want something for myself. Something no one else has a prior, stronger claim to. Then I'm never giving it up."

Marshall shuddered and tightened his hold, reminding me of the strength in his thick arms. "The way you want

447

someone, I get it. I want that, to be that something and to belong with you."

"You don't have to always agree, in order to stay," I whispered, afraid of how much I wanted him to, and that he was only humoring me.

"Stop saying that." He reared back, holding my shoulders and making me look at him. "I could've tried making a place for myself before. I didn't because those towns and people weren't right. They didn't matter. This is right. It's where I belong, with Matteo and Jace because they've cared more than my real brother ever did, and with you. I don't want to stay for the hell of it—I need to be with you. I want all those selfish things for myself, too. To complain if anybody messes with my kitchen, and to grow lemons because Jace likes them."

His voice dropped to a rougher burr. "I want to be yours, and to have a claim to a part of you. It's you, Liv. You're so alive, like walking next to the sun, and I feel alive when I'm with you. You buy comics, and superhero socks, and yell at Bruce the Bastard, which is fucking amazing. Not the buying part, but that you care enough to. You look at me, and you *see me*. Everything makes more sense around you. I want to take care of you that way, too."

"Yes, please." I snuggled deeper, and every muscle in his body seemed to relax.

So did mine, my body recognizing that we were a pair, freed from my compulsively analytical brain and its tendency toward over complicating.

$\mathcal{M}$arshall

WITH LIV'S weight pressed against him and her heart thudding against his, the random sparks and twisty ideas blowing wild in his head slowed. They settled, lined up neatly.

That was another of Liv's powers. She didn't get rattled or impatient or annoyed. She gave him the leeway to breathe and put everything in order, no finishing his sentences for him, no assumptions.

She cuddled closer, while one of her metal ballads wove a backdrop. Her slow, steady breathing, the soft glow from her weirdly decorated lamp, and the room packed with highpoints of her life held him. She was letting him into her world. He got how that was as huge for her as it was for him.

"I'm staying, and we're together." He tested, making sure he hadn't messed up understanding her.

"This is your home and we're all yours." She nuzzled, like she couldn't get close enough, eyelashes brushing his chin.

"Even though sometimes I get sort of fixated. And weird, and freaked out, and I don't even know why." He only stated fact, making sure Liv understood what she was agreeing to.

"I think that's the definition of the human experience."

It wasn't like he was exposing some big secret, but he wanted to be clear. "I'm not like all of you. Sometimes I panic. I'm kind of pasty and freckled and there's a lot of me, and I can hurt myself in my own kitchen. And I get distracted, so I'll probably forget to watch for cryptids tailing me because I'm checking for ripe squash."

A puff of air lifted a curl at his temple. Liv's silent laugh. Her fingers played with his and the laugh included him, inviting him in on the joke. "I'll be sure to take point on our farmer's market trips. As well as on all comic browsing forays, in case. As for the rest—" Liv put a couple inches between them, which kind of sucked, but then rested both hands on his chest, which, any time she wanted to feel him up, was awesome. "I've entertained any number of vivid thoughts."

"Tell me." He couldn't disguise the command.

One hand touched his bicep, traveling on and over his shoulder like she was measuring. Her other hand did even more interesting things, dropping lower, toying with the hem of his shirt. "Things like how your eyes remind me of a chunk of sea glass I found on my first trip to the beach. About your shoulders, because I kind of have a thing for impressive shoulders." Her hand shifted, touching the bridge of his nose, skipping, stopping with a finger on his lower lip. "How I would like to conduct further research."

He tried storing all the impossible-amazing things she was saying, but having her hands all over him, her finger right there, tempting him to take it between his lips and show her other things he'd like to do with her...

Don't be weird. Don't freak Liv out. He settled for, "Research. Okay."

Liv frowned, and stepped back.

One step felt like the Grand Canyon. So much for not scaring her off. He snatched at ideas and words, searching for the right ones to reassure her.

Always faster, Liv spoke first. "You aren't always required to say yes to me. You aren't *ever* required to."

He was. He bit down on his tongue in time to stop words escaping. Liv wouldn't understand and then she'd push him out in the hallway, which might as well be Chicago in January, fatally freezing him to the bone in the same way.

Liv liked direct. She picked what he really meant out of his word jumbles. Go with that. "If I say all the things I really mean, about the two of us together, this soon—I mean, I definitely want to get around to those, but I'm not pushing—you might punch me and then you'd have to write one of those reports you hate. Then you'd be in a bad mood, and for sure it would stop the kissing—you were talking about kissing?" He checked. Liv tilted her head in agreement. "Right. No kissing, which, kissing is really great starting point. Saying okay seemed safer," he finished, then sucked in oxygen.

That tiny crinkle-smile was back. "Ah. Okay it is, then. Good catch."

Hell, yes, it was. He also caught that Liv needed to get out of her head. Stop the over-thinking, her fallback when she was unsure.

She'd said she liked when they were touching. Buzzed on her smile, he went for it. He brought her closer, then wrapped his arm around her back, her skin hot through the thin shirt. The shirt he'd picked for her, and he loved that she was wearing his mark.

Liv let him walk her backward, and against the wall. He

stiffened his arm, shielding her spine from the drywall. Face an inch above hers, he asked, "Is this too much?"

She grabbed his belt loop and tugged.

"I don't want to squash you," he whisper-groaned. Eager Liv, that was a memory to keep and savor. He eased his weight against her, inch by inch. Agonizing and arousing as hell.

Liv wrapped a leg around his thigh and pulled him in the last bit. Pelvises bumped and he jammed his forearm on the wall at head height.

Liv inhaled, and her eyes closed, lashes making lacey shadows. She turned her head into his arm. "Marshall. Damn."

He got that meant *yes*, then long fingers tangled in his hair again, bringing their lips together. Liv caught his lower lip and nibbled. He opened up, ready for whatever she wanted, giving her the sense of control he already recognized she needed in order to feel safe. *See, Liv? It's always yes.*

Like she heard him, her grip relaxed. She curved into him some mystery way, because bodies didn't bend that much. Her hand traced down the back of his neck, drawing short nails over his skin. He shivered, that touch bringing every cell in his body to attention, and he gave into the need to get as close to Liv as possible.

He bent and caught her around the hips, lifting her. A gasp flowed from her lips to his. Then she wrapped her legs around his waist, muscles clenching. He shifted, one arm under her, cupping what had to be the best ass in the universe, the other behind her back. Holding her safe.

He wasn't ready to say it out loud and risk her taking it the wrong, but keeping her safe in his own way was the center of his existence now.

This close and intimate, nose to nose with each other, the world should've shrunk to this one room. Instead it expanded, now made up of the Liv's lips on his, the taste of basil and nutmeg from his meal that he'd put his soul into, for her, her hair swirling around them in a coconut-scented curtain. Her hands bunching his shirt, the warmth of her legs locked around him.

Hours or days or forever later, her mouth left his. Her sigh ghosted over his lips like another caress.

"Damn. Right?" He whispered.

She nodded, cheek sliding against his. She traced around his lower lip, only the tip of her finger, glancing up, checking whether she could, whether he liked it. All it took to shoot a long pulse of *want* straight to his cock.

Sure, they were in a clinch, but he wasn't assuming, yet. He shifted, keeping his hard-on off Liv.

"You can put me down. I'm not exactly petite." She let go of his shirt, expression apologetic.

"I'm good." He'd stand like this forever, Liv in his arms. He settled her closer, arms tight.

Like that gave her permission, her hand rubbed his shoulder, down his arm. Sliding around his bicep, measuring. Over his chest to his other arm, repeating the process. She traced the diamond on his shirt, top to bottom, intent and intense.

"We're raised to be direct about our bodies, sex, and emotions, which I've been informed isn't a common approach for civilians. Basically, I don't think I'm at all accomplished with your type of flirting, so I'm going to stick with what I know. Please tell me if I'm doing anything wrong?" She touched the hem of his shirt. "May I? Because I'd very much like to see you without anything on. Eventually, if it isn't on your agenda yet."

"Yeah. That. Anything like that. Don't yell at me about always agreeing. I say yes because you make sense, okay? When you touch me or kiss me or pretty much anything, it makes sense." He'd seen that Liv liked getting physical. He rubbed his cheek against her face, dragging scruff along her jaw and lips.

At her sharp inhale, he dipped enough to catch her earlobe. He hadn't been sure, since the marks were barely visible and she never wore earrings, but he'd guessed right. A row of tiny holes curved around her lobe and the shell of her outer ear, sweet bumps against his tongue. His teeth grazed along the edge of cartilage, against proof of Liv's rebelliousness, her bucking authority and getting piercings, even if she let them close over. Liv rebelling, like with keeping him, bringing him on the team, letting disorganized him into her neat, ordered life.

It came out rough, a growl-plea in her ear. "Whatever you want to do, I want it, too. Like you can't imagine. I didn't know until you busted in and found me, but this is what I've waited for, all along. So don't let go." He wasn't sure of much, but he did know it would be the end of him if Liv stopped.

iv

I HAD no intention of letting go. Instead, I gave in. Tonight was all about meeting needs, Marshall's and mine. This felt more real, more binding, than any Company oath or contract he would sign, pledging himself to the Company until he drew his last breath. This, what was between us, went so much deeper.

Marshall held me with a strength he'd only hinted at, arms steady and no strain showing on his face.

I touched it again, fingertips learning the feel of him, over the few freckles, and strong jaw. Loving how he leaned into the caress, always trying to get closer to me and not embarrassed to show his need.

The look in his eyes was new. Or perhaps I was only now ready to see it. Raw. Desperate in a completely primal way, a man scoured empty and seeking purpose.

The same way I had felt after realizing I didn't have a

place anymore with Vee, Kimi, and Josh. Then getting slapped in the face with new potential, what I could build with Jace and Matteo. Seeing a future I hadn't envisioned, and a dream I'd do anything to make come true.

Marshall looked at me that same way. Like I was the thing that set his world right.

I let go, trusting Marshall's strength, and caught his face with both hands. "I'm never letting go. You're where you belong, with the people who value you. With the person you already mean the world to."

"You?" The steady blue gaze bore into me.

"Yes. Always."

"I'll live up to that. I'll take care of you. All of you."

"I know, and we need you. I need you, and I lied to myself about that until now, but not anymore. Thank you for being patient with me."

"Anything for you," Marshall rasped, his voice thick.

I whispered against his lips. "Can we work on what you want now?"

"You." No time to think, no hesitation. His demand overlapped my question, answered before my last word died away. "I'm not as smart or creative or whatever, and probably I'm selfish too, since I don't need policing cryptids and vampires, or painting great art, or a cult career on the side. There's only room for our team and you. You fill up every part of me."

"Our team." That sent a contented ripple through me, that Marshall was claiming us.

"Yeah." He shifted me to one arm, easy as breathing, and touched my chin, rough fingers a reverent whisper along my cheekbone. "You're all mine, and I'm all in."

I would reassure Marshall as often as it took for him to accept and internalize that this was his home, deep in his bones. "This is your compound." I kissed the corner of his lips, five-o-clock shadow sandpapery and new and I wanted to explore what it felt like against my breasts and between my thighs. "Your kitchen." I kissed the opposite corner. "As many pots of mini lemon trees and weird herbs as you can think up."

I worked my way inward from the corner, kiss by kiss, promise by promise. "Your B-movie nights. Your primo seat for the gaming marathons." The last was as much a promise for me as for him. "Me. You have me."

"You just gave me everything."

I hadn't, though.

I picked at the tangle of lust, hope, and fear lodged deep inside, isolating the fear, the way we'd been trained when facing predators. Acknowledge it, then get past it so the fear didn't interfere with performance in the field. I couldn't let the fear of losing everything again take over, or I risked a self-fulfilling prophecy.

Marshall remained silent, allowing me to work through my issues. Possibly because my hands still ran a circuit, from his shoulders to his chest, soothing me.

"We don't have to do anything tonight," he said. "I mean sex." His offhand, earnest delivery broke the tension.

I tried hiding my smile, then gave in. Another of his unique powers, the ability to make us smile. "I inferred as much."

"If you're tired, I can go." He glanced at the half full plate, a judge-y scowl flitting over his face. "You should still eat."

"Do you want to leave?"

"The answer to that's always going to be no. Doesn't matter when or why, it's no."

I went down the list. "Short tempered and snappy from marathon Regional calls?"

"No."

"Sweaty. Like, six hours on the training course in the middle of July gross?"

"No."

"After a mission when I come in basted in hostile's remains?"

He looked at me from under his brows. "Stop trying to make me go. It's not gonna work. You're wasting energy when you're already tired, and your dinner is getting colder."

CRUD. He was right. This was more about my insecurities than his. "You are a lot better at this relationship thing than I am. And braver. Got any pointers?"

His voice dropped. "What do you need, Liv? All you ever have to do is tell me. You need to go slower?"

I shook my head.

"You need this?" His grip tightened, fitting me tight against him, arms like iron bands.

I nodded. "I need for us to be as close as physically possible, as soon as possible. Now would be good. I need your hands all over me, and I need mine on you."

Marshall smoothed my hair back, over my shoulder. He cupped the back of my head, and kissed my temple. "Told you—I'll take care of you."

$\mathcal{M}$arshall

ALWAYS. If Liv wasn't understanding, fine. He barely made sense to himself sometimes, when it came to stringing words together. He could show her though. She'd understand that. She always did.

He wasn't a soldier, but he worked all day, every day, twelve hours on lines, loading and unloading, butchering. Not glamorous, but good for something. Now, something Liv liked.

Resettling her legs around his waist, one arm under her, the other touching her hair, he played with its warm-silk waves. He tucked it over her shoulder, then kissed the spot under her ear that'd set her off earlier. His reward was another full-body shiver, and Liv pressing in, breasts crushed against his chest.

He chuckled, and she shimmied at the vibration, practically grinding against his arm. Experimenting, he lightly nipped the corner of her jaw. Getting another rewarding wiggle, he worked his way down and in, nipping, making sure stubble grazed along her flushed skin.

This time he demanded she open up for him. When she did, tongues slid against each other, and he showed her what he intended to do next, once clothes were out of the way— which was gonna be soon.

The eager way she met him, followed his lead, almost undid him. He withdrew by inches, finally catching her lower lip between his teeth, barely denting it, because even if she was into rougher stuff, he'd never be able to bring himself to really hurt her.

Her breathing sped up, hands digging into his shoulders like she was drowning and he was her lifeboat.

Right. *This* was what she needed. His tongue flirted with hers, switching between it and her lips, teasing, until she groaned and tried climbing him like a tree, a move that his cock was all for.

He let her lips go, pulling back enough to admire them, swollen and pomegranate-red. Then caught her earlobe again. Traveling from it down her neck, mixing nips and kisses that were all promise. She dropped her head back, neck a graceful arch, her breasts outlined by the thin fabric of the tee.

He switched, arm around her back. "I've got you. Go with the feelings. Don't think. Don't worry. I won't let go."

Marshall knew more than Liv about this one thing, about brains sometimes lying, and when to ignore them and instead go with what was real, what your body was saying.

Liv hesitated a second, then the weight against his arm increased, trusting him. His chest hurt, like getting punched, except hit with happiness instead of a fist. The feeling spread, and settled into his bones. He didn't know if there was ever a time when someone had completely trusted him, assuming he could, instead of that he'd fuck up.

He caught one of her nipples through the fabric, tongue circling, sucking until it pebbled, the shirt as good as see through now. Liv arched further, offering him free access.

He worked between both peaks, teasing one with tongue and teeth, fingers rolling and lightly pinching the other. Liv's hand knotted in his shirt, kinda choking him, not that he gave a damn. Every twist, every shift of her body, ground rough denim against his cock, shooting as much happiness as lust through him. Every hitched breath and pulled curl cemented his place in her life a little more.

He worked his hand under her shirt, palm flat against her stomach, asking.

"Marshall." She tightened her legs, permission clear.

He rolled the shirt up, and off. He dropped it on the dresser, careful of the photo frames. One day—one day, there would be a photo of him, of all four of them, lined up on there amid the rest of the people Liv loved.

His hand skimmed over tawny brown skin with darker scars, still too perfect to be real, but it was. Around her ribcage, thumbs grazing the lower curve of her breasts. Liv raised to meet his touch. His lips closed around a nipple, nothing between his tongue and her skin now.

He kissed his way down, greedy for every hitched breath and shiver from Liv. He caught the waistband of the tiny shorts, looking up for permission. She lifted up and shimmied her hips, and the clothes were gone like magic.

Stepping sideways, careful of Liv, careful of her life displayed in mementos, he sat her on the dresser between the photos. He took her mouth, because kissing Liv was always on the menu. And because that dazed expression she got— that he was responsible for—it sent answering fireworks through him.

He traced down her ribs, over old claw scars that made him more determined to stay, continuing until his thumbs rested over her navel, pointing down. When she spread her thighs, he knelt in front of her, kissing a new path downward, rolling her panties down as he went.

Impatient, and even sexier, she lifted, jerked them off and kicked them to land on the floor. She was so real and beautiful, and here she was, with him. He was making sure she never regretted her decision. Palms splayed over each of her knees, he slowly swept his way up, and kissed the inside of her thigh. Then almost lost it like some horny teen at her sigh.

He dropped his hands, circling her ankles, barely skimming up the back of her calves. He kissed the softer skin on the inside of first one knee, then the other. She spread her legs, wet and ready, and fucking gorgeous.

She tasted equally perfect. His tongue found a new set of lips, playing and teasing. Not touching her clit yet. Liv moved, restless. Pressing against his mouth. He caught her thighs holding them down, holding her open. Switching for a moment to dragging his stubble along her inner thighs, setting his teeth against skin, not hard enough to mark her. Enough that she bucked and tried escaping his hold, pressing, looking for more.

He gave her what she wanted, tongue flicking at her clit. Circling it, finding the spot and pressure that left her gasping and her thighs quivering, grinding against his face. Her hand not locked around the dresser edge dug into his hair.

His world narrowed to the flex and twitch of Liv's muscles under his palms, the taste of her on his tongue, the way her breath hitched and caught. He switched from holding her down, one hand sliding across her hipbone, continuing south. Finger circling her clit. "I want to know what you feel like."

"Yes." Words squeezed out between gasps, her throaty, fuck-me tone enough to make his balls ache. "That."

He slid a finger in. Liv arched and he added another, thumb rolling her clit as his tongue circled and flicked. His goal was making her forget everything but them, him working her, hands and tongue, for a perfect rose-gold moment.

"Marshall." It came out as a demand-plea, and her fingers tangled in his hair. The best kind of pain shooting through his scalp. He gave himself over to it. Feeling Liv come, clenching around his fingers, as hers knotted in his hair. Like she was staking her claim.

She rode his hand and he gripped her hip with his other, keeping her from coming off the dresser.

The pain in his scalp lessened. Which kind of sucked since it meant Liv let go. When her thighs stopped twitching and relaxed, he withdrew, sliding slick fingers out. Slow, over her clit and lips, getting another mini climax.

He rose, and *damn*. Liv's back was still arched, head thrown back, showcasing the graceful curve of body, her chest heaving. Not ashamed, not hiding that she enjoyed him touching her.

Being even this far apart didn't work for him. He scooped her up, arms under her knees, and brought her against his chest, where she belonged. Liv gave a last gasp, her arms going around his neck. Warm, and relaxed in his hold, trusting him completely.

He wasn't letting her go. Ever, if he had his way.

iv

MARSHALL WAS—WOW.

He wasn't a pile of bulging muscles like Matteo, or five-percent body fat and a carved six-pack like Jace, but he was equally strong.

Strong, solid, and stubborn. I didn't waste my breath reminding him I could walk. Plus, having his arms around me, tucking me close, like I didn't weigh as much as one of our go-bags was different, and surprisingly...exciting. Despite orgasming thirty seconds earlier, heat filled me again.

I nuzzled under Marshall's jaw, the only spot in easy reach, and kissed the side of his neck. "Bed?"

He crossed and sat me on the edge, kneeling in front of me again. His expression was raw. Everything in him laid open, showing on his face. Far too much caution still in his eyes. Waiting for me to change my mind, for one more person to fail him, and jerk this tenuous security from under his feet.

I could talk forever. Marshall needed action, not words. I kissed him, and he met me, eager, that talented tongue sliding over mine. His hands holding my hips, sure and gentle. He hadn't let go of me once since we first kissed.

I nipped his lower lip. "Is naked still on the table?"

He groaned. "Do you even need to ask?"

Letting go, he caught the hem of his tee, arms crossing in that way-sexy move guys did, pulling it over his head. He dropped the shirt out of our way.

I took my time, finally able to look. He was thick and solid. A lot like the compound's adobe walls, still standing and protecting their charges, three-hundred years later. I ran my hand over what I'd only been able to guess at, up his arm, and shoulders, to his chest. My hand was like a shadow moving across the moon, dark against light.

"I told you. I'm not like you guys. What you're used to." His tone was matter-of-fact, face neutral.

"The first time I saw snow, where it really registered as a force of nature, something other than flurries or an annoyance because we had to wipe off our boots, we were on a cross-Region training exercise in the Northwest. A freak early season blizzard hit overnight. We woke up to these walls of snow, and the trees were still in their full Fall glory, red and orange-gold against all this crystalline white." I flattened my palms over his pecs, sliding them down his smooth chest. To his stomach, catching crisp, auburn hairs, the narrow path disappearing under his waistband. Like those bright leaves on pristine snow.

"The other cadets and Instructors were annoyed at being stuck for several days, and having to dig out, or bored."

"What about you?"

"I stared until we had to leave, memorizing the picture. I

hated digging out and ruining it, because it was the most beautiful thing I'd ever seen. Possibly because it was so unexpected, or at least, it was to me. It was special."

Marshall let out a ragged breath and stood. I let my hand trail down as he did, until he was out of reach. He toed his Chucks off. The pop of his jeans tab mixed with the music. Eyes on me the entire time, he let his jeans drop.

I rose on my knees, getting hands back on him. In reverse, I explored, skimming my hands up muscular legs, to broad, strong thighs, hairs ticking my palms. I traced the diamond symbol and S on his boxers, a match to his discarded tee. That he wore the boxers I'd challenged him to get during our teasing sent one of those tingles of possessiveness and happiness spiraling through me.

"What're you thinking?" Marshall asked.

I spread my hands over the erection tenting the S. Marshall was thick everywhere. "I'm thinking that I want to find out what else you like, all the things, and get them, or make them happen."

"You. You're what I want, and you're always gonna be at the top of that list."

I closed my hand around him, and Marshall groaned. "You aren't playing fair, Liv."

He watched me while I tugged the boxers off, and spread both hands, my fingers framing his cock. I burrowed into dense curls, loving how he twitched as I cupped balls in one hand. I wrapped the other around the base of his cock, thumb moving back and forth, velvet skin over the hard length.

Marshall stood, still as if he was made from marble and copper, although I felt muscles clenching with every sweep of my thumb. Especially when he said, "There are free health clinics, and I'm clear. I don't have the proof though, or condoms. I'm not gonna ask for more than this, not until I can take care of both."

"At HQ when you first arrived, and we required the blood as your DNA sample? They also sort of ran a full lab panel." I braced, since neither McKenna or Bruce had taken that practice well, something about laws and privacy. Hoping to smooth over our alleged misconduct, I pointed at the bedside table. "I also have my brand of condoms, if that's okay? Oh, and this." I rolled my arm to expose the implant incision.

"Thank God."

I smiled at his fervent approval. "I meant what I said about enjoying watching you. I'd like to do that with sex, too. I want to watch you."

"This?" He fisted his cock, and I let go. "Why?"

"Um, you are impressive. And—is it okay to tell civilian men they're attractive? Because you are."

He stroked himself, watching me, while I watched him, the play of muscles as he moved, his big hand working his hard length. I wiggled closer, and came up on my knees.

"It's your turn." His bass voice somehow dropped even lower, and deeper. Rich, like it should be edible.

He took my hand and wrapped it back around him. I slid my hand up and down once, gauging what he liked. Hand still over mine, he squeezed, tightening my grip, showing me. He let go, allowing me to learn the feel of him.

I ran my finger around the head, and brought it to my lips. Pulling him in, circling my tongue around, over the slit. Never taking his attention off me, he touched my hair. Instead of tugging or using it to push and set the pace, he lifted strands and ran them between his fingers, sending pulses of heat between my thighs as his calluses and nicks caught.

His balls tightened, his breathing turning harsher, and muscles in his thighs locked. Yet he kept his touch impossibly gentle, with the kind of cast-iron control any agent would envy.

I took him in, as deep as I could, then ran my tongue along the sensitive groove underneath on the way out.

His breath escaped in more of a roar. I rolled my eyes, tip of his cock still between my lips. He caught my chin, thumb following the line of my jaw, stopping to rest under my lower lip. "I want to remember this."

I filled in the rest. In case it didn't last. In case someone came in and took everything away. A surge of anger crashed over me. No one was taking my team away, or my family, or my Marshall.

I pulled him in deep, hitting the back of my throat, keeping eye contact. Tasting his salt on the back of my tongue as I let him go, slow, savoring him.

My mouth, the intimacy, the promise he read in my expression—something finally shattered his iron will.

"God, Liv." He scooped me up, and laid us both down in one hard motion, the mattress bouncing.

The bed settled and Marshall rolled, caging me. Pelvises pressed together, his arms braced on either side of my head, covering me.

He nuzzled under my jaw, scruff lightly sandpapering sensitized skin. I arched into him. He gave a credible growl, and settled a heavy leg over my hips. Not satisfied, he caught my nipple, tugging until it peaked, then switching.

I worked my arms free, and while Marshall mapped my body out, I mapped his. Running my hands over his shoulders, drawing nails over his and up his biceps. Loving the contrast between us. I nudged his head aside and wiggled lower, tongue finding and circling his flat nipples, flicking and teasing. He shifted, giving me room, but kept his leg over mine. I spent time equally, tongue and teeth grazing one, while I tweaked the other.

He swore and rolled onto his hip. "Condom?"

"Drawer." I continued my explorations, running nails down his side as he stretched and jerked the drawer open. He raised up, rolling the condom on, then lined us up. He eased in exquisitely slow, with more of that amazing restraint.

I angled to take him in deeper. He stretched over me again, arms behind me. One hand cupping the back of my head, fingers buried in my hair. Like he couldn't touch me enough, and get close enough, starved for intimacy.

I understood that need. I kept my eyes open and locked on his as he rolled his hips in a slow, deep beat. Putting fully healed abs to good use, I held myself up to wind one arm around his neck, the other hand braced on his shoulder. Relishing in the feel of him under my palm, and wrapping one leg around his waist, keeping us tight. Offering all of me to him, as he set the pace now, powerful hips and thighs doing the work

I arched, kissing him. My tongue slipping in, repeating his slow, languorous motion. He swore-moaned into my mouth, and our rhythm picked up. I met his thrusts, stoking him higher and harder.

Marshall drew on our energy, and fed it back to me. Watching me. Tuned in, reading me and varying his angle and intensity to match. Everything in me was alive, sensitive to the slide of skin against skin, the air blowing over out sweating bodies, the muscles working over and around me.

Marshall felt it, too. Pulling almost out, then driving back in. Sliding over my clit. Pleasure coiled, tighter and tighter. Fed by the primal desire on Marshall's face, the tendon's standing out in his neck, biceps bunching. Holding on, waiting for me to orgasm first.

I let go dropping into the spreading pleasure, Marshall's sure, skilled touch, trusting him to lead the way. My thighs clenched, molten heat exploding, turning my bones and muscles liquid. Still, Marshall waited, watching me ride out the orgasm, expression fierce and satisfied.

When I slowed, it was what he'd waited for. His whole body tightened, grip bruising. Driving in, shuddering. Repeating my name until the syllables ran together.

Bit by bit, his shudders eased, and he drew in a long breath. He kissed my forehead, my lips, the tip of my nose. He shifted, pulling out, ready to roll off.

I wrapped my thighs around his, exerting some muscle and keeping us linked. Marshall propped on one elbow, his other thumb sweeping my cheek, brushing back the sex-loosened hair stuck there.

He tackled my ruined ponytail, working the band off, then fanning my hair out, arranging it to meet his approval. I caught his hand and laced our fingers together.

"That thing you said, about the snow being special to you?" His lashes dropped, shielding his eyes, hiding, for the first time since we'd touched, still double-checking.

"That's you. You're as unexpected and awe inspiring as that September blizzard. Something powerful, and special."

He exhaled, tensed muscles relaxing in relief, like dropping a burden you hadn't realized was so heavy, exchanging it, finally, for comfort. Marshall's forehead rested against mine. His breath whispering against my lips, breathing me in, sharing oxygen. Linking us as our skin cooled, and muscles went satisfied-limp.

It was perfect.

"You didn't finish your dinner."

The stern complaint took a second to register. Once it did, my giggle stutter-snorted out, and wouldn't stop. I clapped both hands over my mouth.

Marshall levered up on his elbow, directing a long suffering look at me. Which made me laugh harder. Big, snorting laughs.

The corners of his very talented lips finally curved up. Then morphed into a smile. He took care of the condom, then rolled on his back, careful to keep us connected, letting me get it out of my system.

I finally did, giggles petering out. Taking with them the last remnants of loneliness and resentment I hadn't been aware I was holding on to.

Digging my shoulder blades into the wrinkled blanket, I stretched, and rolled my head to face him. "Don't tell me your bossy, overbearing switch has been flipped."

His answer was gruff. "My compound, my kitchen, my team. I get to be bossy about the care and feeding of crazy-scary but clueless agents. The days of fridges that only contain second rate cheese are gone."

I laughed again, then shivered, A/C kicking in, and the air raising chills over drying skin.

Marshall abandoned the bed, frown back.

I scooted more or less upright, content to watch. Naked Marshall was awesome. As was the view of his ass, muscles rolling as he tugged boxers on. He collected our clothes from various corners and pieces of furniture, then offered me my sleep set.

I settled for panties and tee. He stood there, holding his clothes. It took me a beat to understand. My chest ached once I did. He was waiting to see if I had gotten what I wanted, and was tossing him out until next time. "I'd like it if you spent the night." Every night, maybe.

Marshall took his time, folding the rest of our clothes, laying them on the nightstand. I now recognized that every job, every meal, every one of our needs he met, grounded him, and made him that bit more sure, letting him claim his place.

I shoveled bed linens straight, and pillows out of the way, then flipped the blanket edge down as invitation. He sat on the edge, one leg bent onto the bed. Surveying my collection, pillows of all sizes and colors, some regular, some decorative. "You weren't kidding about the pillow thing."

"Told you. This is a carefully curated selection, chosen from the cream of pillow-dom."

"Want to add one more of those huggie ones?"

"Are you applying for the position?" There was a lot more going on underneath the teasing than a simple question about bedding.

"Yeah, I am."

"I do have an opening, and upon scanning your resume, you appear the ideal fit. As incentive, I can offer full access to the rest of this collection, plus a private shower." I nodded at the bath.

"Sold." He joined me. "Tired? Want to read? You were about to before. I'll be quiet."

"I'm more incredibly relaxed. Mellow."

"Yeah." He stretched out on his side, facing me.

I scooted so we lined, already kind of missing the connection.

He fluffed the largest pillow, then positioned it so that we could share, my head on his bicep.

I was so okay with that, and turned enough to kiss the center of his palm.

He sighed and seemed to melt, molding around me. Cuddling me like I was his huggie pillow. I drowsed, lulled by the dim, amber light, his warmth, and his even breathing. The kind of happy-content I hadn't experienced in several years.

Marshall played with the ends of my hair, touch tentative, as if he was trying not to bother me. When I made a *yes please* hum and snuggled deeper, his touch became more possessive.

Tracing my brows. My cheekbones and lips. Skimming

up my arms and across my collarbone. Touching each finger, one by one. There was nothing sexual involved. It was intent and focused, totally committed to his task. Proving himself that he was allowed to touch me, to have what he'd longed for so badly.

I practiced breathing evenly, pushing tears back. I hadn't felt this sort of anger since my future brother's cancer diagnosis. Now, the fury was directed at hating that Marshall had ever felt alone, as if he didn't matter to anyone. Because that was what his starved for affection exploration meant.

That? That was over. I'd see to it that he was never left in doubt as to his importance to all of us. Especially, to me.

CHAPTER 58

arshall

MARSHALL FLOATED around the kitchen on a rose-gold cloud, one scented with Liv's coconut moisturizer despite his quick shower earlier. He poked at the feeling. Deciding it was pure happiness, and home. Happy, with no time limit or expiration date. He rolled the emotion around, learning the color and feel as he cooked. It wasn't a frantic snapshot this time. He had the security and space to get to know the feeling, start making it part of him.

Last night Liv proved she meant all the things she'd said. That he belonged to her. That she was entrusting some part of herself to him. She'd also entrusted the most important things in her life—her compound, and Jace and Matteo.

Marshall had given her what she needed, too. She'd released a tiny chunk of her burden last night, sharing it with him. He'd left her tucked in and asleep, and gone to work since the only thing she needed more than rest was food.

Now, boots thumped down the hall and into his kitchen.

"Two more minutes." He flipped a last Belgian waffle onto the plate, and set it at Liv's spot, then placed the caramel container by it, arranging the lemon curd by Jace's, and chocolate-chipotle by Matteo's. Marshall had gone with prosciutto instead of bacon, already doled out on each plate to prevent pork thievery.

"Damn, brother." Matteo whistled.

"It's only breakfast." Pink-tinted pleasure still coiled in Marshall's belly. The team noticed what he did, and appreciated it.

"The hell it is. This is a celebration breakfast, if I ever saw one." Jace thumped Marshall's shoulder on the way to grab a seat.

Heat boiled up Marshall's face. Then he realized they meant celebrating being invited to join the team, not celebrating him and Liv.

He stopped in the middle of picking up the whip cream. He and Liv hadn't talked about telling the rest of the team. She'd said they were together, but she might not have meant everyone knowing.

Marshall took a stab at telling himself that public acknowledgment didn't matter. Being together was the important part, even if it was a private thing.

"Gentleman. Touch that ham and risk losing a digit," Liv said.

Marshall checked over his shoulder, gauging her mood, how she acted around the team today.

She glared at Jace, who'd angled her full plate suspiciously close to his. Prosciutto unloading close.

Jace slowly pushed hers away, big eyed and fake-innocent. "Huh. How did that get over here?"

"Caramel or fruit?" Marshall waved the spoon at the array

475

of toppings, changing the topic and preventing another food-based stabbing.

"Caramel, please. Is there more ham?" Liv headed to the empty range.

"I can do bacon." Marshall's fingers twitched, wanting to touch her. Instead, he skirted around and opened the SubZero.

Liv followed. Shielded by the fridge's metal door, she stepped in and kissed Marshall. He exhaled, his relief brightening the day up again. He hugged her, quick and hard, lifting her off her feet and squeezing a surprise-squeak out of her.

"Sorry." He set Liv back on her feet. They were okay, at least, and if she wanted to keep the relationship private, he'd deal. He closed the fridge. "Go eat. I'll make extra prosciutto tomorrow at breakfast."

"Score." Jace didn't even pretend he hadn't eavesdropped.

"None for you." Liv plopped into her seat. "It's all for me."

"No way."

"Way. Perk of sleeping with the chef."

Marshall's heart did its damnedest to stop beating, waiting for the guys' verdict.

Liv dragged a piece of the ham on her plate through the whipped cream, and took a bite. "Oh, Marshall and I are—" She checked with him. "What's the correct term for monogamous, sleeping together, and committed? Seeing each other? Dating? Is there a difference?"

"Dating is fine." Marshall's face felt neon, but he was also positive he'd never smiled so wide before.

"About time," Matteo grumbled, cutting a bite of waffle.

At Jace and Liv's startled looks, Matteo pointed his fork and the speared waffle square at the pair. "Don't have to be stealth or an intel specialist to see you and Marsh had it bad for each other."

"Man, I'll sleep with you for pork products. C'mon," Jace begged, swiveling to track Marshall's progress. "I like gingers."

Marshall poured himself coffee, and took the chair beside Liv. "You're cool, but I'm a one-agent cook."

$\mathcal{M}$arshall

"Cow rematch after dinner." Matteo stretched, sorta resembling a mountain range shifting. "Kimi's team is going down."

Jace fist bumped his teammate, then Marshall.

Another of those rose-gold waves washed over him, as amazing as the sun slanting out after a storm. He finally, mostly, believed that he had a place here and a family.

"Since I love you guys, I'll be right here to console you after the defeat." Liv clicked the dishwasher closed on the lunch dishes.

A pulse of pure covetousness hit. Liv was serious. Anybody could see she meant it. They weren't only teammates, or even close friends. They were family and she loved them all. Now, Marshall was on his way to being part of that elite category.

He wanted to hear *love* and his name together from her. He added that to his list of things to learn and master.

He was already in love with Liv. That's what all in meant to him. After last night, Marshall could admit that truth. Liv had his heart, even if she didn't know it.

And that was okay. He had time now, and she'd said he was better at relationships than her. Braver. He wasn't. He just didn't have anything to lose the way she did, so he could go all-out. Liv was smart, and he'd teach her.

"What's that look?" Liv tapped the power on the dishwasher and propped her butt against the counter, arms crossed. One brow raised in that thing she did.

Marshall loved that, too.

"What look? I don't think I have looks." He tried out teasing, playing with Liv the way she did with him.

She sketched a wave, taking him in. "That one?" She narrowed her eyes. "I'd almost say it was smug. But that can't be right."

"Maybe it is." He joined her, working to keep from busting out in a grin. "You're the one who said the C.O. doesn't get any respect around here. I have to fit in, follow my teammates' lead."

Her eyebrow went higher. "Seriously? Less than eighteen-hours as Company and insubordination has already taken hold? This is the thanks I get for being basically the most awesome C.O. to ever inhabit this Division?"

Giddiness hit at Liv was playing back. "I guess I'll have to find another way to say thanks."

Last night and her response engraved in his memory, Marshall closed the space between them, using his size, caging her where she'd leaned against the counter. She for real had a dozen ways to take him down, break some bones. Instead, she froze.

He got the satisfaction of her eyes widening, chest rising

in a sharp inhale. Her voice was husky once she got words out. "I suppose I should hear you out."

He spread his legs, and pulled her in so they interlocked. He put an arm behind her so she wasn't rammed into the tile, and caught the back of her neck with the other. He looked down, cock getting into the game as her lips parted, staring at him like she was hypnotized.

He kissed her, lips barely brushing. Tasting the citrus of the fruit salad he'd made his team, and under it, Liv. Coconut and plain lip balm and everything good in his life.

She surged up, ready for more but he kept the kiss soft, lips reverent. Teaching her the first steps, showing her how love worked. That it wasn't scary.

He pulled back tiny kiss by tiny kiss, Liv looking dazed. He ran his thumbs over her eyebrows, her cheeks, the perfect curve of her chin, the way she had with him, loving the softness of her skin. Loving that he could touch her. "How's that as a thank you?"

She wrapped his tee in her fist, standing on her tiptoes, for a fierce kiss.

See? This is love, Liv. You'll like it.

Like she heard him, her grip loosened. Almost tentative, she watched him as she ran her hands up his chest, and stopped. One palm right over his heart. That was fine. Let her feel what she already owned.

Her kiss was nearly as tentative, lips brushing. She didn't pull away after. Instead, she leaned against him. Which was also fine—he'd always be here for her to lean on, to give her a minute away from duty and watching out for everyone else.

He rested his forehead against hers. Her lashes fluttered against his face, like lost butterflies. He'd support Liv any way she needed, any way she'd accept from him, until she figured out he'd do anything for her, and always be there for her.

CHAPTER 60

 iv

HALF LISTENING for the popcorn to finish popping, half watching my guys going down in gamer flames thanks to Kimi, I rested against the arch between den and kitchen.

"The hell—she can't—what'd she just *do?*" Jace yelled at the screen and his floundering avatar.

"Duck man. Duck and roll. She's on your six," Matteo yelled back. "Marsh, man, back me up."

The three hunched over controllers, fixated on CoW.

Mostly fixated. Marshall looked up, checking in every time I appeared. How he knew I was there was a mystery, as if we were connected somehow.

It was weird. And amazing. And weird.

For me, at least. Marshall seemed to have relaxed into his role. When I came in from the shower at lunch, he'd pinked up, but dropped a fast, casual kiss on my temple between plating cutlets, in full view of the guys. He hadn't hesitated to pull his chair flush with mine at dinner, thigh pressed against mine, as we discussed thoughts on mini-grenades, and CoW strategy.

The popcorn dinged, right as my phone rattled out the opening bars of Vee's ringtone. I opened and shook out popcorn, sweeping into the den to hand custody of the bat-bowl to Marshall as the call went to voicemail.

Marshall turned to me, game forgotten. "Is something wrong?" He pushed the mic on his headset away.

"Nah." Matteo answered for me. "If there was, Kimi wouldn't still be online slaughtering us."

I patted his head. "Sorry, kiddo."

"Hey, a little faith. The game isn't over."

"It's over. You simply don't know that yet."

Marshall watched our byplay, absorbing it. I stopped long enough to pat his head, his curls softer and springier than Matteo's. I ended by discreetly trailing my fingers down the back of Marshall's neck, enjoying his shiver. Letting him know that we were okay.

The days of no one caring enough to look below his surface mask, or bother paying real attention, were over. I would be careful of that pitfall, the same way Marshall was careful with me.

I hadn't completely interpreted yet, but I did know he'd been showing me something important this afternoon with our kiss. He was teaching me something, in his lowkey way.

When Marshall trusted me enough to flip his mic down and rejoin the game, I left to check in with my sister.

Vee answered with, "Where are you? Why did you have to wait and call back?"

At her rapid questioning, I backtracked, to my office. This wasn't a for fun call. "What's wrong?" I knew that tone, the same as I could picture her worrying a hangnail right now.

"Nothing. Probably."

"But?"

"Stavros had a feeling?"

Old fear woke again. "Are you still in Monterrey? We can be there in six hours." Four, if Matteo pushed.

Stavros wasn't psychic or any of that supernatural nonsense, but he was something. A combination of intuition, and four-hundred-years of experience mixing in his subconscious.

"It's not us. It's about you guys."

I bent over my desk, flipping my laptop open and hitting keys, pulling up all our feeds, and links to outside sources, sending messages to our network of street contacts, and opening another window on environmental data and real time images. "Do you feel anything?"

Occasionally, Vee did. Most likely, it was Stavros' aura leaking into hers. She'd had flashes of intuition before she was infected though, about the cryptid weirdness, and been correct.

"Nooo." She drew it out.

"I sense a but."

"If I say anything, it might tip your decision, and you'll go all anti-Marshall, basically abandoning him, and I'll be furious. Kimi too. So furious. Then you'll be miserable but refuse to admit it, *then* we will have a huge three-way sister argument and—"

"Stop and breathe. Seriously."

Her inhale carried, loud and clear.

I should tell her Marshall was staying, but... She sort of deserved a minute of squirming, after the whole knife fight thing. "Whatever it is, spit it out, since you've already opened your mouth, meaning I know something is up. What if I obsess over what it might be, and that tips my decision? Ever consider that?"

"Dang it."

My phone buzzed, and I swiped it open to Kimi's text. *Nice. Go with the emotional thumbscrews.*

I texted back. *Seriously? How are you eavesdropping, texting, and slaying the guys?*

She sent a shrug emoji. *I'm trying to be gentle with them but it's impossible. They can't hang.*

Kimi's version of gentle involved evisceration.

"Liv? Are you still there?" Guilt edged Vee's tone.

"Mhm." I refused to give her any potential leverage, by using actual words she could examine for subtext.

"Crud. Fine. Last night B was hulking completely out. Major meltdown over—I don't remember. But all I could do was smile. Like, him being loud, everyone ignoring it or hiding, it all felt so much like a family thing. Then I thought of Marshall and his pie and you guys sitting down to it and I totally saw it in my head, how it would look, and it felt complete. Like you were finally really okay."

Which was as close as we'd gotten to acknowledging why I left, and the pain involved on both sides.

I curled my legs under me and settled in. Vee deserved the truth. "I didn't know how angry I was. Or how raw."

"Liv—"

"I'm not anymore, and the anger was never directed at you, only the situation. Marshall is staying. Jace and Matteo agreed Marshall was our missing piece. He was what was required to bring the team over the finish line. Everything has gelled."

"Family."

"Yeah. My family."

"I'm really happy for you." Vee's voice was soft, all of our arguing irrelevant, because no matter what, we were sisters first.

Me, too. Is that all??? Kimi's text and its million question marks popped up.

She'd earned hearing the news first. She'd been caught between me and Vee. Loyal to us both, and stuck in an impossible position between her sisters, who she loved, but who couldn't live together anymore.

Marshall and I are together. Civilian romance, meet-cute together. Oh, that came after the team agreement.

A victorious whoop went up from the den, audible through thick stucco and thicker oak.

"Liv? Why is Kimi—" Vee's question clashed with Matteo's suspicious bellow. "Where'd she *go?* Her avatar's— it's just standing there!"

I didn't need to be there in person to predict what came next. Three, two, one—

"Oh. My. God. For real? What's meet-cute together?" Vee squealed.

"Put me on speaker phone since you and Kimi are in the same room now." I gave it a beat, and confessed to my sisters. "I slept with Marshall last night. Oh, sleep, as in sex, but then also real sleeping. That kind of together."

My texts lit up, as Vee's piercing shriek rattled the speaker.

"What the hell?" The harsh boom of a door slamming, and Bruce's alarmed bellow sounded from Vee's end.

"Liv and Marshall. They're seeing each other. The dating kind of seeing. Wait, you are dating-seeing each other, right? Not doing that—what did they call it in *The Wedding Date?* The movie, not the book." Voces were momentarily muffled, Vee checking with Kimi or Josh—probably Josh. "Right. You're not doing that hit it and quit it? Because, I'd be furious over that, too."

"For fuck's sake," Bruce's bark was way clear. "That's why the hell you nearly gave me and Josh fucking heart attacks? All over Liv sleeping with that dumbass?" Another whump sounded, followed by more yelling. "Don't fucking *language* me, you fossil."

I scooted the phone a few inches away, as Bruce turned on Stavros, and his irritated Spanish-Nahuatl mashup joined the conversation.

Did you explain team-level togetherness to Marshall? Kimi asked, undeterred by arguing adopted fathers and adopted brothers. *B/c Bruce always says it's invasive lack of privacy.*

Don't forget that co-dependent thing he says, either I added.

Point. So did you?

Sort of?

Better get on that. Which was immediately followed by *Hit'n'Quit? Y or N?*

No.

Was it good?

That one was easy. *Marshall is amazing.*

A horrific thought hit. *Do not—not—text and congratulate M on that! Remember how B's brother reacted and it was only a passing convo about sexual performance?!* I put in a series of daggers and STOP emojis for emphasis.

Positive reinforcement is important.

N.O. Reinforcement is my job!

"Mija." Stavros appropriated Vee's phone. Rattled, his archaic accent back in force.

"Lo siento tanto, papá. I know our emotions are off the charts sometimes."

"Sí. What say your contacts?

He was truly worried, to switch back to business so abruptly. I scanned feeds and results, then opened Terrence's reply. "There was an attack on another team, to our east. We're all clear, though. Perhaps you felt the Bruce drama? That's a fairly unpleasant event."

"That is true. However, that den we walked into only last week was both unprecedented and nearly lethal to us all.

That is concerning. Our visit to HQ to speak to the scientists offered no new information."

I was learning how incomplete relying only on facts and rules was. "We'll step up the staggered sweeps. I'll warn Terence as well, and alert HQ."

"Be aware and be safe, Olivia."

"I will. Watch out for our family."

"Always. I only wish I were able to watch out for you as well, mija."

"Yo también te quiero, papá." I cut the connection, and poured over the data again, mixing, matching, and double checking. Taking sat maps and correlating them with traffic cams and private systems, reports from beat police and dispatchers, even club bouncers.

Nothing unusual, nothing suspicious, even if I stretched the definition of suspicious to its limit. A knock sounded as I stared at the boring normalcy that was a Wednesday evening in Scottsdale and Phoenix. "Come in."

Marshall pushed the door open but stayed in the doorway. "I think Kimi messaged me. But I didn't give her this number, and the message is kinda weird."

"I'm stealing her entire gaming system, and leaving one of those black and white one's from the nineteen-eighties in its place."

"Liv?"

There was no easy way to prepare a civilian for our style of family. "Welcome to the extended family? I told Kimi and Vee about us."

"Yeah?" He came all the way in. "Is that good or bad? I can't tell what Kimi means."

I rolled the chair clear and hopped up. "She and Vee are rabidly pro-Marshall, and pro-us."

"LivMar?" He held his phone up, her text on screen.

I groaned. I should've totally anticipated this. "She gave us a couple name. Like J.Lo and what's his name."

Marshall kicked the door closed, and met me, frown replacing his confusion. "Are you okay? Is all this attention okay with you?"

"This whole *in everyone's business* dynamic is pretty much team life, not a matter of choice." I started to reach for him, then curled my fingers under. I didn't have a Plan B if he hated all the family interference.

"Okay." He played with the tip of my ponytail, curling it around his thumb. There was something new, a new vibe. The feel was similar to the earlier smugness and teasing and the kiss. That kiss had been...wow.

"I don't want to pressure you though. I can ask Kimi and everyone not to push." He let go of my hair. "This is all about going at your speed. What's good for you." He looked over his shoulder, as if he could see through the door. "For the team, too. They're a part of you."

I breathed around the silly lump clogging my throat. "I told Kimi you were amazing."

"Yeah?" Happiness infused that one simple word.

I nodded. "I don't think that does you justice."

"I can be patient. I'm good at it."

"You really are. You're good at so many things." I nudged up against him, needing his certainty.

He wrapped me up, cradling me against his warmth. "For you, I can be."

I worried at the inside of my cheek, but if there was a more appropriate civilian way of asking, I wasn't privy to it. "I'm not giving the impression I'm having second thoughts, am I? I'd very much like for tonight to end the way last night did. Having sex."

"I know that part."

I leaned away, brow up.

"Not like I'm not assuming." He sighed but sure as heck didn't blush. "I mean that sex and hanging out is in your wheelhouse. Your comfort zone."

"It isn't yours?"

"It is. Hundred-percent." Marshall scrambled to correct me. Then relaxed back into his new, slightly infuriating, chill. "I meant the other, the relationship part. I'm weird and don't do anything else like other people do, so it makes sense that I'm already all in on the relationship. Being yours. But I get that my brain works its own way, and that you need more time to go from casual sex and liking me to a real relationship. I'm saying that's okay, too."

"I'm not—" I didn't have the expected sense of indignation. I wanted Marshall here, as part of the team. Certainly in my bed. He was important to me. He was also correct. I wasn't ready to label my emotions yet. Marshall had grasped that fact before I did.

He ran the back of his hand along my cheek. "It's cool. For real. You had this thing, these people you loved. And it was taken away even though you did everything right. It's probably normal that you have to ease back in to loving again. You care, and I'm here with you guys. That's good for now."

In the face of his certainty and commitment, I felt as if I was shorting him. Offering and withholding at the same time. He was right. Part of me was...wary. Waiting for the shoe to drop, for the awful thing to happen. For this to implode, or hear that it was all a mistake, for someone to change their mind.

Marshall hugged me back in, against solid muscle, soft cotton, and a hint of popcorn. "It's cool, Liv. Told you, I'm good at patient."

CHAPTER 61

Marshall

MARSHALL FINALLY GOT what it meant to bask. Right here, right now, he was basking the hell out of the perfectness of the moment. Of Liv telling her sisters, which was the same as telling the whole family, that the two of them were together. That with her weird-cool text, Kimi welcomed him to the family.

So, yeah. He was basking in belonging, at last. The best part was basking in the fact that Liv was letting him in, more and more. Trusting him enough to admit she needed him, and trusting enough to let him know it.

He rested his cheek on top of her hair, silky and catching on his stubble, that bit of roughness Liv seemed to relish. He kept her tucked in, her heart pressed next to his, and breathed her in.

Liv's hands were under his shirt, running up and down his back. He was pretty sure she didn't even realize she was doing it, soothing herself as much as him. Hot skin, with mostly healed scars, slid along his.

He got it. Liv couldn't say the things she was feeling, not yet. So she was showing him instead.

"You matter to me." Her whisper was low, but fierce as she pressed closer.

"I know. It's all good, for real."

She frowned, brows a sharp V. "You shouldn't have to settle."

"I'm not setting. I'm patiently waiting," he corrected her. "Like when you started out as a cadet. You weren't a super-ninja, black-ops leader right away." He snorted, laughing at himself. "Probably you were. This is like cooking, then. I had to practice and mess up and practice more, put in the time to learn knife skills, learn the basics, move to the next step."

"You shouldn't have to wait and work all the time. You deserve better."

He shrugged, making sure the motion didn't shake Liv loose. Even an inch was more separation than he was willing to allow right now.

Liv needed him close. "The thing about stuff you've gotta wait and work for is that it becomes part of you, the way easier stuff doesn't."

Her hands kept up the loopy swirls , down his spine to the waist of his jeans, and back as she thought.

He relaxed into the caress, giving her time to process, same as she'd done for him so many times. Loving that she didn't hide her feelings from him.

She focused on him again, expression clearing. "Our favorite Instructor, she of the hair band fetish, swore you valued the skills you had to really work at more."

"Hm."

She tilted her head, expression sharpening. "What's that look? Don't even try to say you don't have looks."

"Enjoying myself. You're great at petting."

"There's something else."

He smiled—Liv always got him. When she didn't, she wanted to, and tried. "This is a different kind of happy. You were thinking. It's awesome that you can think and be confused in front of me. That you let me see all of that, where you only let others see the leader part."

"Why does that make you happy?"

"It makes it easier to be myself around you. Like, if you're comfortable showing that part—" He loosed his arm enough to tap between her eyes "—admitting being confused and needing a minute to get ideas lined up in your head, then it's cool my doing it. It's not a big deal or whatever. It's something we share."

"A common bond?"

His heart did a funny shimmy. Liv was getting it. "Yeah."

Her hands faltered. "I didn't realize how rarely I showed that side to Matteo and Jace. Until you mentioned it, I would have sworn I was transparent with my team."

This felt important for Liv. Despite the tang of worry about pushing her, he nudged. "But?"

"I suppose I do try to be certain for them. We're a team, yet—"

"Teams need leaders."

"Once the leader starts second-guessing, the team does. With Vee and I, I was her safety valve. She shared those doubts with me privately, because that's the thing. *Every* leader has them."

"You didn't have anybody. That valve."

Liv nodded, and he risked pushing again, catching her chin, bringing her face up, making sure she *saw*. "You do now. I'm your valve. You can unload all your worry on me, and work through whatever issues you gotta solve. Vee did that with you because she full-on trusted you and knew you'd never doubt her, how she was the right person to lead. That's me. I never doubt you. There's a lot of weird in my head, but you're the one thing that always makes sense, because you always do what's best." The words rang through the room, passionate and clear.

He hadn't realized he'd had so much to say. Maybe he'd gone places Liv hadn't expected. He didn't regret it. This was his place on the team—support. This was him supporting Liv.

iv

MARSHALL KEPT SAYING his logic worked differently than the majority of the population. Which was pure crap he'd picked up from some idiot in his past life.

What he'd said seconds before resonated, deep inside me. The same as when we ran drills as cadets, the first one to successfully navigate the course and scale the massive wall at the finish slapping the bell suspended on its peak, the clear brass's peal ringing through your palm and deep into your bones.

Marshall was offering what I still needed, filling the last vacancy. His support wasn't only domestic duties and keeping the compound running, it was supporting my decisions.

I couldn't commit yet. Despite what Marshall said about patience, our relationship felt unbalanced and unfair. I wanted to give him something now. Making doubly sure he

AGENT OF CHAOS: THE REGION TWO SERIES

didn't doubt his value and what he meant to me, until I achieved the same emotional level he'd already attained.

I ground out the tiny voice, whispering questions as to whether I'd ever get there, willing or able to say the three words Marshall embraced. He hadn't uttered them aloud, but they sat there, right under his skin, waiting to erupt into the light.

When I wiggled backward, Marshall immediately loosened his grip. Not completely letting go and putting space between us the way he would've even a few hours ago, though.

He looked down at me, content and waiting. I drew my hand down his arm, finally catching his hand. Tugging, I lead him around the desk. There, I reversed, leaving him in front of my chair. "Sit?"

He easily absorbed my push to his chest. He sank into the chair because *he* wanted to. I tapped his knee, asking, and he spread his legs. I sank between them, one hand on his thigh, enjoying the thick muscles under the denim.

"Yeah?" Surprise flashed over his face. "I mean, this is a good idea. A great one. Just—in your office? Do C.O.s have office hours?"

"We are allowed complete freedom on that issue. As well as how we choose to conduct in-office business." Starting at his knees, I ran my hands along the inner inseam of his jeans.

The closer my fingers got to the bulge underneath the denim, the more intent he got. Thanks to the muted lighting, his eyes seemed darker, closer to a storm over the ocean than to sea glass.

"Should we lock the door?" The question came out gruff.

"That would require time." Time was one thing we learned early not to take for granted. "Nothing is guaranteed, so never waste the now."

A frown intruded, edging out some of the lust. I didn't

want him thinking—able to think, period. He'd advised me to go with my feelings. Time to remind him of his own advice.

I rose higher on my knees, palms meeting in a V, right over the erection testing his zipper's integrity. Experimenting, I increased the pressure. His hips flexed, pressing back and ready for more.

I drug my thumbs up on either side of the zipper. Popping the tab, I dipped in, grazing along the red-gold trail leading lower. Working the zipper down, exposing plain black boxers. As soon as we hit town again, I was getting a dozen pair of superhero themed ones.

Marshall sat back, relaxed and sure as if this was his office. Watching me through half lidded eyes, expression possessive. "What is it you want, Liv?"

"You. This way, watching me while I watch you come so hard you forget your own name."

"Then take what you want."

I bunched the cotton and denim at the waistband and jerked. He chuckled, deep and pleased, and lifted, enough for me to push clothes out of our way. His cock rose.

He wasn't the only one who could do possessive. I wrapped my hand around his base, rewarded with a ragged inhale. I admired the milky white length, veins like shadows on snow, his skin hot and velvety in my grip.

He caught my ponytail, but only spread it over his knee, playing with strands, one at a time, more of that iron self-control. The gentle tugs sparked an electric excitement, traveling from my scalp straight between my thighs.

So did the way he looked at me, like I was the only thing in the universe, or at least, the only thing that mattered. That total focus was heady. Enough to become intoxicated and get lost in.

I stroked down his length, barely touching, and his

breathing picked up. At the tip, I ran a finger under the head of his cock, tracing the slit.

"Liv." One word, rough and potent as mezcal, held a world of meaning.

CHAPTER 63

$\mathcal{M}$arshall

LIV TRANSLATED AGAIN, getting that he meant *yes* and *now* and that she was the sexiest thing he'd ever seen or ever would. Her lips closed over him, and his blood turned molten, the shot of heat spreading from his cock through his body, lightning fast.

Liv didn't hesitate, pulling him in deeper, and cupping his aching balls with her other hand. Rolling skilled as hell fingers over them.

Muscles in his ass clenched. He shoved down on the animal need to drive into her, to take more. He'd promised they'd go at her pace and that meant in bed—okay, in her office and any other place she wanted to go down on him or have him inside her—too. No matter if her mouth felt like heaven, and might be the end of him at the same time.

But Liv wasn't about going slow. She took him deeper, then drew back, tongue following the groove underneath as she did. Swirling around the head like he was her favorite flavor of ice cream, it was a sweltering Summer day, and she wasn't missing one damn melting drop. She finished with a flick of her tongue that wrenched a groan out of him.

She started the same path again, her fist following right behind her lips. Working his now slick cock. Pumping him, grip almost too much, just this side of rough and so perfect he bucked against her mouth, good intentions toast.

Instead of pulling away, Liv purred. Like some big cat, dangerous as hell, but worth the risk. The vibration sent him to a level he hadn't known existed. Her expression..damn. Claiming her territory, no missing the excitement in her eyes.

The combination of the pressure, her hot, talented lips, and that it was Liv touching him, wanting this, and determined to make him come, rocketed him to the bring faster than had ever happened, even as a horny teenager.

He pulled her ponytail apart, digging into her hair, waves wrapping and tangling, needing to touch skin, touch her.

The contact was the last spark, pressure building at the base of his spine, balls tightening. The river of pleasure hit hard, cresting, his hips pumping, bucking and out of rhythm.

He tried pulling away. They hadn't discussed rules, what Liv was or wasn't okay with. She wasn't having any of it, lips tight, that damn brow up, daring him to further and harder. He rode the wave, spilling into her.

The aftershocks finally quit, his harsh breathing slowing, even if his heart didn't.

Even now, Liv was there, watching him. Seeing him, and playing, fingers lightly tracing his thighs, over his stomach, enjoying herself.

A sharp creak penetrated the thick door, coming from outside. Marshall reached to cover himself. Jace didn't always wait between knocking and opening a door. Him and Matteo being chill about Marshall and Liv was one thing. Seeing what was basically their sister, like this, was way different.

Liv stretched, not bothering checking to see if the door opened. "If anyone walks in, that's on them."

Kantor's warning popped up, about agents chasing danger, hunting for that adrenaline high. Which brought up the jerk's other warnings, their stance on violence, who mattered and didn't. Well-practiced at ignoring voices, Marshall pushed it and the accompanying murky twinge of worry away. He rearranged himself, and zipped his jeans.

As Liv stood, he caught her waist. She went with it, settling sideways across his lap. He hugged her, not ready to give up getting lost in each other yet. He coaxed her head against his shoulder.

The sharp alert tone from her phone interrupted the intimacy, followed by the ping of her laptop.

"HQ?" He tilted his head enough to gauge Liv's reaction.

She stayed her version of relaxed. "The usual. I'd sent out a few messages earlier."

Which should've reassured him. Except, even as he brushed a kiss across Liv's lips, brighter and a little plumper from being locked around him, the unease that'd snuck into his head stayed.

* * *

AFTER THE TEXAS CALL, there'd been plenty of time for a night of him and Liv and no clothes, and her falling asleep using his arm as her pillow again. The new unease, or extra layer of his usual weird, still clung to Marshall the next morning.

"S'up , man? Fridge empty?" Hair damp from the post-breakfast workout, Jace ambled in and slouched beside Marshall.

And, yeah, Marshall had been staring into the depths of the SubZero too long. Old habits clung, and before his brain registered that it was Jace, who'd never roll his eyes and judge Marshall for spacing out, his mouth had already taken over. "We're getting kind of low."

Which wasn't a lie. Marshall hadn't nailed down and refined the food-to-person ratio, and having Vee's team visit had further depleted the pantry. He refused to linger over the meals he and Kantor had made, which had gone uneaten.

"First official team trip. Gimme five minutes." Jace held out a fist, and Marshall bumped it, Jace's excitement banishing Marshall's iffy mood.

"More like twenty." Liv deposited her laptop on the bar, and aimed for the coffee pot. "When you're making plans, always triple his estimate."

"Don't hate," Jace yelled from down the hall.

Marshall bumped Liv out of the way, grabbing a mug, and milk to froth.

Liv perched on the stool, heel on the rung and facing him instead of her makeshift desk. When she spoke, it was in that softer tone she used for the two of them. "Are you okay going out with only Jace? I need to—" She tipped her at the tablet beside her laptop, the one that held charts with ammunition and weapon's tallies. Easy to see she was leery of saying things like *bullets.* "If you can wait, I'll be free this afternoon."

"Jace and Matteo are solid." They weren't Liv, but Marshall trusted them, too. Completely. They had his back, like they had each other's.

His reward was a smile that transformed Liv from C.O. to his Liv, made up of real happiness, and relief. He was all about erasing any last doubts she had.

The milk now frothed, he handed her the coffee mug. Then used her shoulders to turn her toward the bar. "Finish your homework, and I'll bring you back a treat. If I can keep

Jace from claiming it first, and get it past Matteo when we unload."

Liv leaned back against him, her surprised, pure-sunshine laugh filling the kitchen. "Clearly, you've got this."

He dropped a kiss on her temple. He'd never realized before how innocent but sexy that spot was. Grabbing his phone, he hit the pantry, dictating ideas and a list of supplies for his team.

* * *

AFTER AN EXPLANATION about new protocols and a quick security sweep through the market, Jace wandered off, chatting up vendors about organic hair products. Liv hadn't been joking about the other agent's self-care routine.

It was freaking awesome that Marshall was on the inside now, getting lessons from teammates like he was an equal member. He nodded at a fruit stand dealer, dropping the treat he'd promised Liv, chocolate covered dried mango chunks, into the bag with his load of fresh fruits. He'd wanted to try out a new idea, so a rustic grilled nectarine tart was on tonight's menu.

Cheese went with fruit, and he scanned the row, pinpointing the stall with local goat cheese, that he'd been too afraid to suggest on his first trip here with Liv. It was hard to remember ever being afraid of Liv and the guys, or stressing they'd hate his food and physically take it out on him. What he'd thought was the worst thing that could happen to him turned out to be the best.

Marshall wove around shoppers, almost at his destination. A shape darted from beside the furthest stall. Whoever it was, they were way too furtive to be a shopper. Smaller, too, like a kid. They paused by one of the trash cans situated throughout the market for a second.

Anyone who'd worked in food service recognized what searching for food scraps looked like. This person's shoulders slumped. Marshall caught a glimpse of wide, dark eyes and a grimy tee.

He'd only seen that face the one time, for a few seconds, but it was burned into his memory. Terror did that, catching memories and cementing them.

Marshall dodged an older couple, and jogged for the trash can. The kid must've caught the movement, jumping like a startled animal, darting right, behind the back of a row of vendors, where the public wasn't allowed.

Marshall picked up his pace. He had to see if the kid was okay physically. For sure they weren't mentally after being hunted by a monster-cryptid. He'd convince the kid to go to one of the Company safehouses Liv talked about. She'd help, make sure the kid didn't have to keep dumpster diving in order to survive.

Ducking into vendor parking, behind the farm pickups and trailers, Marshall caught another flash of the grungy shirt, the kid weaving between vehicles. Thanks to longer legs, Marshall caught up. "Hey. Wait."

The kid whirled, spinning like a human-shaped top, looking for an out, caught between a box truck, a retaining wall, and Marshall.

Marshall stopped, sick that he was scaring a child so bad. He held his arms out sideways, hands palm up. "I'm not gonna hurt you. We've met, kinda. That monster thing and the alley in the city?"

Which probably wasn't reassuring. He hurried on. "I only want to know if you're okay."

The kid stopped, but with his back plastered to the trailer, its shadow concealing him.

Marshall grabbed for ideas, any way to reassure the kid. The hemp shopping bags slid, thumping his side. Food. That, he could do. He'd picked up cured meat before hitting the produce rows. "You're hungry, right?"

He couldn't make out details, but it seemed like the child paused. Marshall shrugged the bag off. "I've got—you want ham?"

A snort, one that could only be called derisive, exploded from the kid. At least their attitude was intact and healthy.

"No ham. Got it. How about—"

"You have fruit." The voice was somewhere between kid and teen, cracking at the end.

Marshall knelt and dug through the top bag. He pulled out one of the nectarines, holding it up as proof.

The kid edged closer, every line of his body wary, finally out of the shadows. In the light, his face was even lighter than Marshall's, almost glowing, under messy, tufty red-brown hair. Big liquid brown eyes were the kind of watchful only gained from constant worry and hiding.

Those eyes were trained on the fruit in Marshall's hand. Moving slow, Marshall reached and rolled the nectarine across the sandy soil.

The kid darted, had his prize, and was back in the shadows between blinks. Scarfing the food down like he hadn't eaten in days.

Marshall wanted to find and punch whoever was responsible for the kid being alone and starving. Instead, Marshall stayed put, doing his best to look harmless.

When all that remained was the stripped clean pit, the kid finally looked at Marshall. "You got more."

Again, not a question. Maybe Marshall could work out a trade. He held out the whole bag, dried and fresh fruit. He'd get Liv more. Even if he didn't, she'd never begrudge it going to a good use.

The kid glared at Marshall, licking his lips, fighting the need for a real meal.

"Seriously. I only want to see if you're all right. That night —" Marshall swallowed against bile threatening to come up. "That was rough. I couldn't tell if that thing—"

"Ghoul," the kid piped up.

Right. So even kids knew more about monsters than he had. "Yeah, that ghoul. I couldn't tell how bad it hurt you."

"I'm cool." The kid squared their shoulders, giving Marshall a better look. A boy, probably a teen, too skinny, tee and basketball shorts hanging on his thin frame. Although he was healthy enough to inch over and in another of those flashes, grab the bag, backing a Marshall-safe distance away.

"That's good." Marshall rolled a pebble around.

Marshall's attempt at harmless worked, the kid digging through the bag, checking contents. He made a happy, high-pitched noise, almost a squeak. "This is good stuff."

Leveraging the opening to keep the kid here and talking, Marshall answered. "Yeah, I cook. For my friends."

The kid quit inspecting the food and hugged the bag to his bony chest, like Marshall was going to try to take it back.

"No, that's yours. They won't care if I share." Which seemed like a solid lead-in. "My friends are pretty cool, too."

The boy made a noise that could've meant anything from 'sure' to 'piss off.' He did tilt his head, staring at Marshall, like the kid was waging some internal debate. He finally spit out, "You should be careful. Things are bad. Big time bad," he added, with a certainty way beyond his age. Like he'd seen stuff no kid should've had to.

The sort of stuff Liv knew about, like kidnapped people and weird cryptid behaviors. Marshall nodded along. "I think you're right. We should both be careful. The friends I mentioned, they can help you. They have safe places to stay, or they know of places like that."

The kid pulled himself up to his full height, practically on his tiptoes, and did that teen *you are old and don't have a clue* thing. "I take care of myself."

"Sure. All I'm saying is, there are options if you get bored. And you wouldn't have to worry so much about finding a real meal every day."

The kid gave an epic eye roll. "Like any of you know what a real meal is."

Marshall channeled Liv, raising both brows since that one brow technique was beyond him, looking at the bag full of produce the boy was guarding, then at the licked clean pit on the ground.

He could've sworn the kid's ears twitched, all embarrassed-offense. But then he gave another of those snort-squeaks. "*Maybe* you do."

"Thanks—uh, what's your name? I'm Marshall," he hurried to add, respecting that this was a fair exchange and Marshall had to offer something as well.

The kid squinted at Marshall, head tilted at that odd angle again. "Kit." Then almost like he'd remembered rusty manners, said, "Thanks, I guess. For the ghoul and lunch."

Everything in Marshall itched to scoop Kit up, understanding both the bravado and the boy's need to act like life was under control even when it wasn't. Especially when it wasn't. Marshall got how acting the way everybody else considered normal was safer.

He'd also seen how fast the kid was. Marshall would never get hands on him. Plus, he wanted Kit to trust him, not freak the boy out more.

He sorted through ideas. "Do you have a phone?"

That got another eye roll.

Right. "Could you borrow one if you really needed to?"

The kid shrugged, which wasn't a no. And of course, Marshall didn't have pen or paper.

As if he read Marshall's mind, Kit said, "I have a great memory."

Marshall hoped that was true, as he rattled off his number. Liv said giving it out wouldn't put the team or the person he gave it to in danger. "Shoot me a text if you're hungry again. Or if things get worse out there. My friends can help, for real."

"Yo, Marsh? You back there?" Jace's voice bounced through the space, echoing off the metal trailers.

Kit flinched. "No way. They don't help people like me. They make us disappear."

Before Marshall could explain, Kit scrambled and squeezed through a space between the wall and trailer Marshall would've sworn was too narrow. He still rushed over but all he got for the effort was a view of an empty lot.

"Marsh." Jace beside him, peering into the parking area, nearly as fast as Kit.

"Kit, the kid from the ghoul attack, he was here." Stumbling over an explanation, Marshall resorted to pointing to the nectarine pit, then the escape route.

"You sure?" Jace grabbed a trailer door and did a pull-up, landing on the roof, shading his eyes as he swept the lot.

"Positive. I caught a glimpse of him in the market, but spooked him and he ran. He's skittish and ran again when he heard you. I swear it was him."

"I believe you. Kid's rabbited now though." Jace jumped and hit the ground with a soft thump and puff of disturbed soil. "These street kids are the next thing to feral. They've been kicked around so much that they won't speak to anyone much less trust them long enough to listen."

Except Kit had talked to Marshall. He'd even taken Marshall's number.

"It's great that you got a name and offered the kid some help."

Jace steered them out of the dead-end and into the busy flow of the market. "Don't go off like this again without letting me know first. This is prime ambush territory. Not your fault—this was on us for not fully briefing you on our public protocols."

"Kit said things were bad on the streets, and getting worse."

Jace grunted as they hit the public parking lot and he unlocked the truck. "The homeless are easy pickings for cryptids. The kid's story corroborates with the chatter Liv's picked up. That freaky party we raided wasn't a one-off according to other Division's reports. We've got to get that kid in, and off cryptid radar."

Marshall buckled in as the truck growled to life. He'd never really thought about what getting picked up by the Company looked like or meant, past his own experience. He hadn't seen anyone like him at HQ.

He also hadn't thought about his old boss and where he went after Company questioning ended.

"Kincaid? My old boss." Marshall added, at Jace's confused expression. Jace didn't understand Marshall's shorthand yet. "Where did he go once HQ was done with him?"

Still misinterpreting, Jace squeezed Marshall's shoulder. "You don't have to worry about that asshole. He isn't a problem anymore."

As awful as the guy had been, ice slid down Marshall's spine at the cold finality of his friend's answer.

CHAPTER 64

Marshall

THE NEW UNEASINESS hovering in the back of Marshall's mind didn't ease when Matteo met them in the pass-through door between the garage and house, his expression serious. "We've got a live lead."

Marshall's gut knotted but this was the job. His, the guys', and Liv's, and he'd promised he could handle Company life. "Go on." He jerked his head in the direction of the armory. "I've got all this."

Without a word, the agents split off to dress and weapon up, while Marshall completed the trip to his kitchen. His domain and responsibility, where he did his share to make sure all three people he cared about were prepared.

He put coffee on, sorted supplies, and pulled out the plug-in cooler he'd discovered in the pantry during his first visit.

When the crew thundered in, Marshall took over. "Here." He scooted the cooler down the counter to Jace.

The agent peered inside, then whistled, checking out the bottles of his sports drinks, and water for Liv and Matteo. "Niiice. I'd forgotten we had this thing. You're on it."

Marshall held up a sealed packet. "None of you had dinner. This is extra high-protein trail mix."

He tossed the first to Matteo. "A custom spice rub."

The next went to Jace. "Extra almonds and dried fruit."

Marshall held on to the last packet, cheating a little, insuring Liv came to him. "Extra dark chocolate for you."

"I like chocolate." Matteo dug through his bag like a kid digging through a cereal box in search of the toy at the bottom.

"You got some, too," Marshall said, casting a quick look at his friend. "Think molé—chocolate and chili."

He switched his attention back to Liv as Matteo made approving noises. Voice low, just for Liv, he said, "But extra for you."

"You are full of good ideas." Liv slide in beside him, taking the baggie and her fingers grazing his.

"No going in hungry and potentially distracted," he decreed, keeping it lowkey and calm. "Coffee, too."

He reached to the side and grabbed her travel mug, already prepared. "I found the cooler and figured you'd need water after. Stay hydrated." He tried out his version of Kantor's bossy tone.

Liv smiled. Her reply backed his worry off a notch. "Yes, sir."

To hell with it. They'd all lived with Kantor, and understood bossy equaled caring. Plus, Liv liked bossy, at the right times. Marshall caught her free hand, and reeled her in. "This is for luck."

He gave her a fast but through kiss, loving how she put an equal amount of intensity into the touch. It hurt, but he turned loose, and put the travel mug in her hand. He addressed everyone even if his eyes were only on Liv. "Be careful, and go on. I've got muffins to create."

He absorbed the backslaps from Matteo and Jace as they passed, and memorized Liv's nod. The one that meant *'thanks'* and *'good job'* and *'I'll come back'*.

As the chime sounded, gate retracting and letting his team roll out to police monsters and protect people, Marshall grabbed his phone, swiping until he came to the infirmary photos. He propped the phone so he could study as he worked, and brought out the muffin pans. With the compound quiet, worry piled back on in a nauseating wave. He'd had a lifetime of being alone with his anxiety though, and now, he had a job to focus on.

* * *

THE PINGING NOTIFICATION of the exterior gate opening jolted Marshall out of his study of medical equipment's arrangement. He squinted, and double-checked the time. The numbers didn't change, confirming the team had been gone less than five hours. The first of the alarm's he'd set on his phone hadn't even gone off.

Not knowing if a speedy mission was good or bad, he held his breath, waiting for the code, the short all-clear notification, or the chilling, piercing one that signaled a wounded agent.

When the crisp three-note clearance sounded, he sucked in a lungful of oxygen and relief. He watched the screen, needing the sneak glimpse of Liv before she even came indoors.

Instead of passing under the camera and into the garage, the truck took a right. He leaned in, watching it take a route he'd never noticed. It was meant for something official, the side road paved, since the tires didn't kick up any dust.

A bay door slid sideways, another he hadn't seen before, on the far side of the armory. The living quarters were here. Medical was here. The team always came this way. Although, he'd only had a handful of missions to go by.

Marshall and the guys hadn't even really started going over rules and the protocols Jace had mentioned. There was a good chance this situation was something Marshall should already know about. Sure, it involved the armory in some way, but he wasn't a guest anymore. This was his compound now, too.

He didn't try to lie to himself—he needed to see his team walking and unharmed. Especially Liv. He headed through the house, for the stairs leading to the yard.

The second he hit open air, pain slammed into him, a band vised around his forehead, trying to crush his brain. Hot liquid filled his mouth.

He stumbled, catching the railing and staying upright. He kept his eyes closed, working on his breathing. Fighting the pain his way. Sliding around it, flexible, the same as the beginning of a panic attack, instead of head-on, which never worked for him.

This wasn't a big deal. The team was home. The alarm hadn't blared. This was a plain stress headache, likely from this being the first call-out since Liv was hurt, and too much caffeine.

The band loosened. Not gone, but easy to ignore if you'd had practice. He scrubbed a hand over his face, and swallowed, short-circuiting the nausea. Steady again, he cut through the yard and around the gym.

Even with his shortcut, the truck was gone, the door closed, by the time he got there. Marshall hadn't tried it yet, but he had security clearance now, his DNA, fingerprints, and a scan of his retina added alongside the team's. All he had to do was touch one of the disguised panels, then the screen that appeared.

He shoved his thumb against the pad.

Nothing happened.

He tried again, leaving his finger there longer. With the same results. Ditto when he centered his eye and tapped it to scan his eyeball.

Relieved he'd automatically stuck his phone in his pocket, Marshall jerked it out, swiping it to highlight his contacts. The mission was over, no worries about compromising security with a call, and he was getting into that building to check his team, right the hell now.

His finger stabbed the first number programmed in, Liv's. The door cracked open before his phone could connect. Marshall jerked back a step, in time to avoid a collision with Matteo.

"Damn, man." The agent pulled up short, door silently closing behind him.

Marshall took in mostly clean camo BDUs, only a couple of stains on the agent's sleeves. No wounds. No internal organ splatter. That was one team member who checked out healthy.

"Jace and Liv," Marshall prompted. "You didn't stop in the garage. What gives?"

Matteo's gaze shifted away from Marshall's face. A reaction Marshall knew too well, one used when people were uncomfortable around him.

"There's a secondary garage out here."

Which, fine, useful to know, but not what he'd asked. "Liv and Jace."

"They're good."

"Don't lie to me. If something happened, I'll deal." He stared Matteo down until the agent met Marshall's eyes.

"I won't ever lie to you. You're team now." Like he'd made a decision, Matteo swore but touched the scanner, then swiped his entire palm across it, to the left. Uncovering a keypad Marshall hadn't known existed. Matteo tapped in numbers.

He held his arm out as the door opened, blocking Marshall from getting closer. "This area is classified. HQ's rules, and all based on safety. You'll get clearance once you're certified."

Matteo raised his voice, and for the first time, sounded like a soldier addressing a higher-up. "Commander."

Marshall might not be able to enter, but he could do like everyone on this and Vee's team, and bend the rules as far as they would go. He leaned around Matteo for a better look.

Jace paced into view, with a rifle in hand. After gaming and gun discussions, Marshall had no problem identifying it as the same type Jace had when he'd stormed into the hotel kitchen, loaded with chem rounds. His face was the same too, schooled and blank as he stopped by Liv's side, though her back was to them.

Liv turned and Marshall made himself stay put. However, he gave his gaze free rein, taking in every detail, head to toe. She was all in one piece, hair neatly pulled back and balled into the tight bun she preferred, no rips in her uniform, no marks on her, no blood.

The worry that was always there dropped by half. Liv wasn't hurt. The world still made sense.

Right. Time for them to do classified weapons stuff here, while he did his part inside. "I'll start hot chocolate to go with—"

At the sound of his voice, a russet head popped up from behind the two agents. Complete with brown eyes and a familiar ragged tee Marshall had seen only hours earlier.

Marshall really looked, taking in the building, and details other than the health of his agents. The truck was off to one side. The rest of the cavernous space he hadn't even guessed existed—this wasn't an extension of the armory, or a garage.

There were machines, some similar to those in the infirmary, others vaguely lab and science-like, some with screens. Shelves lined a far wall, full of nets and chains, and what had to be cryptid-specific weapons. A matched pair of cages sat in the center of the open concrete pad. Metal bars and mesh with the odd silver-gray cast of chem coating gleamed where the evening sun crept in.

Marshall's attention ping-ponged over the room. Taking in the other cage with one of them, a cryptid. This one was humanish, except for rubbery gray skin like the ghoul's, and the feeling of otherness. Evil. It watched him, oval eyes calculating.

His attention bounced back to the second cage and the kid. Kit. Then to Liv, who was still fully armed, her favorite gun and pair of knives in thigh holsters. Whatever she held was new, a cross between a gun and a giant syringe, holding a clear cartridge. One aimed at the cage.

"Wait, no. That's—" Marshall's brain spun, words and images gone wild, trying to line them up in some kind of order.

Matteo's giant mitt locked around Marshall's shoulder. "C'mon. I'll give you a hand inside."

Marshall shrugged out of his friend's grip. "Later. You made a mistake. This is wrong—"

"Agent." Liv's tone was clear and crisp. And didn't hold any of her warm-gold kindness and humor.

Matteo gave a sharp nod and slapped the keypad.

This wasn't right. None of it. "The—that's not who you think it is. I need to talk to Liv."

"She'll be available after—" He twitched "—they'll be in later. Everybody's good. You saw for yourself."

JANET WALDEN-WEST

For once, Marshall wasn't the one a hundred-percent wrong. "It's not *good*. There's a kid in there. One who—"

Matteo's grip closed over Marshall's bicep, hard enough it was going to bruise. "You gotta hear me. That may look human and like a child, but it isn't. That's a shell. Reassuring camouflage. Like those pretty pitcher plants. Something nice or familiar looking meant to fool you, to draw prey in. That's all we are to them. Prey."

Matteo took off, boots hitting the ground hard. Leaving Marshall no choice but to follow. At least until Liv finished— the vision of Jace and the gun jumped into clear focus.

"You aren't killing them." It wasn't a question, and Marshall couldn't keep his voice from dropping, or the rumble of warning out.

Matteo answered anyway, not looking back as the outer compound door closed behind them. "No. We need some answers. If we can't get 'em…" He shrugged. "Then the HQ Lab can try, their way. Liv will get answers or data though. She has one of the highest rates in the Southwest Region."

Matteo peeled off, headed for his room.

Leaving Marshall with a whole list of his own questions for Liv. That murky-green dread enveloping him, he hoped her answers were the kind he needed to hear.

516

iv

"Damn holdout." Jace's sentiment bounced around the annex and off cage bars. He side-eyed whatever this cryptid was. Yet another species new to the Americas.

I'd snapped a series of photos while it was sedated, and would send them to HQ once I was in my office and on a more secure system. This would give the Lab's cryptozoology division a new puzzle to solve. At least they would be happy.

Unlike my lieutenant. Honestly, I shared his frustration. Our prize looked as if it had been bred from the most dangerous parts of half a dozen species. It was bipedal and had the slick, gray skin of a ghoul, though the hide was thicker and its body shape stockier, more akin to the cold-adapted primate cryptids from Eurasia.

The short, serrated teeth were similar to the anangoas we'd had a run in with a few years earlier, the species thought extinct until some collector of exotic creatures imported a pair, and then served as their snack. The broad claws looked more like they belonged on some burrow-digging creature like our chupacabras. With such a confusing set of traits, I was at a loss as to what its natural habitat was, or what niche it occupied in that biome.

Whatever it was, it watched us, through pupilless, irides-cent eyes, weirdly oversized in proportion to its humanoid skull. It hadn't taken its attention off us since the sedative had worn off. That eerie gaze felt as if it was peeling off layers of skin and attempting to dig its way inside of me.

So far, it hadn't spoken, growled, or whined. Or acted particularly frightened of us. The opposite of the smaller cryptid we'd caught during the mission. I glanced at it, and it gave a squeaky, high-pitched trill, then ducked its head away from us and tucked further into the corner of the cage. It stayed as far from us, and the other cryptid, as possible.

"Completely useless." Jace crossed over and jerked the SUV hatch open, tossing the chem-coated netting and chains we'd used to secure the creature, into the industrial sink in a clatter of metal.

He was more frustrated than I'd ever seen him so early in the information gathering process. The patient, detail-oriented finesse that characterized his personality seemed absent today.

"It's early days." I nudged a dial, brightening the harsh UV overheads. There were a few cryptids that preferred daylight to darkness, and this creature's reaction could go into my final report, once our research was complete.

I pointed Jace at the door. "Let them absorb their situa-tion, while we grab a bite." I tweaked the thermostat lower as well, testing their cold tolerance.

Jace rubbed between his brows, scowl deepening.

"Headache?" I'd had a dull throb behind one eye develop on the drive home.

"I think I inhaled enough sand and grit to permanently clog my sinuses. Jackass burrowing cryptids."

The larger creature had tunneled hard, fighting the silver net we'd harpooned it with, like some sort of hooked fish diving for the depths of the river bottom. Yet the thing was slow enough that I'd had time to attach the net's line to the truck's winch and hit the motor, helping reel the cryptid in.

I double-checked that the annex door sealed behind us. "I don't get why it was in that section of town." The spot we'd trapped it was an expanse of open ground, but rocky, the nooks and crannies far too small for the stocky cryptid.

The area was more suited to the smaller creature. After we accidentally flushed it out, I hadn't bet on capturing it, the juvenile whatever-it-was slipping in and out, quicksilver-fast, and unbelievably agile. We'd only succeeded thanks to the larger predator on one side, us on the other, blocking its path.

Its relationship to the other predator was another puzzle, since it acted terrified of the gray creature. It almost seemed as if it looked at us with a flicker of hope for a second. At least, until Jace launched the extra net over it.

Which was a ridiculous thought. I pinched the bridge of my nose, not really helping short circuit the pain. "I need aspirin, and coffee." Better yet, aspirin and a mug of Marshall's indulgent hot chocolate. "And a muffin."

Jace perked up at the mention of pastry. He took the steps two at a time, pulling the door open and holding it, and waving me in.

Instead ,Matteo blocked the entryway, signing "Stay put". He looked over his shoulder, deeper into the house. Apparently satisfied, he jerked his head sideways, to the walkway.

Jace let the door go and we followed instructions, huddling together.

"We gotta talk." Matteo leaned against the pipe rail and faced us.

I copied him, choosing to prop on the wall, the stucco holding a fraction of the day's heat. "Marshall? I didn't think to text him on arriving, and let him know we were fine, and had hostiles. My fault."

II should have already explained basic protocols, well before we left. Instead, I'd gotten sidetracked by our usually jaded street contact's message, more spooked than I'd ever heard her.

Honesty forced me to acknowledge I was also distracted by the novelty of someone once more grumbling at us about staying hydrated and sharp. At having someone concerned, and promising to be there whenever we rolled back in.

The ghost of the earlier good luck kiss surface. My lips still tingled at the memory—the sure way Marshall had moved, confident in his welcome and my reaction. The stubbornness that held far more attraction than I'd anticipated.

Whereas I hadn't warned him we were bringing in cryptids, or reassured him we were all fine. I needed to check with Vee, but I was pretty sure she'd agree that made me a sucky girlfriend.

The learning curve with Marshall was steep, and time consuming.

I lost the thread of our conversation, startled by the thought that came out of nowhere.

"We have to get him to understand, and fast." Matteo jerked me from inside my head to reality. "He kept calling that fuzzy-haired cryptid a kid. He's worked up over it."

"Oh, *fuck me*." Jace shot up from his slouch on the other side of Matteo, turning to me, panicked in a way I hadn't seen since his being brought in on the truth of Vee's team, and the danger his brother was in. "Today at the market Marshall swore he talked to the street kid involved in the ghoul incident, but the kid bolted."

"Were you able to track where he went?" Even that would narrow the search time. At least he was still in the area, and we had a chance at locating him again and getting him the aid he needed.

Jace duck his head, his tell when he was embarrassed. "I found Marshall out behind the vendor unloading section."

"He got that far out of your sightline?" Matteo stared at Jace like his teammate had announced he was giving up gaming.

"I did a quick scan, and went over with him what to say to any curious civvies, but…" He held his hands out wide.

"But we haven't gone over sticking to populated areas, what a dead-blind looks like, where to avoid," I finished for him. Another oversight on my part. Hairs lifted along my arms despite the wall's warmth—Marshall's talk of a kid and his reaction to our second hostile joining together. "What did this kid look like?"

"That's the thing. I never saw him. Marshall said he'd been standing a foot from him, when the kid bolted at hearing me. I checked, and there wasn't any sign of a kid or any other civi, and I'm telling you, there was only a few seconds between him running and my checking. He'd have had to burn rubber, like some junior Usin Bolt-level shit."

The fuzzier cryptids agility and speed, the way it had initially evaded us, resurfaced. The chill pebbling my skin spread to my bones. The creature was small, pre-pubescent looking in a shirt and shorts. Kid's clothing. I closed my eyes, as if that might blot out the horror.

Matteo came to the same conclusion, and swore. "Marshall was back there talking to that damn cryptid."

Marshall, who put himself between armed vampires and a

child, who threw himself on a ghoul to save another kid. *Of course* he followed what he thought was a traumatized child.

It was a good thing I hadn't gotten that muffin and cocoa yet, as my stomach cramped and heaved.

"That fucker lured him in. That's why they were—it and that gray freak work together. The small one looks all helpless and lures prey in for the other to kill. Son of a bitch." The entire metal walkway belled and vibrated under us from Jace's vicious kick.

Marshall had been feet from the clawed horror residing in our cage.

"Enough." My command came out sharper than I'd intended. I opened my eyes and pulled in a breath, held it, then let it go along with the useless burst of fear and outrage. "Go do whatever you need to in order to level out, then clean up. Don't go indoors until then—that's not what Marshall needs right now. He shouldn't be punished for our errors. I'll talk with him and explain."

"You'd better." Jace's reply was as curt as mine, thrown over his shoulder as he stomped down the stairs, headed for the training course. "You're the C.O. for a reason."

"Marsh is seriously wound up about this cryptid." Matteo's response wasn't as dramatic, although equally damning and critical. His expression plainly said I'd come up lacking in his opinion. "We got lucky. Marshall got lucky. This time. He temporarily beat the odds. They'll eventually catch up with him unless you're able to make him see reason, and get him up to speed."

The house door *whooshed* shut. I couldn't fault my teammates. Matteo had said it—he couldn't survive losing more family. Neither could Jace.

I'd been so concerned that bringing Marshall in was dangerous for him, that I'd failed to acknowledge the decision was dangerous for my real team. I'd prioritized Marshall over my true family. My headache increased, like the thought had been physical and slammed into my skull.

I tilted my face to the uncaring sky, and tried ignoring that ugly, factual voice in my head. Jace had made a mistake in the market. However, that mistake was ultimately my fault. I'd screwed up and Marshall had almost paid for my error, all because we didn't know what we didn't know when it came to civilians and training them to survive in our world. My error nearly cost our newest team member his life.

arshall

MARSHALL THREADED a dish towel through his hands, for the hundredth time. He'd run out of anything else to fidget with, and was way too experienced to relax his body and let his brain take over, it getting more and more unrealistically fixated and panicked without a physical distraction.

He eyed the muffins and ham. He probably should've made more food. The smell of browning meat had clogged in his throat. All he could see was Kit, the way he'd turned his nose up when Marshall offered him the meat, and his joy at the bag of fruit.

His memory persisted in messing with him. Reliving how scared the kid had looked, grabbing Marshall's hand for comfort, during the ghoul attack. Then tossing up how Kit smushed into the corner of the cage today, curled up to avoid danger.

No way did it make sense that a monster would want a

recycled bag filled with ripe nectarines. Or bother warning humans about what was going down on the streets, and telling Marshall to be careful. None of it added up, and it wasn't a case of Marshall's brain imagining worst-case possibilities and things that hadn't happened.

At the change in air pressure from the outer door opening, Marshall grabbed plates. He'd talk to Liv and clear this up. They'd fix this together. She needed food and to relax though. As certain as he was that there'd been a mistake on the mission, he was equally sure the other cryptid, the creepy one in the first cage, was a monster. And Liv and the guys had been out there for hours, tracking and fighting and capturing that freaky-dangerous killer.

Jace came into view, an expression on his face Marshall hadn't see before—grief, and anger. He only dipped his head at Marshall and kept going.

"Did something bad happen on the call-out?"

"Give him a beat to get back into off duty mode, and clean up. Same for me," Matteo said, cracking his neck side to side like he couldn't let his stress or tension go. Despite the advice, his friend paused in the kitchen entry like he was waiting on something.

Marshall understood, when the air pressure changed again. Liv's voice carried down the entryway. "Marshall?"

Matteo's rigid shoulders loosened a notch, and he resumed his trip, headed toward the showers.

"In here." Marshall circled the table and met her, barely letting her get inside the kitchen.

Sure, he'd seen her earlier. That had been from a distance, and he hadn't touched her, hadn't really checked her out to evaluate what she might need from him. "Are you—"

"In town today, did you get hurt or—"

Their questions crashed into each other, overlapping.

Some of his ugly worry lifted. This was Liv, checking on

him because that's what she did, what she lived for. Protecting others. Looking out for them.

Fuck it. He gave in and cupped her chin, hit harder than a shot of tequila on an empty stomach by her and her concern for him. "You were the one out in the dark with that monster thing."

He ran his thumb along her jaw, feeling the reassuring, steady beat of her pulse when his fingers slipped from her jaw to that soft spot under her ear. He kept going, hand cupping her neck and sliding down. Gratified by the way her eyes widened and she shivered. He trailed fingers across her shoulder, and over her arm, goosebumps rising as his hand passed.

He stopped with his hand over hers, and Liv rotated her wrist, their fingers interlocking.

She moved closer, so that he had to look down to see her face. "We're all fine, and I should have called as soon as we cleared the gate security. I'll do better next time."

He tugged and she wasted no time snuggling into him, her arms around his chest. "S'okay. This is like in a new restaurant—with a little more practice, we'll get in synch," he said, making sure she understood he wasn't freaking out. It wasn't like Liv would ever purposely hurt anyone, physically or emotionally. "Come eat."

Her hand slipped under his tee, and yeah, that was becoming his favorite out of all her habits. She rubbed her check against him, and her breath tickled his neck. Her arms tightened, surprising a grunt out of him. "Jace told me about yesterday and the market."

This was good. They could talk about Kit. "No, that was fine. I—"

"It wasn't *fine*. You could've been—"

He felt muscles in her jaw clench, and tried to reassure her. "Listen, Kit, the kid, the one you guys caught, he's not what you think. I heard what Matteo said, but that's not true this time. Kit is scared and he needs our help."

As he spoke, Liv stiffened. By the time he finished, she felt more like a hard plastic mannequin.

Her arms dropped and she stepped back.

Marshall tried keeping them linked, knotting their fingers back together, but hers slipped free.

She closed her eyes, and her face changed. Harder, hollows deeper. Like when she'd talked about Vee disappearing.

"Liv, hey, no."

She opened her eyes, pinning him in place. Too close to the impersonal, detached way she acted when they first met. Back when she wasn't seeing him, only another civilian, a problem to be solved. "You have to hear me, Marshall. That thing—"

"Kit."

"That *thing* may have a name, however, it isn't human. It is a juvenile of whatever species." She shrugged like that didn't matter. "It isn't a child. No more so than a freshly hatched rattlesnake is a child."

"He didn't try to hurt me. I think he's vegetarian or the fruit one—fruititarian?" Which wasn't the right term, but he was losing Liv here, her jaw firming into that all-Commander line. "Why would a predator want a bag of fruit, and not try to bite or attack me? It was only me and him back there, not like anybody would've seen or heard if he'd tried. He didn't though, and he ran from Jace."

They don't help people like me. They make us disappear.

Kit's flat statement hit Marshall. It wasn't about Kit thinking that the people sent to safehouses vanished. It was about non-humans getting captured.

Seeing inside him to what he really meant, Liv sighed and her tone gentled. "That was a ploy, a trap. It looks small and

527

helpless in order to disarm people. Then it lures them in for its packmate, alpha, or whatever symbiotic term the Crypto division comes up with. These cryptids are pack hunters of some sort. The innocent façade is well-choreographed hunting behavior."

"Jace though..."

"It bolted when Jace arrived on-scene because the pack leader may not have been close enough yet, or the larger one is nocturnal and the smaller one diurnal and was out foraging alone, or wandered off when it shouldn't have. We can't know that until it gets to HQ for research. However, it identified a threat, evaluated its odds, and chose to run as self-preservation once a threat appeared."

Jace being the threat, Marshall not smart enough for it to bother with or fear. Heat crawled up his neck, part familiar humiliation, part all-new anger. Maybe he wasn't but this situation, Liv's opinion, they didn't feel right. Not completely. "He—it—talked to me. There was no faking how scared it was."

"It was screwing with you." Jace shouldered past them into the kitchen, swiping at his face and head like he'd walked through a cobweb, or like they were wet from the shower, except Marshall's compound was cobweb and dust free, and Jace was totally dry. "Food?"

Matteo elbowed his partner, coming up behind them. He gave Marshall the same expectant, hungry look though. "It's been a hot minute since lunch yesterday, man."

The trill of Liv's phone jolted Marshall, fracturing his concentration and the argument he was piecing together. Liv touched his elbow, and he switched back to her, reaching for their bond. All she said was, "Team needs first, okay?"

Before he could reply, she'd answered her phone, and turned for her office. "Yeah, we need to link the rest of the Region in on this call. Go ahead and pull up the photos I'm about to upload." Her door closed on the rest of her discussion.

He grabbed the plates again, letting muscle memory guide him through the meal. Kit—he or it or whatever HQ wanted to call him—hadn't felt evil to Marshall. He was new to this world that Liv and the guys grew up in, one they'd studied and trained for all their lives. No matter how much he learned, he'd never come close to knowing as much as they did about cryptids and their dangers. He'd told Liv her trusted her, and he did.

They risked their lives constantly. Coming in with throats crushed, insides on the outside, broken bones, and bleeding out. That's what cryptids did to humans.

Guilt edged out his prior conviction. This was his home, his team, his friends. They had his back. He'd promised to do the same, to look out for and protect them the same way they did for all those civilians going through life never realizing how much danger they were in every night. All with the teams never getting thanked for all they put on the line, every day, no breaks.

This was only his first week as a legit team member, and he'd basically acted like he didn't support Liv, doubting her and the guys, and their word.

He handed Jace and Matteo their dinners. "CoW? We can take on Kimi again." They'd understand this shorthand, that he was apologizing.

Except Jace only snorted, then winced like he'd been hit, rubbing at his forehead. "No way. Sleep is the only thing on our agenda."

Matteo nodded, and the pair hunched over their plates, finishing and leaving without another word.

Leaving Marshall's head full of opposite ideas fighting it out, as he scrubbed down every surface in the place, before the mix of adrenaline from arguing, worry, and guilt finally turned into plain tired. The compound was silent, guys already crashed as Marshall trailed through, turning off or dimming lights. One shone from under Liv's office door, proof she hadn't escaped her C.O. duties.

Once in their hallway, he slowed. His room or Liv's?

Technically, she hadn't invited him in last night or the night before, but she'd led him in. They'd shared her bed, but it was still hers, not *theirs.* He compromised, changing and settling on his bed. After he was at the point he kept nodding off, he left his lamp on, door wide, to let Liv know where he was and that she was welcome.

CHAPTER 67

iv

I FINISHED WRAPPING my hair in a fresh bun, and followed the scent of coffee and vanilla to the kitchen, bracing for fallout along the way. I had a mystery predator, wound tight team-mates frightened of losing more, and Marshall to deal with.

I made the first move. "It smells amazing in here."

He glanced over his shoulder, frowning. Although he'd been asleep when I paused at his open door after the marathon Regional meeting, he didn't looked particularly rested.

I didn't know if I was upset he'd chosen his room instead of mine, or relieved. Even then, I had the option of crawling in beside him. I guess neither of us had been up for another discussion.

"Morning." Matteo ambled in, stretching in a crackle of stiff joints.

"More like afternoon." Jace looked as tired as when we'd

rolled in the day before, and a sleep-deprived Jace was a grumpy Jace. "Why isn't breakfast ready yet?"

"Probably for the same reason you two are only now dragging out of bed," I said.

"So are you."

"I've already been out for an early run and a shower." No one else was stirring when I woke far earlier than I'd planned. My attempt at sleep had turned into dreams of endless meetings agents weren't allowed to leave, while civis died, killed by Frankeinstein mish-mashes of every cryptid I'd ever studied in Academy.

The pressure was on for me to ship this new find to HQ for bio-testing. That was standard procedure, and the smart course of action. Jace and I certainly hadn't gathered anything useful from it. I was leaning toward the creature not having vocal capabilities. That, or it didn't have functional pain receptors.

Sending it without having obtained any intel or concrete behavioral insights meant ruining my perfect record though. I'd always gotten something useful. In this case, I'd be at least the first agent in North America to do it with this new cryptid.

The headache I thought I'd gotten rid of tried waking. I ignored it, halted by the idea that my desire and reasoning didn't feel completely right. Rules clearly stated—I winced as the headache stabbed behind my left eye.

The unmistakable clink of a coffee cup snapped me out of whatever I'd been thinking, losing the train of thought. Whatever it was couldn't have been important if I'd already forgotten it. "Eat. Then I want you both in Interogation with me."

Jace grumbled under his breath and grabbed the cup in front of him, already filled.

"That's Liv's." Marshall made a move to block the coffee theft.

Jace glared and sidestepped, fumbling in the narrow cabinet over the counter, and coming out with aspirin. "It's coffee. Pour her another one." He slammed a handful of meds and chased them with the caffeine.

"I would have made you one, but you usually don't drink any." Marshall pulled out another mug.

"Don't sweat it, man." Matteo dropped into a chair.

"Easy for you to say." Jace sat too, but gave the room an impartial glare.

We were all tired and on edge. That fact didn't give any one of us permission to take it out on another teammate. I stared at Jace until he averted his eyes.

He gave a half-hearted, "Sorry," in Marshall's general direction.

Marshall delivered plates with warmed muffins, ham, and fruit, then sat. His leg pressed against mine.

The kitchen suddenly feeling small and suffocating, I scooted my chair away, desperate for breathing room. The entire house felt too full of men demanding things from me —results, my coffee, my attention.

While Jace inhaled his food, I tapped my fork against Matteo's plate, him only picking at it. "Hurry up."

I shared his aversion though. The pastry and ham didn't hold their usual appeal.

"I can make something else." Marshall's soft statement was meant for only the two of us.

"Maybe later." I rose and pushed my chair in.

I made it two steps before Marshall broke. As if I wouldn't hear them, he asked Matteo, "What are you doing? Out there." He tilted his head toward the yard, and presumably the annex and cryptids.

When I turned to face them, Matteo had leaned to

answer. He snapped his mouth shut on whatever he'd been about to utter.

Marshall transferred his attention and frown to me.

"We are doing our jobs, and you aren't cleared for detailed information," I said.

Marshall's frown deepened, but he nodded.

Irritation at constantly being questioned rose as the headache did. Part of me questioned my reaction. The majority couldn't wait to get out of the building, away from all the judgmental eyes, and I left, door slamming behind me.

iv

WHEN WE TOOK A BREAK, Marshall was in the kitchen, like he hadn't left. He darted a fast look our way. "Fifteen minutes."

Jace swooped by the fridge and emerged with electrolytes, before flopping at the table.

Matteo made a pass by the aspirin stash and grabbed the bottle, shaking a couple tablets out and dry swallowing them. Headaches seemed to be all our ways of reacting to the current stress.

"Give it." I curled my fingers in a hand-it-over motion, and he pitched me the bottle.

Marshall left off whatever he was preparing on the range top, and poured coffee, offering me the mug.

He held on a beat too long, fingers touching mine. The intimacy felt smothering and I twitched the cup away, harder than I'd intended, and hot coffee splashed.

Marshall shook his hand, near boiling droplets scattering.

"Can't you speed it up?" Matteo lifted a pot lid, then gave up and dropped into a chair hard enough wood creaked.

"It'll be ready by the time you're out of the shower." Marshall checked the clock, then the pot.

"This dress for dinner thing is getting out of hand." Jace drained his drink, skin ashy like he was dehydrated despite our having been indoors. "This is as bad as Bruce's kitchen tyrant crap."

Marshall turned to me.

Irritation flared to life, out of nowhere. "We're tired and hungry, and we still have considerable work to do. Lunch doesn't have to be perfect, it just has to be ready when we are."

Marshall couldn't hide how his gaze jumped from Jace's shirt, bits of gray hide stuck to a sleeve, or to my hands, and greenish-red blood outlining my cuticles. A streak ran from my thumb to my elbow. There were also cryptids bits on my and Matteo's pants.

Marshall's judgement wrapped around me, squeezing and claustrophobic. My irritation exploded. I plucked my stained shirt a few inches off my chest. "This is part of what we do as agents. Part of what you do is deal with it."

Color stained Marshall's neck and face, anger instead of embarrassment, and he crossed his arms, facing me full on. "My kitchen, my rules."

The guys froze. All except their eyes, attention darting between Marshall and me. Greedy. Waiting to see me back down. Questioning my ability. My right to lead. The urge to bring them all to heel rattled in my head, eclipsing something —a promise?

I shook my head hard enough my ponytail whipped against my cheek, and my objective became clearer. Obedience, from my team and this civilian, immediately.

I pushed into Marshall's personal space, blocking his path

to the oven. "This is your kitchen only for as long as I agree that's so. Let me be very clear—this is my Command and my compound. Do you understand?"

The color drained from his face, leaving freckles standing out in bright contrast.

At the hurt in his expression, like he'd been sucker punched, guilt chewed at the edges of temper. I'd made a promise to him, too. Something important, and it was on the tip of my tongue, just out of reach.

Whatever it was, as the seconds ticked by without an answer, the throbbing in my head and annoyance at being kept from the annex, the cage, and my new prize, pushed out any lingering guilt. "Do. You. Understand?"

Marshall gave a short, tight nod. "Yeah."

I addressed the rest of the team. "Is anyone else unclear as to chain of command and their respective positions and duties?"

The two agents straightened, coming as close to standing at attention as possible while seated. "No, ma'am," they echoed in unison.

"Eat, then report to the annex ASAP." I dumped the coffee in the sink, palmed the aspirin, and sought the freedom of the open air.

As I grabbed the outer door, noise erupted from the kitchen. Marshall spoke again. "The—prisoners. What do I feed them?"

"Damn, Marsh. Are you *kidding* me?" Jace muttered. "Did you not hear—"

"Keep it down." Matteo's deep rumble cut his teammate off. "We don't feed the—"

"Hostile specimens," I enunciated clearly. "We don't have prisoners. We have predatory cryptid specimens." I let the door close on any further discussion.

If I gave them time to process, maybe the lesson would

settle in. There had been too much leeway given recently. Too many rules bent or broken. This blurring of lines, confusion, and insecurity in my leadership ability was the result.

Like an echo, I heard our Instructor's voices, mine when I disciplined the lax cadets. *Breakdown of authority weakens the chain of command. Weak chain of command results from poor leadership. Poor leadership ends in deaths, civilian and agent. Every. One. Of those deaths is at the C.O.'s feet. That blood is on your hands. No one else's.*

Any epiphany sone, out of nowhere. I'd treated my agents as partners, but they weren't, not yet.

We hadn't been together long enough. Cadets knew it. Instructors knew it. Other teams knew it. HQ knew it. That was the reason there were only three of us. Plus one civilian.

I believed that Marshall wanted to belong. As difficult as melding together was for the three of us, at least we had clear goals and an understanding of our roles and what was required of us thanks to years of training and sometimes harsh lessons, and physical wounds.

Marshall...maybe a civilian couldn't ever overcome that gap. At least, not with desire alone.

My chest ached, a band crushing it, a twin to the one vising around my head, feeling as if giant hands were squeezing from both sides.

I left the doubt behind and crossed the dry yard, temples pounding in time with my steps. I'd take this doubt out on the monster waiting for us. I'd find something on what it was, where it originated, what else teams could expect. Proving that my team, Marshall, and HQ could trust me, that they didn't need to stress, question, and second guess my decisions.

If that goal required me to rip through cryptids, people's feelings, all the softer emotions and relationships only civilians could bask in, it would be worth the sacrifice if it kept my team alive.

Ruthless.

The description twined around my worries, then sank into my skin.

Yes. I needed to be ruthless.

CHAPTER 69

*M*arshall

MARSHALL SAT plates in front of the guys, and breathed through his mouth. Not really an improvement, still inhaling the cloying scent of cryptid blood and—stuff. The kind that now decorated wide sections of Jace's and Matteo's uniforms.

When Liv came in this time, she had enough on her to count as clothes. At least she had scrubbed her hands and arms and put on a clean shirt, though she kept the dirty BDUs and boots. He positioned her plate, careful not to accidentally touch her after the way she'd kept retreating that morning.

The guys didn't exactly relax, but they dropped the stiff, eyes to the front posture, once Liv picked up her fork. Marshall had never seen them do that, acting like eating wasn't allowed. Like Liv was a boss. Not a leader or C.O., but a boss, the scary sort like his ex-employer.

Without asking, Marshall also sat the aspirin bottle on the table. Liv took a couple, then rolled the bottle to Jace and Matteo. Chewing was the only sound, as Marshall sat and poked at the enchiladas, his appetite gone.

Liv too, from the way she cut her food then just rearranged the pieces, none making their way to her lips.

He cleared his throat, feeling her out. "What do you want for breakfast? I'll make anything you're in the mood for."

They guys didn't answer, leaving it to Liv. "Whatever is fine, as long as it's on time."

He had to talk to her. To ask what was wrong, what she needed from him. Remind her he'd do anything for her, and he was her sounding board.

There wasn't any of the normal meal-time conversations or goofing, that would give him the semi-privacy to ask her. He couldn't even lean over to whisper. Liv had pulled a chair to one end of the oblong table, and sat there. Removed from him. Removed from her team.

This was feeling less and less like a team. When Liv laid her fork beside her full plate, Jace and Matteo shoveled in their last bites, and drained their glasses.

Liv nodded politely at Marshall. Her thanks wasn't real— if he asked her, point blank, what she'd eaten, he wasn't betting on her being able to answer without checking her plate first.

The guys rose as Liv did, and Marshall made a desperate try at getting them all back on the same page, giving them a way to decompress. "I can make popcorn for now, and whip up some cookies for late night snacking."

"Some other time maybe," Matteo said.

Jace frowned, a moment of confusion passing over his face. Staring at the wall in front of him, like it had an answer. He finally swiped at his eyes, the weird expression returning. "I'm beat."

He followed his partner, both leaving plates and cups on the table, no offer to help. A minute later, two separate clicks marked their doors closing.

That hadn't been Marshall's plan, but he could improvise. This meant he and Liv had privacy. He turned, and got a view of her back, Liv already walking away.

He caught her elbow. She went still, that same brittle stiffness as at breakfast. "Liv."

Her hand covered his, warm, and real and the raised scar at the base of her pinky finger already familiar. For a heartbeat, he thought they were good. She'd explain, let him in on whatever was stressing her out.

Then her fingers worked underneath his, prying his grip loose. She finally looked at him, as she freed herself. "I don't have time for this, Marshall."

He kept his vibe level and reasonable. "I know. These attacks, this cryptid, the meetings and reports and all—I get it. I'm talking about later." Inspiration struck. "It's nice out. I'll take extra pillows to the roof, get those cookies going, and you can come up once you're done. No rush. I'll hang out and read until then."

Something flickered, the strange distance in her eyes retreating, softness spilling in.

She winced and rubbed between her eyes, and the moment was gone like it never happened. "Our routine and lifestyle is new to you. Unfortunately, this is as good as our downtime ever gets. It's probably a better idea if you get started studying."

While he processed that Liv thought this was downtime, like there had never been karaoke, or B-movie night, or drawn-out dinners with joking and easy conversations around the giant table, she...left.

Turned and left. A flash of reddish-brown caught

Marshall's attention. Auburn hairs, scattered along the side of her gray fatigues. Hairs that matched Kit's.

Marshall paced the length of the kitchen, thinking. Liv hadn't outright ordered him to stay in the house. He wasn't doing anything but taking up space inside.

Matteo had mentioned Liv's specialty was gathering information and data. She needed it, and needed it now, with cryptids not acting according to cryptid rules. So yeah, she was on edge. The guys were twitchy for the same reason.

Marshall understood having a responsibility, and feeling like you were failing at it.

If he wasn't helping his team in here, in his usual way, maybe he could in another. Decision made, he jerked open the fridge, loading up on his version of persuasion.

* * *

MARSHALL WAS willing to admit this wasn't the best half-baked plan ever thrown together. He stared at the interrogation building's—the annex's—security panel. The one that needed a scan, plus a security code Marshall didn't have clearance for yet.

He ran his palm over the screen, pausing to let it read his thumbprint. Then he pressed sideways and the seamless cover slid back, revealing the hidden keypad. Like a movie scene playing in his head, he zoomed in and saw Matteo punching in the code. Only half-believing, his finger followed, tapping in the same numbers. The panel light flared green, a click signaling the door opening.

A deep breath, and Marshall plunged inside, slamming the door closed fast enough it skimmed his heel as he entered. He threw his arm up, shielding his eyes from what felt like a blast of pure lightning. He blinked against the glare, swiping watering eyes as they adjusted to the cranked-up illumination.

Giving a clear view of the cages. And too many lethal-looking, sharp tools. Chains. Rows of weapons. Equipment that looked like an evil scientist's lab. They all sat on a concrete floor with drains in the center, and water hoses coiled neatly on the walls. Reddish-green stains had seeped in anyway, no amount of washing able to eliminate the cryptid bloodstains.

Something in him twisted hard, like standing up too fast to process the altitude change, and broke. There was no pretending this wasn't a site where blood was shed. He hadn't wanted to believe this side of the Company existed.

What felt like a frigid wind gusted over him, trying to get inside him, invasive and merciless. Hairs all over his body stood up in a painful ripple. The wind pushed and turned him, or made his brain turn his body, directly at the first cage. Marshall leaned hard, throwing all his weight against the blast, at least keeping himself from moving forward.

He couldn't blink for a minute. Couldn't breathe or move. Only stare, frozen under the cryptid's gaze. He'd seen it from a yard away before and it had rattled him. This close, evil coated it, and the space around it, like a toxic oil slick.

Marshall swallowed, the motion hurting his throat, head going buzzy-light.

A panicked squeak-trill shattered the silence, and the creature turned its head. Marshall jerked and stumbled back a step, like he'd been released from a snare.

Kit curled in a ball, head tucked under his arms, knees pulled up. Making himself as small as possible. Getting as far from the other cryptid-monster as the cage allowed.

Marshall skirted the first cage in a clumsy side-shuffle, sticking to the edge of the room, following Kit's example, not looking at the thing but keeping it in view from the corner of his eye.

He made it to Kit's cage. One liquid brown eye peeked out, then disappeared, covered by skinny arms.

"Hey. Hello, Kit." Which sounded ridiculous even to Marshall. He tried again. "Are you hungry?"

A shiver flowed from one end of the kid to the other, knobby knees knocking against the floor. Because, yeah, Marshall was an asshole.

"Kit?"

The kid's voice came out muffled. "Why? So when I say yes, you can tell me to starve, too? Go 'way."

The flat, hurt tone killed Marshall. He knew that tone, trying to be emotionless but the hurt plain. "No. I'd never say that."

That got a disbelieving snort. "Liar."

"I'm not."

Kit repeated the snort. "Are. *You* said your friends would help. *You* said so. But they don't care, and hate us."

Without thinking about tact and a good approach, Marshall blurted out, "Why do you want to hurt people? Hurt us?"

The kid's head popped up, forgetting to be afraid, eyes hot. "I don't hurt anybody. I've never hurt a human or a Non. I haven't done *anything* wrong."

When Marshall stared, weighing the kid's passionate speech against Matteo and Liv's lectures, the kid blinked, and his face kind of fell, the sliver of hope gone. "Whatever. So maybe I shoplifted once. Or a couple of times. What'm I supposed to do, huh? My flocks all—" he stumbled, sounding closer to tears "—gone. Maybe all dead. I can't find any of them. I chirp and locate, and chirp and locate, but nobody answers." The kid's eyes watered, close to tears.

Marshall didn't get all of the kid's meaning, but understood enough. Kit was alone and scared. Marsh had been right about that. "Then why are you here, with that cryptid? Helping it." Marshall rolled his eyes sideways, not dumb enough to look at the thing directly again.

"I'm not. I was *trying* not to be its dinner. Then the Company monsters got me. Your friends. 'Cause you lied."

Marshall grasped at that last bit, and worked backwards. "The Company. You know about it? You do." Liv hadn't said it directly, but Marshall was sure that wasn't the sort of thing any cryptid they went after lived to talk about.

Kit huffed, for a second looking like any annoyed teenager faced with clueless adults. "Uh, yeah. Most of us Nons know."

"Nons?"

"Non-Humans."

"And you're trying to get even? For the Company policing you?" Marshall worked on piecing facts together.

That earned him an *uber-annoyed* huff. "All of us Nons—us Lesser and non-jerk Nons—we don't mess with the balance. Even if all of you—" his glare called Marshall out "—try to kill us, too, you get rid of the big predator Nons. You *accidently* help us, I guess. *We're* not the kind you humans gotta worry about." He gave a lightning-fast glance at the far cage.

The unbalanced, buzzy sensation intensified. Marshall swallowed and popped his jaw to relieve the pressure, taking a deep breath. At a sharp, electronic beep, they both jumped.

Marshall fumbled his phone out, and silenced the alarm.

He couldn't help looking at the bigger cryptid. He could've sworn a chunk had been missing out of its tree-trunk sized thigh when Marshall first came in, a match to the gunk and flesh on Jace's BDUs. Now, there was only a shallow depression.

His anxiety spiked fast enough the room swam, and sweat

beaded his upper lip. If he missed that, he might be missing other important details. If he missed something as obvious as a wound, what would be next? What if it meant failing the guys or Liv?

Before he completely got lost in his head, he knelt. "Kit." Marshall rolled a couple of apples he'd meant to use for a pie through the cage bars.

His stomach roiled. Liv, the guys, they'd basically forbidden feeding prisoners—because Marshall wasn't calling Kit a damn specimen or creature—but he couldn't refuse the kid the only bit of comfort Marshall could provide. Even if Liv found out and did...

He couldn't finish the thought. Once, he could've guessed her reactions. Not anymore. Marshall stood, his head getting light at the change in position. Kit darted, too fast for a human, scooping up the fruit and back into his protective ball before Marshall blinked twice.

The kid didn't look at him again, as Marshall repeated the sideways shuffle, gaze on the floor, his hand extended and using the wall as his guide. The buzzing and anxiety increased. What he'd done—

His fingers hit the metal of the door handle, and he pushed, stumbling outside. Darkness rolled in, faster than it had since he was a kid. He squatted and swiped at his phone screen, case creaking in his grip.

The app opened, the soft shush of imaginary ocean waves flooding out. Marshall breathed in time to the waves, eyes closed. He pushed back at the worry about falling into an attack, and it being dinner time, and him being late, and Liv noticing, and how bad he was at lying. Instead, he concentrated on what could go right.

Finally, warm, dry desert air registered, along with the tickle of a curl being blown back and forth across his forehead. He let out a last breath synced to the app, and took stock. His head ached and buzzed, but it was bearable. His heart didn't feel like it was battering out of his chest.

When he opened his eyes, it was only to the yard, Kimi's birdbath and an iron bench that needed some outdoor pillows. Right. All good. He stood, dusting gritty dirt off his palms.

He's already done the dinner's prep work, simple sandwich wraps for everyone, since the guys didn't care what they ate anymore, and Liv didn't notice there was food, period. He jogged up the steps, getting there minutes before the team.

It felt like his guilt was sprayed all over him, like graffiti on a wall, and he opened the ocean waves back up, staying centered. He kept his head down, filling the pita wraps with chicken and vegetables.

"Don't you have tunes?" Matteo cruised in, bags under his eyes. He flipped Marshall's phone to face him, examining it.

Marshall had left the apps open before. Matteo had even asked non-judgmental questions about them and the other workarounds Marshall used. After, better understanding what worked for Marshall, he'd sent videos of gun safety rules in place or written or recorded versions.

Now, he inspected the phone, swiping through the app's sounds like he'd never seen it before.

"I can put on a playlist." He wiped his fingers, and pulled the phone his way. He queued up Liv's old school metal and grunge list.

"Liv will love that." Jace took his usual spot, his grin all teasing, and he was Jace, their brother and teammate, with a habit of stealing leftovers. Then he jerked, a pained noise eclipsing the playlist starting. All that liveliness and fun gone, expression hard. Matteo didn't react to his partner's distress.

Marshall was pretty sure they all knew Liv had made him that list. Now, Jace was acting like it was a surprise.

While he was still puzzling out the memory lapses, Liv walked in, frowning at her phone. It vibrated, belting out lyrics, Liv's ringtone for Vee. He held onto Liv's plate, since she wouldn't eat until after the call.

Instead, the phone cut off mid-song, Liv not only declining the call, but turning the phone off. She sat, and gave Marshall and the wrap a pointed look.

"You're not talking to Vee? Is something wrong?" He felt her out.

Her lips thinned out hard enough they lost color before she answered. "I don't need any of her unsolicited advice on how to run my team."

He'd never heard her use that tone when it came to her sister, even when they were arguing. Like Liv was being attacked, or surrounded by enemies, no teammate at her back. He made sure everyone was set, then retreated to the bar. Liv didn't comment on his choice.

No one said anything to him, or to each other. When Liv stood, it was a repeat of the earlier meal, guys jumping to attention even faster.

"The mission yesterday was sloppy. That can't happen again. We're hitting the urban course until we get it right." Ice laced her tone.

The guys didn't groan or fire off the usual half-hearted complaints.

All Marshall got was a curt, "Don't wait up on us," over Liv's shoulder.

He cleaned on autopilot, scenes from the last few days playing in a disjointed loop. Liv's strange coolness and distance. Jace and Matteo not joking or socializing. The growing distance and disconnect between every member of the team. All of them twitching, acting like there was a conversation going on that Marshall couldn't hear.

He let his brain do its thing. It would get to whatever

conclusion his subconscious was puzzling through on its own time schedule. Marshall stared at the fruit salad, the bowl nearly full. And Liv's untouched pita wrap, right beside it.

He gathered them all up.

This time, he kept his app open, only a little muted from where he'd stuck it in his pocket. His fingers tapped out the annex's security code faster than the previous trip, more sure of themselves. He braced for the big cryptid's awful, soul-numbing presence. Eyes fixed on Kit and his corner, Marshall speed-shuffled to his destination.

Without asking, he fit the flat container he'd transferred the leftovers too through the bars. Again, Kit had it and was back in his hidey-hole breath-stealing fast. The kid popped the lid, sniffed, then dug in.

"This is mostly veggies. Some chicken." Marshall held the wrap up for inspection.

Kit wrinkled his nose. "Meat is gross."

Marshall doubted the other creature shared the kid's opinion. He chewed his lip. Was it cruel not to feed it, too? "Will it eat this?"

Kit jumped, plastic container bouncing off the concrete, fruit spilling.

"NoNoNoNo!" It came out one long, panicked word. "Don't touch it and don't let it look inside you!" His voice broke and climbed, a squeal by the end.

The buzzing in Marshall's head roared, like an attack. Bile rose.

Kit gave a pained squeal, like he'd been slapped and bolted back into the corner, head jammed against the bars, like he was trying to phase through them. Or shove against the pain.

Marshall popped his jaw, then crouched, reaching into the cage. "Kit, look at me. Are you okay?"

The kid's only movement was the tremors shaking his body. This close, Marshall couldn't miss how thin he was. He couldn't miss the bruises on the boy's bony wrists and ankles, either, and the mesh-net patterned burns along his exposed skin.

Kit was starving and hurt. Liv and the guys were responsible. They'd done this to Kit, and were gonna do something worse, soon.

Liv, when she was being the real Liv, the one the team looked to, the one concerned with buying socks, and getting innocent people out of harm's way, said she relied on her gut to make decisions.

Marshall's was screaming that this was all wrong. That Kit might not be strictly human, but neither were Vee and Stavros, and that the kid was starving, terrified, and injured. He didn't belong here, in a cage, treated like a dangerous animal.

Kit had been in the wrong place, at the wrong time. The same as Marshall, with his criminal human boss and the vampire cartel.

Except Liv and the Company weren't busting in to save anyone this time. It was up to Marshall to get an innocent to safety.

Marshall held onto that fact, as he bolted for the house, grabbing SUV keys hanging in the kitchen, gathering the odds and ends his mission required, and then his fingers magically knowing the code to get him back inside the annex.

Inside, he held up the dishtowel he'd grabbed on his sweep through the kitchen. "I'm getting you outta here. You have to wear this though, okay?"

Kit peeked from under his arm, curled up tighter than ever. The kid's indecision and misery gnawed at Marshall, a filthy gray-green cloud, drowning out the increased anxiety-buzzing in Marshall's head. "I swear, I won't hurt you. My friends, they're confused, and what they're doing is wrong, and I'm sorry. I can get you out, but you have to trust me, and we have to go *now*."

No matter how hard Liv worked the team, no matter what she demanded, they were incredible. They'd get the drill right, and return. They could be coming off the obstacle course out past the track any minute.

"Please, Kit. It'll be safer this way. You won't know the way here, so no one will take you and hurt you, trying to find out."

Belief or desperation, the kid finally threw himself at Marshall, coming close to knocking Marshall on his butt.

Marshall tied the cloth around Kit's head. What Marshall though was hair in need of a trim felt more like silky fur, the boy's body warmer than usual, despite the building's fridged A/C. Kit's heart beat hard enough Marshall felt the frantic rhythm, way too familiar.

He wrapped Kit's hand around Marshall's left wrist. "Don't let go."

The kid never stumbled, more surefooted than Marshall. He stayed glued to Marshall's side, up the steps, through the house, and into the garage.

Fingers almost numb, Marshall buckled Kit up, climbed in, and cranked the truck. He repeated what he'd watched Liv and Jace do, pulling out the high-tech folding keyboard, and way, way too slowly typed in the clearance code for the gate. Aware Liv would hear the all-clear chime, and the growl of the truck.

He'd deal with that after. Despite the metallic taste of fear coating his tongue, Marshall kept to the speed limit. Concentrated on where to go instead of what he was doing to the team. Breaking rules. Lying. Betraying the trust Liv, Matteo, and Jace offered him.

He pulled into their destination, having driven by it both times he'd been outside the compound, on the way to the market. He leaned over and undid the towel.

Kit blinked. Then tilted his head, taking in the bus stop, the means by which Marshall traveled when a job dried up or he was fired, moving to the next location. Cheap, and more importantly now, no I.D. required if you bought a ticket at the automatic kiosk.

Marshall dug out the cash he'd taken from the guys' wallets, knowing where they were kept thanks to his cleaning binges. Thanks to the market trips and karaoke outing, also knowing they relied more on cash than cards or apps. Another violation of their trust.

He pressed the wad of bills into Kit's hands. "Buy a ticket at the kiosk. Tell anyone who asks that you're sixteen, and going to visit your grandparents." He pulled out his old duffel bag. Nothing in it would fit the starving kid, but the old yellow hoodie would help conceal Kit's face, and it looked more realistic to have a bag or backpack.

Kit watched Marshall's every move, like a prey animal constantly evaluating, checking for threats. Marshall handed him the hoodie. "Don't tell me where you're going. It's better that way." Marshall couldn't spill to Liv if he legit didn't know Kit's destination.

He already felt ripped in half. Part of him was yelling about deceiving Liv, the most important person in his life. The other part was focused, determined to get Kit away before Marshall's people, his new family, hurt the boy.

Liv had kept Vee's secret from Marshall, protecting Vee. Marshall was doing the same with Kit. Liv wouldn't be happy, but she'd at least understand where he was coming from. That was a precedent, and he'd use it to explain Kit was like her sister and father. She'd see reason, eventually.

Marshall was her sounding board, the person she could

double-check ideas, right and wrong with. He'd *felt* it, when Liv accepted his role that night, her trust and relief. What they'd done to Kit was an unfair error, like HQ seeing her sister and father as threats. He'd work on a coherent way to explain that on his drive back.

The kid squashed the bag to his chest, hugging it like a security blanket. His fingers twisted and knotted the webbed handles. "You should leave that place. Your friends are toast, but you aren't. Yet."

Before Marshall could ask more, the kid bolted, truck door slamming, Kit blending in with the crowd of passengers and the people seeing them off.

iv

I GAVE Marshall credit for not hiding or drawing our inevitable confrontation out. He parked the SU, and was out before the garage door closed, his face set in stubborn lines, jaw tense.

He held out the keys. I flipped my hand palm up, not trusting myself to touch him, even an accidental brush of fingers.

He dropped the keys into my palm. "We've gotta talk."

I had trouble hearing him, over the static in my head, in my ears, warning me of another person undermining me.

"My office." I was proud of myself for keeping my voice neutral, in the face of the blatant provocation, the flaunting of my authority, the direct challenge to my leadership.

Marshall fell in step beside me. The hall and kitchen were empty, but I didn't fool myself. Jace and Matteo were keeping out of the line of fire, but they were close.

Watching. Waiting for me to fail. Jace prepared to usurp my spot. Matteo as well. I'd seen the hungry way they'd looked at me, at my office.

Fair enough. I had been weak and was responsible for this disaster. It was on me to clean it up. Reinforce my power. Show them what happened when an enemy crossed me.

As soon as we entered, Marshall closed the door. "Liv, listen before you say or do anything. I know what you and the guys said about cryptids and hunting habits and all. You made a mistake this time. This is like with Vee and Stavros. Kit's like them. Okay, not a vampire, but no evil because he's not human. He only—"

I breathed around the hurt. Freaking Vee, and her damn wild-card plans, and Bruce and his giving Marshall ideas. Vee and Bruce giving *me* unrealistic ideas, like I could fit a civilian into our unit, and into my heart.

She'd set me up to fail. I should've seen it. She wanted my team, to add it to the one she'd already stolen from me.

Soft. The word insinuated itself into my thoughts, slick, and insidious.

Marshall was soft. He made *me* soft. I'd given into always unreliable emotions, and daydreams. I allowed myself to be distracted, and fallen into her trap.

I was soft and foolish, lost in a relationship haze instead of fulfilling my duty to my command and my team.

That buzzing, the clamor of certainty filling my head, doubled.

My gut had known all along. The nagging doubt, my not being able to say what Marshall wanted to hear. It was all because the realistic part of me that I'd been suppressing *knew*. This was the other shoe dropping. Having what was mine jerked away again.

"Liv?"

I blinked at Marshall's question. Whatever else he'd said, I'd missed.

Not that it mattered. It would have been a heartfelt plea—be kind, don't hurt that creature. Because Marshall was Marshall. A civilian. Not one of us. The definition of soft, and incapable of surviving in our world.

An idea scratched at my brain, like a pet trying to get an owner's attention, asking to come in. This one was a faint image, of Marshall facing down a ghoul. I frowned, trying to place the image, but it vanished, the voice in my head that I should have listened to all along blotting all other nonsense out.

I focused on reality, and my current problem—Marshall. He held his hand out, reaching for me. I backed out of range, and his hand dropped.

"Liv, c'mon. Please."

"This isn't your fault. This is mine. I knew you didn't belong here."

Marshall rocked back on his heels, as if he'd taken a physical punch.

I pressed on. "You aren't Company. You never should have had that pressure on your shoulders. It wasn't realistic or fair to you. I was pushing for something outside your skill set."

"Don't." His hands clenched into fists, voice a deeper rumble, momentarily louder than the buzz of truth filling my head and ears. "Don't say those things, because they aren't true."

Another challenge to my authority. "We have to be real. You are a distraction, to Jace, Matteo, and me. Being with you is a luxury I can't afford. I realize you can't truly grasp the magnitude of our current situation, but this cryptid uprising is the most severe crisis the Company has ever faced. Yet I was busy indulging, instead of concentrating on being a Commander."

Another ragged wisp of a scene, like a faded watercolor, surfaced. This one of Marshall telling me he was my sounding board, my safe place to brainstorm and share ideas and doubts.

Pain lanced behind my eyes. I pressed my thumbs over my eyelids, the scorching pulse of agony lessening. My resolve firmed up.

Marshall was speaking, but I held up a hand for him to stop, then resorted to talking over him. "You're confined here until we return. You access is suspended, and you're locked out of every domestic system in the house. Your phone and WiFi service has also been cancelled. I can't trust you to follow my rules."

"You don't mean that." Marshall normal bass changed to a hollow whisper.

"You disobeyed direct orders to stay out of the annex. You freed a cryptid. You released a creature, compromising this compound, the team, and quite possibly, the Company."

"I wouldn't ever do that to the guys or you. I covered Kit's head. He doesn't know where we are, where he was held, or how to get back here."

I sighed, the regret real. "It's done. We'll discuss your move back to HQ when we return."

Marshall flinched. Then his eyes narrowed. "Back from where? Is this a call-out?"

I crushed the stray, out of place inclination to share my plan, and the details, or to reassure him. It, he, might be part of the rebellion, aiding Jace. "We've had a verified tip. We are putting an end to this uprising, today."

"Liv, no." Harsh lines bracketed his mouth, forehead wrinkled. "Wait and I can—"

"You chose a cryptid over humans. You chose it over *me*.

There's nothing left to discuss now." I crushed the last image, of muffins and someone caring whether we came home, not even sure where it had come from. It was inappropriate and had no bearing on our lives.

I held open the door. In a caricature of the past, of Marshall joining us, Jace and Matteo jumped, again surprised eavesdropping, and hastily backed away from the door and me. This time, when Marshall paused in the doorway, neither spoke, looking away from him.

Marshall shoved past them without another word.

I let him and the moment of weakness he represented go. It was time to prove I was still a leader.

ᴍarshall

Nᴜᴍʙ, Marshall watched the red of the truck's taillights pause for the gate to slide closed, then his team disappear down the access road, into the desert evening.

Okay, not numb enough. Instead, it felt like he'd been scoured out, inside, with rusty steel wool, then filled with vinegar. It hurt to breathe. To be.

He'd known the fallout from his decision was gonna be bad. He'd bet on Liv at least listening to him, though. The guys, too. Letting him explain, look at the facts he had lined up and practiced on the drive back to the compound. That Kit was like Vee and Stavros, that the kid was a vegetarian, not a predator, and pass on what Kit had said about other Nons like him, and especially what Kit told him about other cryptids and the Company.

Use that discovery as proof, and show them he had been careful, because he would never put the team in danger.

Instead, it was like they didn't see him, much less hear him. Like it was his voice, but they were hearing something different than the words he was saying, bad dubbing like in a cheap B-movie.

He more dropped than sat in the kitchen chair, feeling like gravity had increased by a hundred-percent. Liv said he didn't even have kitchen rights anymore, but, where else would he go? He dropped his head, digging his hands in his hair.

Staring at the worn antique floor until its pattern blurred together.

This, the whole situation, what they'd done to Kit, Liv acting like a military instructor, the guys not spending evenings bonding, it wasn't right. *Nothing* was right. Like a blockage broke free, questions hit him.

Liv said they'd had a breakthrough, and were ending this, although she hadn't been clear about what *this* really was. Just her and the guys weaponing up.

She hadn't called Vee or Stavros and their team, despite the wounds the crew nearly died from on the last big mission, with both teams in play.

With the dangerous cryptids joining together, basically acting as suicide bombers. No way had Liv finally figured out why the cryptid behavior had changed, or she'd have said so.

She hadn't called in the Texas teams, despite it being the other closest team, and her and that C.O. agreeing about most things, being an ally, and them being in conferences nearly every day with a ton of other Commanders. Despite them tossing around ideas of bringing in backup, talking about group strategies for multiple teams working together.

Fine, he wasn't an agent, like Liv pointed out. But her decision was off. Weird, nothing like her other strategies, or even the strategies the guys and Kimi planned in their damn realistic gaming battles.

Liv's thinking had gotten stranger, more erratic and secretive since—the buzzing in his head intensified. The buzzing he'd gotten so accustomed to, he hadn't even noticed it was a new constant. Which meant that—

A blast hit him, the buzzing scorching and sudden.

Sharp and strong enough tears filled his eyes, blurring the room into terra cota and gray blotches. Alien and direct

Not like his usual low-level noise and worries. Despite the pain, his heart rate wasn't going wild, chest feeling like he was having a heart attack or an elephant was sitting on it so that he couldn't get a breath.

This felt outside him. Not his. Whatever this static and pain was, it wasn't Marshall's. This wasn't his brain, or his anxiety, or panic.

He blinked away the tears, sitting straight, because if it wasn't coming from inside him, then what were the other options?

His vision clear, a blip on the kitchen's surveillance screen caught his eye. Something moving, that wasn't the team SUV, or a desert critter. He hauled up, and pressed closer, nose brushing the screen.

Kit.

The kid stood outside the fence, wearing Marshall's old neon yellow hoodie, the flash of color that had caught Marshall's attention. Kit now jumping up and down, waving his arms, the shirt sleeves falling over his hands and hiding them.

Marshall toggled the camera switch, zooming in.

The kid stopped, like he'd heard the mechanical noise. He stood straight, and mouthed, "Marshall. I need to talk."

Marshall pulled back and blinked hard, then eyeballed the screen again. The image stayed the same. Except now Kit had his arms crossed, sleeves hanging, shooting annoyed *why are adults so slow* vibes at the camera.

The garage side door was one of the few that didn't need a code, the handle a plain doorknob. Marshall let himself out and jogged across the yard, noisy crows waking and winging along over his head.

He stopped, out of breath. "I—how are you here?"

Kit shrugged, looking way too pleased.

"I blindfolded you! I was careful." Liv had been right. Marshall had messed up. God, he'd messed up.

Checking out Marshall's expression, Kit's smirk vanished. "Umm, yeah. Sorry. We have great homing instincts. It's a Non-fruit bat thing."

"Homing—fruit bat—" Marshall tried making sense of...a human fruit bat? Were-fruit bat? Fruit bat shifter? Whatever Kit was, the kid had some sort of freakishly accurate ability to know where he'd been held, despite never seeing where he was, or how he'd arrived and departed.

Kit seemed to get bored waiting. "Your people are walking into a bad thing. An ambush. Which, I don't care. They suck." He crossed his bony, oversized sweatshirt covered arms, trying to look tough.

Then dropped the pose and the attitude. "Except they're part of your flock, even if they're jerks, which they are. You're solid, so I tracked you back down. Like, repaying you."

"Just—wait." Marshall made a slashing motion and the kid quit talking. "Okay. Gimme a minute, here."

Ambush. Marshall understood that fine, and the word froze his blood in his veins. Liv was walking into a trap, one like she'd talked about her sister only surviving because of Stavros. Kit had information, though.

"Right. Explain. Please," he added as Kit's expression verged on belligerent. Marshall couldn't fuck this up.

The kid played with his hoodie string. Despite kinda wanting to shake information out of the boy, Marshall waited.

The patience paid off. "You don't know much, but you gotta understand, we've been around *forever.*"

Marshall took that as all cryptids, not limited to human fruit bats, and nodded encouragement.

"Then, the stupid Company has been around almost as long, some places. Now there's technology and you can do stuff like see almost as well as us at night, and fly, and finally, like, hear stuff other than boring human-range sounds."

Marshall nodded again. Infrared goggles and planes. Got it.

"So now we—them, the big Nons—are using human science, too. Mostly vampires, who are *not* really Nons," Kit glared, as offended as a teen anything could get. "And, you know, being ex-humans." Kit's lip curled, opinion on not being born a Non clear.

Right. Vampires had been human, or were still, their DNA all messed up now. They'd grasp cutting-edge tech, science, research. If they'd been infected in the last decade or two, they might've even worked in those fields.

"Got it. Now, what does that mean? What are the vampires doing, and with the team?" Marshall leaned closer, willing the information out of the kid.

Kit fidgeted. "Science. Science stuff. Labs. Making new Nons? I don't know it *all.* I'm a *kid.*"

Marshall made *sorry, you're awesome,* noises and Kit settled. "Anyway. Humans and Nons don't always see me. They talk in front of me. I hear things."

Marshall understood that phenomenon. If you weren't important, people discounted you. Overlooked you or forgot completely.

"The vampires, the big Nons? I think they're gonna turn some agent jerks, like yours." The kid frowned. "Or maybe they already have with some. They're gonna get them inside the stupid Company. Steal stuff, kill people, I guess. That Franken-Non makes it way easier to do."

Pure terror rushed through Marshall, like nothing he'd ever experienced. The thing, the cryptid creature, the one they'd found and captured so fast, barely gone long enough for Marshall to finish baking... "It wanted to be caught. It's a plant. A weapon."

Kit perked up and nodded, extra hoodie fabric flopping. "See? It got inside your jerk friends, but you were smarter. They kept *touching* it." He wrinkled his nose, as disgusted as when Marshall had offered him meat.

"What's *inside them* mean?" But Marshall already had a good idea.

The noise in his head that wasn't his. The team eating aspirin like it was popcorn, everyone with a constant headache. None of the team talking to each other, chill, easy-going Jace snapping at someone every other word, supportive Matteo not recognizing Marshall's apps.

Liv, being distant and cold. Forgetting to talk to the guys. Not talking to Marshall, and completely ignoring her sisters, and only thinking about rules and regulations.

"The Franken-Non messes with you. It puts in bad memories, and ideas. Pushes you to make *bad choices*." Kit rolled his eyes at the last, saying it like it was something he'd heard over and over.

Bad decisions.

Like Liv not calling in backup teams, or being clear on what their mission was, and heading into a lethal trap she should've spotted in seconds.

With no vampire blood to save them if they were wounded, Jace and Matteo could die. Liv could. Marshall's breathing sped up, even as the band settled around his chest, squeezing his lungs.

"Hey!"

A sharp, sonic-ish burst of noise rattled Marshall. Instinctively, he covered his ears. The suddenness broke the loop and let him breathe again. "Ow." Dampness ran over his top lip, and he swiped, fingers coming away red.

A blush turned the kid's pale skin neon. "Sorry, but you were all—" He made a hands around his throat, choking pantomime, tongue hanging out.

"Yeah." Marshall tilted his head back, pinching his nostrils to stop the bleeding, even if it muffled his voice. "I do that sometimes. Thanks."

He watched Kit, matched his breathing to the kid's, using Kit like an app. The worst of the panic backed off.

Kit twisted the hoodie string into knots, but waited Marshall out.

Marshall's free hand went to his pocket and his phone. The device Liv said was locked. Not that the team would take his call anymore, even if they didn't keep theirs off until after missions.

Think, think, think. There had to be some kind of workaround.

Like a new cooking technique clicking into place, he zeroed in on Kit. "The shoplifting."

The boy took a step away, wary again.

"No, it's okay. Not okay-okay, it's dangerous, and you know, not legal, but—a phone? You've got one?"

Eyeing Marshal the entire time, the kid dug one-handed in the duffle and came out with a low-end disposable model, the kind sold in convenience stores and bodegas.

Marshall held out his hand. "Toss it over to me."

That earned him a glare. Instead, the kid shimmied out of the hoodie, and with perfect aim, tossed it to flutter over the top of the fence. It caught, covering the chem-treated razor wire.

Before Marshall could stop him, Kit took a running start and—leaped. Like gravity didn't apply to him. Arms out, his shoes touched the hoodie for a split-second, then landed inside the fence on his toes, one hand splayed against the ground, not even raising a puff of dirt.

He popped up and grinned at Marshall, enjoying Marshall's shock.

"I'm surrounded by superheroes," Marshall muttered. He held his hand out again, more demanding now.

Kit dropped the phone onto Marshall's palm. With his other hand, Marshall pulled out his phone. He couldn't make calls, but it was charged, and he could pull up the few stored numbers.

He hit Send, grateful Vee had put her number in his phone. The call went straight to voicemail. For all he knew, her team was out on a mission. Marshall barely kept from pitching the phone, out of pure frustration.

Calling the other three numbers on his short list, Liv's and the guys', was out.

The fifth though…Marshall owed past-Marshall, who had been smart enough to enter the scribbled digits Kantor had tossed at Marshall, as Vee's crew left. Kantor didn't go on missions often anymore. Praying that was the case, Marshall stabbed Send.

The number rang, repeatedly. Going to damn voicemail. Marshall tried again, same results. He ground his teeth and texted fast, ignoring misspellings. *its Marshall. Livs n trulbl 911*

Then hit redial. An angry snarl boomed in his ear, the rattle of pans and clink of china loud in the background. "If this is your idea of a fucking joke, I'll shove a cleaver so far up your—"

"They, Liv, they caught this new monster cryptid."

"I'm aware of that. The same as every other agent in—"

He raised his voice over Kantor's. "Shut. Up. It's messed with the team's heads. They're on a mission, alone, and it's a trap. The things are waiting at—" he checked with Kit. "Where?"

"The other side of the fancy financial district. The one with all kinds of research and science stuff. The big flat building with solar panels, and little buildings all around, and they have fresh berries for lunch a lot."

Marshall repeated it word for word to Bruce, minus the lunch description.

"How many? Any civilians? How long have they been gone?" Kantor snapped out the list like it was ingrained, requiring no thought, the kitchen background noise gone.

Marshall looked to Kit, who wasn't even pretending not to listen to both sides of the call.

"A lot. Vampires, another Franken-Non. Ghoul and windigo guards. Like cops with attack dogs. Umm, some plain people for food and work?"

Marshall repeated it, Kantor's swearing increasing, and added, "Thirty minutes, tops. They've been gone thirty minutes. Where's Vee?"

It sounded like a car door slammed, then Bruce was back. "We're right over the line in Vegas. Fuck."

That was close. But not close enough. "Get Vee and Stavros. And this cryptid, it gets in your head easier if you touch it." Marshall cut the call, mid-curse.

The team had left half an hour earlier. They'd be close by now. Vegas was a couple hours out. Too far, too long. Marshall ground the phone against his forehead, talking to himself. "*C'mon. Think.* The team had the SUV. I can't exactly call an Uber out here…"

"Take the one in the other garage," Kit piped up.

"The what?"

"The car. There's one in the garage by the cages and torture stuff."

Marshall stopped, mouth open. "How—you've only been here two days." Marshall hadn't known there was another vehicle. Although Matteo had mentioned something, something about a secondary garage, the day they'd brought the creature in.

"Somebody ate an orange in it." Kit shrugged, fake casual. "I have one fucking kick-ass sense of smell."

"You shouldn't swear," Marshall said automatically. Then —"Where? Show me."

Enjoying his role as know-it-all hero, Kit took off, a red-brown rocket. Marshall sprinted after him.

The kid took them in at an angle, and paused yards from the annex. Marshall halted beside Kit, in unspoken agreement. Neither wanted near the torture building, and *it*.

There hadn't been a car in the cage room, only the SUV. Made sense there was a backup, though. So there had to be another bay, and another way in. Marshall circled to the far side, checking the wall, and yeah, another garage door. No bio-lock and keypad on this one, either. Maybe luck was finally with them. He grabbed the pull and hauled up.

The door rose on well-oiled tracks. A truck sat in one of the two bays. A real pickup, polished white paint, lifted on oversized tires, fancy wheels and grill gleaming.

Kit beelined, opening a back door, sniffing and wiggling in. He came out with another of the mesh bags, a couple of shriveled, head-dried oranges inside. "You humans. Always wasting good stuff." Complaint aside, the kid shook one out, and poked at the peel, pulling a chunk loose.

"Don't eat that." Marshall swatted it out of Kit's hand. "It'll make you sick. I'll get you more food."

The kid glared, and stuffed the mesh bag inside his duffle,

while Marshall opened the driver's side, flipping the visors down, opening the ashtray, checking the cup holders, praying for keys.

"You're probably going to get killed, and then, no food." Kit complained from behind Marshall.

Which, yeah, was likely. Assuming he ever got out of the compound. Finding no keys, he slammed the door, and ran for the house. Inside, he played guess-the-owner, time slipping away. Who'd have the truck? He didn't have time to search all three rooms top to bottom for keys.

Jace liked looking good, and the truck was fancy. Matteo needed space, and the truck had plenty of room.

But there was Liv, who was all rules and order, until she wasn't, who'd once pierced her ears and dyed her hair, and brought a civilian into her life, and who would keep a tricked-out, jacked-up truck because it was fun.

He bolted for her room. Pulling out drawers, checking jeans and pockets. He moved on to her nightstand, coming up empty. Which left only one other possibility. Praying, he checked the little pottery bowls on her busy dresser top. His fingers closed around a keyfob.

He spun and nearly trampled Kit, the kid taking it all in, and the door to Marshall's room open, when Marshall had left it closed. Liv had been furious enough about letting Kit go. But allowing a nosy cryptid to explore the compound? Her head was gonna explode.

Assuming she lived. Marshall caught Kit by the shoulders. "Where is this science building?"

"Past the financial district."

Marshall had no idea where that was. The fact that he hadn't asked to explore his new city was biting him in the butt, again. "Address? Company name?" Something he could put in the truck's GPS.

The kid shrugged. "Dunno. Past the other offices and stuff."

Time sped up, every second moving his new family and the woman he loved closer to death. Kit knew where they were being held. It was time to go old school. "Can you draw me a map?" It wasn't much, but lines and patterns were doable.

"I can write out roads and where to turn."

He'd never be able to read them fast enough or keep them straight in his head, while driving. He was going to lose Liv because of the way his brain was wired.

Unless he had a guide. He was a bag of dicks for what he was about to ask. He put his hands on the kid's shoulders. "Kit, you've got to do something for me. Writing won't work. I need you to ride with me and show me where to go and where to turn."

The boy jerked, shimmying and wrenching, thin shoulders quaking in Marshall's grip. Feeling like the worst bully, worse than the ones who'd taunted him daily at school, he held on. Kit gave one of his high-pitched squeals.

Marshall dropped to one knee in front of Kit, putting them eye to eye, ignoring the new drip of blood from his abused nose. "Listen. Just listen. Get me to the place. That's it. Then, you vanish. Go back to the bus station and get out of town. They'll never know you were there, I promise."

Kit's upper lip trembled. "We could both leave and go someplace without predator Nons and Franken-Nons."

"You can, and you're going to as soon as I'm in sight of the right building complex. I can't."

The boy was shaking his head before Marshall finished.

Marshall tried again. "Please. You lost your flock. You know how bad that hurts. Help me not lose mine. Plus, think about what will happen if I don't, if all those big Nons take over, no Company left to thin them out. They'll wipe all the

JANET WALDEN-WEST

flocks out, all you little guys. I don't want that to happen, and I don't think you do, either."

A tear rolled down Kit's cheek, and he scrubbed it away. Half crying, half angry, he faced Marshall. "You're going to get killed, too. The Franken-Non there will mess with you, and you'll be gone. It's way bigger and louder, and it'll get you."

Marshall froze, not concerned with himself, but with what he'd set in motion calling Kantor. The creature Marshall's team had captured had influenced Liv and the guys so completely that they went out on a suicide mission.

And Marshall had called in a team, complete with an ancient warrior vampire and another trained by the best black ops outfit ever, to crash a building containing an even more powerful psychic monster.

If it took over Vee and Stavros—horror burrowed under his skin to join the fear.

The jolt of terror knocked his brain into action. Out of nowhere, his subconscious completed its process, and pieces clicked together. Vampires had made the Franken-Non. Marshall had seen first-hand, with Stavros, that vampires thought they were the rulers of the cryptid world. No way would they create something better and stronger than them.

"How do the vampires control the monster? How do they not get put under its spell, get looked inside of? And then make other cryptids obey them?" The one thing Marshall had learned from every comic and movie ever was that there was always an out, a weakness, a loophole.

Gentle as possible with their time running out, Marshall shook Kit. "C'mon, think. They talk in front of you. You've seen important things. You're smart and streetwise. You know this, you just haven't realized that yet."

Kit hugged the duffel, his new comfort thing, but finally answered. "The vampires drink the Franken-Non's blood.

Which is super gross, because it's this not-natural blue and they don't act like it tastes good, but they all drink it anyway. They give a drop to the ghouls and windigos, the ones they own now."

Of course. The once human vampires would've created immunity for themselves, and of course it was blood, because, vampires.

Marshall had a source for the blood, to immunize him and Liv and both teams.

Kit came to the same conclusion. His big eyes widened further. "You're going to touch it. No. Way. That's how it gets you."

True, the thought of getting close, much less touching the monster—Marshall's balls tried crawling back inside his body. "We only need its blood."

The supplies were in the infirmary. He'd seen Kimi draw blood. After, he'd been watching the video tutorials he'd found, so he would be ready for the next emergency. "There's a way to get what I need without touching. Stay here. Do not leave—or prowl."

Marshall cut back to the infirmary and grabbed syringes, tubes, and gloves. He wasn't exactly surprised when he caught Kit hanging from the door frame, head stuck in and watching.

Marshall sighed and let it go. "Show me how the team was able to bring that thing in. And—and how they captured you. Please."

"Getting close to it is bad, too. Dumb bad. And it hurts when it gets mad at you."

"My back pocket. Get my phone. Hit the top app. Yeah, that one in the upper corner," Marshall added as Kit basically picked Marshall's pocket, so fast Marshall wouldn't have realized if he wasn't waiting for the kid to grab it.

Kit complied, and the meditation app opened.

"Crank it up. Wait, what about you?" He wasn't letting the kid fall under that thing's control, or hurt the boy again.

Kit perked up. "I can sonic."

At Marshall's blank look, Kit said, "My noise. It warns the rest of the flock about danger. It can keep Franken-Nons out of my head. It might work on you humans except—" He mimed Marshall's nose bleeding.

"App for me, sonic for you. Um, if I start slipping—"

"I'll blast you," Kit said, unsettlingly enthusiastic.

A deep breath, and Marshall led the way out. Imagination or reality, unease cranked higher the closer they got to the interrogation building, each step harder to take.

The buzzing in Marshall's head thickened. Now that he knew what it was, he felt the same oily-evil as when in the cryptid's presence. Buzzing like disturbed hornets, pecking and drilling, searching for a way in.

Marshall clutched the medical supplies in a sweaty hand, Kit shadowing him, all but glued to Marshall's leg. At the entrance, Marshall swiped his thumb across the screen, then carefully entered the code. Praying. Liv said he was locked out of everything in the house, but maybe not out of everything. Not with her fielding calls and planning ops, and this building being on a different system.

It chilled him when the light glowed green, and the lock clicked.

Or, this monster had purposely left a gap in Liv's head. Waiting for Marshall to do just this, because Marshall was actually helping the thing's agenda somehow, it tampering with his reasoning same as with Liv's.

Marshall worked to ignore the doubt. He felt the instant the hornet-things latched onto his worries, and tried twisting them. Showing Marshall scenes of it corrupting him, him walking up to Jace and Matteo and shooting them. Him letting this creature loose, holding the cage door for it.

Liv, Jace, Matteo, and Kit lying in pools of blood because Marshall was too stupid to figure out the creature's plans, or fight them. Because Marshall was weak, and soft, and couldn't fight, hold off the monster, or do anything useful.

Marshall jumped at a sharp pain in his back, and glanced behind him. Kit held a fork—one of the huge serving ones Marshall used for salad, and was readying to jab Marshall in the small of his back again. The kid held Marshall's phone in his other hand, stuck all the way out and aimed at Marshall.

Marshall shoved the door open, holding it long enough for Kit to dart in after him. The kid stayed behind Marshall, but pointed to the wall. "That, and that."

Keeping close to the wall, feeling the monster tracking their every breath, Marshall examined the items Kit motioned at. Something that looked like a rocket launcher, big enough it'd have to balance across a shoulder. Peering closer, Marshall identified netting, inside a clear bullet-shaped casing, chem-treated threads silvery-gray.

The launcher was right out, impossible to get a shot thanks to the cage bars.

Next to the weapon was a smaller gun-syringe hybrid. The one he'd seen Liv holding when they brought the monster in. A clear tube with purple liquid screwed into the top. "Did they use this?"

He felt Kit nod. "It knocks us out. Even predator Nons."

Gingerly, afraid he'd accidentally shoot himself or Kit, Marshall brought the trank gun down from its holder. He examined it, barrel pointed at the floor. It had sights and a trigger, like the Glock Matteo had demonstrated how to use and clean.

Marshall scanned for anything else useful. There were chains on the wall, neatly looped around a bolted-in holder, like a garden hose. Metal shackles hung from the ends, all chem coated. When Marshall added those to his pile, Kit hissed. Marshall had a second of pure fury—these were where the bruises and burns on the kid's wrists had come from. The chains alone were heavy enough to weigh Marshall down.

He used his anger, turning, planting his feet shoulder width apart, sighted on the cryptid's center mass, and squeezed. Enjoying the snap of satisfaction when the dart hit, liquid draining from the cylinder into the creature, before it smashed the dart away.

A wall of swarming hornets slammed into Marshall's brain, drowning out the app. He dropped to his knees, only a wobbly arm keeping him from face-planting into the concrete. Every nightmare he'd ever had, every taunt he'd endured, every slight and mistake roared in, a non-stop assault.

His hands scrabbled against the rough concrete, digging for anything to hang on to, to ground him. The buzzing reduced as the creature moved on to images of Marshall's new life, with the guys and Liv and her family, it crashing and burning. Leaving Marshall knowing what happiness felt like, and then forced to live without it, alone forever.

He grabbed one of the most vivid images. Liv, because she always shone bright. An image of them in the truck the day she'd insisted on picking out a guitar. In his lap, arms around him, telling him every agent had had versions of his meltdown. That, Liv's kindness, was real and true.

He shoved hard and the outside fear lessened. Marshall pulled up every good Liv memory, all the ones he'd memorized and saved. All of them sitting around the bar table, with a beer, talking. Liv sharing his space, reading in the easy silence. Him in Liv's bed, her trusting and using him as her pillow. Him, buried inside her, her nails dug into his shoulders and legs wrapped tight around him.

Marshall wasn't losing any of that. Not to fake memories,

not to monsters and vampires. He concentrated on every visceral detail, Liv's silky hair, the clamor of a CoW game in full play and the faint stink of burned popcorn, the earthy goodness of coconut and plain soap, fresh vanilla, the slide of skin on skin.

His head quieted. Cold from the concrete worked through the knees of his jeans. Wetness dripped from his nose, ending in a soft splat of his blood, droplets hitting the floor. There was a continuous quiver against his left side, and a constant squeaking.

Marshall shoved, knees unlocking, and fell back, butt bone hitting the floor. He scooped Kit, the source of the tremor and noise, under his arm. "It's—" He cleared his throat, coughing at its rawness "—S'okay. It's okay, Kit. Look."

The Franken-Non lay on its side, in the middle of the cage. Its eyes were glassy, their eerie sheen dimmed. Its lids closed in a painfully slow blink.

The quivering and high-pitched squeak stopped, Kit peeking from under Marshall's arm. The kid scooted away.

"How long does the tranquilizer last?"

Kit shrugged. "I was all spacey from it for a long time. Your friends kept giving the Franken-Non doses though. Better hurry."

On the principle that it couldn't hurt to have a barrier between his skin and the monster's, Marshall pulled the gloves on, the latex sticky against sweaty skin. He rubbed his face against his shoulder, wiping away the blood and flop sweat.

He sorta butt scooted to the cage, every muscle rubbery. There, he threaded his arm through the open space, between the last bar and the gate hinges. He reached for its clawed hand, coming up inches short. He pressed harder, metal digging into his chest and bruising.

Marshall's fingers brushed empty air. His plan to clamp chains on the monster, and anchor it against the bars, crashed and burned.

Going inside the cage was the only option. Hands shaking, he secured one end of the chain, and tossed the length inside. Grabbing his supplies, he forced fear-stiff muscles to move. Lied to them that this was no biggie, no real threat, only his body overreacting.

He pressed his finger to the lock on the cage and put in the code, pin disengaging. "If I don't—if it gets me, run," he ordered Kit, not looking back. "Run. Take the truck if you can, but go."

A sniffle that sounded like snot being sucked back in answered, before Kit said, "Yeah. I'm outta here."

Every hair on his body standing on end, smart enough to recognize the danger, Marshall eased inside. Every mystery creak and ping twisted his nerves tighter, expecting the thing to roar to life.

An arm's length from it, Marshall crouched, and pulled up every bit of courage he didn't believe he possessed, until Liv had. Keeping the image of her front and center, he reached. He worked to keep from puking when he touched the unnatural flesh. Evil flowed off the cryptid, marching along Marshall's skin like angry scorpions.

He gritted his teeth, and pulled the arm-paw out straight. He'd seen plenty of its blood all over the team, so it had veins, somewhere. The rubber tourniquet barely fit around its arm. The things joints were human enough, and Marshall jerked the band as tight as it would go, not hesitating to bruise a monster that'd set Liv against her team and him, and sent them into an ambush.

Thick, ropy veins sprang up. Replaying how Kimi had worked, how the video demonstrations went, he unwrapped the catheter, and careful as moving a souffle, eased the needle in. He stuck a tube on the end.

Viscous blue goo welled. The tube filled at a painfully slow pace. As soon as it did, Marshall jerked it out, and replaced it with another.

The creature's eyelid dropped. Lifted. Hate gleamed from its eye. Like the tube filling, the buzzing in his head slowly returned. Filling his skull and bringing doubts.

This wouldn't work. He'd never finish. He'd never find his team. He'd walk in and they'd all be dead, torn apart, nothing but unidentifiable chunks left. He'd fail.

Marshall popped his jaw, and dragged in a long inhale of the cold annex air. He concentrated on the sound of the app, and followed its mechanical rhythm. Fingers clumsier, he switched tubes. The monster's eyelid dropped, and rose. Immediately dropped again.

Sweat dripped down Marshall's spine, soaking his waistband. Three tubes nearly full. One for each of his teammates. Except there was Vee, Stavros, Kimi, and Josh. Marshall had no clue how much blood they needed in order to become immune.

The thing blinked, a fast blip-blip. Out of Marshall's sight, a claw *skreed*, twitching against concrete.

"Hurry!" Kit's squeal sliced over the soothing shush of waves.

Marshall fumbled another tube out, attaching it.

The *skree* repeated, longer this time. Its paw twitched. This tube and one more, that was all Marshall needed. He grabbed the arm, kneeling on it, dry heaving at the contact. He just had to—

It jerked hard, muscles contracting. Marshall lost his grip, hitting his ass. He scooped up the filled tubes, scooting on his rear, sneaker soles slipping instead of gripping the concrete.

The creature rolled, uncoordinated but fast as a striking

snake. Claws arced by Marshall's face, breeze pulling curls into his eyes. Bunching thigh muscles, he hauled himself to his feet.

The monster rolled again, dragging its anesthetized, limp legs. It slashed, way faster, catching Marshall's jeans. He heaved backward, the thing hanging on, a dead, vicious weight. Digging in, a claw grazing his shin in a line of fiery pain.

It heaved again, and Marshall tripped, going to one knee. He threw a hand out to catch himself. Blood tubes shattered, glass digging into his palm in a dozen pops of pain. A burning tingle, like the worst case of pins-and-needles, started in his palm, and spread.

Adrenaline shot through him, and he hauled backward, muscles protesting. Denim gave with a harsh rip. Marshall stumbled, aimed at the gate, and fell through, whirling and slamming it a half heartbeat before the cryptid rammed it, metal ringing.

Kit's squeal was continuous, and more painful than the cuts and Non blood. Marshall coughed and cleared his throat. Squeezed out, "You gotta quit sonic-ing."

After a second, silence fell. A warm weight pressed against Marshall's hip. "You're bloody."

Marshall wiped his face on his shirt, fabric filthy and damp. The stinging in his leg and hand fully registered. Along with the memory of his tubes, smashed against the ground. He opened his hand, the one clutching *a* tube.

One tube.

Kit leaned in, sniffing at the vial. "That's not much."

Marshall glared at the kid, then regretted it. Snark was probably the only thing powering Kit at this point, panic clear on his pale face.

Marshall picked a couple of bigger shards of glass out of

his palm, gagging again at the blue creature blood smeared in the cuts.

With the wall's help, he climbed to his feet. Time for part two of his plan. "When you said a monster party—did you mean a party-party?"

arshall

So, monsters did throw parties. Expensive ones. Kit had been right about the party, and Marshall had been right about the sort of high-brow taste vampires might have, thanks to his ex-boss's boss, with his chauffeur and expensive looking suits.

The other sleek glass and chrome buildings in the research sector were closed for the day. Leaving only the largest, and the buildings radiating out around it, the business complex nearly large enough to have its own sector. Tasteful landscaping hid a lot of the building unless you were as close as Marshall.

He crouched behind an understated sign, avoiding the in-ground lights, all burning and throwing artful splashes of illumination. Enough for him to watch white-clad servers go from the caterer's enormous truck, and into the building's back entrance, using an empty loading dock as their staging area.

Warm fuzz brushed Marshall's arm. He jerked, plastering his back against the sign and choking back a horror movie shriek.

"Shh!" Kit shushed him.

"What the—I left you with the truck, so that you could leave. Be gone already," Marshall hissed, heart doing high-speed flips. Paranoid, he patted over his chest, checking the pocket and his last tube of Franken-Non blood.

Marshall had borrowed the shirt from a go-bag he'd found in the truck. Matteo's bag, from the size of the clothes, raided after Kit pointed out Marshall couldn't walk in smelling of Franken-Non, blood, and fear-sweat. The bundle under Marshall's arm was all Marshall's though.

"Kit." Marshall tried for authoritarian.

"You'll mess up without me." The kid stood tall, completely lost in the soft blue hoodie, the one Liv had picked for Marshall. Guess he wasn't the only one borrowing other people's clothes.

He rested his hand on the kid's shoulder. "You taught me a lot, okay? I've got this. You need to head out. Get to the bus stop, and leave town."

The doubt gnawing at Marshall reflected back at him from Kit's face. "But—"

He squeezed Kit's arm. "I know. Whatever happens, you can't be here for it. I need to know you're safe, so I can concentrate. Deal?"

Kit's lower lip trembled. He finally nodded. In a blink, he was out of sight. Lost in the darkness and maze of businesses and landscaping.

Like it was his good luck charm, Marshall touched the tube, then crept around toward the catering truck, sticking to the shadows. Quest achieved without anyone or anything sweeping out of the night to grab him, he pressed his back to the trailer's metal side, peering around into the interior.

And came nose-to-eyeball with one of the employees. The guy blinked, but his eyes stayed glassy, like he was listening to something inside himself. The caterer finally frowned at Marshall. "Get in uniform. Now."

Marshall shook out the white jacket balled under his arm, the last item he'd grabbed from the compound. His from months before, the one he'd had on when Liv loaded him into the team's SUV and changed his life. He shrugged into it, hoping this guy didn't notice the faded reddish-brown bloodstains at the cuff, that wouldn't wash out.

Marshall had barely gotten it buttoned when a sharp push to the back propelled him forward. He fell in line, grabbing a tray of hors d'oeuvres, heavy on tartare, from a rack. Hot liquid filled Marshall's mouth and he forced himself to think about his plan, not what the raw meat meant for a vampire party might be.

As he passed from the lot into the building, Marshall kept his head down, wishing he at least had a hairnet, anything to cover his hair, the red standing out among a crowd of darker shades. He stole sideways glances. More servers passed him, their trays empty. Others clustered in the mini-kitchen, more of a really nice break room, filling crystal glasses, some with red wine, some with liquid too dark to be a merlot.

Nobody spoke, no orders flying, none of the usual bustle and routine that kept an event kitchen in order. They also didn't pay him any attention. Braver, Marshall slowed and took time to really check out the area. Everyone from the better dressed pair in suits, to the workers filling the glasses, had that spacey, not quite there expression.

The same disconnect the guys had at the end, whenever Marshall mentioned gaming and got blank looks, and when Liv said the team didn't take downtime, despite all the evidence proving otherwise surrounding them. The same as when he tried talking to them, but they heard someone else's words instead.

Hypnotized, compelled, monster-whammied. Had to be.

Marshall inhaled, let it out, and repeated the calming exercise. So far, his head was—fucking terrified. The terror was all him, his thoughts and worries, not outside ones being jammed into his brain.

He flexed his hands, cuts stinging under the hastily applied bandages. Kit said vampires drank the Fraken-Non's blood. Guess it didn't matter how it got into your system, though.

Either way, he needed to move. Find his people, wherever they were being held. Immunize them. Then let them do what they specialized in—escape, and create a real plan to kill these creatures once Vee arrived. He glanced at the clock on the closest wall, right above a microwave. Still too long until the other team arrived, as backup or distraction.

"Here." He cut in line and shoved his hors d'oeuvres at a girl reaching for one of drinks, nabbing the tray she'd been after. She took the switch without a word.

Marshall aimed himself at the party, leaving the relative safety of the humans-only room, passing through a narrow corridor, all of Matteo's CoW lectures about bottlenecks and ambushes returning.

He came out into an open room, more of an auditorium-meeting space. He'd get the layout. Then sneak off to his team, immunize them in private.

The event space was set with linen-draped tables, matching slip covered chairs tied with frothy bows in the back, like for a quinceanera or wedding. Candles on the tables cast an intimate circle of light. A full bar had been set up in the opposite corner, a glassy-eyed human behind it, mixing drinks for those wanting more than wine or blood-wine.

All familiar so far, easing some of his anxiety. Until he got to the center of the room, and the Franken-Non standing there. Kit had said it was bigger. Not a great description, because this was one was at least twice the size of the one at the compound, wider, taller. It towered over the crowd. Claws laced together, like a sick parody of a Company soldier at parade rest.

Clustered all around it were vampires. The uncomfortable, edgy thing that had hit him the first time Vee and Stavros walked into the compound poured in waves off everyone not in a white serving uniform. Vampires at the tables, chatting and sipping from the crystal glasses. One pulled a server into her lap, lifted the other woman's arm, rolling it and exposing the underside of a delicate wrist and—

Marshall jerked his gaze away, disgust and fear mixing. He'd assumed real vampires survived like the ones in pop culture. Assuming, and seeing for real, weren't the same. He had to find the team and get out of here.

He inched sideways, focus on the floor, and the polished loafers, colorful stilettos, and the random servers' practical black or white sneakers. And a pair of scuffed black combat boots. Out of place at a party, but already as familiar as Marshall's face, boots that clomped into his kitchen every day.

The glasses on Marshall's tray clinked as he stopped too fast, gaze jumping. Relief washed over him at finding an even more familiar lean frame, and elegant face. Jace, alive and in one piece.

Matteo's reassuring bulk stood beside his teammate. Marshall started to speak, then snapped his mouth closed.

The third person in their group wasn't Liv. Wasn't even a human.

The fitted, tailored suit was the same, today's tie aqua. The last time Marshall saw the vampire flooded in. Women huddled in a freezer, their whispered prayers, a traumatized kid in a cartoon shirt, and a man's face turning from normal to a misshapen, blackened corpse's as it targeted him. Then the whistle of a machete and a head rolling free of its body inches from Marshall, and soldiers, guns, and chaos.

Part of Marshall fell into that memory. But now, another, bigger, part stayed in the here and now. This wasn't real. It was only a memory, and not capable of hurting him, no matter that he felt the crunch of broken security glass under his soles, and heard the screams.

If he let the memory win, and froze, then he was dead. So were Jace and Matteo and probably every human server in the place, and Liv, who he hadn't seen yet.

The Franken-Non twitched, and its head moved. Those disturbingly round eyes took on a bright, iridescent sheen. Like an owl, its head twisted in an almost complete circle, surveying the room. Searching for Marshall, who was shooting emotions all over, when everyone else in here was either hypnotized-numb or pleased.

Marshall curled his fingers under. Digging them into his palm and the bandage, reopening the cuts. The creature would smell blood, but between the blood-wine and the vampires already feeding on staff, it was less risky than either melting down or catching the creature's notice.

Pressing harder, pain radiated up his wrist. Marshall held on to the real, immediate sensation. Added the weird-awesome feeling of Matteo's affectionate backslaps, and Jace's fist bumps, the warmth and friendship. Digging deeper for the citrus of Jace's favorite lemon curd, and the smokey heat of Matteo's chili and chocolate, the rose-gold of pure happiness whenever Liv was near.

The simple details worked. Marshall sidled closer, yet one more invisible server. The vampire, Welch, Marshall's boss and head of a trafficking ring, lifted a glass, never glancing at who held the tray, as Jace and Matteo stood quietly.

Too much like the Franken-Non, eyes forward and at parade rest. The guys were busy scanning the crowd, with that vigilance they always held a trace of, even when sprawled out for B-movie night.

They weren't glassy-eyed and checked out the way the rest of the humans looked. Hope unfurled in Marshall's chest. Maybe the guys were biding their time, waiting for the right distraction, or at least not as far under the Non's mind whammy.

He did a quick inventory of his team—none of the guns they'd left the compound with, holsters empty. They'd kept the huge knives in their thigh rigs. Marshall dared raise his face. Looking Jace dead in the eye, holding his gaze.

Getting nothing in response, except a cold once-over, and quick dismissal, not recognizing Marshall or cataloguing him as a threat.

"Are these.."

Marshall tensed at the cultured voice, practically in his ear, then dared a side-glance. A blond man—vampire—in another expensive suit, though no tie, joined Welch. Both studied Marshall's friends.

Welch took a sip of his drink. "A set of the Company's most proficient killers? Indeed."

The blond circled the guys, predatory enough that the hairs on Marshall's arms stood up. "I'd heard the rumors that you'd succeeded, but assumed that's all they were."

"When will you learn not to discount me, Phineas?"

The blond, Phineas, drew a finger along Jace's arm. "Even

you have to admit one of your mad science projects aimed at grafting together a trainable psi-cryptid sounded like a drunk's hallucination."

"You never were an early adopter. It's a wonder you haven't gone extinct." Welch lifted the other vampire's finger off Jace.

Phineas' eyes turned flat silver, his face thinning out as Welch smiled, fangs now on display.

The tray shook, Marshall unable to stop the fear. Glasses clinked, and Matteo's gaze landed on Marshall.

In a wild bout of inspiration, Marshall angled, putting himself more clearly in Matteo's line of sight. Marshall shifted the tray's weight to one arm. Under its cover, he signed, "help. Please."

At least, that's what he hoped he signed. He'd lined up ASL teaching videos, but had only been through a few.

Matteo frowned, and Marshall's pulse sped up, tapping out *please, please.* After a second, the agent looked away. Still engaged in their argument, the vampires never noticed. The blond took a glass, no more aware of Marshall than of the furniture.

Welch wasn't done needling the other vampire. "This process has gone far beyond barbaric grafting procedures, and training a psi. Phase One is complete and has been for some time." Carelessly, he waved at the guys. "These are intended for Part Two, which has exceeded my expectations, and far quicker than we had projected."

Phineas snorted, a thoroughly human noise. "Company thugs aren't much of a lure. Well trained junior nest members are easier to create, and hardier."

Moving faster than Kit had, the blond drew a finger, now tipped in a claw, down Jace's arm. The heavy camo fabric split, and blood welled in a line along his friend's arm.

Marshall clenched the tray hard enough his hand cramped. Jace didn't even flinch.

Welch frowned, irritation slipping through his haughty mask. "Careful, or you'll be paying for one, and they far exceed your Master's yearly budget." He snapped his fingers and both agents came alert, attention on Welch, but like well-trained dogs, not the animated way they did with Liv.

"These aren't personal toys. They're part of the first wave of infiltrators."

Marshall's blood iced. Kit had said there might be spies, but this was way more. A catastrophe.

Phineas didn't appear any more impressed than when he'd hurt Jace. "Lobotomized drones aren't a step forward. We've seen those demonstrations for years. All they're good for are as shock troops and distractions. They couldn't function a day inside a headquarters or on a team."

"These go beyond any sort of drone." Welch looked at the guys, and tilted his head. Jace and Matteo flanked him, gazes colder and attention on Phineas.

Welch strolled to stand by the Franken-Non. Without a word, Jace spun, one of his smaller chem-coated knives flashing in a vicious arc.

The blonde hissed and grabbed his arm, jacket and shirt sleeve sliced open, blood dripping from the gash Jace's blade left, a match to the one the vampire had left on the agent. Welch laughed, low and rich, as the agents stepped in front of him, knives out.

He spoke from behind the living wall of protection. "This is what I have been working for, in order to insure our Nests' futures. I've replicated the portion of our virus that codes for the bond between Masters and those they create. Augmenting it with the advances you have seen before, in our cryptid breeding trials. These infiltrators are responsive, maintain an identity, and seemingly, their free will. Members of their groups won't notice a difference. Yet they are bound, in this case, to me and my will."

Vampires tuned into the spectacle, questions flying. Welch's voice filled the room, not vampire abilities but a professional speaker's tricks. "This advance is why I asked you all here, and am asking your support in funding, and recruiting."

Marshall drew back, way from the force of focused vampire attention, and probing eyes. Sweat dampened his hairline. If there had been anything in his stomach, he would've lost it on the spot.

Commanding the room, wooing his audience, Welch continued. "I am getting closer to isolating the code and biological substance psychic cryptids use." He motioned to the Franken-Non. "As useful as this version is, there's room to refine the process. Eventually, my labs will synthesize the DNA codes to ensure obedience and maintain personality, as well as to exchange psychic conversations and orders over longer distances. I'll admit, these two are little more than soldiers, and as you noted, we can already produce those via our nestlings."

He did the finger snapping thing again, and Marshall had never wanted to run anyone's hand through a meat grinder until now. A spotlight came to life, centered on the small, raised stage. Welch took his place on it, and the light moved to shine on the wall. The well concealed door opened. Liv stepped out.

The spotlight followed her, like for some awards show, as she stalked across the stage. "Here, we have an elite agent, a Division leader with full clearances through Level Seven, with unfettered access to come and go from their Regional headquarters. As of this afternoon, she. Is. Ours. She, and others we capture, will prepare the way for the next part of our agenda."

Conversations erupted all over the room, voices raised. Shouting at each other in high-speed bursts that ran like a grater over Marshall's frayed nerves.

All he could do was stare at Liv, obsessing over every detail. She was here and alive. Her hair was down, out of the bun she wore for missions. The gray-scale sweater they all wore was gone, leaving her in the black undertank. Bruises ran from her cheek and chin, down her chest and across her shoulder. Dozen of cuts, or claw marks, decorated her hands and arms.

All of her holsters were empty, thigh rigs gone. From the rips in her pant leg, even her last-ditch backup pistol had been used. She'd fought. Of course Liv had.

Now, she halted on the stage, the light picking up the copper and gold strands in her hair, those dark cocoa eyes fixed on Welch. One brow lifted in that perfect Liv question only she could do. The one Marshall had last seen while in her office, daring him as she unbuckled his jeans. Showing him she cared, that she was giving him part of herself, a promise that she would get to where he already was in their relationship.

Except now, she was waiting for an answer from a vampire, one she'd sworn to eliminate. One that had been behind the fight that'd nearly killed her and her brothers only a week before.

Marshall must've made a noise. Jace frowned, focusing on Marshall's spot in the crowd. Marshall dropped his head, and shuffled to the closest group of vampires. Offering the tray like his only thought was the one the Franken-Non had planted in his head. Offering food and drink to creatures who intended to kill him before the night was done.

As Welch's voice filled the space again, Marshall dared another glance. Jace's attention was dancing over the room, assessing risks to his new Commanding Officer.

Not Liv. Not even another human. His loyalty stolen.

Welch, so much more than a cog in a human trafficking ring, in reality some vampire scientist and leader, strode across and joined Liv. She gave him a small smile, one of her intimate in-the-know ones reserved only for her family. The vampire lifted her hand, ignoring the scrapes and cuts, and kissed the back of it.

Marshall couldn't give in to his rage, the fury that the sight brought out of him. Needing to keep moving and planning, instead of storming the stage and carving the vampire's lips from his face, Marshall drifted from group to group. Getting ever closer to Liv. His heart pounding too hard. Too aware the vampires could hear, if they took a second to pay attention.

The vial of blood in his pocket felt like there was a flashing neon *Look Here* sign attached to it. Pointing out his guilt and his plan. He couldn't help the guys. Liv was it, chosen to receive Marshall's one vial.

He had to free her. She was the only one with a genuine chance of then freeing Matteo and Jace. Marshall only had one chance at waking her. He tuned out the excited crowd, and their cult leader scientist detailing plans to own the Company. Use Liv and the guys to bring Welch more C.O.s, to bend to his ugly use.

When he checked, Welch was off the platform and mingling, Liv beside him. The vampire showing her off to the other monsters. Proving she wasn't some zombie, calling over a server.

The woman held out here tray politely. "Hors d'oeuvre?"

Liv looked over the tray's selection. Then motioned a different server over, one that had tiny desserts instead of the awful tartare. "I prefer to indulge my sweet tooth."

Her voice hit Marshall like one of the mini-grenades. Welch's knowing laugh hit like another.

Fine, then. Marshall had a hell of a lot better understanding of what Liv enjoyed.

He made a wide circle to the bar, now deserted except for the bartender. Keeping an eye on the crowd, Marshall took over. Pouring tequila, which Liv did drink. Adding pomegranate syrup, for its camouflage ability and sweetness. He palmed the blood tube, using his thumb to pop off the rubber top, pouring the blood goo in and using a cocktail stirrer to mix. He stashed the empty tube back in his shirt pocket so no one accidentally found it.

He circled the room again like a good, invisible server, betting on the vampires being too interested in Welch, or only interested in the blood-wine. Heart slamming hard enough his breastbone ached, he approached the clique around Welch. With his head down, Marshall made it through, and stopped by Liv's elbow.

Some naïve, fairy-tale loving part of him still believed. Okay, Jace and Matteo hadn't recognized him despite their being friends. With Liv, what he and Liv had shared meant more, and went deeper. She'd *seen* Marshall in a way no one ever had. She knew the parts of him he hadn't guessed existed. She'd know him now, on some level.

Throat tight, he asked, "Drink, ma'am?" Ma'am, what he'd called her when they first met. The title Matteo teased her about, one she kinda hated, insisting Marshall call her Liv instead. Working so hard to convince him she was one of the good guys.

Those perfect eyes met his. And looked through him, same as Jace had. "I'm sorry. I don't care for wine."

Marshall held up his lure. "Pomegranate tequila cocktail?"

Oblivious to a bit of him burning away, her expression brightened. She accepted the glass.

Marshall held on a moment longer, under the guise of

making sure she had a secure hold on the cocktail. Allowing her fingers to touch his.

With the same results as meeting Jace's eyes, and signing to Matteo. Nothing. No recognition, no storybook flash of true love winning through, breaking the curse, and saving the day.

Welch, the new most hated thing on Marshall's list, smiled at the group of vampires, predatory and victorious.

"How did you manage such a level performance in so short a time? She seems freshly caught." The petite vampire who had snacked on a server earlier inserted herself in the conversation. Diamonds sparkled on her fingers, ears, and neck.

Maybe because buying an agent, and funding experiments, was in her budget, Welch gave her a respectful nod. "We don't waste time reinventing the wheel. We co-opted and used the Company's training regimen against them. With a pre-induction process we're still refining, plus the DNA breakthrough, we reinforce their existing training and beliefs. We've only changed one element—who they are loyal to and fight for. We study our subjects pre-capture, in order to tailor the process and deepen emotions already ingrained from birth.

"Olivia?" He caught her chin. "Does any of this distress you? Our discussion tonight or having humans present, and near my cryptid creation?"

Liv laid a hand on Welch's arm, the way she did the guys and Bruce—and Marshall. "Never doubt my, and my team's, loyalty to the cause. Sometimes, we have no choice but to do difficult things in service to a greater outcome."

"Human emotions make them ours. We own them on their deepest level." Welch patted Liv's hand.

The diamond vampire whispered, "Exquisite. I apologize for my skepticism all those years ago, as this is—"

595

Whatever else the vampires said was lost to Marshall. Eclipsed by a molten blue-white tide of rage like he'd never felt. Novel, and tempering him, like heating a new cast iron pan, to make it usable. Finish turning it into what it had been made to be.

His hands steadied. These trash vampires were stealing Liv's emotions, the thing that under it all made her Liv. This was so much worse than trying to steal and own her physically. Liv would *hate* this invasion, with everything in her.

She didn't deserve this treatment. Nobody did. Marshall wasn't letting it happen. Fuck vampires in general, and brilliant millionaire vampire scientists, and Frankenstein-psychic lab experiments. Marshall knew the real Liv, and her real emotions.

He stepped closer, interrupting the cozy circle, catching Liv's eye and enunciating clearly. "Your drink, ma'am. You don't like it?"

Marshall felt dozens of pairs of vampire eyes fasten on him. His pulse sped up, echoing in his ears. He raised his voice over the terrified whump-swoosh of his blood pumping out a survival warning. "I made this especially for you, ma'am. If you don't like it, I can make something else."

Liv raised the glass, taking a long sip before Marshall finished his question. Because Liv hated needlessly hurting people's feelings even more than she disliked being called ma'am. That kindness was a basic part of her that nothing could change or erase.

The air seemed to condense around Marshall, pressing in.

Vampires circled his group, like those nature specials where hyenas circled a bigger predator's guaranteed kill. Picking up on something that shouldn't exist—Marshall and his free will.

"It's very good. Thank you," Liv said into the pocket of silence Marshall had created.

"May I?" Confident of her answer, Welch took her glass. He sipped at the alcohol, then handed the remainder back to Liv.

"Well. That was interesting." Welch gave Marshall a slow once-over, nostrils flaring, taking in Marshall's scent. He finally snapped his fingers. "I know you. The spy who escaped during the attack on one of our business ventures. You did an excellent job not leaving a trace of what you knew or where you disappeared to. At least, until I heard someone fitting your description was at their Headquarters."

Marshall couldn't hide his twitch. If the vampire had heard about Marshall, that meant there was either a plant already inside the Company, or they were seriously watching his team's HQ. Possibly all the HQs Liv had mentioned.

"Humans and their useless emotions." The expensive diamond vampire strolled around Marshall. Inspecting him like he was a new purchase or toy. She reached for his head and he shied away.

His side slammed into a wall that turned out to be Matteo, stopping Marshall.

The vampire caught one of Marshall's curls, twirling it around her finger. The same way Liv played. Marshall jerked his head away, okay with the sharp pain in his scalp and losing hair. She didn't get to ruin Liv's thing.

The vampire didn't seem to care, wrapping the torn free curl around her ring finger. "Ooh, he matches my color scheme."

"Give me five minutes. Then we may be able to work out a deal, and you add him to your menagerie." Welch's amusement was evident. "I believe he's waiting for his doctored beverage to wake Olivia up. Even a few ounces of Subject Twelve's blood can't alter the work done on her though."

The spot where Marshall's hair had been torn out burned, probably bleeding. Another wound, at least not as bad as

Marshall's hand where he'd accidentally broken the tubes, stabbing himself and losing the Non blood that would've saved them all.

The cuts and blood which *had* helped Marshall. Marshall glanced away from the smug vampires, to the giant Franken-Non, feet from Welch.

Marshall went all in. He dove, more a clumsy fall, and snatched the knife from Matteo's thigh rig on the way down, ripping it free in a crackle of ruined Velcro. Marshall lurched sideways and grabbed Liv.

Liv gave Welch a raised brow, waiting for orders. Not worried about herself or Matteo.

"Your performance substantiates my guess. You aren't an agent, merely one of their civilian Assets." Welch shook his head, taking fake pity on Marshall. "You stand no chance of escaping. Olivia certainly won't leave with you."

"Whatever. I can hurt her. Damage your property." Jesus, he hoped Liv would forgive him.

"I will promptly heal her wounds."

"What if giving her your vampire blood makes her immune and not listen anymore? Huh? Your Franken-Non can't control you. What if *you* fix her up and then you can't control *her*?"

Welch raised a finger, stopping Matteo from grabbing Marshall. The agent halted immediately.

"One. To me, now."

Before Marshall's brain processed the words, he was on his toes, hanging from the Franken-Non's claws like an old shirt, the creatures speed more than anything in Marshall's worst-case imaginings.

Marshall still clutched the knife, the monster not bothering disarming him. It didn't consider him any more dangerous or important than Welch did.

Liv was the one to knock the knife from Marshall's grip, a quick, professional tap that left his hand and wrist numb.

That was okay. Getting her and the monster closer was the point. Marshall smashed his good hand against his chest, putting all his fury and determination in the blow.

The test tube shattered with a crunch, glass biting into his chest. Marshall jerked, popping a button enough to get his hand in, scooping up a handful of glass. Then stabbing the rubbery gray skin of the Franken-Non's arm, not even getting a snarl as the cryptid's skin split, the creature not reacting.

Marshall drug his hand across the arm holding him, covering his hand and the shards with peeled off gray skin, the creature's blood, and Marshall's. He swiped sideways, punching the whole gory mess against Liv's bare, bruised shoulder. Grinding, forcing glass and thick blue blood and his bright red into Liv, her skin shredding. He put his weight behind the blow, pressing the blood into her.

Praying to the one thing he truly believed in—Liv. This was it, his Hail Mary play. Like in CoW, the stealth avatar that'd either win the game or end it for him. The little blood from the captured Franken-Non, that Marshall had accidentally partially immunized himself with had sorta worked, keeping the monster's thoughts shoved to the side, letting Marshall fight back.

Now, Marshall had gathered as much blood and skin DNA from this Non as he could scrape off, and jammed gunk into Liv. That and whatever she shipped from the cocktail might break the hold over Liv.

Welch seemed to come to the same conclusion or was pissed that some of his super-secret process wasn't so secret anymore. Silver flooded the vampire's eyes, skin thinning to transparency, fangs popping down over blackened lips. "Silence him."

The weight of this Franken-Non's power fell over Marshall, like the nets the team had used to capture Kit. Heavy, slowing Marshall's movements. Making everything an effort—thinking, talking, breathing. Dragging Marshall's mind down into the monster.

Marshall focused on Liv. "C'mon, Liv. You know me. Marshall."

The invisible net tightened. His tongue felt too big and clumsy. Marshall forced words out. Putting his heart in them, because the vampire was right. Emotions, the good ones, those were what was important. The thing that made the real difference between monsters and not-monsters.

He threw all those good emotions at Liv, throwing her a lifeline. "It's Marsh. Maple leaves on snow." He fed back to her the pure awe she'd shared with him. "I belong to you. You belong to me. Remember? We're making a team and a family."

Frown lines wrinkled Liv's forehead. Her cheek dented in, biting it.

Darkness edged closer, dimming the lights, and the sight of heartless vampires watching the spectacle. Liv was silhouetted in the light even as the dark closed in, and Marshall wasn't stopping talking to her, not until his heart quit beating. "Me and you and *your* team, that you worked and fought for, helping Matteo and Jace live again. Your family no one else can take away, except these jerks are trying to. They're stealing your happiness and purpose."

Breathing becoming harder and harder. Marshall sucked in air, chest and lungs aching like they were being crushed, from the bottom up. He couldn't feel his toes or fingertips. "This...this is our compound and our city and—and our comic store. Our home. That thing you want as bad as I do."

The vampires' laughter mixed with the buzzing in Marshall's ears.

"One, proceed." Welch snapped his fingers.

The monster lifted Marshall higher. Its other clawed hand rested at his throat, then started a slow glide down to his chest. The exact same pattern as Liv's wounds after the mission, the monster getting ready to gut him. Open Marshall like a beef carcass, let his guts slide out and him die here, Liv and the guys watching, but Marshall all alone anyway.

Liv watched Marshall, head tilted. But only like he was an unusual occurrence at a party. She'd moved a few feet to the side, her hip now resting on one of the spotless linen-covered tables, littered with wine glasses and candles.

Marshall might lose, but he was going for what he wanted. Lips numb, he said it. The thing. "I love you, Liv. Always." The last came out slurred, the burn of claws slicing through his jacket the only thing he could feel.

The last thing he saw was Liv, lifting the cocktail, like she was toasting. He didn't know if it was to love, or his death.

iv

I RAN my finger around the rim of my glass, concentrating on the cool solidity of the crystal as I listened to—a server. A fellow human. One talking about snowstorms and home.

A nagging headache rose and fell, as if it was alive and fighting with something inside my skull. When the headache hit a lull, images exploded across the back of my eyelids. Snow. The mahogany and gold of Fall leaves. I remembered that training exercise.

Another memory fit itself in with the first. Pale skin over sturdy muscles, a sprinkling of fascinating freckles. My hand on a solid, warm chest. Soft auburn curls and sea-glass blue eyes. Those eyes looking at me as if I was the most wonderous, important thing in the world. Making my world complete. My home.

My shoulder throbbed, an immediate, real hurt. A match to the hurt in Marshall's voice.

Marshall. I had…misplaced him somewhere. His voice, too hoarse, was also real. *"I love you, Liv."* He ended on a gasp-whisper, barely audible. *"Always."*

I lifted my eyes and met his perfect blue ones, familiar and dear. I jolted out of my slouch, and liquid sloshed, splashing my hand. Bringing the equally familiar smell of tequila.

I flung the cocktail in an arc, anointing the creature holding Marshall in a grip meant to eviscerate him. Blood already stained Marshall's chef's jacket. Snatching the candle from the table centerpiece, I shoved it against the alcohol-drenched cryptid.

Fire sprang up, licking away at its gray skin, the creature making no sound, although vampires all around shrieked, clutching their heads and each other. Probably the oldest, and most resistant to the psychic attack, turned into a hissing, swearing mob, rushing by as they tried avoid the creature and the spreading fire.

Diving for the floor, I grabbed the knife I'd knocked from Marshall's hand, then launched upward, severing tendons in the cryptid's arm. Its hand flopped, useless, no longer attempting to open Marshall's chest.

I slashed again and Marshall fell, free from the creature's killing grip. I grabbed Marshall and rolled us both under the table, in a clumsy tangle of limbs. Kicking out, I knocked over and flipped the table sideways, a flimsy temporary shield. A hoarse, ugly wheeze blew across my cheek.

I turned my attention to Marshall. "Hey, stay with me here."

I patted across his head, down his chest, searching for wounds. My hand came away red, and I jerked, buttons on his shredded jacket popping. Dread, worse than when I'd realized I had walked my team into a trap, swamping me. "No, no, no. Do not do this."

Marshall coughed, and levered up on his elbow.

My heart, the one that had threatened to shatter, gave a hard, relieved thump. I tore his ragged shirt the rest of the way. A dozen tiny, mostly superficial cuts clustered over the left side of his chest. A nasty row of claw marks ran from under his collarbone, ending over his pecs. Ugly, but not deep. "Damn it."

"S'okay." Marshall coughed, then inhaled, deep and long, restoring oxygen. "You woke up and saw me, and it's okay."

The guilt and horror threatening to choke me said otherwise, but we weren't safe enough to stop and give in. "Jace and Matteo?"

Marshall nodded his head toward the crowd. A tiny measure of horror receded—my brothers were still alive. The whole sequence of events, where we were, was foggy. Us storming into a building, but not the one we were in now. Then stopping.

Heat licked the tablecloth behind us, close to my calf. "Can you stand?"

Marshall nodded and held out a bandaged hand. I grabbed on and hauled us both to our feet. Shaking my head, I tried knocking free the memory of the science complex's schematics I'd memorized for the mission. Which building and wing we were in, entrances and exits. Moving us so our backs were to a support pillar, I scanned the chaos.

Vampires and humans were everywhere, the vampires rushing around also looking for exits, the humans mostly standing or huddling together, faces looking lost. A few were already coughing from the smoke. At least they were all in white, and easy to identify.

I didn't want Marshall out of my sight, but he was part of the team, and damn good in a vampire crisis. "Get everyone human. Side exit." I pointed, knife blade catching the fire light. Marshall nodded and sprinted for the largest group.

I kicked, sending the flaming table rolling into a pocket of vampires. The long, red carpet-worthy train of one's dress caught fire. She stumbled and fell into another, his jacket sleeve igniting.

When I spun to search the crowd, Marshall was herding the original group of people, plus a handful more he'd gathered, aiming them all at the exit. All of them now looking to him. He gave me a fast thumbs up, shoving the herd toward freedom.

While under Welch's control, I'd still retained all my knowledge of the Company, my training, the guys, and my role. I had been the one to order Jace and Matteo to act as personal guards for Welch, the two obeying me exactly as they had before we were under Welch's psychic influence. The only fuzzy parts were my personal life, time spent gift shopping with my sisters, balling with the guys, touching Marshall.

Vaulting to the stage, I raised my voice in the Company's call and response, the phrase one of the first things cadets learned.

A deep bellow answered from my right, another from straight ahead. Matteo and Jace, coherent and alive.

Jumping to the floor, I laid the knife on a chair, careful to keep only the hilt touching the wood. I couldn't lose any of the gore coating the blade. Whipping my tank top off, I stomped on another chair, breaking a leg free, tied the cotton shirt around my makeshift torch, and dipped it into the fire.

Grabbing the knife in my other hand, I joined the fight. Shoving the torch into anything fanged or not in white, blade flashing after, hitting throats and chests. Working to find and free my team.

The room narrowed to the increasing heat, the flex of muscles, and spray of blood. I called again.

A solid weight wedged against my hip, barking out our

call and response, saving Matteo from a reflex slash. He roared out the call again. This time, Jace's response came from a foot away.

Our partner emerged from the smoke, whirling to put his back to ours. Taking the risk, leaving my back exposed, I turned and grabbed Matteo's arm. "Don't move," I ordered, in the same tone I'd used for the last year, to call them to attention, ask for input on missions, talk with them about lost loved ones, and joke about terrible movies.

I shoved the Company sweater past his elbow, sliced along the outside of his arm, then pressed my palm over the wound, smearing the creature blood in deeper. I spun to Jace, his sleeve already cut open, and did the same, rubbing the last of the blood gunk in. Hoping it was enough.

"Look at me, now." Two sets of eyes fastened on me. Both scowling. "Think about—foul fake-mango sports drinks. Skin care regimens. The impossibility of ever beating Kimi's CoW record."

They stared at me. Giving me nothing. No clue they remembered our real life, outside of fighting.

Then Matteo frowned. "Hey, have faith. We'll take Kimi out one day."

Jace scrubbed at his face, and added, "Yeah. What he said." He rubbed at his temples, nearly taking an eyebrow off with the blade he was holding. "Also, *what the fuck.*"

"How do we feel about vampires and serving them?" I shoved the torch into one's open mouth as it came at us, frantic with pain and after blood to heal.

Their answer was Jace hammering a punch to the vampire's stomach, doubling it over, as Matteo swung, his blade cleaving its skull.

We flowed into formation, and created a tripod, knives hacking through vampire flesh, fewer and fewer left in our path, many already burning too quickly to repair themselves.

"The Master and that psi-cryptid?" I got out between kicking a silver-eyed vampire's knee, it going down with a satisfying crunch, Jace's machete taking its head.

"Negative," echoed from both my teammates.

"They are now our objective." The creature had to be eliminated, as did its creator. The Master had enjoyed giving us his speech about vampire superiority before he tossed us to the creature. Allowing them to escape meant repeating this nightmare in another Region.

Time was against us though, fire climbing the organza wrapped columns, jumping from table to table, claiming anything flammable. The sprinkler system rained a fine mist, but it was no match for the inferno I'd brought to life.

Smoke thickened around us, and instinct demanded I grab the guys and go. Get away from a molten death. Heat not from the fire but from the rush of fear-adrenaline prickled my chest and throat.

I closed my eyes for a second, facing my old phobia, and acknowledging it was still with me, but didn't have to rule me. Marshall fought his fears, and I wasn't doing any less.

"I'm going to try something, locating the cryptid." Relying on our bond, I trusted Matteo and Jace, my brothers and partners, to keep claws and fangs away, not to let me trip and end up screaming as we died the most horrible way I could imagine.

I concentrated, blocking out smoke, the death shrieks, and scorching heat. Isolating the weak throb hanging on in my head, the creature's influence still there, waiting for me to weaken. Latching on to it, I turned, following the pull. Believing in me, the guys moved in synch. No questions or hesitations.

The vague pull turned into a full-on tug. I opened my eyes to a towering hulk, swathes of charred black skin mixed with its normal gray. The injured monster was ramming through vampires and furniture, clearing a path in a parody of our teamwork, the Master sheltered behind it.

They were only yards from the front reception area and a wall of plate glass the creature would rip through like damp paper. Unholy yipping and howls reached us from the outdoors. Muted by the walls and fire, but closing in. Beside me, Matteo swore.

The Master's half-dozen ghoul and windigo pairs, that shouldn't exist, but did. They had formed an honor guard when we'd arrived, funneling us into the lab as our will dissolved with each step. The bit of us not yet under the psi-cryptid's control fighting and losing, forced to watch.

"If they get inside—" Jace's voice was rough from the smoke.

"We're fucked," Matteo finished for him.

They were right. My arms ached from the non-stop fighting, sweat rolling to soak my waistband, and into every cut and scrape. Our lungs burning from the smoke, fast approaching intolerable levels. We couldn't hold off ghouls and windigos that were fighting in unison, especially since the psi-creature had stripped them of their sense of self-preservation.

Welch was flinging them at us, on a kamikaze mission. Time to finish this. Like we were one unit, we surged forward. Aimed at the biggest threat we'd ever faced, the pull cresting as we got close enough to see it.

The creature was moving slower, but like our captured version, it was already regenerating. One arm still hung useless. The first, that I'd severed tendons on, flashed at my face, claws red with human and vampire blood.

We split, the guys flanking it on each side as I dropped and rolled. Slicing at the backs of its legs, hamstringing it. Close to a ton of flesh and bloodlust wavered.

I scrambled to stand, slipping in water and ash, sprawling

flat instead. The creature stumbled, sliced muscles and tendons failing, bulk crashing downward.

Matteo's strong grip locked around my elbow, heaving me out of the way.

The monster hit the floor, but wasn't truly down. It rolled, good arm slashing, claws catching my boot and pining me for a heartbeat.

Jace's machete flashed between us, driving deep into burned flesh and through to bone. Blue goo splashed, mixing with the water.

Matteo locked his knee, and I used his leg as a springboard, and launched, blade out. Burying my knife in the thing's eye, all the way up to my elbow. Angle wrong to bite me, its teeth clicked together enough to pinch skin, scouring a line down my shoulder.

I wrenched my knife free and plunged it into the other eye, until it hit bone. Jace's blade joined mine, punching through the misshaped socket into brain. The creature's psychic shriek echoed, ping-ponging around in our heads, only the grip on my knife keeping me upright-ish. The Master vampire's scream joined his monster's, one pummeling us from inside our brain, the other our eardrums,

Welch wavered, and fell against the windows, the link between him and his dying creature still intact, dragging him through its pain. A sharp snap cut over the wail. A crack traveled through the safety glass, like an ice flow breaking up.

The crimson of windigo eyes shone from the darkness on the other side of the glass. A yard away, and closing fast, their baying drowning out the injured vampire and the roar of the fire.

Matteo latched onto my arm again, hauling me to my feet. He did the same with Jace, on my other side. Then flipped the short punch-blades from his boots. I snatched one out of the air, Jace snagging the other.

We closed in on the last of our prey. Welch snarled, his back to the glass. Fanaticism gleamed from his silver eyes, nothing left to lose and readying to take us with him. We met in a clash of knives and vampire claws, fists thudding. No finesse on either side.

He snapped, fangs centimeters from my neck. I bent my head, tucking it into my shoulder, only giving him a face full of hair. I'd only get the one shot with the short knife. He grabbed hair and jerked me close, fangs glancing off my scalp. With the last of my energy, choking om smoke, I angled my hand and shoved.

The blade slid between his ribs. Not long enough to hit his heart. On either side of me, Jace and Matteo hammered punches and slashes. I threw my weight against the vampire, yelling, dumping all my anger and fear for my team into it. Ribs broke, and I fell against its chest, blade caught between us, finally ramming into his heart and through the tough muscle.

I let go, shoving away from the Master's chest, just avoiding his snap, jaws where my ear had been a heartbeat earlier. Skidding in the swamp of water and debris, I fought to stay upright.

Bloody froth, with that freakish blue tint that had to have come from the cryptid, coated the vampire's lips. Even as the silver in his eyes faded, he held onto the hate. Using his last breaths, he choked out, "Your Company is infected. I won't live to see it, but its already dying, right under your noses."

His eyes went back to human brown, and he fell in a graceless heap.

Exhausted and clumsy, we whirled to face another threat.

Windigos hit the windows. Standing on their hind legs, muzzles against the pane, and clawed front feet digging at the glass like they were digging through dirt. The cracks fast forwarded, spreading through the entire panel, bits already chipping, leaving tiny openings. What had to have been the horde's alpha reared back, then jerked forward, slamming both paws against a weak spot.

The center of the window shattered, air rushing in, fire rising higher. The windigo stuck its muzzle through the hole.

The canid's head exploded. A delicate spray of blood and brain decorated the window shards. The rest of its body heaved, speared on vampire claws.

Our vampires. Vee flung the carcass off, and hit the ground in a crouch, black jacketed back to us, snarling at the ghoul attached to the dead 'digos leash. The ghoul growled and snapped wide jaws.

Then shook its head like a dog shaking of water. It retreated, not taking eyes off the threat in front of it. Finally turning to bolt for the desert.

The neat snap of rifle shots popped, an accompaniment to the growls and whines. The rest of Vee's team appeared, cutting down confused windigos and fleeing ghouls.

The entry door disappeared in a squeal of twisted hinges, Stavros heaving the metal and glass to crash into the landscaping. Bruce's swearing rushed in with the fresh air, Stavros' "Ninōs?" coming a split second later.

I grabbed the guys by soaked shirts, propelling them outside ahead of me, into the blessed coolness of the dry night. I propped a hand against Stavros shoulder, coughing, and he grabbed me.

Using his hold to stand on my tiptoes, I located Vee, stretching and shaking her arms out amid the downed cryptids. "Do not even think of claiming official primary credit for this mission. You guys are only mopping up our leftovers."

From where he squatted, upper torso bare, using his

slightly less filthy shirt to scrub his ash and blood covered face, Matteo said, "You guys are strictly junior varsity B-team."

"True, that," Jace said, half-coughing, half-laughing. Both laughed even harder as Josh tried arguing with our logic.

I ignored them and let go of our father, elbowing Bruce and his pat-down off, searching for the last member of our team. I had sent him and the humans outside. But outdoors also included the ghouls and windigos, and I'd forgotten about them. I spun in a circle, checking and hoping. The only bodies strewn over the landscaping were cryptids though.

The parking lot was empty, except for what looked like my truck in the neighboring lot, Vee's SUV, and a big white box truck with a catering logo emblazoned on the cab door.

Heart going faster than during the fight, I ran for the truck. Able to breathe again, Jace and Matteo were a step behind me. We skidded to a stop, my palms slapping the metal side. The rear door didn't budge when Matteo heaved at it, locked from the inside.

"Marshall!" I put every ounce of command in the word.

"It's us," Jace yelled from right beside my ear. "The vampire and that lab experiment are toast, man. We gotta haul ass. That lab may blow, and this truck is in the blast radius."

Like talking about it brought it on, a boom echoed from the building. I banged on the truck. "Marshall, please. I swear on—on the sanctity of our B-movie nights that we're us again."

In microscopic increments, the door inched up, then stopped. Marshall, blood and gore streaked, hair sticking up in clumps, knelt on one knee in the sliver of open space. Heartbreaking suspicion written all over his face, while humans in white jackets and shirts and one in a suit with no tie huddled behind him, sheltering between metal racks. "Prove it."

"Man, we don't have time—"

I cut Matteo off, bending to peer into the truck. "How?"

"What are you, Kimi, and Vee getting Kantor for his birthday?"

"An adult sized Bride of Dracula onesie. Kimi ordered a life-size cardboard cutout of the British chef who's name we aren't allowed to say, to put it on. He and Bruce loathe each other."

Marshall stood, hauling the door the rest of the way up, and waved the truck's refugees out. "Go. Follow the soldiers, and hurry."

I stepped aside, letting confused and frightened civilians pour out, scanning them for obvious injuries. Kimi quickly headed them, in now-orderly lines, to the SUVs and our first-aid kits. Vee was already on the phone, calling in our local LEO Assets to back up our story of a designer drug-fueled party gone wrong.

Marshall jumped out of the truck and I started for him, needing to touch him and prove he was really here and not skewered on a monstrous cryptid's claws, and somehow apologize. I made it one step before I jerked to a stop, as the wiry little cryptid we'd captured hopped out behind Marshall.

And me without one damn weapon. No way had we come this far to lose one of our own to some stealthy animal.

"Marshall, *move*." I whirled to face Vee's team. "Josh, knife."

He tossed it to me, sprinting our way, and going for his backup piece.

When I spun back, Marshall had his hand out, warning me away. "No, Liv." He tucked the cryptid behind him, out of sight, tension pulling his shoulders tight. "This is one of those times I need *you* to pay attention and listen. That goes for all of you," he said, as the guys joined Josh.

Every bit of my training warred with my promise to Marshall, that he was part of this team, and had the same right as Jace or Matteo to have his opinion heard. Tonight should have ended any possibility of leniency toward anything non-human on my part. Whatever name Marshall called it, the thing was still a cryptid.

The rules said what Marshall had done in releasing a cryptid, and now preventing a fellow agent or team from eliminating the escapee, was treason. His actions had undercut our mandate to protect humanity. The terms set out by Oversight were detailed, strict, and unbreakable.

Bending wasn't breaking, though.

If I'd only gone by the rules, my sister would be dead, and our adopted father along with her. We would've lost Bruce, too shattered by Vee's loss to keep going.

Instead of treason and putting humans in jeopardy, Marshall, and presumably, the slight creature, had done the exact opposite. Somehow, they had shown up here, done the impossible and destroyed the psychic cryptid's hold on me, allowing me to save our team, and the civilians.

"I'm listening." I owed Marshall that.

"You aren't hurting Kit. I could tell you he's the reason I got here, and helped, and kept all the other humans safe, but that's not the important part." A squeak easily translated as offended disagreement came from behind Marshall. He glanced over his shoulder, tone apologetic. "Okay, sure, it is still important. Definity." He faced me again. "The most important part though, is you either trust me, same as you do Matteo and Jace, not strings attached, or you don't."

I tilted my head back. Stars still laced the sky, but the horizon was a lighter navy, dawn flirting with the night. Smoke spiraled to join the stars.

The air wavered to my right as Vee materialized, her long ponytail lashing my shoulder. "The one boomer was the extent of the danger. Stavros and I got the fire contained. What are we doing—" She went from conversational to predatory, head whipping left. Taking a long inhale, she held the breath, sampling the scent that caught her attention.

I flung my arm out, blocking her lunge as she identified the smell as a cryptid. We both grunted from the impact. I shifted a hair further into her path, so that she had to focus on me instead of the prey she'd discovered, also bringing Josh in on the conversation. "How did you know to get here at all, much less in what? Three hours?"

There was only one possible answer. The rest of our extended family needed to hear that answer, though.

"An hour-fifty-eight. Ish," she said.

"No police or State Troopers, huh?"

"B was going too fast to be sure." Some of the vampire dropped, more of my sister coming out.

As the rest of the team arrived, Kimi last, since she'd passed out water to the confused civis, I prompted Vee. "How did you get the intel that sent you here?"

Bruce shoved into the group and the conversation. "Your roommate called. Repeatedly." Since he'd already checked the guys out, Bruce resumed his interrupted job, examining me, bitching under his breath when he hit the glass shards and claw mark combo, and I winced. "What the made that wound pattern?"

"A now deceased Master vampire, a creature that Oversight needs to take apart and examine in meticulous detail, and Marshall."

Bruce exhaled, and didn't swear at Marshall. "Because?"

"Because Marshall intuited that the creature's—"

"Franken-Non," Marshall said.

"Thank you. Marshall intuited that the Franken-Non

blood, ingested or injected, conferred a measure of resistance to its compulsion. When it was taking us over, and we were still aware enough to understand what was happening—it was one of the worst experiences I've ever gone through on a mission." I shivered, that violation and inability to move or fight back too raw, as Matteo grunted his agreement. "It was pure malevolence, pouring into my head, and there was nothing I could do to slow or stop it."

Speaking to Marshall while still corralling the team, I said, "Sorry about the tequila, by the way." Marshall was *brilliant*. This had to be enough to secure Oversight's permission for him to join.

"S'okay. I don't think the cocktail would've been strong enough, even if you'd finished it. Guess the Franken-Non we —" he paused "—the one you guys caught, wasn't grown and as powerful."

I hated the pause, that I had made Marshall feel as though he didn't belong with us. "Hero-ing isn't an exact science."

A pale, elfin face topped with reddish-brown fur popped into view, ducking under Marshall's arm. "*I'm* the hero. He only helped."

Then the cryptid—the cryptid kid, because he was so a kid, attitude and all—disappeared behind Marshall again as everyone stood in stunned silence, then erupted, talking at and over each other.

I held Marshall's gaze, putting fingers to my lips, and whistled. The blast caused Vee to give me a *was that really necessary* glare, and Stavros to sigh at the assault on his super hearing. "As lead C.O. on this mission, I have the floor for now. Marshall?"

"Yeah?"

"The cryptid—"

"Kit," he corrected me firmly.

"Right. Kit's role in this series of events?" I tried letting

Marshall see that I trusted him, and I'd been wrong to doubt him.

"Kit came back after—you know. After I let him go."

I ignored Bruce's colorful description of Marshall's parentage and I.Q.

Marshall did as well, raising his voice. "Kit came back and warned me that you were walking into a trap. That the other Franken-Non was a plant. Then he told me where to find you."

From behind his human shield, Kit piped up. "I *got* you here, not just told you. And waited and made sure you got out, even though you said to leave, but you never abandon your flock, even when they're being dumb. *And* told you about vampires drinking Franken-Non blood."

Kimi's rough laugh carried, appreciating the kid's highly advanced snark level. I sort of had to agree with her.

"Uh, yeah. All that." Marshall's attention stayed glued on me, the way mine was on him. "I told you, Liv—Kit's not bad. He's not a killer. He helped even when he didn't have to, when he had everything to lose. Even after what you did to him."

"Kind of like you."

Marshall closed his eyes, resignation and hurt plain. Only the fact that if I moved, Stavros and the guys might take it wrong and go for Kit, stopped me from throwing myself on Marshall for the world's longest hug, and promising him I would do better.

His shoulders squared, and meet my gaze. "Do what you have to, arrest me, or send me to wherever you sent my old human boss. I know I broke rules, lots of them. You can have Stavros do that thing with draining most of my blood and scrambling my memories, and drop me on the side of the road, and Kantor put out word for no kitchen to ever hire me. But you aren't hurting Kit or putting him in a cage."

"For fuck's sake." Bruce finished his exam and jerked a thumb at someone, probably Josh. "Let's get this done, finish cleaning you two idiots up—" that would be Matteo and Jace "—otherwise Liv will never get around to having those wounds cleaned. My threshold for unnecessary, self-sacrificing, bullshit is at an all-time low."

Bruce understood what I'd decided, and wasn't questioning my authority, or love and dedication to my family. I smiled, already feeling lighter. "You're cooking. Marshall earned a day off."

"I was part of this damn mission, too."

"Agreed. However, Marshall did the heavy lifting."

Bruce snorted. Which was a yes.

"I don't—Liv, I've got no idea what that means." Marshall's determined mask slipped, revealing the soul deep pain, twin to mine, at the idea of him leaving.

"It means, you had me at 'Our comic shop'. You aren't being reported to the Company. As far as we are concerned, you broke no rules. I know you'd never betray us or doing anything to put us or others in harm's way." I channeled the emotions I wasn't able to say yet, into the short explanation. That he had been right. That I still cared. That I was sorry, and would work to prove it and regain his trust.

"Oh." Vee's soft sniffle meant she understood, too.

"What about rules, and my bio-code is gonna show for the torture roo—the annex—and the gates. There's probably footage of me and Kit on that security camera, and—" he went to shove his hand through his hair, then grimaced and quit when he hit a gooey patch. "And there's Kit."

Kimi wiggled in, signing, "Consider your digital footprint gone. I've got your back."

She understood, too.

"Special dispensation for heroes." I frowned, cataloging what we might have between both SUVs and my truck that we could put together as supplies for the Kit, when Marshall took him to wherever he'd originally meant for the kid to go.

They'd be too large, but Kimi's go-bag clothes would still fit Kit better than Marshall's hoodie. I couldn't remember if there was an ATM nearby, to grab some cash. "Our behavior was so off from handling the creature, that I didn't file complete reports, or mention anything except the creature. The kid was never at the compound, or here."

"I was so!" Kit darted in front of Marshall, hands balled into fists, eyes suspiciously watery and red. "I am too a hero. Plus, heroes get paid, so I should too."

"Come again?" I folded my arms, holding a smile in, as Jace muttered an awed, "*Damn*, kid."

The boy retreated beside Marshall this time, instead of behind him, braver with Marshall as his protector. Which is exactly what Marshall was, not only toward Kit, but toward all of us. "I need a job and money. You—" He pointed at all of us "—you don't know much, and you all mess up. A lot. The predator Nons had an inside spy. You need one too. Humans are pretty slow." He folded his arms, mimicking me, although sleeves trailed past his hands. "You need me. Like, a specialist."

"Ah. I see." Even aside from my gratitude for him saving my brothers, and aiding in exposing a far-reaching project to take down the Company, I was starting to like the kid. He was a smaller, more feral version of Kimi. "To be clear— you'd like an official position?"

"Yeah. The one with benefits and stuff. Asset."

"Daaamn. How'd he even know about that?" Matteo muttered.

"Told you. I'm smart and I know things. I hear way better, too. You need me."

Stavros placed a hand on my shoulder, pure fatherly concern now. "While the boy has earned our aid, you cannot be considering this. You are on trial with Oversight, no less than we are."

Bruce's response was non-stop swearing. Vee turned to me, eyes cartoon-huge. "I'm all for livening up HQ's day, but maybe take a beat here."

I looked to Marshall. "Do we trust this kid? Do you trust him with your family's safety and security?"

Marshall's face softened, either at my acknowledging Kit was a kid, not an it, my calling us family, or my getting smart and asking his opinion. "Yeah. Yes. Kit is solid. I vouch for him. I'll be responsible for him. I swear. I'd never put you, and Matteo, and Jace in danger." He swept the crowd. "Any of you. Even Kantor."

I checked with Jace and Matteo. "Well?"

Matteo scrubbed a hand over his scalp. "After all that went down tonight, there's no question. I trust Marshall's word. Marshall trusts this crypt—"

"Kit! I have a name, you know." The kid certainly knew how to make himself heard, for sure. Bruce even grunted in grudging approval.

"Uh, Kit." Matteo course corrected. "I vote yes."

"We got vampires in the family, so why not?" Jace shrugged, calculations going on in his head the same as when planning a sniper shot on the fly. He recognized the implications of our discoveries, and how a double agent benefited us, meaning both *us,* in the sense we were Company, and us, as in our and his brother's teams. "I like not being some vampire's experimental puppet, and a lot of that is thanks to Marsh and the kid. We're gonna have to finesse a pitch to Oversight first, then HQ."

I came clean. "Kimi and I have some ideas. We worked up a number of potential eventualities regarding pitfalls, changing circumstances, and leverage should we need to address Oversight again. None precisely for this scenario, but we have a place to start."

Vee gave a victory squeal. "I knew you two were up to something even more off-book than our daily off-book-ness. I'm putting my faith in Kimi's creativity. Which is another word for crazy-brilliant, and invading all sorts of files and privacy, and Liv's equally crazy-brilliant way with rules."

"We made most of the plan outlines with vampires in mind, but we can pivot," Kimi signed. "The shortage of agents mixed with the surge in cryptid activity was a key point for us. We need more boots on the ground, immediately, and a theoretical alliance is the most realistic avenue."

Bruce looked between the two of us, and Kimi angled enough to speed-sign, "A vegetarian humanoid cryptid who is also a child and undeniably cute will be more palatable, since the first stage is introducing a cryptid as an ambassador, *not* a fighter."

"The groundwork is laid. This is us being proactive, as opposed to continually reacting to a problem," I said.

Bruce had pulled the Star of David pendant out, and was compulsively running his fingers over it. At last, he tucked it back under his shirt, a tiny measure of the terror he lived with siphoned off. "Fine."

He was trusting me despite my martyr status, the way he'd entrusted me with his blackmail stash.

Only Vee's being occupied for the last few minutes, talking Stavros around to our way of thinking, had kept her out of the conversation. Now, she gave a tiny nod. We didn't need to discuss why she and all the guys had unconsciously softened to Kit, it having little to do with the kid's heroics.

Proving me right, Stavros addressed Kit. "You have no family? None of your kind here?"

They hadn't missed the thing about Kit needing money and food. Or his defending his actions saying you never left your flock behind. The worst thing any of us could think of was being without our year-mates, and most especially, our team siblings, our family. Stavros was nearly as bad.

Kit squeezed tight against Marshall's leg at attracting Stavros' attention, looking up to Marshall, who gave him a nod. "My flock is gone. I've looked and looked, and chirped, and..." He lifted a shoulder, trying to seem tough and unaffected.

"I can't make promises as to what your role will be, but I'll begin a report detailing your help, and I will put my weight behind creating some type of liaison role, with you reporting to me. It will take time, but it will happen," I promised.

Kit needed a sense of security as much as he did food and supplies. Before Vee came back to us, while Stavros was teaching her how to control the vampire virus, they'd had unofficial, primitive bases. One of those might work as a means to get Kit off the street and into a safer environment.

"Nuh-uh. I report to Marshall. He's the only one I trust," Kit said.

I caught Matteo and Jace sharing a guilty expression. Kit had every reason not to trust us.

"You can trust Liv now. Seriously." Marshall laid a hand on the kid's shoulder, very much as Stavros had with me earlier.

"No way. Better careful than a dead little bat. Marshall or no deal." His pointy chin jutted out. "And Marshall feeds me, too. Until I get cash."

Kimi shoulder bumped me and signed, "I like him."

"You would." It seemed my crew was suddenly at full strength.

Though I had a major apology to figure out. I hoped Marshall hadn't changed my status from someone he loved and needed, to his platonic teammate and Commanding Officer.

CHAPTER 74

$\mathcal{L}$iv

GETTING the civis taken care of, Cleaners called and briefed on specifics, then home, took more time than usual.

It didn't help that the compound bio-security wasn't designed to accept a long term free-ranging cryptid, especially one zooming all around the base like a hyped-up road runner. The non-stop emergency alerts had taken both Kimi and Jace's skills to bypass into accepting our newest resident's DNA.

Kit was here since Marshall had refused to leave the kid behind, out on the streets, even with money, and a go-bag of supplies. Honestly, after seeing the rail-thin kid as a kid, drowning in Marshall's hoodie—which, hadn't figured out what that was about—I couldn't bear to leave him to fend for himself, either.

I also had a lot to make up for. It didn't matter that I was under the Franken-Non's influence—I had hurt Kit, physically and emotionally. He didn't have his family to comfort him and help him heal. There had to have been other kids in his group, and whether they were captives in the vampires' other facilities, or dead, Kit's siblings were lost to him.

I saw that same realization on Matteo and Jace's faces. Kit had lost his brothers and sisters the same as they had, and to violence, possibly even to the same creature. There was a kinship forming.

The guys' losses were fresh enough that I wouldn't bet on Oversight getting their hands on the kid now if they tried. The guys were already seeing him the same way they did our cadets, whom they'd spent months with while healing from their injuries after their teams' massacres.

For now, my report to Oversight would detail the mission, and Kit's part in aiding us. They could make the call on whether our official report to HQ included the cryptid child or not. For now, we weren't mentioning that Kit was ever on the base, much less currently residing here. This was one more secret to keep, and one more risk for both of our teams to juggle.

Both of my reports would include Marshall, and his brilliance and loyalty in coming up with a rescue plan, and executing it despite his slim chances of success. That he had gone in alone among a mob of vampires and cryptids to save his team was pure Company. This rescue was enough for Oversight to agree—part of the testing for adding a new member was to ensure they didn't hinder the team's performance. There was no arguing Marshall had enhanced ours.

There was also the Franken-Non to deal with. Matteo had filled it so full of tranquilizers that I'd had to concentrate to see its chest moving while he drew its blood. We'd all been immunized with its blue gunk ASAP, and everyone's headache was history.

Oversight, then HQ, had been notified the moment the

house system was tamed, and Kimi had erased the evidence of Kit being held here, Marshall taking him away, and Kit returning. That this new mega-cryptid was lab grown, and had terrifying powers, was keeping both sections of the Company occupied for now. The Cleaners had taken the dead Franken-Non's blood and DNA, and the Lab was synthesizing a version in order to immunize all Company members and Assets.

In other words, I was out of excuses, and it was time to woman-up. I hadn't had the chance or privacy to speak to Marshall since finding him sheltering the human victims in the truck. After checking the kitchen, his room, and the gaming pit, I climbed the ladder steps, lifting the trapdoor.

Bingo.

Out platform swing looked to now be a bedroom. Kit had done that next-to-unconscious sleep truly exhausted kids did, and the pillows were mounded around him like a nest. Marshall was draping a blanket around the boy.

I chewed on the inside of my cheek, then crept out, careful not to let the door bang, going to the far side of the roof, in the corner where the walkway wall met this end of the house.

Propping against the wrought iron railing, I stayed quiet and out of the way. The kid might not be comfortable sleeping indoors, but I suspected the real reason he was out here was that he wasn't comfortable sleeping indoors with us.

We'd begun the steps to make our behavior up to Kit. Now I needed to do the same with Marshall, whether he saw me as his romantic partner, or only C.O., no matter that I was pretty sure it was the latter.

When Marshall finished tucking Kit in, he halted a body length away from me, hands in his pockets. "Hey."

"May I?" I motioned at his chest. Vee had donated a few

drops and taken care of his wounds, and ours. Facts didn't hold much sway though. I'd see Marshall hanging from the creature's claws in my nightmares.

"It's good. I swear." He didn't come closer.

I sighed and slumped against the solid stucco wall behind me. If he saw me as a sort-of-friend now, I had no one but myself to blame. Even before the creature's manipulation, I hadn't been willing to commit, and say what Marshall needed to hear. An issue he couldn't, or wouldn't, ignore now, not on top of all the other drama. I'd ignored the chance to tell him so many things, and this was my punishment—Marshall distancing himself from me.

"I deserve that. I wouldn't want me around right now, either. Certainly not checking out your shirtless self." I sucked at romantic apologies. I should've cornered Bruce and demanded his expertise and how-to-apologize-for-being-an-epic-ass cheat sheet.

"What? Why wouldn't I want that?" Marshall moved within touching distance, brow furrowed.

"Why would you? Parts are hazy and disjointed, but there are enough memories left to know I was awful to the guys and you. Beyond awful to you. I said some unforgivable things."

"That was all Franken-Non."

"I didn't talk to you, after I swore I would. I turned my back on you, I didn't trust you, I didn't keep my end of our deal." A stupid tear escaped, running down my chin and I swiped it away. "I didn't even recognize you. I didn't defend you, here or against a room full of vampires taunting and threatening you."

Familiar, protective hands caught my arms. Marshall pulled me against him and wrapped his arms tight around me. I buried my face in the curve of his neck.

"Hey, no," he said. "We've both—I didn't want to assume.

Once the mission was wrapping up, you said I was part of the team, and Kit's liaison. Not anything about us, or where we're at now. We didn't agree on some stuff before all this went down, about some cryptids deserving a chance before being executed, and all."

"I'm so, so sorry," I whispered. "I nearly lost you and wouldn't have even *known*." More tears trailed down my face, making wet splotches on Marshall's superhero tee.

"Shh." He fit me in, chin on top of my head.

"I can't. I could've lost you, and not gotten the chance."

"For what?" Marshall went still, and stiff against me. "What chance?"

Saying it meant that it was real. That I was going all in, involving my heart and accepting the possibility of losing all that again, when I'd only now recovered from the last time.

I'd recovered because of Marshall. My fears, in comparison to Marshall's bravery, him risking his life even after he thought I'd abandoned him, and him still fighting for us—it wasn't even a fair contest. I could be a different kind of brave for Marshall.

Dread and hope balled together in my stomach. "I almost lost the chance to tell you that I love you. I do."

The noise he made rocked us both, and his fingers tunneled into my hair. We clung to each other, relearning the feel of the other, taking and giving comfort.

Marshall loosened his hold enough for me to see his face. His eyes were damp too, but his smile welcomed and warmed me the way the first rays of a desert sunrise did, everything new and hopeful. "I love you, too. You already know that. But I do, and I don't mind saying it as much as you need me to. I like saying it."

"You're all in on this, and us, even after monsters and almost certainly a war on the horizon? And I took your phone?"

"Always." He bent and I raised the inch so our lips met. Every bit of his strength and belief in us flowed through where we touched.

I matched him, sealing our promise to each other. I ran my hand under his shirt, scrunching soft cotton up as I went. Fingers gliding over hot skin and muscles, double-checking that he was whole, and not hurting, and that he had someone who cared now.

He jerked his shirt over his head and out of our way, then put my hand back, pressing my palm flat over his heart. "Go ahead. This is all yours."

CHAPTER 75

M arshall

MARSHALL SCOOTED THE SQUAT, gnomey-looking statue wearing a Christmas scarf—Chupacabra on a Counter, their version of Elf on a Shelf—to safety, as Jace and Josh careened off walls, each vying for the winning headlock in their wrestling face-off.

It didn't help that Matteo was taking bets, as Kimi rained red and green glitter over them, while also recording the entire event. Marshall wasn't getting near that blackmail-in-progress.

He also nudged the eggnog bowl behind the remnants of the cookie platter, the eggnog mostly vodka with a splash of cream and nutmeg tossed haphazardly at it, Kimi and Liv's version of the holiday tradition. Which Bruce kept pouring down the sink, and the sisters kept refilling as soon as his back was turned.

There was a giant, antique menorah taking up the center

of the kitchen island, despite it being past Hannukah. Before things had gotten as wild that morning, there had been a video call involving the group, and what looked like Bruce's entire family, plus a not very well behaved but cute dog. Even Stavros got involved, discussing wines with Bruce's sister.

It was a way-twisted tradition, kinda like everything else Company. Marshall leaned to open the outer door and pitch damp swim trunks out on the balcony walkway. Since the two teams couldn't hit the beach this year, somehow an adult-sized, heated, aboveground pool had shown up, located between the birdbath and gym.

Matteo swore it was a holiday miracle. Not so much, unless miracles involved appropriating a fire department water tanker to fill the pool.

Liv could deal with that red tape.

Now, the still freaking scary vampire sat with a glass of wine and Kimi's laptop, watching some old Christmas movie she'd pulled up for him.

The joint Christmas Day was crowded, loud, and chaotic, and the kind of weird Marshall had never associated with a holiday, and awesome. It was awesome. Marshall's cheeks ached from smiling so much.

"No cleaning, and no work today." Liv smacked his wrist, the playful kind of tap, and kicked the sandy towel that'd been with the trunks out the door, closing it.

"My compound, my rules." He reeled Liv in for a kiss.

He ran his hands up and down her arms, sun-heated skin not as scorching as the way she nipped his lower lip, then dove in, their tongues tangling. An echo of what they'd done hours before, greeting Christmas morning their way. He wrapped his arms around her, hungry for more. He'd never not be hungry for Liv, no matter how long they were together.

She ended the kiss sooner than Marshall would've

preferred, and leaned backward, letting him brace her and hold her weight. Trusting him, and that shot joy through him every time it happened.

"The bedrooms are down *that* hall, not in *this* kitchen," Bruce grumbled, aiming for the doomed eggnog again.

Kit trailed Bruce, immune to the guy's grump and volume. "Yeah. You're gross. It's not even breeding season."

Kantor nagged the kid, and had him get haircuts and brush his teeth, and barked about random bowls and blankets and earbuds disappearing into the kid's rooftop retreat. Except Kantor was also constantly buying organic fruit and vegetables, dicing them and leaving them in Kit-reach.

Marshall was also pretty sure who'd had the idea of ordering the hand-felted fruit bat, and tying it on top of a huge basket of clothes that fit Kit, sneakers the same style as Josh's, and a higher-end phone and game controller. Even if Bruce only swore louder when his team or the guys suggested he was responsible, and Liv played clueless.

But Marshall had found the receipt for the expensive stuffie, and ribbon matching the bow on the basket, on Liv's dresser.

Whoever wanted to claim or deny responsibility, the toy was already tucked in Kit's pillow nest, no one else allowed to touch it.

"Privacy isn't a bad idea." Liv got Marshall's attention, wiggling and requesting freedom. He let go, already missing the connection.

Light sparkling off the glitter that had ended up in her hair, she caught his hand, fingers tangling in his, and tugged him out of the crowd and down the hall to her room.

Liv kept saying it was their room. A little more of him believed that every day. He got to the door first, pushing it open. Needing to see it all again.

Their new king size bed. His guitar, on its stand, beside

her bookcase. His and hers stacks of comics on each of their bedside tables.

Two tables instead of one, two lamps instead of only Liv's single leaded-glass one. The lamp on his side routinely left on. Right after the Franken-Non mission, Marshall had woken up from nightmares multiple nights. One bad enough he'd melted down, the scene a mashup of his old kitchen, the alley, and the burning lab, him not being able to get Liv out in time in his version.

Liv was always there, though. Ready to banish nightmares with her touch. There, holding him, when an attack ended and he realized where he was, and was messed up and exhausted. Never acting like it made him less, or a problem. Never expecting him to be cured, whatever *cured* even meant.

"Close your eyes." Liv shut the door, cutting off the outside noise.

He obeyed, his way of convincing Liv he'd meant it when he told her whatever she wanted, he did too. Giving her a sense of control that let her trust him and learn more about what being in love meant. She was a fast learner.

"Here."

Instinctively, he reached out, eyes opening. His hands closed on another wrapping paper and glitter-bow wrapped object, this one square.

"You already gave me my gifts." A set of knives from the entire team, the elite brand Kantor favored, plus a mono-grammed case. The gift nearly brought Marshall to his knees, at the cost and at what the knives meant. That his team, his family, paid attention to what he liked, and what he needed. That Liv, Matteo, and Jace saw him the way they did Bruce—as professional and important.

"Wait. Does this glow in the dark?" Marshall eyed the gift. It was the right size. Since this was also irreverent Liv, Kimi, and Vee they were talking about, there had been gifts of boxers. Mostly cool superhero ones. But thongs, too. Weird ones, with glow-in-the dark...pouches.

"This is my personal gift to you." Liv shoved the package into him, and let go, tucking her hands behind her back like she was nervous. "Open it?"

He took his time, untying the ribbon and peeling paper away. Savoring it, because before landing here, it had been a long damn time since anyone had bothered with presents for him. The novelty—he probably oughta be embarrassed at how much it mattered.

He turned the exposed square over to reveal a photo frame, one of those distressed, handcrafted ones from the farmer's market. This one was the shade of mellow blue that Liv swore was his color. The photo centered in the matching mat—emotion clogged Marshall's throat.

He traced his finger over the image. Matteo, Jace, and Liv —and him. All of them crowded around a bar table. Matteo's arms thrown over Jace and Marshall's shoulders, Liv in Marshall's lap.

That night hadn't been a special occasion. They'd been out for karaoke and beer, no ghouls this time. Liv had handed her phone to a bartender and asked him to get a couple of shots.

No gift had ever meant more to Marshall. "I—" He couldn't get words out. Couldn't figure out how to say what he truly meant.

Liv's cheek dented in. "Is it a silly gift? It's a silly gift. No one prints and frames photos. Civilian guys don't do that. Let's go back and see if there are any cookies left." She edged away.

Marshall put his bulk in front of her. He caught the back of Liv's neck, coaxing. Asking her to be here, in the moment, with him.

Liv got it. She always did, like with the photo. She snuggled against his chest, that spot meant for her, arms around his waist. He buried his face in her hair, loose and glittery and perfect. Because being with her made the world make sense, he was able to put what he felt into words she'd understand. "This is the best. The best gift anybody every gave me."

"You don't have to say that. I won't be upset." Liv laid her head on his shoulder.

"Why did you do that? Frame it and all?" He knew part of the answer. This was his Liv, breaking more rules. Liv showing him that he belonged with the team and her.

"We aren't supposed to be memorable. The Company values us and cares, yet we're supposed to be interchangeable, so if one falls, another can step in and keep the team and our mission going." Her tone was fierce.

"All these, your photos, prove you're real, and that each person matters. They show that you see them and know that." Like Liv saw him.

Her answer was a whisper, like she felt how important this moment was, an intense red-gold coloring her words. "Exactly that. I love who and what we are, but we aren't clones or replaceable, and life wouldn't ever be the same if one face from any of these photos was missing. I keep them where I can see them, so that I never forget what else we are and what I'm fighting for."

"We'll keep our family safe." Marshall would stand beside her, doing his share. No one, Company, cryptid, or vampire, was taking away what he'd searched for, for so long, and finally found.

IF YOU WANT MORE Region Two, check out Book Four, Agent of Change, Kimi's story.

ACKNOWLEDGMENTS

All my gratitude to the amazing Anne Raven of Black Bird Book Covers, as well as to the incredible PR teams at Psst Promotions and Let's Talk! Promotions.

To the Omegas and our monthly Zoom accountability/cheerleading/problem-solving, you all helped make this series happen.

Thanks to my sis, Amy, other-sis Deb, and ride-or-die BFF Sybil, for listening to endless rambling monologues concerning book plots and publishing world details, as well as to Cathy for creating a published-by-my-daughter-in-law bookcase display. Thanks also to Favorite Cousin Bill for the mini-library, and his impeccable taste in Shiny-Pretty Things.

Thanks to Sonya for making me laugh when I needed it most.

A special thank you to the Quarantine ICU Team at Sweetwater Hospital. They are true real-world heroines and heroes.

A huge thank you to all the readers who have fallen as hard for the Region Two crew as I have.

Finally, all my love to Mr. WW for his support, patience, and buying the good coffee.

ABOUT THE AUTHOR

Janet Walden-West lives in the Southeast with a pack of show dogs, a couple of kids, and a husband who didn't read the fine print.

She writes intersectional sexy-times romance and boss-girl fantasy heroines.

A PitchWars Mentee/Mentor alum and RWA Golden Heart finalist, she's the author of the contemporary romance series, SALT + STILETTOS: South Beach Romances, and the Region Two Urban Fantasy series.

She is represented by Eva Scalzo of Speilburg Literary Agency.

Visit and sign up for her newsletter to be the first to hear about giveaways, bonus content, and new releases!

Janet Walden-West
www.janetwaldenwest.weebly.com